# More praise for
# ACQUIRED MOTIVES

"If you don't have any travel plans for the last days of summer—or even if you're staying in your backyard—read Sarah Lovett's new mystery, *Acquired Motives*. . . . Lovett is a talented writer of the Patricia Cornwell genre."
—*Albuquerque Journal*

"A potent novel . . . Best of all . . . is the complex and charismatic heroine . . . Lovett offers an exceptional plot, unusual characters . . . and vivid forensic details in this off-beat but satisfying story."
—*Booklist*

"A fascinating mystery that was so hard to put down."
—*The New Mexican*

"A rip-roaring story."
—*Kirkus Reviews*

By Sarah Lovett
*Published by Ivy Books:*

DANGEROUS ATTACHMENTS
ACQUIRED MOTIVES

Books published by The Ballantine Publishing Group
are available at quantity discounts on bulk purchases
for premium, educational, fund-raising, and special
sales use. For details, please call 1-800-733-3000.

# ACQUIRED MOTIVES

## Sarah Lovett

IVY BOOKS • NEW YORK

An Ivy Book
Published by Ballantine Books
Copyright © 1996 by Sarah Lovett

http://www.randomhouse.com

Library of Congress Catalog Card Number: 96-95500

ISBN 0-8041-1298-3

This edition published by arrangement with Villard Books, a division of Random House, Inc. Villard Books is a registered trademark of Random House, Inc.

Manufactured in the United States of America

First Ballantine Books Edition: August 1997

10  9  8  7  6  5  4  3  2  1

*This is for Flor and Mom*
*And for Robert*

# ACKNOWLEDGMENTS

My very special thanks to David Rosenthal

And Leona Nevler
Miriam Sagan, Carolyn Gilliland, Melissa White, and Julia
  Goldberg
Bernard Baca, Ph.D., Jacqueline West, Ph.D., Susan Cave,
  Ph.D.
Rick Smith
Jim Burleson
Doug Beldon
P. J. Liebson and Barbara Gordon
Lawrence Lee Renner, Dr. Karen Greist, and Dr. Bruce Mann
Lew Thompson and Richard Folks
Adam Rothberg, Brian McLendon, Tammy Richards, Dennis
  Ambrose, and everyone at Villard Books for going the
  extra mile
Peter Miller, Jennifer Robinson, and PMA Literary and
  Film Management, thanks guys

And Timoteo Thompson, the Book Doctor

# ONE

ANTHONY RANDALL DIDN'T look like a self-confessed sadistic rapist. His large blue eyes were free of guile, his cheeks were tinged pink, his lips habitually worked themselves into a soft frown. He looked younger than his twenty-two years.

He looked like an altar boy.

Sylvia Strange shifted in the hardwood chair where she had been poised for more than thirty minutes. The glare of the fluorescent lights made her head ache. Her navy silk skirt was creased. She hoped dark circles of perspiration weren't visible under the arms of her suit jacket. It was her job to maintain the illusion of control even when the courtroom resembled the inside of a pressure cooker.

Sylvia noticed sweat easing down Judge Nathaniel Howzer's throat to the collar of his black robes. The judge had summoned opposing counsel to the bench three times during the past fifteen minutes. Clearly, he wasn't pleased with the most recent turn of events.

Just days earlier, Erin Tulley, an officer with the New Mexico State Police, had admitted that Anthony Randall had been reeling under the effects of drugs and alcohol when he confessed to rape. The law demanded that confessions be knowing and voluntary—tricky when the confessor's system was toxic.

Immediately following Tulley's turnaround, the defense had filed a motion to suppress the confession. If granted, there would be no trial, and the defendant would walk. The judge had refused to render a decision on the motion until he heard the testimony of the evaluating forensic psychologist: Sylvia Strange.

As Judge Howzer conferred yet again with defense and prosecuting attorneys, the bailiff fanned himself with both hands. It had to be pushing ninety degrees in the courtroom. A female journalist in the gallery lifted a ponytail of graying hair above her neck and strained forward to catch the breeze from a portable fan. The nose and mouth of another reporter were covered with a white mask to filter out environmental impurities.

Behind the press row, the family members of the rape victim were huddled together. The victim's mother looked as if she was shell-shocked. Sylvia could hardly bear to glance at the woman.

Judge Howzer finished his murmured consultation with the attorneys. Sylvia took a deep breath to regain her focus as Tony Klavin, the defendant's attorney, approached the witness stand. Klavin was thirty-five, athletic, and aggressive; he committed every ounce of energy to this examination.

"Dr. Strange, at any time during the fifteen hours you spent with the defendant Anthony Randall, did you discuss his family history?"

Sylvia saw Randall seated at the defense table, his blond head held perfectly still. She said, "During the examining interview I obtained a clinical history to establish the individuality of the defendant's background, his family, education, and life experiences."

Tony Klavin nodded sagely and the dark curl that licked his forehead bounced ever so gently. He'd earned a reputation as a cunning and oily defense attorney by taking on offensive clients and winning their high-profile cases. He jammed both hands into his pants pockets and hunkered down. "Did Anthony Randall have a tragic childhood?"

"Objection." The prosecutor, Jack O'Dell, was on his feet. He shook his head in disgust. "Dr. Strange has not been qualified by this court as a dramaturge, Your Honor."

"Mr. Klavin, rephrase the question in less theatrical language."

Tony Klavin touched the tips of his fingers together; his hands formed a triangle. "Dr. Strange, did Anthony Randall become a substance abuser when he was eleven years old?"

For a split second she locked eyes with the defendant; it was like looking into the eyes of something dead. Six weeks ago, during the final clinical interview at the jail, Randall had been cocky, convinced that his ability to manipulate would get him whatever the hell he wanted. He wasn't sophisticated enough to be cognizant of the MMPI-2 validity scales, which detected "fake bad" crazies—those hard-core cases who wanted the world to think they were too sick to take responsibility for their crimes. But he had a good handle on his sociopathic skills: deceit, control, exploitation.

To hear Anthony Randall tell it, *he* was the victim.

Sylvia felt the dampness between her shoulder blades, and one droplet of sweat slowly traveled down her spine. She ran her tongue over her lips and willed herself to speak. "Anthony Randall was hospitalized for alcohol abuse when he was twelve."

"At what age did he begin to drink?"

"Between the ages of ten and eleven."

"And did he also begin sniffing glue?"

Jack O'Dell interjected, "Your Honor—"

While the attorneys argued another point of admissibility, Sylvia took a breath and centered her mind on the business at hand. In this case, she was a witness for the defense. As a forensic psychologist, she worked for prosecution, defense, or the court—whoever requested her services. Impartiality was a professional requirement.

Sylvia had evaluated hundreds of criminal offenders. She had heard enough truly horrific life stories to fill volumes. And most of the time, she felt empathy for the defendants. But Anthony Randall left her cold. He enjoyed inflicting pain.

Sylvia continued to answer Tony Klavin's questions, to build a case for Anthony Randall, the conduct-disordered child who had grown into a dysfunctional, antisocial adult. With each response, Sylvia felt her stomach muscles clench. Months ago, when she first read the police crime reports, she'd wept. Anthony Randall had beaten and raped a fourteen-year-old girl with a metal pipe. And then he'd left her for dead.

Flora Escudero had survived—just barely. But she had been unable to identify her masked attacker.

Sylvia was no proponent of the death penalty. It was an archaic, unjust system—racially and economically biased, outrageously expensive, imperfect, and inhumane.

But she couldn't deny the intensity of the primitive emotion that welled up inside her: she wanted Anthony Randall to die.

"Dr. Strange? I'll repeat the question." Tony Klavin was staring at her, puzzled by her slow response. "Was the purpose of your evaluation to determine the defendant's competency to stand trial as well as his mental state at the time of the incident?"

*Here it comes,* she thought. "Yes."

"When you questioned him about the incident, did he

indicate whether or not he remembered making a statement to the police?"

"He said he couldn't remember much." Sylvia's voice was flat, stripped of emotion. "He said his memory was clouded and he was suffering the effects of Valium, marijuana, and alcohol."

"When Valium and marijuana are combined with alcohol, can they impair a person's judgment?"

"They could."

"Could they impair an individual's memory?"

"It's possible."

"Did Anthony Randall indicate whether or not he remembered making a confession to the police?"

The words lodged in her throat, and she glanced at the defendant. No one else would have seen it, but Sylvia was attuned to Randall's every movement. His left eye narrowed for an instant as the soft skin around it responded to a muscular contraction—an involuntary reaction—and even that minute loss of control was exceptional for Randall. The public Randall.

Sylvia heard the click and whir of cameras going off along the press bench.

"Dr. Strange?" Tony Klavin prodded.

"He said he did not."

"Could the defendant remember even one word of his so-called confession?"

"No."

"Why not?"

"He said he was too intoxicated, too high."

The hum of voices in the gallery reminded Sylvia of cicadas. Judge Howzer's face darkened as he wordlessly castigated his courtroom. Silence returned.

"Dr. Strange, in your work, have you had the opportunity to observe substance abusers?"

"Yes, I've observed them in various stages of addiction, withdrawal, and recovery."

"The first time you met with Anthony Randall, what was he like?"

"His voice was a monotone, his mood was blunted, dull. He was depressed, and he said he felt suicidal."

"Is that consistent with the way someone would act who has recently withdrawn from drugs and alcohol?"

Although the heat in the courtroom was stifling, Sylvia felt cold. "It could be."

Tony Klavin stepped toward the witness stand. "Dr. Strange, Police Officer Erin Tulley has testified under oath that when Anthony Randall made his *alleged* confession on the night of April sixteenth, he was"—with a grim flourish he quoted slowly from the transcript in his hand—" 'stumbling around, sick and dazed, blacking out.' " Klavin paced a tight circle, making no effort to hide his scorn. "Does that sound like the behavior of a man who made a knowing confession?"

"Objection!" Jack O'Dell was on his feet. "This pantomiming and playacting is unnecessary and prejudicial."

"Sustained. Just ask the questions, Mr. Klavin."

"I'm sorry, Your Honor. I wasn't aware I was making *faces.*"

Sylvia tried to stay focused on Klavin's line of questioning, but her thoughts kept coming back to Erin Tulley's turnaround. State Cop Tulley had shocked the state when she recanted earlier evidence concerning Randall's confession. By now, the rumor of choice was that Tulley had broken rank because she was dying in a gender discrimination lawsuit against the state police; she claimed she'd been denied promotion because she was female. The agency's response to the civil action was simple: Erin Tulley had spent only two years in uniform; a promotion to the Criminal Investigation Division would be premature for anyone—male or female—after two years' service.

But Tulley wasn't the kind of woman who would take a lonely fall. Pale, visibly distraught, and vehement on the witness stand, she had given the defense the wedge it desperately needed to demolish the prosecution's case.

And Sylvia felt as if she'd been set up to follow Tulley's act—her testimony would be the clincher, the last scene before curtain.

Tony Klavin interrupted Sylvia's racing thoughts. "Dr. Strange, at the time of the defendant's arrest, if he was under the influence of drugs and alcohol, would you say that any confession he made would be made knowingly?" For an instant Klavin had to work to hide his impatience with his witness.

"No, I would not."

"Thank you, Dr. Strange. We have no more questions, Your Honor."

Sylvia noticed the fleeting smugness that breezed across Anthony Randall's perfect features. For an instant, she felt her veneer of control slip—she hated the system, she hated her role in it, she hated Anthony Randall.

Sylvia raised an eyebrow and caught the compact smile on Tony Klavin's lips; it was his way of saying, *You done good.*

The prosecutor, Jack O'Dell, prepared to launch a last-ditch assault. He didn't have the slick good looks of his opponent, but he cultivated an earnest, professorial demeanor. He was a man who, when the time came, would welcome the addition of white strands to his dark brown hair because distinguished gray would be an asset with a jury.

At the moment, O'Dell wore the grim expression of a man who knew he was beaten. Today's decision on the motion to suppress would be based on the fact that law enforcement had *coerced* a confession from a guilty defendant. The prosecutor had considered the variables—public outcry over crooks going free on a "technicality," the weight given a cop's recanted testimony, the odds of ever making it to trial without a confession. He moved heavily, almost sluggishly, from his chair.

As O'Dell scanned his notes, a rangy man wearing a tan jacket and cowboy boots entered the courtroom and stood by the door. Sylvia barely glanced at State Police Criminal Agent Matt England before she returned her attention to Jack O'Dell. She'd worked for the prosecutor on other cases, and she knew from the look in his eyes that he had sensed her enmity for Randall.

She waited for him to ask one more question: *Will Anthony Randall rape again?*

*Yes.*

Her answer wouldn't change the decision, but it would be a public indictment of Anthony Randall.

But it was Judge Howzer who spoke, and his voice wavered with emotion. "Mr. O'Dell, what does the government have to say in closing?"

The prosecutor dropped all pretense as he said, "You know, Your Honor, if you suppress this confession, this is all we've got."

Judge Howzer took a labored breath. "I am all too well aware of that."

Tony Klavin bolted forward. "Your Honor, we have clearly demonstrated that the defendant was incapable of making a legally valid confession. Without this bogus confession, the state has no evidence to implicate Anthony Randall—"

Howzer snapped, "Enough, Mr. Klavin." The judge's skin had an unhealthy yellow cast and it drooped from his square jaw; he looked like a man melting from heat and disappointment. He said, "Motion to suppress the confession is granted."

The courtroom came alive with the hum of voices expressing protest, shock, grief. Howzer was forced to wield his gavel. He gave a weary nod to Sylvia to release her from the court.

Sylvia stepped down from the witness stand. As she passed the defense table, Anthony Randall drew his lips into a smile. Light glinted from the diamond stud that he wore in his right earlobe. He whispered, "Thank you."

She couldn't wait to get out of the courtroom. As she strode past the reporters and the small group of spectators, a woman in the gallery sprang to her feet. Angie Escudero had been lovely before her daughter's assault. Now, her naturally soft features were twisted with rage. Her skin was blotched and shadowed. Her eyes burned dark furious holes in her face.

She pushed away the restraining arms of her husband and son. In a terrible voice she hissed at Sylvia, "You're a bad woman. He hurt my Flora, and *you* let him go."

# TWO

SYLVIA FOUND CRIMINAL Agent Matt England waiting just outside the courtroom door. She shook her head—frustrated, angry, unable to speak. She wanted to be far away from the accusations and the suffering that surrounded this failure of justice. She walked straight for the double glass doors at the end of the long hall. Matt matched her stride.

"What happened in there?" he demanded in a low voice.

"Randall's going to walk because of Erin Tulley."

Like every cop in the county, Matt had already heard about Tulley's turnaround minutes after she began recanting her testimony; the courthouse had been swarming with cops and at least one of her supervisors, all ready to get in some digs. It burned him too when somebody in the ranks screwed up. He took it personally. Tulley had been a good cop—top of her class at the academy; idealistic and smart. She should have come clean three months ago about Randall. Come clean or shut up—he could have lived with that, too. But not this last-minute spin that set a rapist free.

Matt clenched his jaw. Tulley had been more than a friend.

Behind them the courtroom door flew open. Sylvia heard keening—it could only be Flora's mother—and

10

then someone called out: "Dr. Strange!" When she turned, she felt the hot lights on her face before she saw two reporters and their minicams.

She gripped Matt's arm so hard her fingernails cut into his skin. "Get me the hell out of here."

They passed the security guard, and Matt pushed open the doors of the Santa Fe Judicial Complex.

Outside, the air reeked of rotting apricots and smoke. The fifth of July had produced record-breaking temperatures, continuing the trend of the previous three months. The mountains surrounding Santa Fe were besieged by forest fires—already more than twenty thousand acres had been destroyed.

A dry wind swept Sylvia's shoulder-length hair from her face. The sun's glare was blinding. She pulled sunglasses from her briefcase and took the steps two at a time.

"Dr. Strange! How do you feel about today's hearing?" At least one reporter was going to rate a "P" for persistence.

Matt pressed the car key into Sylvia's palm and nudged her forward with a command: "Get in."

His unmarked Caprice was directly in front of her, blocking entry to the lot, illegally parked as usual. Grateful for the chance to escape more questions, she used the key, yanked open the passenger door, climbed inside, and reset the lock. The interior was still slightly cool and quiet—an island of tranquillity.

She saw Matt pivot suddenly. The reporter—a gawky man with a hawkish nose—backpedaled to avoid a collision with the big cop.

Matt loomed over the reporter. His grin was standard issue for the criminally insane. His voice was an ominously pleasant baritone when he said, "Hey, McPeavey, why don't you get yourself a day job? I hear they're hiring the handicapped at Lotta Burger."

McPeavey fired back, "They'll be happy to have you on staff, Matt."

Matt jogged around to the driver's side and hitched a farewell finger at McPeavey. "Just remember to wash your hands before you handle the meat."

He slid behind the wheel, started the engine, and backed so close to McPeavey that the reporter stumbled on the steps.

Sylvia groaned, shook her head, then laughed as Matt guided the Caprice onto Grant Avenue. "You're crazy."

"Don't go all technical on me, Doc." He glanced at the woman sitting beside him as they pulled up to a stop sign. She was slumped against the seat, but she wasn't relaxed. Her opaque brown eyes gave her away; they were focused too intently on a fire truck as it inched across the intersection. The rumble of the truck's engine made speech impossible for fifteen seconds.

She picked at a loose thread on the hem of her skirt. If she tugged in the wrong spot, the entire seam would unravel, but she couldn't keep her fingers still.

Matt turned left onto Catron Street and said, "You better stop appearing as witness for the defense."

"Then tell the prosecution to give me a call." Her skin had lost its usual olive warmth, her lower lip was trapped between slightly crooked front teeth.

When she spoke again, her voice was a whisper. "Flora Escudero's mother stood up in court and blamed me for letting Randall walk."

"She should be blaming Erin Tulley and the case investigators."

The words were meant to soothe, but Sylvia heard

something else in her lover's voice. She stared at him. "Don't tell me you think she's right. You think I'm responsible?"

He caught the dangerous glint in her eyes, and he knew it was too late to convince her that her instincts about him were off base. A part of him couldn't stomach the fact that she had anything to do with a scumbag like Anthony Randall.

He said, "I don't always understand your career choice."

"Is this the I-work-like-hell-to-put-them-away-and-you-let-them-off speech?" They were on opposite sides of the fence when it came to professional issues. That wouldn't change. His job was enforcement and control; hers was evaluation and treatment. They'd had their share of fights, but so far they'd managed to avoid a showdown. They agreed on one crucial point: the protection of the public had priority.

Matt's voice was soft. "No. Not that speech."

"Good." Sylvia brushed an unruly strand of dark hair from her face and tried to shift internal gears. But she felt overwhelmed by the constraints of her professional identity. She shrugged off her jacket, pulled her blouse loose from her skirt, and stripped off damp pantyhose. Then she dug her fingers into her hair and brushed it into wild disarray.

She was edgy, volatile. And right now she was wired. Matt knew that. But there were times when she let her guard down, when she let go, and a different woman emerged. A vulnerable woman. She kept him off balance.

She asked, "Where are we going?"

He glanced at her. "I thought you said the Zia for lunch."

"Did I?" She tucked her legs under her butt and

touched his shoulder gently. "Let's go back to your place instead."

"Hey, I'm happy to take advantage of your mood swings." His delivery was deadpan, but one arched eyebrow gave him away.

"Or we could fuck in the car." She turned and stared out at a school playground. It was empty except for two teenage boys perched on tires that swung beneath a large cottonwood. The air was hazy with smoke and dust and gave the scene a soft-filter quality like a Hallmark memory, trading nostalgia for gritty reality. While Sylvia watched, the smaller boy eased himself back, his knees hooked over rubber, and hung upside down. His hair brushed dirt and weeds. Both boys grinned.

"Will somebody keep an eye on Randall?" Sylvia's voice was suddenly harsh.

"Yeah ... but when we get too close, his lawyer's going to scream harassment."

"Somebody better ride Randall's ass."

"Hey, relax." Matt reached across the seat with his right hand and touched her bare knee. He could smell the soft scent of her perfume intensified by heat. His eye caught the curve of one breast, visible where the fabric of her blouse puckered between buttons.

Sylvia smiled. "Hey, yourself." She glanced at her watch and groaned.

"What?"

"I've got a session in forty-five minutes. With Kevin the Terrible." She didn't usually talk about her clients with Matt, but he knew about this particular case. He had made the initial arrest that resulted in probation and court-ordered counseling.

Matt nodded. "Kevin Chase. Lucky you."

They were approaching Guadalupe Street, and Sylvia

pointed like a kid. "I can't go back to work without my chile fix."

Muttering under his breath, Matt cut the wheel to the left, and the Caprice swerved across the curb into the parking lot of Bert's Burger Bowl. It was a fifties-style takeout stand where locals had been ordering chile-cheeseburgers for forty years.

Before the car rolled to a complete standstill, Sylvia was out the door.

Matt followed her past a cherry 1960 Buick filled with teenagers. At eleven-thirty, the lunch rush had barely begun; only a handful of customers waited inside Bert's. When the order was ready, Matt carried out iced tea and burgers wrapped in wax paper. Tin umbrellas provided tiny islands of shade for the tables. Sparrows patrolled concrete surfaces for crumbs. One bird hopped across the table where Sylvia waited.

She tore off some bun for the sparrow and then she took a bite of burger. Matt watched her eat. He saw a striking woman. Her bone structure was all angles, almost too sharp. Her brown eyes were wide set. Her lips were full, lipstick worn away, mouth fixed now around a thick green-chile cheeseburger.

He asked the question that had been on his mind. "Why did you agree to evaluate Randall?"

She set the burger on the paper plate and wiped mustard from her chin. Her gaze was unflinchingly direct. She said, "He was accused of false imprisonment, criminal sexual penetration, attempted murder. Stacked, those felonies carry a maximum stretch of fifty years. If the prosecution had requested the evaluation, the results would have been the same—the outcome was inevitable. Bottom line, the man had the right to a competent psychological evaluation."

Matt nodded slowly. "That didn't have to be you.

There are other shrinks out there." His expression went dark, suddenly unreadable. "You've handled more than your share of creeps lately. Why didn't you just let this one go?"

She tipped her head; her look said, *You're out of line.*

"You knew Randall would be a high-profile case—"

"So what? I take low-profile cases, too. It's my job."

"I have a small problem with the fact Randall's out again. And he'll hurt another girl just like he hurt Flora Escudero."

Sylvia stared at him. "You think I don't know that? Randall could be meeting his next victim as we speak. And I'll make you a bet: next time, he'll kill." Her voice hardened. "But maybe next time, the state police will get a valid confession, and someone like Tulley won't have the chance to recant. And maybe the sadistic sonofabitch will be caged in North Facility, which is the only place in this world for Anthony Randall."

Matt swallowed the last of his iced tea, and then he crumpled the waxed cup. "You still haven't answered my first question. Why didn't you let this one go?"

When she didn't respond, Matt pressed. "Every time a scumbag rapes some poor kid like Flora Escudero, you've got to be there. Why?"

She gathered up the food wrappers on the table and then raised her eyes to his. "Today, in that court-room . . . that was one of the hardest things I've ever had to do."

"So why not walk away?" Matt stood and followed her toward the car.

When Sylvia reached the Caprice, she turned to face him, then stood stock still. "You shouldn't have to ask that." She took a deep breath and shook her head. "Not everybody can do what I do. Most people can't stomach working with these guys. But I'm good at it. At my best, I help people. At my best, I make sure someone like Anthony Randall doesn't get the chance to hurt another human being."

A sudden gust of wind blew her hair back from her face. The branches of an old cottonwood rustled. Paper and other debris skittered across asphalt. She stepped toward Matt and touched his cheek. "Now, can we go? I've got to be back at my office in five minutes . . . and it's been a shitty day."

Instead of a verbal response, he pushed her against the Caprice and kissed her. His mouth was rough, needy, and she let him suck the air from her throat and lungs. His hand crumpled silk as his fingers found her breast.

She was caught off guard; heat traveled along her thighs, up her belly. They kissed until the teenagers began to honk the Buick's horn in appreciation.

Inside the Caprice, the fight started again.

He said, "I think you should lighten your caseload. We could spend more time together—"

"My schedule's no worse than yours. You want me to stay at home with an apron on?"

Matt just rolled his eyes.

They'd been over this territory before: a familiar trail where the traveler was smart to avoid a misstep. Neither of them was ready for marriage. They loved each other, but they weren't good at sharing territory.

"We're both happy with the way things are, right?" Sylvia didn't like the strident tone of her voice.

To her surprise, Matt blushed. He turned crimson from neck to ears. Then, to cover his embarrassment and frustration, he turned the key in the ignition, revved the engine.

He dropped her off outside the building that housed

her office. As he drove away, she was left with the
beginnings of panic; she wanted to call him back. She
couldn't shake the feeling Matt was withholding something. But then, so was she. She'd never been able to
relax with the idea of commitment. Her brief and
unsuccessful marriage was evidence of that fact. So was
her more recent affair with Malcolm Treisman. Before
his death from cancer, Malcolm had been her mentor,
her associate, her surrogate father—and the man she
loved.

Desertion, divorce, death. She had a bad track record
when it came to men.

It took her a moment to calm herself. She stood on
the hot sidewalk and listened to a dog barking frantically
in a nearby yard. Thirty thousand feet overhead, a jet left
a shaving-cream trail in the sky. The usual summer
thunderheads were nowhere to be seen; instead, the fir-
mament was smeared with smoke from the Dark Canyon
fire that burned in the Jemez Mountains to the northwest.
Closer to earth, the blue-gray foothills of the Sangre de
Cristo Mountains set the northeast boundary of Santa Fe;
above eighty-five hundred feet the air would be notice-
ably cooler.

Sylvia tucked her briefcase under one arm and began
the short walk to her office. She tried to focus on her
upcoming session with Kevin the Terrible, but her
mind replayed the recent scene in the courtroom—
Flora Escudero's mother crying out, "You're a bad
woman!"

Matt was right, she should have walked away from
Anthony Randall.

Each day she dealt with men who had psyches as
twisted as shrapnel. She probed, explored, contained their
darkness. She had the ego strength and the endurance to

commit herself completely to her work. But because she had come so close to evil, Sylvia knew her immunity to it was less than perfect.

# THREE

ANTHONY RANDALL SLOUCHED across the intake desk at the Santa Fe County Detention Center and licked his lips. The female clerk scowled and slid the release form across the counter.

"Sign it."

*"Cunt."* He mouthed the word when she glanced away. Then he smiled and scrawled his name at the bottom of the form. Overlooking the desk, glassed-in detention cells housed offenders and indigents taken into custody the night before, or those inmates awaiting transport to other facilities. Vapid faces pressed against the reinforced glass; they were the witnesses to Anthony Randall's release. At 1:55 P.M. on July 5, he was officially a free man. He pocketed his thirty-two bucks and change, took the paper bag with his few possessions, and turned his back on the prisoners, the orange linoleum, the intake clerk. He walked out the rear door, the same way he'd entered three months earlier.

Outside the detention center there were no cops, no reporters, there was no crowd. Randall's lawyer, Tony Klavin, had encouraged interviews in front of the courthouse after the hearing. Anthony had given his statement: "In my case, justice won out, and I want to thank God for His help. I offer my sincerest condolences to the

Escudero family because somewhere out there—the real rapist is free."

Klavin had filled in the rest: "Law enforcement should be concentrating on finding the real perpetrator instead of destroying the life of an innocent man."

Randall figured "law enforcement" would be on him like ugly on a frog. But he didn't see any cops as he walked past storage sheds, trailer parks, and minimart gas-ups. It was a three-block stretch to the intersection of Rodeo and Cerrillos roads, where the Villa Linda Mall occupied eighty acres. Here and there, clusters of poplars and juniper had escaped bulldozers. For those who had been in the area long enough, the trees touched a memory of high-desert prairie, of ranches, meadowlarks, and Spanish land grants. But Randall had no such memory; he, his mother, and his younger brother had drifted from Van Nuys, California, three years earlier.

No, the cops hadn't shown, and neither had his mother. He didn't expect to see her for days. She was keeping a safe, alcohol-dulled distance from her bad seed.

He turned north, thumb out, cocky smile. *My lucky day.* It took him only minutes to hitch a ride on the back of a Honda 750. The biker cruised him the twelve miles out to Pojoaque—past the Santa Fe Opera, past piñon-studded hills, past Pueblo bingo parlors and Camel Rock—to his final destination: the Cock 'n' Bull. He would be hammered before the sun even began to set beyond Nambe Valley.

It was a roadside bar, weathered and faded, with a cracked billboard. The dusty parking lot was filled with pickup trucks, gas guzzlers, and enough Harleys for a biker convention. On the fifth of July, the holiday weekend was still a party at the Bull.

The Honda skidded to a stop behind a turquoise

pickup, and the engine throbbed while Randall nodded thanks for the ride. A fat and very drunk man wearing a leather Harley vest stumbled out the bar's saloon-style swinging doors. Randall slapped road dirt from his Levi's and strutted into the Cock 'n' Bull.

Instant noise and irritation. His regular bartender was gone; he didn't recognize the black-haired witch who was setting up draft beers by the dozen. In fact, it was hard to see anyone in the dim, crowded room. Nobody looked familiar, although he'd been gone barely three months. Anthony Randall didn't expect a hero's welcome—he wasn't a man who had friends. But he did expect somebody to pay some attention when he entered a room.

*I beat the fucking system.*

He shouldered his way to the bar, yelled, "When's Kiki working?"—and got smoke in his face. He paid for a double shot of Herradura Gold and a Bud chaser. The only empty table was wedged into a corner at the back of the large room. Randall pushed his way past revelers and serious drinkers. The air was stale with sweat and alcohol, the noise level was harsh. He sat down, did the shot, and slammed the glass on varnished wood just as a string of firecrackers exploded across the room.

A girl in skintight black pants had jumped up on the bar. Surrounded by a crowd of onlookers, she was chugging a pitcher of draft. Randall shook his head in disgust. The bitch was looking for a good time.

He finished off his Bud just as the girl drained her pitcher. Beer had soaked her face and neck, and her T-shirt stuck to her skin.

Above laughter and applause for the chugger, a voice sounded in Anthony Randall's ear: "It's cool, what you did."

Randall glanced up and found himself staring into a

face obscured by black sunglasses. The guy from the Honda 750.

The biker set four double shots of tequila on the table. He straddled the chair opposite Randall.

Anthony Randall grunted. The guy wasn't a cop; he'd smell that shit a mile away. One-handed, he slipped a pack of smokes from his shirt pocket, shook one out, and slid it between his full lips.

Broad-shouldered, pumped up, sporting a three-day growth of beard, the biker was wearing a brown leather jacket even though it was hot. His skin was chapped by sun and wind. He jerked his head in disgust. "Nobody else understands about what you did. You stuck it right up the ass of the cops, the judge, the whole stinking system." He held up a glass, raised it to Randall in salute. "To you, man."

Anthony Randall took the second double shot and poured oily tequila down his throat. Heat streaked through his belly; his muscles began to loosen up. He wanted to get drunk. He wanted to get blind. He had it coming after all that time inside. Maybe this motor-dude could do him a favor.

"Baby Did a Bad Thing" blasted from the jukebox.

Randall gripped another glass, and tequila slopped onto the table. "You got any smoke to go with this?" He did the shot.

The biker's face slowly transformed behind a stupid grin. "Outside."

In the parking lot, a sudden gust of wind shot Randall's hair with static and left grit in his eyes. An empty beer can clattered across gravel until it lodged behind a tire. Randall followed the guy to the edge of the dirt where the 750 was parked next to a white panel truck under a stand of elms and cottonwoods. The groaning tree branches leaned into the wind. Two cars pulled out of the lot and turned onto the frontage road.

Randall slapped his new friend on the back and stumbled toward the biggest cottonwood. The cords on the thick tree trunk stood out like veins. He reached down and unzipped his fly with unsteady hands. He had to take a piss. Beer and tequila always did it to him, made him piss like a faucet. His urine spattered off a handmade wooden cross planted at the base of the tree.

What did they call them, the crosses that marked where somebody died on the highway? There was some word in Spanish he never could remember.

This cross was made of rough pine stakes, maybe twenty inches by twelve, nailed together and planted deep in earth. The ribbon had faded from sun and dust, the plastic flowers looked new. So who the fuck got wasted?

His urine cut a yellow rainbow through space, and Randall flashed on the girl gazing up at him, legs splayed out, face all bloody. The way he left her to die. But the stupid bitch had stayed alive, almost got him a long vacation. Almost. It was his lawyer's job to keep him out of the joint. And the shrink's. Other guys got caught, did hard time, not Anthony Randall. He had plans.

He heard footsteps—the motor-dude back with the weed—and he didn't look over his shoulder. Instead, he bent forward to read the name burned in the cross.

That was the last thing he did. One slam to the back of his head, the letters scrambled, his mind jammed into free fall, and he fell forward.

ANTHONY RANDALL COULDN'T breathe. It was hot and dark, and he had lost all sense of time. Maybe hours had gone by since the bar . . . maybe minutes. His mouth had been taped, he was blindfolded, his hands had gone numb. The acid taste of bile filled the back of his mouth; tequila and dread.

His body rolled to one side, then back again. He was in a moving truck or van. Who was driving? His mind dissolved into shiny fragments.

When he came to again, his first thought was that he must be naked. There was no breeze to brush against his skin, but he felt exposed. Someone had taken his shirt . . . his jeans. But even naked, he was so hot he felt like he was burning alive. Abruptly something covered his nose and mouth—he went under.

When consciousness returned—hazily, painfully—he discovered he was sitting up inside the truck. He could smell sweat—someone else's, and his own. What did they want with him? That question filled him with fear, something he rarely felt. He hated fear. The fear exploded into rage and gave him the strength to fight against whatever held him. He strained forward, muscles flexed, blood pounding up to his head, a growl exploding from his throat. The duct tape around his wrists cut into his skin—but it held. So did the tape that kept his legs spread wide.

He was trussed like an animal. His throat was raw, his tongue swollen behind the gag.

"Aaaaa." He tried to call for water but the word was only a ragged cry.

He sensed the presence of his captors. More than one. Three or four? Maybe they were the crazy family of that girl he'd done. He mustered himself. The gag was ripped from his face, and a voice whispered, "We want to hear you scream when you die."

"Who—?" Randall couldn't finish the question.

"Call me Killer."

He heard the hiss of a match, and the air filled with a sweet, sickening stink. Incense; it smelled like church.

Mercifully, his mind drifted again. He remembered a birthday many years ago. The sound of laughter, the taste of a white cake with pink frosting.

Perhaps he fell asleep, or maybe it was only a daydream. But his eyes shot wide open, and he tried to scream when he heard a click.

He wrenched himself back to consciousness. What? No one had touched him, but there had been a bright light, a popping sound.

He strained to lift his chin and found he could see under the edge of the blindfold. He could barely make out a shape in front of him. A hand, gripping something.

His heart began to pound. He thought he could smell his own blood for an instant. But that was impossible. Scared . . . he was so scared he knew he'd shit where he sat.

Suddenly someone stretched his knees wider. He fought against the force, the naked vulnerability. He'd seen goats right before slaughter. His old man had been a master of the kill. He was quick with the blade, but animals always knew what was coming. They could smell death . . . and you could see death in their eyes.

"So you fancy yourself a ladies' man?"

There was laughter just as a sickening, red-hot pain radiated out from his groin.

"Pain is a great teacher, Anthony."

He was unconscious when the mask was ripped from his face, and the second photograph was taken. He didn't see the flash, and he didn't feel the blood that drained down his legs and pooled at his feet.

# FOUR

LATE WEDNESDAY AFTERNOON, the Dark Canyon fire burning in the Jemez Mountains northwest of Santa Fe was declared seventy-five percent contained. Teams of firefighters working deep in the Santa Fe National Forest had spent two days and nights trenching a three-foot-wide fire line to encircle the flames. A Forest Service dispatcher confirmed that the fire had burned twenty-eight hundred acres, was still active in small areas, and would not be fully suppressed for a day or two.

Three hours later, a new pressure system rolled in from the Chihuahuan Desert bringing hot forty-mile-per-hour gusts and not a drop of moisture. The previously lethargic Dark Canyon fire reacted to the transfusion of oxygen and opened up like a giant blast furnace. The ground fire had become a crown fire, one of such heat and intensity that it raced from treetop to treetop driven by its own winds.

Benji Muñoz y Concha, a first-year fire rookie, fourth-generation firefighter, and furloughed minimum-security inmate at the Penitentiary of New Mexico, witnessed the explosion near San Antonio Creek. He said a fast prayer that he wasn't watching a blow-up, a blaze that literally shoots hundreds of feet skyward and might devour a square mile within a minute.

He took off running uphill—like the flames—but veered west up the safety lane the crew had devised. The

27

safety lane fed into an existing Forest Service road. Eventually, the road would intersect Highway 4.

Night was lit up like day. Benji lunged over the rough road and felt heat lick at his heels. The runt end of the Dark Canyon fire was going to dog him until he reached the ridge top and his comrades. His heavy logger boots slowed him down; the fireproofed green pants clawed at his sweat-soaked legs. His yellow shirt was gray with ash. Somewhere along the way he lost his "salad bowl," the plastic hardhat all firefighters wear, as well as the backpack that contained his goggles, headlamp, gloves, maps, and first-aid kit. Also gone were ax, brush hook, and shovel. Two canteens still dangled from his nylon belt. So did a portable fire shelter—the tent–sleeping bag that was every firefighter's worst nightmare; once it became necessary to use the shelter, odds were the fire-fighter was a ghost.

Benji felt confident he could outrace the fire. He was a runner trained for endurance, an athlete who had logged hundreds of high-desert miles. For Benji, running con-nected him to his Spanish and Pueblo ancestors—it was a spiritual exercise. He never lost stride—at least not until he spied the man.

At first, Benji thought he was one of the other fire-fighters, maybe injured or smoke-blind. He sat—no, he was propped—against the grandfather of all trees in a stand of old-growth piñon. And he was buck naked.

Benji veered toward him and called out. Then he stumbled, retching.

Smoke oozed from the man's pores, flames tickled the bottoms of his feet and turned his skin black; his eyes glowed red like those of a mad dog, he howled, writhing as the fire ate the flesh from his body.

*This man is alive with fire.*

A sharp eruption of light and noise jerked the burning man forward and he teetered in front of the firefighter.

In that terrifying instant, Benji's mind closed like a door. Locked inside were faint memories of feast days and masked dancers with painted bodies, visions of *curanderas* and *arbularias*—healers and those who offered protection against black witchcraft—and all the ugly prison mojo he'd ever seen.

He was without defenses when he saw the second apparition: a witch.

It rushed toward him, skin painted with blood and earth. In Benji's eyes, the witch was a two-legged bird of death—an owl that flew directly in his path. He heard a death rattle, felt the owl claw at his soul—and fear clutched his heart, held it between icy fingers, and refused to let go.

AT EIGHT-THIRTY P.M., Cerrillos Road was crowded and every motorist in the southbound lane was on a blind collision course with the sun's final rays. Cruising lowriders cut across white lines to sniff rival tailpipes. The heavy beat of car stereos gave a bass rhythm to the stop-and-go traffic and rising tempers.

Stranded at a red light, Sylvia eased her head out the window. She tasted warm exhaust fumes, and smoke from someone's barbecue; the day's heat settled over the city like a lid.

Her home was still twenty minutes away, in La Cieneguilla. The adobe house would be surprisingly cool, and dim, except for two automatic security lights. The recently installed alarm system made her feel more secure, but it didn't make the house less lonely. No one waited for her at home, not even her dog. For several months, Rocko, her terrier, had been staying with her former partner's son, six-year-old Jaspar Treisman.

Sylvia slumped down behind the Volvo's steering wheel. Before her relationship with Matt England, solitude had always been desirable, pleasurable. A relief. Now, nothing was quite so simple.

At the corner of St. Michael's and Cerrillos she turned right. Matt wasn't coming to her house tonight, but she would go to his. She touched the bag next to her on the seat. Through paper, the thick bottle of Absolut chilled her fingers. In addition to the vodka and some jalapeño-stuffed olives, she had focaccia sandwiches from Portare Via. She wanted to feed her lover, then she wanted to fuck him. She wanted to drink too much vodka. Get stupid. Gain distance from her professional life for a few hours.

The Volvo's engine whined as the revs slowed in second gear. She patted the steering wheel; the car seemed weary and worn out, and she identified with it. Not a good sign.

Salazar Elementary was deserted for the summer. The only structure in the illuminated school yard was a white trailer. It sat in the far southwest corner. Tires dotted its roof. Next to the trailer, a small patch of earth had been transformed into a lush garden. Matt's garden. Planted in neat rows, green chiles, tomatoes, and corn thrived. Between rows, giant sunflowers—great floral babushkas—seemed to nod their heads reverently. Mounted on a pole, a big yellow beach ball mimicked a predatory owl with huge black-and-red eyes. It was designed to repel jays, crows, and magpies. The ball bounced off the pole in a sudden gust of wind. An automatic sprinkler ticked insistently, and the air was tangy with the scent of moist soil. Beyond the garden's fenced border and the wooden compost bin, an elm tree had grown up through weeds like a leafy flagpole. Matt had an agreement with the school: they gave him free rent and a trailer pad; he brought his own trailer and kept an eye on the property when he was off duty. It was typical of state cops to choose a trailer over a real house.

The Caprice was gone; Sylvia parked next to Matt's battered pickup truck with its wrought-iron calf rack. She watched a dust devil chase itself across asphalt and dirt. At the trailer door, she balanced groceries and briefcase under one arm and used the key Matt had presented to her three months earlier. She opened the door and was greeted by a throaty meow. The old tomcat, not yet adjusted to domestic life, liked to complain. His head was misshapen, and his nose bore scars from his recent career as a stray. Matt's new pet was fodder for "kitty" jokes at D.P.S. A cop with a cat simply wasn't manly.

"Hey, Tom," Sylvia murmured. "Lonesome?" The cat brushed against her bare leg as she switched on the trailer's overhead light and stepped into icy cold—Matt had left his air conditioner at full blast again.

The small entryway led into an almost equally minute kitchen. The groceries landed on the counter, the Absolut went straight to the freezer.

The living room accommodated a couch, stereo system, and television. The master bedroom was located at the trailer's west end. During late June and July, it took the day's full heat. When the air conditioner was off, the result was hot enough to bake a cherry pie.

Sylvia threw her jacket and briefcase on the couch and stripped off her clothes. She pulled on one of Matt's extra-large T-shirts, this one sporting a law-enforcement academy logo—like most cops, he was never completely out of uniform. And then she splashed cold water on her face and blotted away makeup.

Maybe she could finally let go of the day, the court-room, the office. She intentionally set her briefcase beside the couch, out of sight. Not quite out of mind. Her partner, Albert Kove, was on vacation, due back in four days. He was sorely missed; for Sylvia he was both a peer and a boss, a teacher and a friend. She sighed; Albert had better be in the office of the Forensic Evaluation Unit on Monday morning. Negotiations on the renewal of their state contract were set to begin. Professional do-or-die time.

In the kitchen, the snap of the pop-top elicited mews from Tom. While the cat scarfed his dinner, Sylvia made herself an Absolut martini, straight up, double olives. She switched on the television, sprawled on the couch, and sipped the drink, which wasn't quite cold enough.

Everywhere she looked, she saw Matt. His fly rod propped in the corner behind the couch. A baseball bat and a basket of balls. On the wall, a framed photo of his wife and young son, both killed years earlier in a car crash. Three state police certificates of commendation next to the photograph. Tacked to a closet door, a paper target—a man's torso outlined in black against a white background. Bullet holes neatly etched a happy face on the target torso. On the end table, a copy of *The Rise and Fall of the Great Powers,* part of Matt's self-education program.

She could count on the fingers of one hand the possessions she had in his trailer. She had a new pair of underpants tucked under the pillow on the bed. Her toothbrush, floss, and hairbrush were in a bathroom drawer next to his razor blades and shaving cream. She kept a box of tampons under the sink. She knew he wouldn't mind if she left clothes in his closet, CDs, or bath oil, but she didn't want to make the present arrangement comfortable.

Comfort always came with an unpleasant edge.

She needed an escape route. She needed to feel she

could retreat into her own world. No doubt that need could be traced back to her father's desertion and disappearance. Sylvia made a face and downed the rest of the martini. She wasn't in the mood for her own two-bit analysis. She let her body settle deeper into the cushions of the couch.

If she had a problem sharing territory, Matt was the opposite. Shirts, undershorts, books, gardening catalogs—these were the prized possessions he kept in abundance at her house. She was constantly finding his strays: fountain pen in the washing machine, bolo tie under the bed, one sock in the toolshed.

She yawned and stretched just as her briefcase emitted a quick series of chirps. Her cell phone. She retrieved the handset and greeted a woman from her answering service. Kevin the Terrible, her court-ordered client, was on the line. Sylvia's eyebrows rose in surprise. He'd missed his appointment that afternoon. Unless Kevin had a note from home signed by God, his probation officer would almost certainly begin the revocation process.

She said, "Put him on."

"Hey, Dr. Strange? Listen, I know I messed up." There was a rumble of traffic in the background. The noise became louder, then it was suddenly muffled, and Sylvia imagined Kevin had cupped the mouthpiece with his hand.

He continued, excited, really full of himself. "I had something I had to do."

"You know the deal, Kevin. If you miss a session, you may be revoked." Sylvia examined the remaining stuffed green olive in the bottom of her glass. "I have one bit of advice: be in my office tomorrow. Twelve o'clock sharp. We'll talk about this."

Suddenly, Jackie Madden, Kevin's legal guardian, was on the phone. She sounded distressed. "Dr. Strange. I'm really sorry Kevin missed his session. He had a job interview for a dishwasher at El Comal. But I'll make sure he gets to your office tomorrow."

"I'll see him at noon." Sylvia disconnected, let the phone slide out of her fingers.

Tom landed suddenly on her stomach; sharp claws began to knead flesh. Startled, Sylvia moved the cat aside, stood, and walked into the kitchen. She wanted another drink. She needed food. She looked longingly at the focaccia sandwiches—she had no idea when Matt would return, but she was determined to wait. She stole a quick bite of provolone cheese and closed the refrigerator door firmly. In a small cupboard she found a bag of pretzels and a squeeze-bottle of mustard. With a fresh shot of vodka, she reclaimed her position on the couch next to the cat.

Two of three network affiliates had the same lead story on the ten o'clock news: "Anthony Randall walks in sensational turnaround."

On Channel 7, against the background of the Santa Fe Judicial Complex, reporter Mike McPeavey summed up the half-day hearing and the intense community reaction to Randall's release. McPeavey told his anchor, "Apparently, there have been threats of vigilante justice in this case."

Anthony Randall faced the camera with his lawyer to say, "Somewhere out there, the real rapist is free."

Sylvia drained the last of the martini and used the remote control to turn off the television. Anthony Randall's cocky smile stayed with her, and she tightened her fingers on the cat's fur until Tom yelped indignantly.

She left her empty glass in the kitchen sink and switched off all the lights in the living room. She stood in the dark. Anger, blame, frustration—acute and discordant reactions. She felt them all.

\* \* \*

OUTSIDE, KILLER CROSSED the dark school yard, moving from shadow to shadow. The trailer stood out like a big, ugly rock. Or a stranded ship. The windows were dark eyes. Empty eyes. Wind buffeted the trailer's aluminum walls. It knocked about the ceramic wind chime on the back porch, and the pottery chips made a soft, urgent sound. Wind prowled through the corn and tomato plants like a hungry animal.

Killer saw the doctor's car parked in front of the trailer, near the front door. The cop's Caprice was gone. Good. That was just the way it should be.

Words played through Killer's mind on a loop: *You see it all behind their eyes—evil thoughts, evil lies.*

SYLVIA PULLED ON her wrinkled skirt and stepped barefoot from the trailer. Outside, the low howl of the wind overlaid the steady hum of traffic from Cerrillos Road. Horns honked in the distance, followed by the screech of brakes and a siren. She walked to her car, opened the door, and began her search.

Glove compartment. Visors. Ashtray. She turned away empty-handed, but before she closed the door, she remembered to check under the front seat. A lonely Marlboro had rolled around on the floor for weeks. The car lighter glowed red in seconds. She inhaled gratefully, with illicit pleasure. She welcomed the bite the smoke took from her lungs.

On the trailer steps, she sat and drew the cigarette down to the quick. The wind had picked up, and it slapped her face with a warm, dry palm. In the garden, cornstalks danced and whispered. She felt someone's presence, eyes on her skin, and she looked up at the moon. The fine hairs on her arms stood up. She was edgy as hell.

With great care, she tapped the cigarette butt against asphalt, then she pressed the tip together with finger and thumb. She slipped the butt under one of the cinder-block supports beneath the trailer skirt and took a last look at the garden. When she was back inside the trailer, she locked the door.

Sylvia lit three scented candles. Earlier in the evening, she had craved sex as a frenzied antidote to her anger and frustration. Now, she would gladly accept sleep. But her body and mind refused to relax.

She dimmed the lights and left the first candle burning in the kitchen, the second in the bedroom, and carried the third to the bathroom. The flame sent shadows scurrying up bathroom walls to escape the confining space. She dropped her clothes in a pile, reached into the shower stall, and opened the cold spigot.

When she stepped in, the water was frigid and goose bumps instantly dimpled her skin. She gasped and dipped her head under the flow. It hurt. She forced herself to stay under the water even after her head began to throb with pain. Finally, she turned on the hot water, full force. The spurt warmed, became hotter. The bathroom overflowed with steam and the scent of jasmine from the candle. Her body polarized, then centered itself. The heat began to work its magic, and a deep sense of relaxation lulled her senses.

KILLER HEARD THE message like an internal whisper: *You are the wings of vengeance and death, vengeance and death, vengeance and death.*

A three-quarter moon highlighted silky tassels and slender leaves. The earth felt cool and cushioned, and it filled the air with loamy scents.

Killer skimmed gloved fingers over the white painted surface: siding, vent, drain spout. The exterior of the trailer was home to tiny beetles and spiders; an orb-weaver had spun its complex web in the corner of an air vent beneath a window. The web glistened in the restless night air. A moth struggled in vain to free itself from silken chains. Flickering candlelight escaped through the screened window and danced on the web with the spider.

Window, siding, door, handle. The dried blood on Killer's hands and arms gleamed dully in the moonlight. The crowbar fit neatly between door and jamb; it took steady pressure—prying the area below the knob—before the lock popped and the door swung open.

SYLVIA RINSED OFF shampoo suds and reached for soap. The bar was thin and hard—she remembered seeing a bar of Ivory in the sink. If she worked fast, she could reach out and grab the soap and her toothbrush without flooding the floor. She snapped the shower curtain open.

The Ivory was there, within reach. She gripped the smooth bar in one hand. As she retreated behind the curtain again, a shadow passed the open bathroom door.

Sylvia's heart stuttered. She caught her fear instantly, held it back, and rationalized: *Matt's home.*

She called his name.

The silence stung. She left the water running but stepped out of the shower. Another shadow across the doorway. This time, candlelight. She allowed herself a full breath. But still she moved quickly. She pulled her T-shirt over her head; it clung to her wet body. Telling herself she was overreacting, she checked the hall and moved into the bedroom. The walls seemed to slant inward; the room appeared smaller than usual. She perched on the edge of the bed and reached across the Pendleton blanket. Matt's off-duty revolver was in the bed holster—loaded. She used a two-handed grip and

started back toward the hall. Something caught her eye.
The back door had been forced. It hung ajar on its hinges.
   Someone was inside.

# FIVE

SYLVIA FROZE IN her tracks. Her heart was pounding against her chest, her breath caught in her throat. A voice in her brain kept screaming, *Get out.*

She shifted the revolver and pivoted to escape through the door. A shadow hovered, disappeared, just as sharp pain raced across her right side. No shadow could deliver such a blow. Heat followed pain. Her eyes filled with tears. She stumbled from the force of the kick, her torso twisted, knees buckled. The air had been knocked out of her lungs. The room swam.

Candlelight caught the side of her attacker's face, and Sylvia cried out.

Teeth white against the wide, blackened mouth. Skin coated with a muddy pigment. No eyes, just dark holes the size of fists. Reddish stripes smeared across both cheeks.

Before Sylvia could react defensively, a gloved hand shoved her against the bed. Metal cleats on a black boot tore through her T-shirt and her skin. The pain was searing.

The fingers of her left hand closed around the butt of the revolver. She shifted her body, transferred the gun to her right hand and raised it to defend herself. Her attacker was gone.

She stayed there, numb, unable to move even when she felt the blood ooze across her abdomen.

MATT CUT THE turn sharp, and the Chevy's bumper scraped the fence that bordered Salazar Elementary. An S.F.P.D. patrol car was parked behind Sylvia's Volvo. Two uniforms were bent toward the Volvo's passenger window. The cops looked tense. One of them tried the door handle.

It was midnight, but Matt's beeper had gone off thirty minutes earlier when he happened to be trekking an arroyo by moonlight a half mile from his vehicle, in search of a stolen U-haul. To cover the eighteen miles between Budaghers and his trailer, Matt topped one hundred miles an hour up the interstate. Cars in the right lane were buffeted by the wake of the Caprice. Bumpers pulsed red. He only slowed when he exited I-25 at Cerrillos Road.

Matt parked the Caprice next to the Volvo. One of the uniforms raised a hand in recognition. Manny Ruiz was the shortest law enforcement officer in the state; rumor had it he perched on a telephone directory when he drove. Matt knew him from the academy; Manny had aced Criminal Procedure.

"She locked herself in the car," Manny said.

The second uniform was a woman. She pressed both hands to her hips as she spoke. "We got her statement, checked out your trailer. We can dust, but she told us the guy wore leather gloves." She nodded toward the Volvo. "She wouldn't let us in—"

"Shock," Manny Ruiz explained to the night air.

"The bleeding slowed down," the female uniform said.

Matt brushed past the officers. He leaned against the Volvo's flank and pressed his hand to the windshield.

Sylvia was seated behind the steering wheel. Her eyes

flicked upward and focused on his. She unlocked the door. He opened it, bent down. He saw his revolver clutched in her right hand. Blood was smeared on her oversize T-shirt.

He said, "Slide over."

He did not try to touch her at first. He signaled Manny Ruiz and friend to take off. In the rearview, Sylvia watched the blue Buick roll out of the school grounds. A moment later she said, "He got in when I was in the shower. I don't think he took anything." Her voice was flat.

Matt said, "You're bleeding."

Sylvia shook her head. "I'm all right." Gingerly, she released the revolver and let her fingers trace her rib cage. She flinched in pain. "I bet I have a cracked rib." Matt kept his hands off. He would move at her pace.

Sylvia sighed. "He kicked me with his boot." Finally, she turned to look directly at Matt. Her eyes stayed on his for seconds; tears welled up. She blinked them back and let her head rest against his chest.

Her voice was muffled when she said, "Tomorrow, this is going to hurt like hell."

Matt found a five-milligram Valium in a bathroom drawer. Sylvia swallowed the sedative. He helped her clean the abrasion on her ribs. It was a little more than four inches across, deep in places where boot cleats had penetrated. The skin around the wound had already begun to darken; it was purplish and swollen. Because she refused to go to the emergency room, he smeared the area liberally with antibiotic ointment. Hopefully that would ward off infection.

He found a way to rig the back door so no one could get in—or out. It would do until tomorrow.

With the television providing white noise, they both stretched on the couch, their bodies arranged for maximum contact. It took another twenty minutes before Sylvia's breathing became deep and steady.

Matt hadn't told her that he expected one of his supervisors to show up within the next thirty minutes—the attack had occurred at the residence of a state police investigator.

While he waited, he almost fell asleep. But his muscles began to cramp, and he had sharp pains in his shoulders and neck. He knew aspirin and a cold beer would help. He eased Sylvia's body from his, stood cautiously, and walked into the kitchen.

He put a hand out to open the refrigerator, then stopped. Amid grocery lists, postcards, and a stick-on calendar, a photograph was trapped beneath a magnet. He was about to lift it from the door when he felt breath on his neck. He turned and found himself staring into Sylvia's dilated pupils and deep brown eyes. Without a word, she reached around him and took the photograph. The magnet fell to the floor with a soft sound.

It was a Polaroid of a man. There was no way to know if he was dead or alive. His nude body was trussed, his face was visible. He had been castrated.

Anthony Randall.

Horrified, Sylvia dropped the photo. When Matt reached to retrieve it from the floor, he saw the message scrawled on the back: "Take a good look at the only True Justice. One for the Killers' Doctor."

"HE WAS TORCHED." Hansi Gausser, head of serology at the Department of Public Safety crime lab, cleared his throat and used his sleeve to wipe grit from his eyes. The outdoor crime scene west of San Antonio Creek was a bear to process: rough terrain, ceaseless wind, and the devastation of the Dark Canyon fire. Gausser sighed;

just his luck to be on call the week after July Fourth. Holidays brought out humanity's nasty streak. He smiled vacantly at Sylvia and Matt, then brought himself back to the business at hand: Anthony Randall's corpse.

Gausser's fingers hovered over burn patterns on the dead man's body. "The forest fire missed him altogether. But he was doused with accelerant. Fortunately, there's enough of his face left to identify him—it looks like your guy."

"It's Randall." Matt nodded at the serologist. Hansi Gausser was Swiss-born and -educated and a perfectionist. Pronounce the "au" in Gausser like the "ou" in "house" and you were on his good side immediately. Pronounce it like the "a" in "gas"—as almost everyone did—and the Swiss mercenary soldier emerged. In spite of, or perhaps because of, his peculiarities, Gausser was a first-rate criminalist.

And he was known for his olfactory tolerance.

Matt tried his best not to breathe. Sylvia kept a bandanna over her mouth and nose. It was too early in the day for anyone but Gausser to brave the stink of burned, decomposing flesh. When the wind gusted from the south, the stench was unbearable.

Sylvia stood clear of Gausser. It wasn't the smell that kept her outside the perimeter, or fear of contaminating the scene—the techs had already completed a grid search and most of their evidence collection. Her need for distance wasn't physical. She had wished death on Anthony Randall. However irrational the thought, she couldn't shake the nagging sense of complicity in his murder.

*"One for the Killers' Doctor."*

Gausser pointed to a fire trench to the west of a stand of piñon. "Look at the layout: the edge of the burn was thirty feet from here and stretched all the way to Dark

Canyon." He turned back to the body. "This tree trunk, and the duff around it, weren't even touched. The fire didn't jump the trench."

Sylvia forced herself to ask the question: "Was his body burned postmortem?"

"That's an interesting question," Gausser said evenly. "The autopsy results will tell us the answer."

She swallowed, but the lump stayed lodged in the back of her throat. "If he was burned alive, how long did it take him to die?"

Gausser was suddenly more animated. "That depends. A person who is immolated, who inhales corrosive fumes and superheated air—or even a fireball—will lose the tissues that line his airway. That could kill him, but most likely not instantly. Poisoning or air exclusion—a common problem in house fires—could be fast- or slow-acting. Loss of homeostasis—for instance, if you were to fry off all your skin—that's a burn unit issue." Gausser paused, then continued. "In cases of true immolation, like those Vietnamese monks who barbecued themselves to protest the war—it's usually not an immediate death. Seconds, minutes . . . very *long* minutes." Gausser chewed on his lower lip thoughtfully. "However, I think Anthony Randall got lucky."

"What?"

Gausser pointed to an area just behind what remained of Randall's left ear. "Gunshot to the head. Entry wound, exit wound. Notice the angle. The shot was probably too shallow to kill him outright, but it would have stunned him."

Sylvia leaned forward to get a better view of the darkened area. She said, "A mercy shot?"

"Whatever it was, lousy aim." Gausser tweezed a charred fragment and placed it carefully in a brand-new paint container. He shrugged. "Matt, I don't think your friend from the F.B.I. believed it was a mercy shot."

Sylvia caught Matt's look of surprise.

Gausser continued. "Special Agent Chaney left right before you all arrived."

Matt took in the information without comment, but he was curious as to why a federal agent based in Las Cruces would show up at this particular crime scene.

A gust of wind brought with it the stench of burned flesh; Matt groaned.

Without looking up Gausser said, "Help yourself to my private stock of Charlie. In my back pocket."

Although Matt had already applied a liberal coat of Vicks VapoRub around his nostrils, he accepted the offer and pulled out a worn plastic bottle. When he unscrewed the top he was overwhelmed by the sweet stink of Charlie cologne. Gausser swore it was the best way to mask the stench of the dead. The criminalist's theory was that somehow the cologne's fragrance chemically bonded with one of the world's most loathsome odors; the result was at least tolerable for inhalation.

Matt offered the bottle to Sylvia. She shook her head and kept one arm crossed beneath her breasts. Matt wasn't sure she should be here, but she hadn't asked for his opinion. The call had come in somewhere after four-thirty A.M.: a body discovered by a firefighter in the Jemez Mountains. It didn't take a genius to figure out the dead man might be Anthony Randall.

Inside the scene perimeter, Matt took a breath, stepped close to Gausser, and pointed a gloved hand toward what remained of Randall's right arm.

"Bindings," Gausser said.

To Matt's surprise, Sylvia slipped under the perimeter tape and squatted next to Gausser. She lowered the bandanna from her nose. Her eyes were invisible behind dark glasses. She was thinking of the image on the Polaroid. She said, "I'm guessing the castration was pre-mortem."

Gausser said, "Again, I won't be able to tell you until we get the autopsy report."

"No. But it looks like this killer—or killers—wanted to inflict pain."

"Payback for rape." Matt stared down at the swollen torso, the burned thighs.

"Flora Escudero's family?" Gausser wiped his upper arm across his forehead and gazed down at Randall's corpse. "If he'd raped my daughter, I'd think about doing something like this."

Silently, Matt agreed. When you made a career of law enforcement, you faced the fact early on that the bad guys got away with murder . . . and rape. If someone you loved was a victim, it could be easy to take the next step, make your own justice.

Criminal Agent Terry Osuna was the D.P.S. investigating officer on this one—she'd been out at the scene earlier, working with the special agent from the U.S. Forest Service. When Osuna questioned Flora Escudero's family later today, Matt would make it a point to be there.

Gausser said, "How are your tomatoes doing, Matt?"

"My first Cherokee Purple is about ready to pick."

"You promised me a basketful."

"They'll produce until October first. You'll get your fill of tomatoes."

"You ought to get Sylvia to put them up for you." Gausser winked.

"Right." Matt looked down at Sylvia, who wasn't taking her eyes from Randall's body. He tried to picture her in an apron slaving over 180-degree water and a canning kettle.

Matt let his gaze slide slowly over the damaged

corpse. His detachment and curiosity never managed to block out quite enough. People who died of unnatural causes often wore the same disappointed expression, as if they had known their last moment was imminent, felt the injustice, but were too weary to protest. But Randall's corpse had the face of a macabre jester: his lips had burned back to reveal a grotesque smile, his skin was pulp, his eye sockets blackened and empty.

Matt turned away from the body and listened to the distant throb of helicopter rotors above the noise of the wind. The fire crew was dumping water and retardants on the last of the burn just a mile west of the scene.

Sylvia stood and closed her eyes. Matt reached out a protective arm. She stiffened, then moved out of reach. It took him a moment to realize that he'd grazed the wound on her rib cage. He felt clumsy and inept.

His frustration transformed into desire for action. He wanted to nail her attacker, tear him apart, make him hurt. At this instant, Matt didn't pretend to be broken up by Randall's death—he could almost believe that somebody had done law enforcement a favor—but he hated the idea that Sylvia was involved in this mess, that she'd been hurt. And, ultimately, it sickened him that another killer was loose.

On the other side of the piñon grove, between Gausser's state vehicle and Matt's Caprice, a van from the Office of the Medical Investigator pulled up. The deputy M.I. picked his way through the trees. It was his job to make the official pronouncement of death—as if without it Anthony Randall might surprise them all and suddenly walk away—and then to transport the remains to the O.M.I. in Albuquerque. The deputy M.I. walked up to the crime scene perimeter and ducked under the yellow tape.

He said, "Got lost and couldn't find you guys. They

gave me directions up at the staging area." He peered closely at the corpse. "That is one sorry crispy critter."

Sylvia stared through the stubby, potbellied man; her thoughts were far away. She envisioned the fire raging up the canyon, and then she tried to imagine Anthony Randall's last few hours of life. Why drive him all the way into the Jemez to kill him? It wasn't likely the killer—or killers—had expected the body to be destroyed in the forest fire. Clearly, they wanted to make a public statement. And they wanted to make sure the "Killers' Doctor" was included in that statement. So much so that they risked a trip to Matt's trailer after the murder.

Sylvia turned to Matt. "I'd like to talk to the firefighter who found the body."

Matt closed his eyes, stretched, then nodded. "I'm going to be a while. If I don't catch up with you, I'll call you at noon. You know your way to the staging area?"

"I'll find it." Sylvia moved with more energy now. She cocked a finger at Gausser. "About those canned tomatoes, Hansi . . . dream on."

DAYS EARLIER, WHEN Santa Fe National Forest officials set up a staging area outside the village of La Cueva, the Dark Canyon fire had been an unknown force. During the last ten hours, the fire had peaked. Now, officials gambled it would burn itself out.

When Sylvia turned off the access road, she saw buses, trailers, and emergency vehicles parked in a meadow that was smaller than a football field. This was where dispatchers communicated with the world, journalists prowled for scoops, and the all-important firefighters slept, ate, and got themselves patched up. At the moment, a dozen people, some in yellow-and-green firefighter uniforms, waited while a helicopter touched down.

Sylvia parked her Volvo next to a school bus. Directly

ahead was a trailer with a sign: U.S.F.S. COMMUNICA-
TIONS. She knocked, then entered. Communication
equipment lined one wall and maps and aerial charts covered most of another. A man wearing headphones bared
one ear.

She said, "I'm looking for the firefighter who found—"

"In first aid." He replaced his headphone. "That big
RV next door. You better hurry. They're gonna ship him
back to Santa Fe."

Sylvia stepped through the trailer door and collided
with a petite, copper-haired woman dressed in a tailored
tan shirt and a trim black skirt, silver belt buckle polished
to a sheen: Rosie Sanchez, lead investigator at the Penitentiary of New Mexico.

"Hey!" Sylvia's eyes opened in surprise. The helicopter had taken off again and the noise overhead was
deafening.

Rosie held her arms wide, and the two friends hugged.

Sylvia mouthed, "What are you doing here?"

As the helicopter moved out of range, Rosie shouted,
"I've got inmates on furlough, fighting the fire. What are
*you* doing here?"

"I need to talk to the firefighter—"

"—who found the body." Abruptly, Rosie lowered her
voice. "Benji Muñoz y Concha."

"He's an inmate?" Sylvia knew that any inquiry
related to an inmate on furlough was part of the pen
investigator's bailiwick.

"One of my best boys." Rosie's expression was
quizzical.

"Let's go see your inmate, and I'll fill you in."

Benji Muñoz y Concha wore the vacant expression,
the glassy eyes, of a zombie in a B horror movie. His
wiry body seemed fragile, his normally dusky skin was
pale. He was huddled on one of four cots.

Rosie said, "Benji? This is a good friend of mine."

Sylvia stood next to the cot and spoke softly. "How are you doing, Benji? Can you talk for a minute?"

No reaction. Benji stared through Sylvia. When she looked closely, she saw that the firefighter's pupils were moving, involuntarily tracking some invisible current of air or mind.

His eyes were a rich sable with a marbling of chestnut highlights. Spanish and Anglo blood had been mixed somewhere in the not-so-distant past with Pueblo. The genetic consequence was regal: high cheekbones, straight nose, chiseled chin.

Sylvia sat on the edge of the bed. "I hear it was rough out there last night."

Silence.

Sylvia snapped her fingers suddenly.

Benji blinked, and a sharp spurt of sound issued from his mouth. It wasn't English—and Sylvia didn't think it was a Pueblo language—but it had the rhythm of some exotic speech. It reminded Sylvia of a client who, in times of stress, had reverted to the frenzy of speaking in tongues.

Sylvia turned to Rosie. "How long has he been like this?"

"When I got here, he was sitting up and talking, but it was mostly *that* kind of speech. The E.M.T.s brought him in early this morning; they said he made sense one minute but not the next. There's an M.D. on call. He examined Benji."

"Where is everybody now?"

"They went out with the helicopter. Two firefighters were injured in Dark Canyon."

Sylvia gazed at Benji. Malingering was a common problem with inmates, and some of them were amazingly adept at faking physical and/or emotional trauma. Evaluating health professionals had to rely on corroborating or discrediting data.

She stood and tipped her head toward Rosie. "You know Benji . . . is he faking?"

Rosie shook her head vehemently. "Benji's a fire-fighter—it's part of his heritage, it's who he *is*. He takes great pride in his skills, in his ability to face fire. His father was a firefighter. And his grandfather before him." She waved a hand at the inmate. "Benji has nothing to gain by faking this—trance. In fact, when he's himself again, I believe he'll feel as if he lost face today."

Sylvia nodded. "Okay. Let's assume he's traumatized. Without a neurological exam, the doc can't completely rule out seizures or head injury, but I doubt the Department of Corrections wants to shell out four hundred bucks for a scan?"

"You guess right." Rosie handed Sylvia a long form that a Dr. Cooper had filled out; it was a report on Muñoz y Concha. Sketchy, but still interesting. According to the doctor, the firefighter had shown no sign of head or neck trauma. Dr. Cooper noted that the most disturbing symptom was Benji's amnesia: "Patient has no memory of discovering a body."

At the top of the page, someone, probably Cooper, had scribbled "?mental? B R psychosis?? dissociative amnesia?"

Sylvia stared at the report and guessed the initials "B R" stood for "brief reactive." She considered both diagnoses. Brief reactive psychosis was short-term, sudden psychosis, in which there would be severe disturbances in mental functioning, i.e., the inability to tell reality from fantasy. Brief reactive psychosis might be induced by a heavy-duty stressor—say, for instance, the discovery of a mutilated and burning body. In contrast, dissociative amnesia was contained memory loss or disturbance caused by a trauma or by traumatic events. Simply, it was a change of consciousness—a disconnection between an individual and some part of himself or his environment.

She glanced at Rosie. "Would you say Benji's been catatonic for thirty minutes? An hour?"

"A half hour or less."

"No one was with him on the hill when he found Randall?"

Rosie shook her head. "Benji was out there for hours, wandering around." She frowned and worry altered her features. "You heard him just now."

"Has he said anything you could understand?"

Rosie pursed her lips. "When I first got here, he blurted out something about an owl of death . . . and something evil stalking the city."

"What, like Godzilla?" Sylvia massaged the muscles of her neck. "Tell me about Mr. Muñoz y Concha."

The women moved to a small table in a corner of the RV and sat down. Rosie leaned back against the hard wall. Usually in her job she was dealing with inmates who overdosed on pills, crack, or heroin, or inmates who shanked other inmates, or inmates who shanked staff, or correctional officers who used excessive force. There was nothing supernatural about the system—it nurtured a very down-to-earth breed of monster. Normally she didn't have to deal with witches and death owls.

"Rosita." Sylvia interrupted her thoughts.

"Ummmm?"

"How old is Benji?"

"Twenty-two."

"And he's in for—?"

"He's in the murf."

Sylvia knew that the Minimum Restrict Facility housed a wide variety of inmates—everything from first-time nonviolent offenders to murderers awaiting parole or unconditional release.

Rosie said, "Benji got popped for working with this hot-car ring in Las Cruces. They just zip them across the border. He swears he didn't know about the ring—got suckered in."

"And you believe him?"

Rosie turned to study Benji; the inmate didn't move a muscle. She said, "No. Not a word." She ran a hand through wild curls and smiled. "But I like him, and I want him to make it. Why are you so interested? You think he saw something last night? You think he saw Randall's killer?"

"I think he saw something that scared him out of his wits." Sylvia narrowed her eyes and leaned forward, chin propped on her knuckles, elbows braced on the table. "Tell me about his family background."

"He pretty much lives in his own world. His parents are dead. I think his mother was Pueblo, and his father was Spanish and Anglo . . . old-world, a healer."

"So he grew up with more than one reality?" Sylvia nodded encouragingly. So far, Benji sounded normal by New Mexico's multicultural standards.

Rosie weighed her next words. "I've known him now for more than a year. He *sees* things. He *feels* things before they happen."

Sylvia leaned forward until the edge of the table pressed against her abdomen. "You're saying he's psychic?"

Rosie shrugged. "I'm saying he *thinks* he's psychic."

"I'm not big on psychics." Sylvia shrugged, then smiled. With one finger she had traced a series of invisible stars on the tabletop. "They're my competition." She eased back and turned to watch the prostrate form of Benji Muñoz y Concha. She had read about *susto*—the frightened state that came with bewitchment. Many people had ways of expressing a similar idea. She thought of "ghost sickness." Some Southern Plains Indian tribes believed that the ghost of someone recently dead needs to haunt the living. And there was Rosie's grandmother-in-law, Abuelita Sanchez, who was clever, witty, a devout Catholic, and who believed in evil as a force of nature. Abuelita lived in a world already crowded with *brujos,* spirits, demons and their curses—*el mal ojo,* the evil eye. The woman made regular visits to a *curandera*—a healer whose seventeenth-century ancestors had brought their traditional practices from Spain to Nuevo Mexico. Sylvia knew Rosie wouldn't think of trying to dissuade her husband Ray's grandmother from her beliefs—Abuelita would give *her* the evil eye.

Rosie stood slowly and walked back to the cot where Benji lay curled in a ball. "Look at this."

When Sylvia was standing by Rosie's side, she saw what her friend had noticed: a long, deep scrape ran the length of Benji's right forearm. She said, "That wasn't on the medical report."

Rosie murmured, "It's almost like Benji's haunted."

Sylvia said, "He is."

# SIX

BRIGHTLY COLORED FOOD booths lined Santa Fe's downtown streets, and Sylvia had to dodge tourists and locals who lined up for burritos and Indian fry-bread on their lunch hour. A summer craft show overflowed the plaza. Costumed mariachi musicians filled a makeshift plywood stage, and traditional marriage songs blared from loudspeakers. On the brick street, two clown-faced jugglers on Rollerblades tossed water balloons. When a balloon splatted on the ground, wide-eyed children in the audience shrieked with pleasure. Sylvia found herself laughing out loud, and one of the painted jugglers winked a pie-eye as she passed by. Just forty-five minutes earlier, she had left the fire staging area, Benji Muñoz y Concha, and Rosie Sanchez.

But the city felt like a completely different world.

Sylvia stepped up to a red-and-white-flagged booth that advertised lamb stew and Navajo tacos. A woman with skin the color of chestnuts and eyes as soft as brown velvet took her order. Sylvia paid two dollars for a huge taco. It was hot and spicy, and she finished it as she walked the short blocks to the office.

It was noon; time for Kevin the Terrible.

"SHEE-IT." KEVIN CHASE mouthed the profanity, and then tried to hide it behind a smile. "People don't like it

55

when a guy like Anthony Randall gets away with rape and sodomy and whatnot." He glanced around Sylvia's office, knees jiggling. His eyes never settled: not on the white walls decorated simply with prints by local artists, not on the Taos-style couch, not on the heavy oak desk, and *not*—God forbid—on another human being.

Sylvia took a deep breath and tried to focus. The respite she'd gained on the plaza was gone. She was completely unsettled; her thoughts were all over the place. Fatigue threatened to overwhelm her senses. Her injured ribs ached.

She tried to ignore the fact that Matt had promised to call. She missed him. Anxiety accompanied her feelings of vulnerability. She wanted to drive straight home, fall into bed, and pull the covers over her head.

Instead, she faced her client, and reminded herself that she had ordered him to be here today *or else*.

A nineteen-year-old probationee. A petty thief about to graduate to hard-time. Cocksure and kid-stupid. *Pissed off*. Not scared enough. Not a clue. In her court-centered practice, Sylvia saw ten "Kevins" each month. Maybe *one* out of a hundred ended up with a real life.

Chase adjusted the 49ers cap on his head, tugged it down over his eyes. "See, that's why the dude was burned up and whatnot."

Sylvia groaned inwardly. The *New Mexican* wouldn't carry the story on Randall's murder until tomorrow's morning edition. But local radio and television stations had already run sound bites and footage. Kevin's feedback was just the beginning. Her thoughts were interrupted by a single sharp knock.

Sylvia stood, opened the door a crack, and found herself gazing at Kevin's legal guardian, Jackie Madden. The woman spoke softly. "I just wanted to make sure

Kevin got here, so I drove him myself. Can I speak with you?"

Sylvia turned to Kevin and said, "Would you give us a minute?" When he nodded, she joined the other woman in the hall.

Jackie Madden had been appointed Kevin's guardian by California courts after his parents were killed in a commuter plane crash four years earlier. She had been the Chase family's neighbor and Kevin's church counselor. Madden was young—in her mid-twenties—but she was responsible.

Jackie kept her voice low and urgent. "Please, you can't just take away Kevin's probation when he's cooperating." The woman was plain, sandy blonde and freckled. Her rangy body projected only nonsexual energy. Her hands were big for her arms, and her fingernails were manicured. Phlegmatic and languid, she was the motor opposite of Kevin. However controlled, her passion came through. And real distress altered her coarse features. "Kevin made a mistake, we don't argue that. But he needs another chance."

Jackie Madden knew what happened to kids who took a bad turn. As a clerical employee of the Department of Public Safety's state police, she spent her days entering data into the computerized National Crime Information Center, N.C.I.C. Her computer screen was filled with details of crimes committed by known criminals in every state—serial murderers, kidnappers, rapists. And most of those offenders had started their criminal careers when they were adolescents. Like Kevin Chase.

Sylvia said, "That's not my decision. You both know, as part of the contractual agreements Kevin made with the courts, his probation officer is notified when he misses a session. I spoke with Frankie Reyes yesterday afternoon when Kevin didn't show up. This may affect his probation. That's all I can tell you."

"But he did call—" Jackie Madden cut her protest short and nodded her resignation. "I'll wait for him in the lobby."

When Sylvia was seated across from Kevin again, he said, "What did *she* want?"

"Jackie's concerned that your probation will be revoked. I don't know what your probation officer will decide, but you and I may need to process that possibility."

"I got here, didn't I?"

"No bullshit, Kevin." Sylvia's dark eyes flashed. "You're facing prison time. Is that getting through to your brain?"

"Yes, ma'am."

He was a well-fed calf. Moderately intelligent, an emotional runt, passive-aggressive. When he talked, his hands moved constantly, drawing pictures in the air. When he was silent, his fingers still fluttered, drummed, or curled into fists. A scar ran from his left elbow to his wrist; he said it was a memento of a motorcycle accident. His shoulder-length reddish hair was neatly layered and framed round features. Translucent blue eyes peered restlessly from a pink face marred by adolescent acne.

For an uncomfortable moment, an inner voice warned Sylvia she was missing signals. But unless Kevin Chase was an obvious danger to himself or someone else, Sylvia's job was to present the facts to Probation and Parole.

Kevin blurted out, "I just wanted to say it, you know, I'm sorry for missing and whatnot." Although he curled his lips into a smile, he did not relax his grip on the arms of the oversize chair. "What was I supposed to do?"

"Get here."

"Oh."

*Ten minutes before the hour.* It was time to end the session.

In the outer office, she watched as Jackie Madden ushered Kevin Chase toward the stairs. She was struck by their odd symbiotic connection.

When Sylvia was alone, she dialed Matt at the Department of Public Safety. The phone rang six times before someone answered. She didn't recognize the voice: "Matt's out, but try his pager."

Sylvia scanned the appointment book. Her afternoon was clear; she had already canceled a three-hour evaluation session. Her five o'clock client had canceled himself the previous afternoon when he was arrested on a parole violation.

She made the only intelligent decision: get out of the office and call Matt from her house. She notified her service that she had closed shop for the day. A stack of papers—psych tests that she needed to score—went into her briefcase, along with a paperback of Patrick O'Brian's *Desolation Island,* the fifth volume in a series she enjoyed for its heroes—a scrungy naturalist and a lusty sea captain.

She locked the office door and took the stairs of the Forensic Evaluation Unit two at a time. The courtyard of the Diego Building was filled with apricot trees, thick green cornstalks, cosmos in rainbow colors, and petunias. Water gurgled from a stone Spanish-style fountain in the courtyard's center, then flowed through narrow *acequias,* water channels, that fed the garden. The soft sound was refreshing. A quick breeze stirred the residual tang of smoke, which mingled with the Russian olive tree's scent like that of fresh-cut lemons.

In the office parking lot, Sylvia ran her index finger

along the Volvo's trunk. When she examined her hand, the tip of the dusty finger showed a perfectly defined print, an accidental whorl pattern. Ash from the Jemez fire had coated the city, and everything glowed with a faint orange hue. Sylvia rubbed thumb against finger just as a hand clamped down hard on her shoulder. She spun around. It took her a moment to recognize the F.B.I. agent's familiar features.

MATT SENT THE Cock 'n' Bull's lady bartender a sleepy— and he hoped halfway sexy—smile. The Pojoaque watering hole was a down and dirty party spot for drug dealers, bikers, and your everyday working stiffs. The bartender looked like she could hoist her Harley overhead, one-handed. In contrast to her strapping body, she had a delicate, heart-shaped face.

She reminded Matt of a bartender he'd known in Enid, Oklahoma, when he was a sheriff. More than twenty years ago. He kept his voice soft. "So Kiki . . . that's a pretty name. Kiki. What about yesterday?"

Kiki lit a hand-rolled cigarette and inhaled so deep that the smoke went all the way to her toes. She washed down the nicotine with a shot of Black Jack. "I wasn't here. Got a day off for once." Her sweet mouth pulled into a smile. She set down the almost empty shot—but not the cigarette—and picked up a damp rag with her free hand. She began to wipe down the rough pine bar with a steady stroke.

Matt thought about the stark contrast—this bar and the home of Flora Escudero and her family. He'd visited the Escudero residence on his way to the bar. Criminal Agent Terry Osuna had been there, too. They'd both had a long talk with Flora's mother and older brother. Their home was small, meticulously and lovingly kept, and filled with objects that symbolized their faith in God:

paintings and statues of the Madonna, Jesus on the cross, and various saints; an ornate, leather-bound Bible.

But it wasn't the religious effects that convinced the investigators that Flora's immediate family was not involved in Randall's murder. It was the fact that they had spent the night in a hospital waiting room while Flora Escudero had aspirin and Valium pumped from her stomach after a suicide attempt. Matt's heart went out to the girl and her family.

Still, there were probably a hundred Escuderos who were more or less related to Flora's family, and they did not all have alibis to cover the hours of Randall's kidnapping and murder. Terry Osuna and Matt were both convinced the crime was one of revenge that could be traced back to *la familia*.

Now Matt leaned closer, nosing the bar with his cowboy boots. "You ever take your bike out by Little Peaks?" He kept his breath shallow. The sour stink of rubber bar mats and margarita mix was close to lethal.

"Yeah." This time Kiki's smile was shy. "You?"

He nodded. "My buddy's got a three-fifty trail bike and I put her through her paces."

Kiki gave up on wiping the bar. She raised a soda gun in her right hand. "You want something? Pepsi? Seven-Up? A beer?"

"I'll take one of your smokes." He'd been able to lay off cigarettes a few years ago, but the inevitable replacement was a tin of Copenhagen. He was trying to break the habit. In a pinch, he still smoked the odd cigarette. Like now.

Kiki shrugged, secretly pleased, and went to work with a little American Spirit shag and a rolling paper. When she sealed the cigarette by moistening the paper with her tongue, Matt said a silent prayer that her shots were in order. He slid the cigarette between his lips as Kiki struck a match. She held out the flame, and Matt sucked in smoke.

Kiki drained the last of the Black Jack from her shot glass. "I liked him."

"Randall?"

She nodded. "Nobody else did. But we were friends, kinda. And I know he didn't rape that girl. He wasn't all bad like people say." Her hands pressed down on the bar. "I don't like cops."

"Who does?" Matt tried a smile.

"You guys have given me some rough times."

"I'm sorry about that, Kiki." Matt pushed his tongue against one cheek.

"But Robbie says you're different."

"Robbie's an okay guy." Robert Wiggits, owner of the Cock 'n' Bull, biker, speed freak. Occasional snitch. For some reason—which probably had something to do with Robbie's bisexual preferences—he'd taken a shine to Matt.

"So . . ." Kiki picked up the bottle of Black Jack, tipped it until the metal pour spout clicked glass, and reached a decision when the gold liquid formed a soft dome at the top of the shot glass. "Yesterday, I wasn't here when Anthony came in." Her expression darkened. "I wish I had been. He'd still be alive."

Matt watched the bartender closely. Some twist of her delicate mouth made him question her true feelings about Randall's death. Matt thought that maybe this large, rough woman had fallen for the man's pretty face and sociopathic charm, but now, the reality was starting to sink in about Anthony Randall.

Or perhaps something more ominous was going on, something she wasn't talking about.

Suddenly, Kiki yelled out, "Hey, Shoshone!" The shrill sound pierced Matt's ears.

A few seconds later, another full-size Anglo woman—hair dyed black, late thirties—stuck her face between the saloon's swinging doors.

Shoshone said, "What?" Then she stomped into the bar, kicking off a parade: two guys followed—one sporting worn Levi's, a faded T-shirt, work boots, and a billcap, the other in manure-spatted cowboy boots and duds.

Matt thought they looked like they were buzzed on meth.

Kiki set up beers for her friends. She told Matt, "These guys were here. They saw Anthony Randall, the whole thing."

Matt's heartbeat revved as he stubbed out the last of Kiki's cigarette. He leaned casually against the bar. "Anybody see who he was with?"

Shoshone had a rumbling voice, a deep bass. "He was looking for Kiki so I poured him a shot of tequila."

Matt said, "You were a friend of his?"

"That little shit?"

Matt saw a sulking Kiki ease down to the end of the bar, where she began to roll another smoke. He said, "It must've been really busy in here."

Shoshone stuck a finger into her mouth, and retrieved a wad of gum. "I know what Randall looked like. And I saw him yesterday."

Matt believed that much was true.

Billcap sniffed and wiped his nose. "I remember him, too, and he sat back by the pool table. A guy sat down with him—a black dude."

"No way." Cowboy shook his head. "He sat over by the toilet. Him and a tiny Mexican chick—"

Billcap shrugged, then chugged his beer.

For an instant Matt's excitement level plummeted.

These guys weren't going to tell him squat about Randall. Not if they could help it. They talked like Randall was drinking with a shape-shifter.

But Matt's curiosity was piqued. Why all the bullshit? Just for his benefit? Just to mess with a cop?

Shoshone growled in Matt's face: "I remember the guy Anthony Randall was drinking with. Tight body, you know? Guy was buff. But he was kinda short."

She turned and chopped a hand halfway down Billcap's back to indicate height, or, more accurately, lack of height. "And I hate short guys. Short guys got—" Shoshone held up her little finger. Billcap and Cowboy snorted derisively.

Shoshone took a slow pull on her beer. "This short guy had eyes like Charlie."

"Charlie?"

"Manson." She leaned close to Matt until he felt her breath like a small, hot wind. "I thought Manson was cool. I mean he was crazy and weird, but he had a philosophy. About war and society and shit. These days, nobody's got a philosophy."

Kiki moved back along the bar until she was standing opposite Matt. She caught his eye, and emotions scuttled across her features. Anger, shame, disgust.

Shoshone was caught up by her own words. She said, "Manson, he controlled those Manson girls . . . he willed them to kill. How many people you know have that much will?"

Billcap looked suddenly worried. He mumbled, "It was all the acid they took."

Shoshone shook her black hair. She smiled slyly. "I think Anthony Randall's killer has that Charlie Manson kind of will. Better watch out, Mr. Cop."

\*    \*    \*

"YOU SCARED ME, Dan!" Sylvia took in the familiar features of Special Agent Dan Chaney. He was an old law enforcement buddy of Matt's. Broad, muscular, and gray-blond—normally she would describe him as handsome. Not today. Today, he was hollow-eyed and haggard.

She said, "Are you all right?" Then her brain caught up with her mouth. "I was so sorry to hear about Nina, Dan. I know she was a good friend."

Special Agent Nina Valdez had been Dan Chaney's lover for more than a year. It had been one of those secret affairs that everyone seemed to know about—everyone except Chaney's wife and his supervisors. The F.B.I. morals code of conduct was so strict that agents were subject to discipline for extramarital affairs.

Now, she tried to pull together recent details: Nina Valdez had been dead for almost two months—killed in Las Cruces. She, Dan Chaney, and other F.B.I. and D.E.A. agents had closed in on suspects just as an arms deal was going down. When the suspect warehouse exploded, Nina went with it.

The media had christened the incident "Blowout at Las Cruces."

Sylvia reconsidered the man standing next to her: Dan Chaney looked just the way a burned-out federal agent burdened by grief should look.

"I've got to talk to you." His voice was a hoarse whisper. He still gripped her shoulder. She looked into his eyes—they were light blue with pinprick pupils. They were the eyes of someone who suffered from sleep deprivation, caffeine overload, and maybe something more ominous. Sylvia had seen speed freaks more relaxed than Special Agent Dan Chaney.

"What's this about?"

"We can't talk here." Abruptly, he let go of her shoulder.

Sylvia felt infected by the federal agent's profound unease. His anxiety was palpable. "Have you seen Matt? We heard you were—"

"I know about last night," Chaney interrupted sharply.

"You were up at the crime scene, where Anthony Randall was murdered. . . ." Sylvia's voice trailed off.

Chaney nodded once. He said, "Sylvia, I know what's going on. I know who assaulted you." For an instant, his face softened, and the old Dan Chaney appeared like a ghost. Curious, diligent, oddly gentle. Then he was gone, buried under this taut mask.

"You know who broke into Matt's trailer?" Sylvia surrendered to Dan Chaney's urgency. Her instinct to help Matt's old friend was shoved aside by the pressing need to hear what he had to say about her attacker. Chaney might be functioning on emotional overload, but he had always been an excellent federal agent.

"Sylvia, you've got yourself a problem." He gestured to a tan Lincoln Town Car double-parked on the street. "Follow me."

Sylvia was two cars behind Dan Chaney's Lincoln, driving south on Cerrillos. They were headed to his motel instead of the Santa Fe office of the Federal Bureau of Investigation. Chaney had insisted on an informal meeting. Sylvia guessed he was working a stakeout.

As she passed Siler Road, a cloud cleared the sun, and the light became brilliant. Luminous. This was the high desert's familiar and legendary summer light: crystal clear and achingly beautiful. For the past few weeks, the sky had been hazed by smog and the residue of wildfires.

Sylvia braked at a red light. Forty years earlier, Cerrillos Road had been a dirt lane fronting farms and orchards. Now, because it connected downtown with the interstate, a hodgepodge of fast-food joints, franchises, and minimarts lined its shoulders. The light went green, and traffic crept forward. Just ahead Sylvia saw Chaney turn off to the right. She followed and parked in the lot of the Rode Inn.

Elbowed between Burger King and Carpet World, the Rode Inn rented by the week or the month. The interior hallway smelled of cigarettes and soiled laundry. The frayed carpet was a sorry clash of orange and red. Sylvia took a shallow breath. Special Agent Dan Chaney was definitely living on the fringe these days.

Uneasy, she followed him down the hall. He kept his body erect and butt flat; Sylvia noticed the right shoulder canted slightly. She hoped he hadn't been trying to bust through doors. When he reached Number 222, he used a key.

Inside, Sylvia squeezed past Chaney. The odor of sweat and apprehension hit her dead on. She stepped over a T-shirt, between stacks of what seemed to be files, newspaper clippings, official reports. A map of the Western states lay open on the bed.

The only window in the room was curtained. Straight ahead, the television was on, humming softly, but the screen glowed blue. The agent had placed a framed photograph of Nina Valdez on top of the TV. Sylvia felt wooed by the high cheekbones, deepset eyes, and wide mouth; she knew how the woman's lovely face must haunt Dan Chaney.

Now Sylvia was also certain that Dan Chaney wasn't working a case—at least not officially.

And that made her feel worse. Her heart sank. She paced the room, glanced out the curtained window for a view of the parking lot, Chaney's Lincoln, and her Volvo. The motel windowpane was cracked. In the tiny open closet, one shirt hung limply over a hanger. The bathroom's fluorescent lights revealed cheap tile and fixtures. Chaney fit right in.

She turned to face him now. "How did you know about last night?"

He ran a thick hand over his stub-cut hair and shrugged. "Shit, Sylvia, I'm an agent. It was all over the scanner." In the next room, a door slammed and the plywood and plaster motel walls vibrated. Chaney's body went rigid.

Sylvia fought her own instinct to tighten up. The man was behaving like a crazed alcoholic coming off a binge, not a law enforcement professional.

She faced him, and her dark eyes explored his limpid blues for a moment, but that particular entrance to his soul was closed. Her voice was gentle when she said, "Dan, does anybody know you're here? Can I call someone?"

He ignored her questions, hunkered on the edge of the bed, and eased a photograph from a dog-eared file. "See if this reminds you of anything?"

The photo was an enlargement. The subject was a corpse. The victim had been bound and burned, just like Anthony Randall. Sylvia said, "Where did you get this?"

When Chaney saw the fear in her eyes he gave a quick nod of approval. "California law enforcement raided a ranch south of Mojave earlier this year. They found Polaroids of two other victims—both adult males—and they found home movies of the murders."

She sat wearily on the bed. "So are we talking about a serial killer? Vigilantes? I don't understand what's going on."

Chaney leaned toward Sylvia, took the photograph from her fingers, and lowered his voice until it was sensual in its intensity. "The dead man in this particular photograph was a child molester until he met up with our mutual friend Dupont White."

Although the name sounded only vaguely familiar, Sylvia knew that Dupont White must be Chaney's enemy—the man responsible for Nina Valdez's death. Then instinct was bluntly shoved aside by facts.

"Dan, this man—this Dupont White—he was the gun-runner who was killed in Las Cruces. In the warehouse blowout. I remember now."

Without moving a muscle, Chaney pulled himself back, reined in his emotions—almost invisibly, but Sylvia saw the transition.

"Dupont White's death"—Chaney stood and cocked fingers to sign quotations around "death"—"his death is an official lie. The Bureau has no proof. All the evidence went up with the warehouse."

Dread ran through Sylvia's body like a chemical. She didn't know if Chaney was delusional or a whistle-blower. The mattress springs dug into her buttocks. She was hot and sweaty. And she wanted to get the hell out of Dodge. But she also wanted to hear what proof Dan Chaney had—if any.

It was a hard sell, and Chaney sensed his narrow window of opportunity. He paced a few steps and continued quietly. "Dupont White hawks black-market hardware to skinheads in Idaho, the Aryan Nation in California, and Lone Star Nazis. It's all part of his para-noid mission to fuck over the cops, the feds, his daddy—everyone who fucked him over first." Chaney stopped moving, rubbed his neck with short, thick fingers, and studied Sylvia for an uncomfortably long time. She refused to veer her eyes under his gaze. Finally he sat down next to her, and his lips turned up into a crooked smile. "For your own safety, you really should believe me, Sylvia."

"Believe you? Jesus, Dan, you're talking about a dead man." She took a breath and set her palms on her thighs, fingers spread. Apprehension pushed her to act, to get out of this room, this motel. She didn't move.

In a quieter voice, she said, "It's been two months since the warehouse blowout. Hasn't the F.B.I. completed DNA tests? Don't they have proof of Dupont White's death?"

Wearily, Chaney ran a hand across his temple to ease a throbbing pain. "It's more complicated than that. The Bureau won't release their findings. They don't want any of this made public."

"Oh, come on, why the hell not? Are you suggesting this is a federal conspiracy?"

"Don't forget, I was there," he answered quietly. Sylvia was startled when an image appeared suddenly on the television screen.

"When they raided the ranch in California, they found this footage." Chaney nodded toward the screen.

The camera panned, jumped, and a grainy image pulled into focus: a desert moonscape.

Sylvia glanced at the agent. His mouth hung open— eyes glommed on film he'd seen a hundred times—his hand gripped the remote. Sylvia's attention was drawn back to the video. The quality was poor, black-and-white and grainy, but watchable.

The camera's eye slid to the ground and closed in on something long and white. Rope. Sylvia swallowed uncomfortably as the camera moved again, jerked along, as if it were a hound following a ripe scent.

The camera stopped on a man's face. Eyes stared blindly out at the viewer. His mouth was open, he was breathing hard and fast. Then there was blurred motion as if the camera had been dropped. For what seemed an interminably long time, the screen was gray. When the camera finally pulled roughly back to reveal the captive's naked body, Sylvia heard herself groan. He was on his back, arms and legs outstretched, lashed between four metal stakes. His skin was wet.

She could hear Chaney's drawn breath; but it wasn't Chaney, it was her own quick inhalation. Nothing else. There was no soundtrack to the homemade video as it became a montage of horrific images: a hand gripping a burning flare, an arm extending over the man's naked body, the flare dropped.

And then, in an instant, flames exploded from the prisoner's gasoline-soaked belly, chest, face.

Sylvia put her hand to her mouth, but she couldn't take her eyes from the burning man—not even when the camera pulled in for a blurry close-up. The body became alive and breathing with flames. Chaney leaned forward on the bed.

Abruptly, the camera pulled back, refocused on a pair of black combat boots, panned up the legs of the killer.

Sylvia knew this must be Dupont White.

He was wearing army fatigues. He had his back to the viewer. A dark ponytail spilled over his broad shoulders.

As he turned toward the camera, Sylvia realized she was holding her breath. Her lungs hurt, she was aware of sharp pain along her ribs.

*His face is smeared with mud or paint.* Black pigment circled the whites of his eyes and spread up over his broad forehead. Dark stripes had been smudged along his cheeks. His thick, flat lips—smeared with black—pulled into a grin.

Like the face of her attacker.

He was arrogant, grandiose, a dark pagan god.

Chaney froze the image.

Sylvia felt numb with fear. She forced herself to speak. "If he's alive, if he's doing this, the authorities—"

"I *am* the authorities," Chaney said tersely. "My superiors didn't believe me, and they won't believe you."

Her fear exploded into anger, and she bolted up from the bed. "That's not good enough! You bring me here to tell me this crazy s.o.b. broke into Matt's trailer after he murdered Anthony Randall? You're telling me I was kicked by a dead man? If you really believe your story, let's talk to Matt, and then we'll go back to the F.B.I. and we'll deal with this in a sane way."

"It's too late for that."

"Well, come on, dammit." She was angry and she was scared. It was bad to think that Chaney might be on the run, paranoid, obsessed with a dead man. It was worse to think he might be telling the truth.

Chaney wiped sweat from his forehead. His eyes were bloodshot. The stubble of his beard shaded the lower half of his face. He shoved a thick manila file folder into Sylvia's hands. "Read this if you want to know more about Dupont White."

Sylvia stared down at the folder.

Chaney's voice dropped to a whisper. "Everyone Dupont touches turns up crazy or dead. Violet Miller—his girlfriend—ended up in a California hospital for the criminally insane. His partner—a killer named Cole Lynch—he's at the pen."

Sylvia shook her head. "Why would Dupont be after *me*?"

"You'll have to answer that one—you're the shrink. But my guess is he doesn't like your clients."

Chaney grasped Sylvia's hand, and he steered her across the room. When they reached the door, he said, "I brought you here to scare you, to warn you, Sylvia. We tracked Dupont to Santa Fe right before he came to Las Cruces for the deal at the warehouse. He was here—now he's back. He's alive. I hope to God you listen to me."

Her voice was soft when she asked, "What about you, Dan? Do you need money, a place to stay? You need help."

"Me?" Chaney stared at her vacantly. "I'm going to find the sonofabitch, and I'm going to kill him."

Sylvia felt his eyes on her back as she retraced her steps down the motel hall.

In a daze, she pulled out into traffic on Cerrillos Road. Her car radio was on, playing an old Righteous Brothers tune, but she did not hear the words. She couldn't shake the images of Dan Chaney or Dupont White.

Five blocks beyond the Rode Inn, she turned into the parking lot of a paint store. An old man driving a fat Pontiac swerved to avoid a collision with her Volvo. She didn't see the other driver's fist raised in anger because she was already dialing Matt's pager on her cell phone. She entered her own number and hung up immediately.

Within minutes her phone rang.

"Hey, what's up?"

Sylvia heard voices in the background. "Where are you?"

"Waiting for a green-chile burrito at Baja Taco. Should I order a couple for you?"

"I need to talk to you. I just spent an hour with Dan Chaney. He told me some really crazy things about Randall's murder and that Las Cruces warehouse blowout—"

"Whoa. Slow down. Where did you see him?"

"At the Rode Inn. I left him in his room, but I don't feel good about it. I think he needs help. I think he's gone AWOL."

She believed she knew what Matt would be thinking about his old friend. An F.B.I. agent gone over the line was an F.B.I. agent without a country. The Bureau would be tracking Dan Chaney down. And when they found him, his career would be dead.

Matt said, "Meet me there, in the motel parking lot.
Don't try to go back to Dan's room. Don't spook him. I
can be there in five minutes. I have to hear this from
him."

Sylvia hung up the phone and drove back to the motel.
She had barely turned off the Volvo's ignition when Matt
pulled the Caprice into the next parking space.

Quickly, Sylvia led Matt back up the metal steps of the
motel's side entrance. When they reached Chaney's
room, the door was ajar.

Matt knocked once and pushed open the door. "Dan?
It's Matt."

No answer. There was no one in the room. Except for
some trash and the odor of fear, all traces of Dan Chaney
were gone.

# SEVEN

"JITA, LET ME get this straight. Dan Chaney thinks you should talk to Cole Lynch because then maybe you'll believe this Dupont White is alive?" Rosie Sanchez caught her lower lip between very even teeth and raised her eyebrows.

"Dan Chaney didn't tell me to meet with anybody. I made the decision to see Cole Lynch because he was Dupont White's partner."

"So you show up on my office doorstep. Well, I wish you'd give me warning, an hour or two, at least. You know what Fridays are like." Rosie clucked in gentle admonition. "Does Matthew know you're doing this?" In electric-blue high heels, the penitentiary investigator still managed to move briskly along the gravel path that fronted the dog runs at the penitentiary kennel.

Sylvia followed, shortening her stride to match pace with her friend. She said, "Matt won't talk to anybody until he tracks down Chaney. He's left messages on Dan's voice mail in Las Cruces. And Chaney's acting hypervigilant, so you can bet he'll check that machine to see who's calling." A German shepherd growled as Sylvia passed by.

The canine unit at the Penitentiary of New Mexico consisted of a small cinder-block building bordered by a kennel. In contrast to the functionally contained kennel space, the surrounding flatlands had a plain grace. The short grasses gained softness with distance. The almost invisible slope and dip of the land reminded Sylvia of a grassy sea. Reluctantly, she brought her attention back to the kennel.

Each of twelve runs was defined by an eight-foot-high chain-link fence. Dobermans, shepherds, and rottweilers paced their cages. A hundred-pound rotty wagged his stubby tail and pressed his wet muzzle against metal when Rosie murmured, "Hi there, Maxwell."

Sylvia found her gaze drawn to a fawn-colored shepherd in the farthest run. The dog had keen brown eyes, sleek fur, and a lean body.

"A Belgian Malinois," Rosie explained. "Her name's Nikki; she's in training. She's going to be a sniffer for drugs, contraband. Maybe."

Sylvia said, "Maybe?"

"Nikki's on probation. *Pobrecita,* she can't keep her mind on her job. Not everyone's cut out to work at the pen." Rosie led the way toward the run. When they were several yards short of the Malinois, she stopped. For a moment Sylvia stood by Rosie's side; then she advanced two more feet. Nikki growled.

Rosie said, "You should know the other inmates call Cole Lynch the Counselor. He *lives* in North's law library. He's our best jailhouse lawyer."

Without turning her head, Sylvia focused her eyes on her friend. "Isn't the Counselor in for murder?"

"It was almost murder. He beat a Hell's Angel just shy of death; part of a business deal." Rosie's milk-and-coffee skin gleamed under the summer sun. With one hand she shielded her dark eyes from the glare. The heat felt unnatural, foreign to New Mexico's high desert. "You really believe Dan Chaney is AWOL?"

"He's acting that way."

Rosie's eyebrows arched again. "He gave an excellent speech two years ago at the New Mexico Correctional Association Conference. Wasn't he good friends with that murdered agent, Nina Valdez?"

Sylvia's skin was damp with sweat. She pushed up her sunglasses until they rested again in the small of her nose. "He was in love with her."

"Poor Dan. I met his wife, Lorraine, at the conference."

"Poor Lorraine."

The Malinois began to pace the six-by-nine run. Every few seconds she'd stop, set all four paws like table legs, and stare at Sylvia. When her canine attention broke—and she could no longer stand her ground—she'd bolt again.

Sylvia whispered, "Keep your focus, Nikki."

The Malinois growled.

Rosie said, "You think Chaney might be right that Dupont White is alive?"

A single, abrupt bark escaped from Nikki when Sylvia turned to face her friend. The stale, hot air made her feel short of breath. "No. I think Dan Chaney's acting like a conspiracy nut."

Rosie studied Sylvia critically. She saw a woman who was strung too tight—that much contained energy had to explode somewhere down the line.

Sylvia closed her eyes, suddenly aware of the pain along her ribs. "But I can't just ignore his warning."

"If Dan Chaney's right, then maybe Benji saw Dupont White out at Dark Canyon."

Sylvia tried to picture her attacker. In her mind's eye, his image had merged with Dupont White's painted face as it had looked on the video.

She jumped sharply and covered her ears when Nikki barked. The shrill sound echoed off concrete. Then she squatted down and rested her elbows on her thighs. This time, she faced the dog like a beta dog in the pack hierarchy—eyes downcast.

Rosie said, "What do you think you can learn from the Counselor?"

"Maybe he'll start screaming and come apart at the seams when I mention Dupont's name." Sylvia kept a straight face and shrugged. "Rosita, what are we doing at the kennel?"

"We're waiting for somebody *I* need to see."

Sylvia shifted her feet; her knees were beginning to ache. Although a low growl was audible at intervals, the Malinois had stopped pacing. "This dog likes me."

"She loves you to death." Rosie frowned.

Still crouched, Sylvia scooted forward toward the shepherd while Rosie watched an off-white sedan raise a cloud of dust along the gravel road. At the far end of the kennel the car pulled smoothly to a stop and a man climbed out. Rosie waved and then returned her attention to Sylvia.

"You've got to do something for me."

"Anything, scout's honor," Sylvia said. She inched forward, and the dog growled.

"I've known you for twenty years, jita. You were a delinquent, never a scout." She glanced at her watch, then at Sylvia. Finally, she couldn't contain her exasperation. "Why don't you leave the poor dog alone?"

"What's the favor?" Sylvia could feel the Malinois's breath tickle her cheek. Out of the corner of her eye, she saw teeth, gold fur tipped with black, and liquid brown eyes.

"Don't tell anyone we were out here."

Sylvia turned to stare at Rosie, and she caught sight of Colonel Jose Gonzales approaching the runs. Gonzales had worked at the penitentiary for more than twenty years, and he was part of New Mexico's old-line corrections network that was based on family connections and nepotism. Wardens came and went, but the network stayed put like a rock foundation. Why was Rosie being so secretive about a meeting with the colonel?

Sylvia frowned. "You know I won't say a word." Then she made a mistake; she let her gaze slide over the Malinois's face. For an instant, dog and woman locked eyes.

The Malinois let out a ferocious snarl, her lips pulled back from serrated teeth, and she lunged forward; the cage vibrated from the force of impact.

Sylvia heard the snap as the dog's jaws closed on metal. Saliva flecked her arms and face. Her heartbeat accelerated to a flat-out run; adrenaline followed the rush. There was a single smear of the dog's blood on chain metal.

Sylvia stood and her knees trembled. "She likes me."

"Jita, they don't know how to *like*." Rosie shook her head. "Too much prey drive."

SYLVIA WAITED BESIDE Rosie's Camaro while, fifty feet away, the penitentiary investigator talked to Colonel Gonzales. Her curiosity was piqued, but Rosie had been unusually reticent. Gonzales hovered protectively, unable to hide the fact that he was totally enamored of Rosie; she patted his arm in a friendly way, but there was tension in her posture. Whatever they were discussing, it wasn't good news.

Waves of heat rose from the Camaro's shiny candy-apple roof. Sylvia positioned herself under the stingy shade of a lone poplar. She thought about the night she had spent with Matt at her house. They'd both been keyed up. Neither of them had slept. Now, her eyes ached from dry heat, smoke, and fatigue. And the wound along her rib itched like hell. Maybe she should stop by First Care on her way home—pick up a supply of antibiotic ointment. Maybe she should get an AIDS test. *Maybe I'm turning into a hypochondriac.*

But she wasn't ready to believe a dead man had attacked her in the trailer.

Matt had agreed with her skepticism: "Dupont White died two months ago. Whoever did this isn't some goddamn serial killer. These are angry locals, these are vigilantes."

"What about Chaney?"

Matt had pulled a beer from a six-pack and slammed the refrigerator door. "From your description, I think he's seriously over the edge."

Still, Matt had insisted on reading the file on Dupont White that Sylvia had taken from Chaney's motel room; a picture began to appear.

Thomas Dupontier White, a.k.a. Dupont White, was a heterosexual male born in Santa Barbara, California, in 1970. His adoptive father, Roland White, now deceased, had been heir to the Smith & White manufacturing fortune. Dupont's mother, Roland's second wife, had been employed as a secretary at the company offices when she met her future husband. Her marriage had been opportune, both financially and socially. It had lasted thirteen years, until Roland White was killed in an unsolved hit-and-run accident. Dupont was sixteen at the time of his adoptive father's death.

At age eighteen, against his mother's wishes, Dupont entered the Los Angeles Police Academy. Almost instantly, White encountered problems with authority. A psych evaluation—part of a recommendation to expel—labeled White as an antisocial personality with sadistic tendencies.

Although Dupont's dream of a law enforcement career had been crushed, his criminal career began to flourish. He trafficked in illegal firearms—and Cole Lynch worked as his partner. Their interstate dealings ranged over Idaho, Texas, California, Oregon, and Nevada. It would make sense for Dupont to have a jacket the length of a novella. But after 1994, the official entries stopped dead. No mention of vigilante murders. No mention that Dupont burned his victims alive. On paper, the man vanished.

Sylvia was startled to see Rosie standing next to her. For a moment she marveled at her friend's tenacity. *Only five feet two on tiptoe. She is hell in high heels.*

Rosie raised an eyebrow at Sylvia. "What are you staring at? Let's go find the Counselor, Mr. Cole Lynch." She navigated the Camaro along the dirt road that skirted the penitentiary's security perimeter. They passed a white sedan on perimeter patrol, and the C.O. in the vehicle raised a hand.

"How did your meeting go with Colonel Gonzales?" Sylvia asked too nonchalantly.

"He told me the warden wants me fired."

"What? Why?" Sylvia jerked around in the seat *"Why?"*

"He wants a man in my job. He wants a college grad. One of his own kind." Rosie raised a placating hand. "That's all I know at the moment. This is a big secret, and Jose risked his job by telling me."

Sylvia sank down in her seat and caught her thumbnail between two teeth. "If they try anything, we're going to sue." Her sunglasses slipped down her nose and she pushed them back.

*"We?"*

"I won't let you go through a lawsuit alone. Does Ray know about this?" Over the past few years, Sylvia had become good friends with Rosie's husband. He was a warm and loving man who adored his wife and their teenage son, Tomás.

"Ray would be happy if I just quit. You know he wants me out of the prison." The Camaro's windows were open, and Rosie let her elbow rest on the lip of the door. Warm, dry wind swallowed the sound of radio chatter.

Rosie nosed the Camaro to forty-five m.p.h. as they approached the Corrections Academy, where a new class of officers was currently in training. A ragtag group of men and women attempted push-ups out on the field. Heat undulated from their bodies.

Minutes later the penitentiary's main facility was directly ahead: dull gray, institutional, lifeless. With fingertips on the wheel, Rosie eased right at the fork and continued past Main Facility, where her office was located on the second floor.

Cole Lynch, the Counselor, was housed at South Facility, medium security, three minutes away. But they would find him at North—the maximum-security facility—on the job.

ROSIE SANCHEZ TAPPED on the reinforced glass window that topped the door to the law library. Inside, the inmate looked up from a stack of legal texts he was organizing. He had the ridged forehead of a Neanderthal man and a hook nose, his dark hair hung in short ringlets, his eyes were almost hidden beneath thick brows. Recognition soothed his wild features; he stood slowly, walked to the door, and opened it a crack.

"Ms. Sanchez. To what do I owe this pleasure?" Cole Lynch's voice had the clipped, concise syllables, the theatrical enunciation, of a practiced attorney. He was clearly pleased to see Rosie Sanchez.

"Could you spare us a minute, Counselor?"

Cole Lynch, a.k.a. the Counselor, was custodian of North's law library; he was also a self-taught paralegal who helped inmates in disciplinary seg when they needed to file an appeal or write a brief.

Usually, the Counselor supervised three separate and secure study cells, each occupied by an inmate, each a spoke off the hub of the compact reference library. This was where men who routinely spent twenty-three hours a day in lockdown could work on getting out. *Legally.* At the moment, the study cells were unoccupied.

From her vantage point behind Rosie, Sylvia thought the Counselor looked like a law student she had dated years ago at U.C.L.A. Maybe it was the hook nose or the *L.A. Law* hair. It wasn't the D.O.C. duds.

Rosie smiled. "We need to talk." She stepped past Cole Lynch and entered the library followed by Sylvia.

The Counselor's eyes gleamed with intelligence and dead-on animal instinct; they slid over Sylvia while he spoke to the penitentiary investigator. He said, "I have reshelving to finish before my next clients arrive." He motioned to the books stacked on and around his desk.

Rosie pulled back, and Sylvia took over. "We'll stay out of your way." She knew the Counselor had already recognized her—inmates knew everyone whose work took them inside the joint—but she introduced herself formally, and then she motioned for him to proceed with his task. He picked up two heavy volumes. He was well over six feet tall and he reached the top shelves, balancing books, with ease.

Sylvia leaned her butt gingerly against a table that already bowed under the weight of *Black's Legal Dictionary* and *Landmark Supreme Court Decisions*.

"Have you heard from Dupont White?"

The Counselor slipped one of the tomes into place.

"Killer? The last I heard, he died in that warehouse explosion eight weeks ago—'Blowout at Las Cruces,' as CNN said."

"Killer?"

The Counselor nodded. "He liked people to call him that." *Constitution and Society* slid into the row.

Sylvia watched Cole as he worked. His thin fingers caressed each binding like it was skin. Here was a man who valued books for the power they could bestow. She knew he would tell her exactly what he wanted to tell her—and nothing more.

She spoke casually. "How long did you know Dupont?"

Cole's lawyer persona was neatly in place. "Since we were kids in California. From the time we all spent at the ranch." He looked at her, gauging what she already knew. "My father was caretaker at Devil's Den. That's what they called it out there. All fifteen hundred acres." He selected another text and glanced at the clock on the wall. His patience was wearing thin.

Sylvia said, "It's possible that Dupont White is still alive."

The Counselor spoke softly. "Don't play games with me, Dr. Strange. I'm one of the *smart* ones—don't let the inmate greens fool you."

Sylvia heard Rosie exhale.

He reached around and picked up four volumes from beside the desk. They were heavy—at least eighty pounds of paper and leather—and the muscles on his arms bulged. As he moved back to the shelves, he said, "The feds were here six weeks ago. They were closing the case on Dupont White." A leather text landed roughly on the shelf.

Cole hefted another into the air. "DNA from hair and skin fragments will provide proof that he went up with the warehouse." The book slammed next to its relation.

Cole continued, "Dental records are also admissible in court as evidence of death." The next book hit so hard that the entire shelf shook.

Sylvia said, "You were his partner—but you seem happy to believe he's dead."

Cole faced Sylvia. "The last deal we did together, I ended up here, and Dupont walked." He gave her a cold smile.

There was a knock on the glass. An inmate stood just outside the door.

The Counselor nodded to the man. His mouth barely moved when he spoke to Sylvia. He said, "I can name four cons who will refuse treatment from you because the last man you evaluated was burned alive." He raised one eyebrow. "What is it with you prison shrinks? I think you overload on the dark side. Maybe you need some perspective?"

The waiting inmate tapped on the glass again.

Cole addressed both women, "Now, if you'll excuse me, I'm busy."

Sylvia said, "Thank you very much for your time, Counselor." She picked up her briefcase.

Rosie was standing by the door, key in lock. As Sylvia turned to follow her friend, she glanced up at the bookshelves. *Model Penal Code and Commentaries* was upside down.

She found it appropriate that the Counselor had laid out his legal argument like a lawyer. Clearly, he needed to prove to "the court" that Dupont White was dead. But she believed that he didn't buy his own argument. And that upset the Counselor.

\* \* \*

IN THE HOSPITAL of the penitentiary's Main Facility, firefighter and inmate Benji Muñoz y Concha lay supine on his mattress. He had not moved a muscle since the nurse and the C.O. had arranged his body under clean sheets. But he did have one of his waking dreams.

He saw himself racing up a hillside chased by flames. He knew exactly where he was—in the soft cleft between tuba rim and dirty canyon—just an easy jog from Dark Canyon. As he raced, he struggled to breathe. His throat was scorched, his lungs felt blackened and withered by the kind of heat that devours every last molecule of moisture. The muscles in his legs filled with blood and contracted until he thought they would rip apart and leave him crippled and powerless to escape the hungry flames. He heard the fire's roar like the great storm waves of the Florida ocean he had seen when he was seven years old. The water had terrified him more than fire.

He knew he would make it to the hilltop; he was a fourth-generation flame warrior.

When he was twenty yards from the crest, he heard the rhythmic *ffoof* of wings above the noise of the burn. It was night, but the flames cast a light as great as the sun. A pulsing shadow on the rugged earth kept pace with him. He felt a presence, and finally, he looked up. A great owl was flying directly above his head. Its eyes were hot orange. The tips of its wings were aflame. Smoke trailed from its beak.

Benji stumbled, fell, and that's when he saw the woman who was Rosie Sanchez's friend, the doctor. At first he didn't recognize her in Levi's and T-shirt with her hair tied back from her face. She was ahead of him surrounded by flames. He tried to call out a warning, but when she turned his way, he saw that her eyes were the hot glowing eyes of the owl.

Benji sat up rigid in his bed, felt the cinder-block walls and the dead air of this hospital, and knew that the owl had sent him a message.

# EIGHT

"YOU'RE BACK!" ON Monday morning Sylvia crossed the office reception area and hugged her colleague, Dr. Albert Kove. "You're so tanned and beautiful," she said, "I'm jealous. How was Tobago?"

Albert Kove was in his mid-forties, but with his cropped, salty-blond hair, collegiate wire-rim glasses, and rolled-up shirtsleeves he could pass for thirty-five. His movements were habitually slow and deliberate, in direct contrast to Sylvia's impulsive edginess. His careful speech and measured physicality always made his female associate want to jam at warp speed. Silently she ordered herself to slow to his pace.

He considered his response. "The island is lush, the snorkeling is incredible. It's not too touristy, and the locals don't seem to mind the intrusion. I give it another three years before it's overrun—"

She interrupted. "Did Carlos have a good time?" Carlos Giron was Kove's longtime domestic partner.

Kove grinned. "Too good. Too many rum punches, too many coconuts. He has to do penance for the next month. A low-fat diet."

"We missed you."

Kove had created the Forensic Evaluation Unit in 1984. Its purpose: provide top-notch forensic psychological services to state divisions and the criminal justice system. He'd courted the first contract from the state of New Mexico, and he'd negotiated renewals ever since. The F.E.U. was his baby. He also happened to be an excellent forensic psychologist.

Roberto Casias and Sylvia Strange were the two other members of the unit. Sylvia had joined the team five months earlier. In addition to the contractual triad, both Sylvia and Roberto were in limited private practice. The offices of the Forensic Evaluation Unit were within shouting distance of the Santa Fe judicial complex—just down the street from Sylvia's former office.

Albert Kove said, "If you schedule with the airlines now, you could be in Tobago within the week." He allowed a long therapeutic pause while he perched on the edge of the receptionist's desk. When he leaned back, Monday's unsorted mail slid everywhere.

Without success Sylvia tried to stop the landslide of letters, magazines, and journals. She gave up and balanced on the other side of the desk. Her fingers drummed wood.

Kove continued. "I heard all about Randall—Erin Tulley's testimony, the motion to suppress." He paused, then said, "That must have upset Matt. Didn't he work with Tulley?" He saw the distress on Sylvia's face and touched her arm gently. "You're not responsible for anything that happened with Randall."

"Somebody thinks I am." Quickly she filled Kove in on the details of the last few days—including Dan Chaney's suspicions of a federal cover-up, and his insistence that Dupont White was alive and killing. She said, "At first, I was absolutely convinced Chaney's paranoid."

"I imagine he is." Kove took off his glasses, rubbed his eyes.

"I watched the videotape of one of Dupont White's

kills—the m.o. is almost identical to Randall's murder. I
talked to Dupont's ex-partner who's doing time at the
pen; he wasn't happy when I suggested Dupont is alive."
She swung one leg nervously. "I'm beginning to think
Dan Chaney might not be completely crazy. What if the
killer *is* Dupont? Is that possible, Albert?"

"There are other explanations. What about a copycat
killer? The kind of experience you had, the assault in
Matt's trailer, will influence your perceptions—"

"Albert, I'm not a hysterical female—there needs to be
an investigation into Chaney's allegations, I know that.
But I can't just call up the F.B.I. and say, 'Are you covering this up?' "

Kove readjusted his glasses and studied Sylvia's face.
He thought he saw her brown irises darken. The ferocity
of her gaze made him uneasy. He said, "What does Matt
think?"

"He suggested that I stop evaluating perverts."

Kove snorted. "He's got something there." He stretched,
one hand collided with metal, and Sylvia just managed
to catch the high-intensity light as it fell.

Stooped beside the desk, she tugged at a large brown
package. "What's this?"

Kove peered down. "My coconuts from Tobago."
While Albert opened the package, Sylvia picked up a
letter opener and began work on the envelopes. One by
one they landed in appropriate piles—correspondence,
bills, announcements.

He said, "It's going to take me a day to recover from jet
lag." He cleaved plastic, reached inside the box, and produced a large brown fruit. "How about lunch tomorrow?
We can review pending cases."

"Sure." She sliced the blade through creased paper.
A neat white square fell from the envelope and landed

on green plush carpet. "Oh, Jesus." She dropped the envelope.

Albert leaned instinctively toward the Polaroid, and Sylvia said, "Don't touch it."

He knelt next to the desk. "Damn . . ."

Sylvia hunched beside him.

In stark black-and-white, the Polaroid pictured an adult male, nude and trussed. His bound wrists were caught overhead on a large steel hook. His body was suspended, knees buckled, lower legs sagging against the floor. The upper half of his face was concealed by a dark hood.

Sylvia took a deep breath, puffed out her cheeks, and touched Albert's knee gently. "Hand me something—a postcard, anything—so I can get it up off the carpet."

She took the large postcard he offered and slipped it carefully under the Polaroid. She set postcard and photograph on the desk. Then, with two fingers she tweezed the lip of the envelope and set it out of the way. She watched while Kove used the tip of the letter opener to lift a corner of the photo.

He said, "There's a message on the back."

It had been printed in tiny, precise, and upright script:

> When you slide the knife between the ribs of the betrayers, when you cut out the tongues of liars, when you burn the seed of the destroyers, you are following your own star.
>
> Two for the Killers' Doctor

Forty minutes later, Matt slid the envelope into an evidence bag.

Kove nodded toward the Polaroid on the desk. "That should be a woman."

"Say what?" Matt frowned.

Sylvia had moved midpoint between the two men.

Kove said, "We're used to seeing women victimized by sadists; it's routine." He tucked a pencil behind his left ear. "We don't expect a male unless it's a terrorist act."

Matt shook his head. "If the victim were a boy, I'd say we were dealing with a pedophile."

"Or a gay lust crime," Sylvia murmured. "That's what your average cop would say."

Kove nodded. "This jogs the imagination: male bondage and ritual behavior—body paint, birds of prey, a sophisticated message—and it all lands on Sylvia's doorstep."

"He's using a dissociative voice," Sylvia said. "*You* slide the knife, *you* cut out the tongues, *you* burn the seed . . ."

"So what's your theory?" Matt asked.

Kove straightened his shoulders and adjusted his spectacles. "The killer is a thirty-one-year-old Libra who loved to fingerpaint in kindergarten; his teacher punished him when he touched his genitals. Sylvia reminds him of his mother. He's a latent homosexual, insecure as hell about his sexuality. He's a law enforcement shadow because he believes guns can restore his masculinity. And he's a show-off."

Matt kept a straight face and said, "I hate show-offs."

Sylvia said, "Albert's kidding, Matt."

"Yeah, but it sounds pretty damn good."

"He *is* a show-off." With a crooked smile, Kove opened the receptionist's desk drawer and rummaged around until he produced a rectangular magnifying glass. "And he *may* be a law enforcement shadow—a wanna-be."

Matt said, "He's very kindly interjected himself into the investigation. He's officially notifying us of kill Number Two."

Sylvia asked, "What about his sexuality?"

Kove scratched his cheek slowly. "A gender bender. I think we could be talking about latent homosexuality."

"Vigilantes," Matt said. "Last week, in Texas, a man hanged his daughter's rapist."

Kove coughed. "That's a fairly fancy message for vigilantes. From what Sylvia's told me, the kidnap and torture of men is Dupont White's style." He held the magnifying glass inches above the Polaroid and studied the photographic image.

Frustrated, Matt moved around the desk and stretched across it to get a look at the photo. "You're telling me the motive here isn't revenge?"

Albert Kove said, "It might be if the killer—or killers—had stopped at one murder. But now we're into a whole different ball game. It's become much more complex, and more interesting."

Sylvia hunkered closer to Kove and the Polaroid—effectively excluding Matt. "If it's Dupont White, we're talking about displaced rage. The source object is not available, so he transfers his hostilities to available victims. He's reliving his fantasy murder over and over."

Kove nodded. "We're dealing with someone who's *driven* to kill, and he does it in a specific, ritualistic manner. The ritual gives him as much reward as the kill. Whoever it is has acquired a taste for a particular type of kill," Kove said flatly.

Sylvia studied the Polaroid. "He's acquired a motive."

"Quite a nasty one." With his eye to the magnifying glass, Kove leaned over the photograph, unintentionally blocking Matt's view. After a moment he said, "This victim is probably Anglo or Hispanic—he's olive-skinned, but I can see tan lines."

Sylvia nudged Kove gently and peered through the glass. Her hair fell around her face and she pushed it back behind one ear. "His ankles are bound with duct tape. Ditto his wrists. But there's no unnecessary bondage, no noticeable symmetry, so it's probably not the work of a sexual sadist." She swallowed and closed her eyes. "Thank God he's not a child."

Kove said, "I don't see any mutilation marks, no wounds. Take a look at his head—"

"Give me the damn glass," Matt snapped. "You've got to start at the margins and work in toward the victim." He groaned when Sylvia took the magnifier from Kove's fingers.

"In a minute." Sylvia's words were muffled. "I've seen morgue photos where I never would've known the subject was dead. Even when the eyes are open, some trick of the lights . . . with a hood it's impossible to judge." She sighed.

Matt wagged an index finger at the Polaroid. "The background is black. Garbage bags or plastic from a roll? It's a small space. A torture chamber?"

Sylvia leaned in closer. "There's a toolbox . . . and a bucket . . . some rope."

Matt shrugged a shoulder to loosen a muscle. "He's got a torture kit."

Sylvia said, "Our guy is definitely obsessive-compulsive."

"A neat freak," Kove said dryly.

Matt said, "It might be the back of a van or a truck. The ceiling is low." Once again he moved around to the other side of the desk. "So that's how the kidnappers got Randall from the bar to the Jemez. In a portable torture chamber."

Sylvia said, "The victim's genitals are intact and clearly visible."

Kove asked, "Is there any indication of sexual excitement? Can you see if the penis is erect?"

Sylvia stepped back and handed Kove the glass. She said, "It's flaccid."

Matt raised a brow. "The Polaroid's overexposed; can you really make out that much detail?"

Sylvia said, "I know an erect penis when I see one."

Kove adjusted the focal length of the magnifying glass until the tip of his nose was six inches from the Polaroid. "This is interesting. . . ." He moved back and gestured with one finger. Matt stepped close to the other man and took the glass.

Kove asked, "What's this look like to you?"

Sylvia was hot and thirsty, and her mind was filled with unpleasant images: the mask . . . the victim's bound wrists and ankles . . . and then she pictured Anthony Randall's corpse.

It took Matt fifteen seconds to find what could've been a slight stain on the victim's penis. "A birthmark?"

Kove shook his head. "I'll bet you a dime it's a tattoo."

THE NEW MEXICO Department of Public Safety crime lab was part of the south Santa Fe complex that included the law enforcement academy and state police head-quarters. If Matt pitched a brick out his office window it would land in the reception area of the crime lab. He preferred to walk.

Just before five on Tuesday, as he passed through the long carpeted halls, he thought about the computer print-outs that he'd left on his desk. They were case reports of vigilante assaults and homicides that had occurred in Texas, California, New Jersey, Colorado, and Idaho. The list was long—courtesy of his fellow investigator, Terry Osuna. She was still convinced that local vigilantes had a vendetta against sex offenders. Matt wasn't rock-sure anymore.

But one thing was clear to anyone in law enforcement—know the victim or victims if you want to know the perpetrator.

He'd delivered the second Polaroid to Hansi Gausser just over twenty-four hours ago. He was hoping that Gausser had worked a miracle.

He found the serologist hunched over a comparison microscope.

Without looking up, Gausser gave Matt a small salute. Gausser said, "Your tax dollars at work—and a rush job to boot. After I promised to hand over my firstborn, Los Alamos lab supplied us with a beautiful enlargement of your hostage."

He straightened and gestured to a packet on a table. "They also returned the original Polaroid by courier. I'll check it out and let you know if I find anything interesting, but I wouldn't hold my breath, pardner." Occasionally, Gausser tried to affect a cowboy drawl, Swiss style.

"The photo will be clean just like the first one," Matt said. Both Polaroids would be sent to the F.B.I. lab at Quantico. There, analysts would enlarge, enhance, and assess behavioral markers and search for identifying factors. By the time they came up with anything on the second victim that could be sent out to law enforcement agencies for a possible I.D., there would already be a corpse. Matt and Gausser shared the conviction that the second victim was dead or would die soon.

"Can I speak to you for a minute, Matt?" Both Gausser and Matt looked up. Captain Elizer Rocha stood in the doorway of the lab. Rocha nodded to the serologist and turned away.

Matt joined his commanding officer in the hall. Rocha said, "What's the latest on Anthony Randall?"

"Terry Osuna's running a Crimestoppers bulletin and

pushing the anyone-who-has-information angle. So far, none of the calls have led to much. We're working on an I.D. on the second victim—"

"Fine. Keep it at that." Rocha nodded curtly. "And I want those Polaroids sent off to Bureau analysts ASAP. This afternoon." He opened his mouth, as if to add something to his orders, then turned and walked away.

The brief exchange left Matt feeling uneasy. Rocha tolerated the F.B.I., but he wasn't partial to their attitude. State cops never were. So why was the captain so eager to hand over jurisdiction?

Matt joined Hansi Gausser at his desk with another question. "Can you do something with the handwriting on the photographs?"

Gausser lowered his voice. "If I get a known sample, then I can compare. If not, you'll have to wait for the guys at behavioral science." He held up an eleven-by-fourteen-inch photo enlargement. "Your Polaroid. Subject: male groin and penis . . . complete with tattoo. Isn't technology fabulous?"

Matt took the enlargement and examined it for a few seconds. "Damn . . . Albert Kove was right. It is a tattoo. A snake?"

"Snake or sword." Gausser tapped at the enlargement. "See, this could be the hilt. How many men do you know who tattoo their cocks?"

"I know one." Matt whistled. "Jesse Montoya."

"That's right." Hansi scowled. A felon with a trademark tattoo on his penis became instantly notorious within law enforcement circles. "Jesse Montoya, a.k.a. Zorro."

THERE ARE TWO types of blacktops in New Mexico; those that twist like a snake on the end of a stick, and those that drive themselves straight across the plains.

For the first fifteen miles out of Santa Fe, State Route 14 fell into the second category. In darkness, illuminated by headlamps and a three-quarter moon, the white stripe seemed drawn toward a distant, straight-ahead point. Matt kept one hand on the steering wheel.

Sylvia watched a shadow land of trees, trailers, and homes blur together in the passenger window. They passed the Corrections Academy and the Penitentiary of New Mexico. The Main Facility was lit up by the flat white glare of perimeter lights.

Jesse Montoya—Zorro—had done time at the pen. But not very much time. Most recently, Montoya had been convicted of criminal sexual penetration of a minor and sent to South Facility. With "good time," his original commitment had been reduced to less than three years, and his release two months ago had garnered heavy publicity.

Neither Sylvia nor Matt had spoken a dozen words since they left her home. They were on their way to the village of Cerrillos, eighteen miles south of Santa Fe. In the 1880s, it had been a thriving mining community funded by the Atchison, Topeka & Santa Fe Railroad. Cerrillos, "Little Hills," was named for its surrounds, the mineral-rich Ortiz Mountains. There was some historical evidence that seventeenth-century Spaniards had forced Indians to mine turquoise in the Ortiz. A few hardy individuals still sought wealth in the hills, but for the most part, Cerrillos was a marginal community whose residents included surviving hippies, a few artists, Spanish families, and a scattering of rich folks.

They were going to pay a visit to Augustine Montoya, Jesse Montoya's grandfather. Sylvia had seen the old man at Jesse's trial. Stooped and twisted like a root— that's how she remembered him. Grandfather of a convicted rapist.

Jesse Montoya was what behavioral scientists classified as a "power/reassurance rapist." He raped young women to reassure himself of his own masculinity. His fantasy was about relationships—he forced his victims to consent "voluntarily." It made him feel like a *man*. The tattooed penis was out of character because it was a little too macho. She'd done an evaluation when the defense toyed with the idea of going for "guilty but mentally ill." They had not used her testimony when it failed to support their theory.

Maybe Jesse had paid a very high price for his crime, after all.

When they passed the railroad tracks at Cerrillos, Matt said, "Augustine's road is a half mile from here."

The turnoff to the property was almost hidden behind a large boulder and scrub brush. Rinsed by moonlight, the hills looked larger than they actually were. Sylvia gripped the dash as the truck bounced over a bar ditch.

Matt negotiated a tight turn. The truck slammed into a rut that almost qualified as an acequia, and Sylvia felt her teeth grate. She was relieved when he pulled over and parked at a slight widening of the road.

"Wait here." Matt climbed out and closed the door quietly.

She watched him traverse the smooth rise of the hill. She'd never accompanied him on the job, and she didn't particularly like his attitude tonight. Moody, withdrawn, cold. But they were both jittery, expecting bad news— and another body—any minute. The killer or killers had acted very quickly when they kidnapped and murdered Anthony Randall. There was no reason to believe Jesse Montoya would receive different treatment.

She glanced at her watch: 8:36.

A faint breeze ruffled her hair, and crickets kept up

their incessant song. She leaned her head against the half-open window and closed her eyes.

She wasn't sure how much time had passed when she became aware of a sputtering sound; a fire had started somewhere nearby. Acrid smoke curled into her nostrils. She coughed and woke with a start.

THE TWO-ROOM HOUSE was filled with the hiss of kerosene lanterns. The yellow light delineated the two wooden chairs, the handmade table, the plywood counter propped next to the deep old-fashioned sink. It washed over the neatly stacked tin plates, the lidless Mason jars, the pot of pinto beans that simmered on a hot plate.

There was no sign of Jesse Montoya or his grand-father, Augustine.

Matt's boots crunched earth and sand as he crossed the dirt floor. When he pulled the handle on the old gas refrigerator, the heavy door swung open with the groan of rusty hinges. Inside, a bright red can of Coke, an almost empty bottle of ketchup, half a loaf of Wonder bread, and a jar of cocktail franks occupied the two shelves. He closed the refrigerator door quietly.

The only other furniture in the room was an armchair and a television set with wires that fed out the window; Matt figured the old man ran the set off car batteries. He ducked through the doorway that led to a tiny bedroom.

The earth floor had recently been sprinkled with water and swept. The bed was a cot. From a *retablo* on the north wall, the Virgen de Guadalupe kept watch. Next to the Virgen, in a *nicho,* burning votive candles framed a photograph of Jesse Montoya. Tiny flowers had been placed between the candles. A faded *ojo de Dios,* eye of God, hung beside the altar.

Matt guessed Augustine Montoya believed his grand-son was dead.

He heard the rueful hoot of a barn owl as he retraced his steps to the front of the house. The chorus of crickets came to an abrupt halt when he appeared in the doorway. In the distance, the soft swell of two voices drifted up the hillside.

"*¿Comprende?*" THE MAN stood inches from Sylvia's face. She caught the scent of malt and cigarette smoke as she slid toward the driver's door. There was a small explosion—the crack of a pop-top.

The owl called again.

She could see the man now. He was thin and stooped, and he clutched a cigarette and a beer can in one hand, his hat in the other. He grinned at her. She opened the truck door and stepped out.

"*¿Bebe, jita?*" He offered her the can. "You want Schlitz?"

"No, *gracias.*" Her heartbeat slowed to normal as she shook off the confusion of sleep. This was Augustine Montoya.

He said, "*Su chota*, he's looking for me, *pero yo* . . . I'd rather talk to his *mujer.*"

*Chota*—she'd heard it before. It meant something like prick. Augustine had defty insulted Matt and stated his preference for the cop's woman; he had expressed himself politely, and she wasn't the least bit offended. In fact, she found herself liking Augustine Montoya.

He shuffled around the front of the truck, took a drink, and offered Sylvia his free hand. His skin was rough as sandpaper; his handshake felt good.

"*¿Buscando a Jesse?* You want to find him?" He shook his head softly. "No . . . you come to tell me, *está muerto.*"

Sylvia caught it: he's dead.

She studied Augustine's face in the moonlight. She

saw a ghostly topographical map of canyons and valleys. His mouth fell slack to one side. It was difficult to read the expression in his eyes; she felt more than saw a mixture of sadness and resignation.

Sylvia shook her head. "I don't know that," she said softly. But she couldn't shake the image of the bound body in the Polaroid.

Augustine was matter-of-fact. *"Muerto."*

"Why do you think your grandson's dead?" Her voice was a whisper, but she thought it sounded loud.

Augustine took a last swig of beer and used one gnarled hand to crush the can and toss it into the bushes. He eased closer to Sylvia, and she felt his eyes like delicate fingers on her face.

*"Mi esposa . . .* Elena . . ." His voice broke when he said his wife's name. "She told me to take care of Jesse."

He gazed up at the sweep of stars overhead, and Sylvia followed his lead. The Big Dipper and Hercules hogged the sky. Other summer constellations proved more timid. For an instant, the gleaming planets, asteroids, and stars clustered together to form a woman's profile, a shoulder, the rump of a horse. Just as quickly, they blurred and melted back into infinity.

Augustine said, "Jesse went missing three nights ago—*el sábado*." Saturday.

"Does he have friends?"

*"Nadie.* He's not staying with nobody." The old man turned his head away and spit at a rock. "People want him to pay."

"For his crimes?"

*"Sí."* He nodded. "His time in prison . . . it wasn't enough." Augustine's body swayed for a moment, then he caught himself. *"El juez* . . . he warned me that someone might try—"

"What?" Sylvia crossed her arms around her waist; she

was frustrated by her lack of Spanish. "Did someone threaten your grandson?"

"*Una troca.* One, maybe two nights it parked on the road."

"Which nights? Did you see the driver? What kind of truck?"

He shook his head. "It was . . . *amarilla* maybe, *una troca de panel.*"

*A yellow panel truck. That would fit with the Polaroid.*

Both she and Augustine heard a stone tumble down the hill thirty feet away. Neither looked toward the sound. She said, "You think they came for Jesse?"

"*Su chota . . .*" Augustine gave a low growl that turned into a rasping cough. "He's got big ears, no?"

Matt called from fifteen feet away. "Hola, Augustine."

Augustine ignored the greeting and touched Sylvia hesitantly on the shoulder. "*Una troca* Ford, maybe, but I only see it from far away."

Matt rattled off a long string of Spanish; its meaning completely eluded Sylvia, but from the inflection she recognized a series of questions. She watched Augustine's posture stiffen.

He said, "*Mi nieto, Jesse . . . fue un bad hombre.*" His voice dropped to an angry whisper. "*Vienen las llamas de juicio,* the flames of hell. *El juez,* the big judge, told me they would come!"

Augustine swayed toward Sylvia; he touched a shaking finger to his forehead. Then he turned away, and his feet scraped the ground as he crossed the road and disappeared behind a stand of Navajo willows.

Matt slid behind the wheel of the truck. When Sylvia was next to him, she touched his arm. "Augustine believes Jesse's dead."

"I think he's right."

"What else did he say?"

"The flames of judgment, the flames of hell are on their way."

Sylvia found her cotton jacket on the seat. She draped it over her legs. "The judge told him that?"

"The judge warned him there would be justice."

"The judge as in God?"

"I don't think so." Matt started the truck's engine. "From what he said, I've got a feeling he means your judge."

"Who?"

"Judge Nathaniel Howzer."

THEY WERE TWO miles down the main road when Matt turned onto a dirt track that led past livestock chutes. He cut the headlights and accelerated.

Sylvia's eyes failed at the abrupt loss of light; the world passed in a blur of smells and sounds. The blind motion was exhilarating and frightening.

Finally, Matt let the truck coast to a stop near the old Atchison, Topeka & Santa Fe tracks. The moon stared down like the yellow eye of a black cat. Under its milky gaze the landscape appeared bare, a relief of oblique angles. The earth was caliche. Where it allowed any visible growth, dark spears of yucca plants probed the air and native grasses resembling clumps of hair marked the rusty tracks.

With the truck windows open, the night's sound and scent were surprisingly complex. A chorus of crickets, the mating trill of a spadefoot toad, a barking dog, the musty aroma of pond water, manure, and creosote. When Sylvia took a deep breath, she imagined she could taste the earth. Her skin felt like paper, sweat evaporating unseen, no dampness visible between the tiny hairs that covered her arm. Sylvia settled back and closed her eyes.

Matt took a tired breath. "Jesse Montoya deserved

more punishment than he got." A soft breeze crossed his cheek. "But he doesn't deserve to die the way Randall died. Nobody does."

Sylvia said, "When I was a kid, I used to lie awake at night, in bed . . . and I'd think, there are people out there doing bad things right this minute, and I can't stop them."

Even without the moonlight, Matt would have been able to tell she was turning toward him. He watched, wordless, as she negotiated the claustrophobic space. With almost desperate energy, she slipped off pumps and hiked her skirt up bare legs until it bunched around her waist. She straddled him, and he heard the cotton fabric of her underpants tear when he tugged at the side seam.

Through her silk blouse, the steering wheel dug into the small of her back. She could feel the heat where his hands had gripped plastic. The warmth felt good. *Alive.* She silenced him with her mouth; her fingers found his zipper. Callused fingers slid up her thighs, moved roughly over belly and breasts. With a quick animal cry, she let him inside.

# NINE

JUST AFTER SUNRISE, Sylvia stepped out of the shower and dripped water all the way to the bedroom. As she stared down at Matt asleep in her bed, she was disconcerted by the sensation of unfamiliarity. Maybe it was only the milky sunlight that paled his skin and highlighted signs of age and fatigue—but for a moment, he was a stranger.

Partly for reassurance, she kissed him on the mouth, and his eyes opened slowly.

"Good morning, sleepyhead."

He said, "Do that again."

"Good morning?"

"The kiss."

She smiled. "Should I leave you alone?"

He rubbed his face like a drowsy kid, focused, and then let his eyes play over her nude body. "Too late for that." His hand moved down his belly. She could see his erection pressing against the blue cotton sheet.

She scrambled over him, fell onto the mattress, and pulled him on top. He brushed her hair from her neck and kissed damp skin. His mouth moved to her breasts, and she willingly lost herself in a wave of physical sensation. She almost missed his whispered demand.

"Let's make a baby."

Sylvia pushed him away and sat up abruptly. "Shit."

"What?" He propped himself on one elbow.

She stared at him, her eyes compressed into dark slits. "Forget it." Her skin was flushed, she was breathing hard.

He watched her grab her robe and stalk out of the room. He heard the refrigerator door open, then slam shut. The soft hum of the answering machine's message playback went on for a long time. A jet streaked overhead, and its rumbling vibrations could be felt inside the adobe. Matt sighed and lay back on the bed. The words had popped out of his mouth; worse, they'd come out of nowhere.

"So, you want a baby?" Sylvia had appeared in the doorway.

He folded his arms over his bare chest. "You're overreacting."

Sylvia started to protest—her anger flared again, then died away. She held back tears and shook her head. Her emotions were shifting so quickly, she couldn't keep up. But she knew this reaction was connected to her own internal struggle. A part of her wanted a child, a family. Another part of her was committed to her career. And she was torn in an even deeper way—she was estranged from her mother, and her father had disappeared years earlier pursued by twin demons: alcohol and depression. Sylvia knew her biggest issue around having a child: she feared that she would prove unfit as a mother.

All this raced through her mind, but she couldn't share her thoughts with Matt. She realized she still felt the distance between them. A distance she didn't know how to bridge.

She shook her head. "I don't know what's wrong with us."

Matt said nothing, just stared at countless dust particles visible in a shaft of daylight until Sylvia turned and left. When she was out of view, he sat up in bed. Suddenly, he felt weary and exhausted. It was going to be one of those full-moon days when the bars filled up with howlers, gang-bangers partied, and lovers did bad things to each other with kitchen knives, baseball bats, or just plain words. He and Sylvia were off to a great start.

For the first time that morning, he remembered that Jesse Montoya was missing. Dan Chaney was missing, too. Matt had left three cryptic messages on the federal agent's voice mail. Now, *he* was getting paranoid. He'd made sure his words didn't betray Dan's possible whereabouts. What he wanted was a meeting—somewhere neutral, like Tommy's Bar during off-work hours. Face-to-face, he could assess Chaney's mental state. Maybe figure out if his old friend really had something solid on an F.B.I. cover-up. So far, no response.

Matt groaned when he stood. His back ached and his right shoulder was tight. As soon as he got his clothes on, he'd pop a couple of Advils. Painkillers and coffee, the breakfast of champions.

He found Sylvia seated at the kitchen table sipping coffee, tearing chunks off a fat frosted cinnamon roll. While she ate, she studied the front page of the *Albuquerque Journal North*. Matt could see where she had doodled a series of eerie masklike faces in the paper's margins.

Without glancing at him, she said, "There's a story on Jesse Montoya's disappearance." She pulled the newspaper off the table, away from Matt's over-the-shoulder view, and read: " 'A spokesperson for the Department of Public Safety revealed that a local psychologist has received messages from a possible perpetrator.' " She looked up and shook her head sharply. "When are you going to talk to Dan? You should see the videotape—"

"I'll see it when I track Chaney down." Matt was

dressed in the same jeans and rumpled khaki shirt he'd
worn the night before. His Luccheses needed a shine. His
hair stood out from his head in weedy clumps.

Self-conscious, he straightened his collar with unusual
care. "Before, in bed, I don't think I said anything
wrong."

"Oh. Then you do want to have a child?"

His finger discovered a belt loop and tugged nervously. "It was a figure of speech."

For an instant, sadness clouded Sylvia's features. Then
it was gone, replaced by cool efficiency. She said, "There
was a message for you on the machine. From Erin
Tulley, about her lawsuit. She sounded upset." Sylvia
raised an eyebrow.

Matt almost looked nervous. "She still wants me to
testify at her hearing."

"And you're going to?"

"I haven't made up my mind."

Sylvia frowned and shook her head.

He said, "About you and me living together—"

"Let's talk about it later."

Matt took his car keys from his shirt pocket. He'd been
dismissed, and that angered him more than a no-win
argument. He started to say good-bye, but Sylvia turned
her back as he walked out the door.

ON SANTA FE'S east side, the high-pitched hum of cicadas
electrified the hazy summer air. Matt stood on the veranda
of Judge Nathaniel Howzer's Upper Canyon Road home.
An hour earlier, he'd stopped by D.P.S. headquarters to
smooth-talk Captain Elizer Rocha. Politically, N.M. State
Police was a hypersensitive organization. Any investigation involving a district judge usually included the "big
guns." Now he watched as the red glow of a new forest fire
near the Tsankawi ruins warmed the sky over the Jemez

Mountains thirty miles to the northwest. The distant mountain range included the vast caldera of a volcano that had erupted and collapsed roughly a million years past. Now, the sky between mountain and city was hazed with ash and smoke.

Matt took a last look at the view and reluctantly returned to the subject that had brought him here. "You told Jesse Montoya's grandfather that the flames of judgment were on their way. Why would you say that?"

"Did I?"

"That's what Augustine Montoya remembers."

"I remember a little differently. At the trial, Augustine seemed very distressed by his grandson's crime. I reminded him that justice has a way of catching up with each of us." Howzer smiled ruefully. He was almost six feet tall and heavy. Thick white fingers clutched a glass. He took regular sips of what looked like tomato juice but Matt guessed was a Bloody Mary.

Howzer continued, "You and I both know Montoya's release wasn't popular in the community. He's a registered sex offender."

"He's also a missing person," Matt said quietly.

Howzer used his free hand to shelter his eyes from the sun. "How do you like my view, Matt?"

Matt finished his coffee, set the cup on the rail, and said, "The fire's changing course." And the judge was changing subjects.

"Is it?"

He didn't answer, but he thought about the fact that the judge had lived in the city for ten years. Funny how some people could stay so unaware of their surroundings. Unaware even of the prevailing summer winds. They almost always blew up from the Pacific Ocean and swept across Mexico, southern California, and the Arizona desert. This time of year, they usually brought rain. But the rains were long overdue, and the sluggish winds had shifted.

The judge was still staring out at the distant fire as if a keen eye could steer the conversation away from Jesse Montoya. Matt took the opportunity to study the older man. Strong features—high forehead, aquiline nose, full mouth—were undermined by a weak chin and blurred by a weariness that went deeper than physical fatigue. He looked pale, and he seemed restive. Matt wondered exactly what was going on with Nathan Howzer.

"Shall we go inside? I need to freshen my drink."

Matt followed the judge through French doors. Although he had known Howzer casually for years, he'd never been to his home. His first impression had been that the living room was humble for a house of such grandiose scale. But the judge explained that the room was simply his library. Bookshelves lined with legal volumes bound in blue, red, and black stretched the entire length of three walls. Later, Matt had seen the actual living room; it boasted eight times the square footage of the library, and it was as large as a Spanish Colonial church.

Somewhere along the way, the man had accumulated *beaucoup* bucks. This house wasn't built on the salary of a district judge.

Every wall in the pueblo-style mansion—interior and exterior—was constructed of double-brick adobe. The central ceiling was supported by thirty-foot-long vigas that were as thick as a fat man. Many of the mansion's rooms seemed to exist only to contain daunting ornamental displays—pots, kachina dolls, masks, pipes, and other ceremonial objects all much too small and too simple not to be expensive.

"Matt . . . ?" The judge held a crystal decanter in the air, but Matt shook his head. Howzer returned the decanter to its tray and took a sip of his Bloody Mary. "Do *you* believe Montoya is the second victim of some . . . vigilante killer?"

"Yeah, I do."

Howzer said, "I was a lawyer for twenty years in California and New Mexico. I've held a judgeship for more than a decade. Imagine having the audacity to think one could actually dole out justice." He kept a straight face and waved a fleshy arm toward one of a set of matching armchairs.

Matt sat and faced Howzer across a Persian rug. He knew the judge had a dry sense of humor as well as a reputation around chambers for being secretive, enigmatic. He'd testified in Howzer's courtroom, and so had Sylvia. He pushed away the memory of her . . . of their morning argument.

The judge spoke quietly. "Adobe lost his nerve a while back." At his feet, a timeworn black-and-brown Doberman had come to rest, legs crossed, chin on paws. Howzer patted the dog absently and said, "He's a pitiful coward—but we become very attached to our family, don't we?"

"I've got a cat." Matt shrugged.

"I worry about what will happen to them after I'm gone." The judge closed his eyes, gathered his thoughts. "Just look at my docket; within three years, Beck, Martinez, Tafoya, Dolan . . . those are just the trials that became media circuses. Then, there were the plea bargains, suspended sentences, dismissals. And, of course, both Jesse Montoya and Anthony Randall passed through my courtroom."

Matt studied the judge. The man spoke with a certain bravado, but beneath the veneer, the intangible something might be fear or dread . . . or resignation.

" 'To me belongeth vengeance and recompense.' "
Judge Howzer's voice was barely a whisper.

"Deuteronomy."

"You're a religious man?"

"I was raised on a well-thumbed copy of the King
James, but my Bible's rusty these days."

"Vengeance seems to be what the public wants."

"Do you blame them?"

Howzer shook his head slowly, then he swallowed a
third of his drink. "But personal vengeance is very
impractical." An odd smile flashed across his mouth.

Matt thought it was a false smile—asymmetrical,
involving only the lower portion of the face, dropping
away abruptly like a mask.

Howzer continued. "And who really knows what
makes the guilty suffer most cruelly?"

Matt leaned back in the leather chair and tried to get a
bead on the judge's state of mind. He said, "You passed
judgment on Randall and Montoya."

"Montoya, yes. Randall got away. But only for a few
hours." There was a sudden twinkle in his eye. "You
don't think I'm a secret vigilante, do you, Matt?"

Matt was surprised by something warm and wet that
rubbed against his hand. He looked down and saw a
long-haired dachshund gazing shyly at him.

Matt patted the dog, stood, and faced Nathan Howzer.
He said, "Have you heard of a man called Dupont
White?"

The judge swallowed, then frowned, as if he were
thinking back through the years. After a long moment he
said, "Of course. The blowout at Las Cruces . . . He was
the arms dealer who died. Why do you ask?"

Matt shrugged. "Just following up a loose thread. By
the way, I spoke with your secretary this morning. Ellie

tells me you've received several threatening letters in the last two weeks."

"Ellie has too much imagination." Howzer summoned the dachshund to his side. Very gently, he stroked the animal's silky ears.

Matt moved to the door, then stopped. "I don't know why, Judge, but you're lying to me."

Judge Howzer looked up from his dog, and his expression was ironic. "You and I should find new careers, Matt. Life is too short."

"Is someone after you?"

The judge threw back his head and laughed. He was still chuckling when Matt let himself out.


THE PENITENTIARY'S MAIN hospital was a mind-numbing institutional infrastructure, outmoded and sullied by the ghost of a 1980 riot. Built as part of the original pen structure, its thick walls had absorbed the accumulated misery of forty years of incarceration. Scuff trails had been worn along its dull linoleum floors. Fluorescent lights illuminated loose tiles and peeling plaster. Exposed wires crawled across the beveled ceiling.

The staff did their best to create a healing environment—brightly colored posters and inmate crafts decorated the walls—but they did not have an easy task.

Sylvia found a nurse in the hall between examination rooms. She introduced herself.

The woman nodded. She was small and blond and she had a nicely wicked glint in her eye. "I've been expecting you. Rosie Sanchez talked to Dr. Cray, the psychiatrist, about your visit."

She beckoned for Sylvia to follow and stepped briskly toward the stairwell. "We've got Benji Muñoz y Concha upstairs, where he'll get some peace and quiet." She took the stairs easily, talking nonstop. "He's really improved, knows where he is, good spirits and all."

"So he's talking?" Sylvia reached the top of the stairs behind the nurse.

"Some. He started on his own yesterday morning." As the nurse moved, she trailed her fingers along a white stripe painted over green walls. "Dr. Cray thinks it's a cultural thing." She pursed her mouth in disapproval.

Sylvia said, "*What's* a cultural thing?"

The nurse offered Sylvia an apologetic smile. "You can ask him yourself; Dr. Cray's waiting for you." She stopped and held her arm straight out as if she were directing traffic. Sylvia peered into an open office and saw a man standing by the mesh-covered window. He turned in her direction.

A number of psychologists and psychiatrists worked on staff at the penitentiary, and turnover was frequent. Sylvia didn't recognize Dr. Cray.

He was somewhere in his thirties. Pale and thin with earnest eyes. He wore a cotton dress shirt and a suit coat—in the heat. Sylvia recognized the cropped hair and the black-rimmed glasses as an effort to add maturity to his presentation.

She braced herself. At first glance, Dr. Cray appeared to be chockful of learning-by-the-book. He walked toward her, arm extended, and she saw his fingernails were gnawed down to the quick. A job at the penitentiary would quickly test the doctor's mettle; then again, it was less a job than trial by fire.

She smiled, introduced herself, and shook his hand. "Welcome to the fray."

"Thanks." As he tucked a clipboard under his arm in a gesture that reminded Sylvia of a fledgling bird adjusting its wing, he began a slow walk down the hall. "I know you've come to see Benji Muñoz y Concha."

"How's he doing?"

Dr. Cray coughed quietly. "I've been observing him pretty closely." He tugged on his ear—the lobe was pink from constant irritation. "I've never seen a case of cultural psychosis before."

Sylvia came to a standstill, and the doctor shifted to face her. She said, "Cultural psychosis?"

"Well, yes." He puffed up his chest, but his smile wavered when he said, "I don't believe in witches, do you?"

Sylvia widened her eyes, tipped her head. She couldn't afford to offend Dr. Cray; he was penitentiary staff, she was the outsider—and the walls at the joint had ears. She kept her mouth shut.

Cray looked discombobulated. "I don't think you understand, this inmate believes he was poisoned by a witch. Literally." Dr. Cray's pitch went up a notch on the last word.

Sylvia considered her response, then said, "Let's look at it from another angle. What you call cultural psychosis is a physical and emotional reaction to something very *real*—in symbolic terms."

"Well, yes . . ."

Sylvia began to walk and the psychiatrist kept pace. She said, "Dr. Cray, you're making a judgment of pathology, but I don't see it. I don't think Benji is psychotic."

He said, "Fine. So Benji saw a *symbolic* witch." His voice was peevish.

Sylvia smiled reassuringly. "Fine. We can agree on that."

They had come to a standstill beneath a window at the end of the hall. On the other side of embedded wire and dingy glass, Sylvia caught a glimpse of perimeter fence and guard tower. She turned toward the psychiatrist, who frowned as if he were silently replaying their recent conversation.

She said, "May I stop by your office after I speak with Benji?"

Dr. Cray nodded. He pulled a key ring from his belt and unlocked the door to Benji's room. He said, "I'll send the nurse up in five minutes to let you out." He stared at Sylvia's back as she entered the hospital room alone.

It felt like a cell. Single bed, bare walls, a small window with a view of the maintenance building. The room smelled of old linoleum and institutional cleansers. The hydraulic door pulled shut with a soft tick as the lock engaged.

Seated in a plastic chair, Benji Muñoz y Concha looked younger than his years. Thick black hair was pulled into a long braid. Wrists and fingers were bare. The T-shirt and baggy faded jeans did nothing to hide a wiry body.

"I remember you." His voice was soft and low.

Sylvia studied him quizzically, watchful for signs of confusion or depression. But when Benji turned toward her, his eyes were alert; they were also the rich hue of burnished walnut.

"I remember you from the fire . . . you're Rosie's friend."

She smiled. "I'm Sylvia Strange."

"A doctor." His voice was guarded.

"Psychologist. Sometimes I work at the penitentiary. I'm not on staff with the hospital. Do you mind if I sit?" She perched on the edge of the bed when Benji didn't protest.

"Are you here to decide if I can go back to the murf?"

The murf was the penitentiary's Minimum Restrict

Facility. "I don't have any say about whether you stay or go."

Benji shrugged.

She said, "I'm amazed at the work you do—fighting wildfires."

He pointed at her face. "How did you get that?"

Sylvia's fingers went instantly to the small scar at the corner of her left eye. She was surprised to discover she felt self-conscious. She said, "It's old."

"Did you win the fight?"

For an instant, Sylvia remembered another institutional room, and the painful slap of the angry matron. "No . . . I thought so then, but I was only sixteen."

Benji's face settled like a quiet pool of water. "My family has always known about fire, but I'm the only one left to fight." His fingers tapped the smooth skin at the corner of his eye. "Like you. They're wrong about my forgetting. I'm not crazy." He was quiet for a moment. He closed his eyes, and a shadow seemed to fall across his handsome features.

"Benji, a man's body was found on the hill."

He nodded. "They told me I saw him burn. Owl always brings death."

Sylvia waited. She knew the owl was connected with witchcraft in some belief systems. Night predator, raptor, and highly skilled hunter. She reached into the pocket of her shirt and fingered a thin notepad.

Dan Chaney had told her there were no recent photographs of Dupont White, but she could still visualize the man on the videotape—his painted face was seared in her brain. She set the pad and pencil on the bed next to Benji. "Can you draw the witch you saw?"

It took him a moment to make the decision. He seemed to have a clear sense that the image might affect him strongly. He said, "I saw you . . . in one of my dreams.

You know someone who's going to die soon . . . like the other man."

Sylvia closed her eyes and thought of Jesse Montoya. When she opened her eyes again, Benji had picked up the pencil. Intently, Sylvia watched a primitive being take shape on the page.

She studied Benji's face as he worked; she saw apprehension re-form his features.

Abruptly, Benji drew back. "That's him. He poisoned me."

Sylvia picked up the drawing. It was rough and childlike—oval-shaped head, shaded circles for eyes and mouth, slashes across the cheeks. The painted face of Dupont White.

Benji stood and began to pace. He was clearly agitated, apparently in the throes of making a decision. Finally, he turned to face Sylvia. He stepped toward her, studied her—read her. He said, "I need to see Velio Cruz."

Sylvia knew the name. Just as Cole Lynch was the pen's jailhouse lawyer, so Velio Cruz was the joint's inmate shaman, "psychiatrist," all-around healer. Most important, he came from Benji's own culture: not Spanish, not Pueblo, not Anglo . . . but *prison* culture.

She asked, "Why Velio?" She heard a soft knock; the nurse was at the door.

Benji said, "Because he's the only one who can drive the witch from my body."

Sylvia believed Benji was right. She stood, nodded, and said, "I'll see if I can arrange it."

Benji's entire aura softened, and a shy smile transformed his face. He murmured his thanks as she left the room.

Cray was waiting for Sylvia in his office. He wasn't alone. The deputy warden, a squat, middle-aged man

with small eyes and an apostrophe mustache, was by
Cray's side. He didn't pause for an introduction.

He snapped, "Benji Muñoz y Concha is not under your
care. You will not visit him again unless you have permission through *proper* channels. Is that clear?"

Sylvia bit her lip and nodded. She didn't say a word.
And she didn't mention Rosie Sanchez.


OUTSIDE THE PEN, behind the steering wheel of her
Volvo, she found herself staring at the cell phone in her
lap. She'd placed three calls to Matt; she had left three
messages. So where the hell was he? She dialed again
and checked her own messages. Finally, after an inter-
minable wait, she heard Matt's voice.

He said, "I thought you'd want to know, I checked
out a body this afternoon, but it wasn't Jesse Montoya. It
was a hitchhiker, a hit-and-run off Old Las Vegas Highway. Listen, I'm sorry about all this—you and me this
morning."

She was sorry, too, and she regretted her angry out-
burst. A few seconds passed; she thought Matt's message
was complete. But he had added a postscript: "I'm
working late tonight, so I'll just stay at my place."

She heard the sharp beep as the message cut off, but
she sat with the phone still clutched in her hand. Overhead, a layer of gray cloud and smoke veiled what should
have been a clear summer sky. Sylvia felt as though the
pall had blurred her mind. The weather was unnatural;
the normal pattern of the winds was shifting.

# TEN

SYLVIA WOKE FROM a dream while it was still dark outside. The illuminated digital clock showed three-fifteen. She lay in bed under a thin sheet. Her skin was damp, she was uncomfortably warm. In the dream, at twilight, she and her terrier Rocko had hiked up the ridge behind the house. By the time they reached the rocky spine, night had fallen. In the floating time of dreams, they found themselves trapped between two large coyotes who stared with gleamy yellow eyes. The largest coyote lunged at Rocko, but Sylvia fought it off. It bit her hand as she hurled it over a round boulder. Blood poured from the toothmarks on her palm. When she looked to see if the coyote was dead, she saw her father, and he rose up and flew away like an owl.

Awake, she couldn't shake the sense of dread that hovered over her like a shadow. Her father had walked out of her life when she was thirteen. She still had no idea whether he was dead or alive. He would be in his sixties now. She thought of the way Anthony Randall had died. Jesse Montoya was missing four days now. Her thoughts and her dreams were occupied with absent or disappeared men.

Automatically she whistled for Rocko before she remembered her terrier wasn't staying at the house. She kicked the bedsheet away and switched on the small fan next to the bed. Warm air brushed her skin and brought little relief. When she managed to steer her mind away from Jesse, she found herself picturing Matt. By now he must be sprawled in his bed with Tom the cat. She rolled over and hugged the pillow where Matt usually slept. The whisper of lemon scent made her want to cry. The bed was suddenly depressingly large and unwelcoming. She fought the light-headed panic that came with the fear their relationship had shipwrecked. She felt like someone who was trying to complete a puzzle with missing pieces.

It was four-thirty when she gave up on sleep and brewed a pot of espresso. She carried her coffee outside to the deck, stretched in a chaise longue, and watched the sun peek over the Sangre de Cristo Mountains. A ghost of the full moon still hovered in the western sky where the fires had turned gray clouds pink. Liminal time, no longer night, not yet day. An interim she usually loved.

She closed her eyes, and her fingers grazed a glossy page; the book lay on the table next to the chaise. It was a museum edition—*Art, Ceremony, and Religion*—from her own shelf. It was just the way she had left it late the night before, opened to a full-color photo of a Papua New Guinea totem mask and a smaller black-and-white inset of a warrior mother kachina doll used in a Hopi Pachavu ceremony.

Sylvia found her reading glasses folded in the seam of the pages. She put them on and studied the images once more. In many cultures the mask traditionally expressed an alternate identity. It might transform the wearer into an animal or human spirit, invoke the soul of the dead, or impart transcendent, godlike powers.

The mask itself might be the actual dwelling place of a particular spirit. Masks were almost universally thought to hold great power—dangerous power if the wearer was not properly prepared and protected.

Sylvia had marked several other pages. She turned now to a Zairean initiation mask that was passed from male to male in families of royal lineage. That ritual was about the transference of power and potency among earthbound gods.

Finally, she let her fingers trace the simple sketch of an Anasazi petroglyph. This was a masklike face stained on rock. Better than the other images, it expressed the aggressive, poisonous rage of Dupont White.

Sylvia stood, stretched, and walked inside her house. She found a weathered Marlboro under a wooden spoon in her kitchen drawer. She lit it, inhaled, and stepped outside to exhale. She had already tasted smoke on the air, and last night's news had featured footage of forest fires burning in the Sandias and the Gila, and a new fire in the Jemez. This summer was proving itself to be the burning season. A gust of wind stirred the salt cedar that had grown up next to the deck. Behind the house, gray-blue sparrows bobbed on the telephone wire like a strand of live ornaments. A feather caught up on the air currents skittered past Sylvia's bare toes.

As she smoked the last of her cigarette and drained her coffee cup, she stared out at the dirt road at the end of her driveway. Her eyes skipped to a more distant focus—the pastures that belonged to her neighbors, the Calidros. Heat-browned grass offered skimpy grazing for the chestnut mare and the paint gelding. She thought again of her father, and how he had walked across those fields so many years ago. Was he still alive somewhere? Or was he dead?

Ghosts, witches, and Dupont White. If Dupont was alive, what dead spirit was he resurrecting with his painted mask? Or did his mask allow him to become *God*?

\* \* \*

HER LAST PATIENT—at the end of a very long day—was early for his appointment. Kevin Chase walked into the waiting room of the Forensic Evaluation Unit at eight minutes before the hour. He looked pale and reeked of musty tobacco and smoke. Sylvia told him to help himself to coffee and join her in the office.

Her goal was to follow up issues raised in the previous session. This would be a last chance to assess Kevin before she met with Frankie Reyes, his probation officer. She had little doubt Frankie had decided to begin the revocation process.

They were twenty minutes into the session, when Kevin turned to gaze out the small window overlooking a neighboring garden; his sleeves pulled back on his arms and Sylvia saw what looked like rope burns on both wrists.

She confronted him: "Kevin, what happened?"

His hands quickly disappeared under crossed arms. "Nothing . . . I cut myself."

"Those aren't cuts."

Kevin's head moved ponderously, and he refused to look at her.

She said quietly, "Show me your wrists." She waited while he made up his mind whether or not to comply. Finally he stretched out both arms, and she saw a band of irritated skin encircling each wrist where a restraint might cause abrasions.

Sylvia's first thought was sexual bondage. Her second thought was of the Polaroids, the bound men.

Kevin looked up at Sylvia and there were tears in his eyes. "Ja—she didn't do anything."

"Jackie?"

"No." He took a deep, apparently painful breath and Sylvia heard him swallow. "I didn't mean that." His head swayed back and forth like a clumsy metronome. "I got to feeling crazy, so I burned myself."

"Those aren't burns. Did you try to kill yourself?"

"No!" He looked shocked.

She believed he was self-destructive—*not* suicidal. "Did somebody restrain you?"

"What for? No."

For the next fifteen minutes, Sylvia tried to get a clear read on Kevin, but he was guarded and evasive. After he left, she stood on the second-story landing and gazed out at the parking lot of the judicial complex across the street. A gold Toyota Tercel was idling in the lot. Barely visible behind the steering wheel, Jackie Madden puffed on a cigarette.

Sylvia watched as Kevin left the courtyard and crossed Griffin Street. He sprinted around the vehicle on his way to the passenger door. After he was inside, the car remained stationary. His guardian was talking intently, and she drew circles with her cigarette. After several minutes she turned to look up at Sylvia. She raised her hand limply, put the car in gear, and drove slowly out of the lot.

Sylvia left her office two hours later. As she drove the few blocks to Adult Probation and Parole and her meeting with Frankie Reyes, she pondered Kevin Chase. After seven weeks of treatment, Sylvia was reading his overall clinical diagnosis as borderline organization with narcissistic and undersocialized features. He was adept at passive manipulation, he blamed the world for his problems, and he would desperately form dependent relationships and then ride an emotional roller coaster.

Were Kevin and Jackie Madden enmeshed in an "incestual" sexual relationship? Or had Kevin done his best to plant that false accusatory seed in Sylvia's mind? By the time she was seated across the desk from Frankie

Reyes at the offices of Adult Probation and Parole, Kevin's revocation process had begun.

Her client was on his way to prison.

BY EARLY EVENING, the Tsankawi fire had consumed three hundred acres and cut dangerously close to Tsankawi ruins between Los Alamos and Bandelier National Monument. Firefighters had gained a foothold on the blaze since it had been spotted two days earlier. Still, from his vantage point on the Highway 4 lookout, Matt saw pockets of flame explode at uneven intervals. He stepped out of the Caprice and walked to the edge of the gravel. Below him, the ground sloped down steeply. Gamble oak, chamisa, and dwarf juniper clung to the rocky soil. So far, these native plants had escaped the wrath of the fire. Two hundred feet lower, the vegetation and wildlife had not been so lucky. The burn pattern looked like a glowing crazy quilt.

Matt heard a small landslide, and he was startled to see the shadowy form of a young deer barely fifteen feet away on the slope. The animal scrambled up onto the gravel and stood in front of the Caprice. A doe. She snorted, nostrils wide, eyes luminous. He heard the harsh quick intake of her breath. He caught her dense musky scent. His heartbeat quickened the way it always did when he encountered a wild animal.

Headlights cut across her flank as a car rounded a curve of the highway. The animal bolted, and Matt grimaced as he heard the screech of brakes followed by a dull thunk. He sprinted out toward the highway, but the deer was already racing up the other bank.

Matt followed the Lincoln as it slowly turned off the road and pulled up next to his Chevy. The door opened, two booted feet hit the ground, and Special Agent Dan Chaney climbed out. A cigarette dangled from between his lips. He'd lost weight, his face was hollowed out—so changed Matt barely recognized his old friend, who had called for this out-of-the-way rendezvous.

"Where the hell have you been? I've been tracking you for a week." Concern became anger when it reached Matt's lips.

"I've been moving around." Chaney held out his cigarettes, an offering. Matt didn't make a move so Chaney stuffed the rumpled pack in his shirt pocket.

Matt said, "When I couldn't reach you, I finally called Cruces, Dan. Someone I can trust. He says your S.A.C. and the agency psychologist are both wondering where the hell you are. You haven't shown up for your counseling sessions. You are AWOL, guy."

"Yeah, well fuck it, I'm crazy." Chaney's voice was harsh. He tossed a manila envelope at Matt. His cigarette glowed deep orange while he inhaled. The residual smoke dispersed like a very light fog.

The special agent continued. "I still have friends I can trust, too." Smoke streamed from his mouth. "That's the forensic report on the bodies from Las Cruces—the blowout."

Chaney flicked his cigarette on gravel and ground it out with the toe of his boot. "No remains, no DNA match for Dupont White." He had already jammed a fresh cigarette between his lips, and he lit it. Still containing the smoke in his lungs, he said, "Proof my man is alive."

Matt opened the envelope and pulled out two sets of stapled reports issued by the state crime lab and the Federal Bureau of Investigation. He clicked on his belt flashlight and scanned the photocopies. While he read, Chaney walked to the edge of the turnout and stared out at the Tsankawi fire.

Chaney said, "What do you think . . . you got yourself a fire starter?" Matt grunted, and the federal agent continued. "Did you see the *New Mexican* today? That one-column short about a federal inquiry into the blowout at Las Cruces?" His voice went flat and hard. "They'll try to cover their asses. Just like they did with Ruby Ridge and Waco."

Matt lowered the report he had been scanning. "Who's *they*? Are we talking about your S.A.C.? The F.B.I. director? The attorney general? Shit, Dan."

Chaney's grin was cockeyed. His teeth reflected light from Matt's flashlight. "I think we can leave the President out of this mess."

Matt tried to curb his impatience. He waited for his old friend to offer more information.

Chaney picked up gravel in his palm, shook it, and then tossed it over the slope. He said, "Dupont was a federal snitch. That videotape I showed Sylvia? The agency had it—and the Polaroids—months before Las Cruces went down. Somebody knew Dupont White was a serial murderer. Somebody knew how dirty he was."

"They didn't pull him in."

"Because he was too dirty—or too damn valuable." Chaney's eyes shone with manic light. "If he was going to give them something big . . ."

"What?"

"I don't know, but I think he came to Santa Fe to get it."

Matt shook his head. "The N.C.I.C. database has him for a couple of possessions raps and some interstate trafficking—no murders, no assaults. It was Dupont's partner, Cole Lynch, who got sent up."

Chaney snorted derisively. "Who you gonna believe, guy? Dupont was a killer and a snitch—and somebody didn't want him to exist any longer, so they set him up in Las Cruces. They finally decided to kill him. But they missed. I know. I was there."

Abruptly, Chaney slapped the stapled pages Matt held. He said, "Read the last lines of the summary."

Matt turned pages, moved his light over the text, and began to read. "Existing DNA samples obtained from the crime scene were matched to known samples originating from Special Agent Nina Alcon Valdez, Special Agent Frank Teahouse, Ronnie Lee Hatch, and Jay Dennis Hatch."

Chaney said, "The Hatch brothers were supposed to make a buy from Dupont."

"There's no evidence Dupont was even on the premises." Matt switched off his flashlight.

"Oh, the scumbag was there, all right." Chaney snorted derisively. "We saw him go in. And I saw him run out of the warehouse just before it went up. I think I got one round into the asshole."

Matt stared at his old friend. "You reported all this?"

"I was put on stress leave for my trouble."

Chaney's Lincoln was parked nose to tail with the Caprice. The agent opened his door, then he stood staring up at the sky. "I talked to Sylvia this afternoon. I called her—told her where to reach me—which is more than you seem to do these days."

Matt shook his head to warn his friend off sensitive territory. After yesterday's argument, he'd decided to keep his distance for a day or two.

The special agent shrugged and climbed into the car. "She told me you're waiting for Jesse Montoya to turn up dead. He will." Chaney chuckled. It was an eerie sound, without mirth.

In the shadows, Matt saw only the rough, broad strokes of Chaney's features. He swallowed, glancing out at the fire. It cast a halo in the sky. Orange and sienna. It was beautiful. Deceptive. From a distance, the light was seductive; up close it was deadly. He didn't say a word.

Chaney shifted the Lincoln into reverse but kept his foot on the brake. "I just want to know if you're with me now."

"Yeah," Matt said softly. He turned to face the other man. "I'm with you."

All of Chaney's raw emotions seemed to tangle in his voice. He said, "When Nina died, it was like suddenly, I was bigger. There was more substance to me because I felt responsible for her. I wanted to carry on her laugh, her thoughts, her life. Now, I feel diminished. There's this hole inside me. And it keeps getting bigger."

Matt thought he heard Chaney crying.

Chaney continued. "Nina was everything . . . my life. I should've divorced Lorraine, married Nina, had kids, the whole bit." He rubbed a hand over his face. "I know you, Matt. We've been through a lot together. Don't you screw things up with Sylvia. You better clean up your act." He slammed the Lincoln into drive, and it lurched forward, out of the turnaround.

Matt stood for minutes on the edge of the mountain. He could taste the bitter ash in his mouth. The fire had spread out, wild and terrible.

He focused again on Chaney. Was the man too far gone for credibility? Matt no longer believed so. He gripped the envelope between his fingers. It wasn't just the report that changed his mind—it was Chaney himself.

The federal agent's story was growing more and more credible—at the same time Chaney had a dangerous edge. The man was disintegrating with grief. Matt knew Chaney was looking for trouble—and he'd find it.

Matt wished Sylvia had been here to witness the encounter. He trusted her judgment, her training. He trusted her intuition. His already low mood crashed.

Why couldn't he just come clean about Erin Tulley?

Their affair had been brief, and he'd broken it off months before he met Sylvia. But Erin still claimed to be in love with him. Maybe he was just ashamed of the whole thing. Ashamed that he'd almost rekindled the affair in March. Maybe he was ashamed that she still had some power over him, however small.

MATT PARKED THE Caprice under a streetlight in front of a tan stucco house on Agua Azul. The street was narrow and short and part of a newly suburban maze in south Santa Fe. Each home had a porch, a garage, a patch of lawn, a tree. Children were still at play down the block. The faint sound of their laughter caught and broke on the night air.

For a long minute, Matt studied number 67: the curtained windows, the brown stubble of grass, the weed-ridden flagstone path that led to a faded blue front door. The weeds were new; four months earlier, the yard had looked immaculate.

How many times had he been here? Almost every night for the brief time their affair had lasted. And then again in March. It had been a ritual; this time alone in the car, waiting for the porch light to go on.

And now it did. Bright yellow light flooded the cement foundation and the weathered slatted flowerpots.

The affair was over; so why hadn't he ever told Sylvia about Erin?

He approached the house and stood on the doorstep, arms at his sides. Almost instantly Erin Tulley opened the door. She looked tense. And angry. And very young. He asked, "Are you all right?"

She stared at him with contempt. When he recoiled, she stepped back so he could enter the house. He had to turn sideways to fit through the space she allowed, and his movements were clumsy. He could smell her scent, a hint of rose.

Matt reached out to touch her face, but she pulled away. "Forget it." She clutched her terry-cloth robe tight to her throat. "That's not why you came."

Uneasy, Matt glanced around the entryway, into the beige living room, into the yellow kitchen. He felt eyes on his back.

Erin said, "We're alone, if that's what you're wondering." Her hand brushed against his sleeve and emotion flickered over her face; he couldn't tell if it was bitterness or sadness. She didn't let him get another look.

"You want coffee?" She had already turned toward the kitchen.

Matt shook his head. "I'm fine."

She wasn't listening, or else she couldn't stop moving. She opened cupboards, found a clean mug, filled it, and refilled her own cup.

Matt accepted the coffee. He didn't want to sit, but he forced himself to settle on the edge of a white plastic chair. The room was small, square, made of prefab materials, and had absolutely no relation to the heavy molded adobes of east side Santa Fe. The stucco walls were bare except for a photograph of the Sandias at sunset and a poster of impossibly perfect habañero peppers. A toaster oven took up half the counter space. A blender and dish rack demanded the rest. Dirty dishes filled the sink.

Erin kept her head low as she sipped her coffee. Her robe was loose and Matt could tell she was naked beneath the terry cloth. Where the fabric gaped, the inside of one thigh was visible. He averted his eyes.

She turned to face him, chin square and defiant, and she saw that he was embarrassed. She said, "Why did you come? Aren't you taking a big risk, coming near such a pariah?"

"Erin," Matt said softly.

Her eyes filled with tears. "You wanted me a few months ago—before Sylvia took you back."

Matt stood, moved a step toward her, but she raised the flats of both palms. "No."

He stopped and shook his head. He wanted to escape . . . he had no idea what to say to her. He'd dreaded finding her like this. That's why he'd avoided a meeting. But she was calling again—her lawsuit was the excuse now.

Her voice shook like a child's when she said, "I messed it all up. My career, everything. I wasn't tough enough to take the heat." Although he didn't respond, she turned on him and her eyes burned.

"I had a valid case, dammit. I should've been promoted. I had a valid gender discrimination case, and everyone at D.P.S. knew it. But you didn't stand behind me. Where were you when I needed you?" Fury shook her body and stretched her voice to the breaking point. "You're a coward!"

Matt moved into her space and grabbed her by both shoulders. He outweighed her by sixty pounds, and she only resisted for a few seconds before her strength seemed to give way. She collapsed against his chest and wept.

When most of her tears were spent, Matt sat her down at the table and got her a fresh cup of coffee. She drank half the cup before she could speak.

"Do you hate me?" she asked.

"Why would I?"

"Because I screwed up on Randall."

He kept silent for a few seconds. Really, he didn't understand why she'd lied and then broken rank. Except she was so shaken by the long, drawn-out lawsuit. She looked like a different woman from the one he'd thought he loved—and different from Erin, the cop. She'd been good at her job. He said, "It didn't matter in the end."

Erin released her breath in a long sigh. Matt was afraid she would cry again, but the storm passed.

She said, "I needed your support."

"You had the police officers' association on your side."

She shook her head. "I got so sick of the way you all shut me out."

"What did you expect?" Matt asked her wearily. "You accused the department of discrimination. Did you think they'd applaud you for it?"

"I thought you might."

Her words stung him. Just as quickly, he knew most of the anger was meant for himself.

He studied Erin now. Behind the exhaustion, the emotional havoc, she was still striking. For the first time he was shocked to realize she reminded him of his wife. Mary had been nothing like Erin in temperament. But she had seemed incomplete without her husband or son by her side. Erin had that same air of incompleteness. Sometimes she was like a lost kid. She had a neediness that Matt rarely saw in Sylvia. And Erin wanted him—she'd made that clear ever since their affair.

And he had been equally clear that he was unavailable. But when Sylvia had asked for some time alone last March, Erin had been eager to renew the relationship. Remembering that final encounter made Matt feel ashamed. He'd hurt Erin again because he felt rejected by Sylvia. Guilt washed over him, made him even more uncomfortable. He glanced surreptitiously at his watch.

Erin said, "I know it wasn't easy for you to come." Her face was shiny and pink from crying, as if she'd scrubbed it too hard. She tried to smile and got halfway there. "Thanks."

He stood and started to tell her he was sorry: she was right, he hadn't stood behind her because he didn't want to get involved in her problems.

She shook her head, and brought her fingers gently to his mouth. "Before you go, I need to know . . . are there any leads on Randall?" Suddenly, she looked stricken. She pulled back and covered her face with her hands. "I messed up bad—if I could do it over—" She fought for control, gulped air. Slowly, she let her arms drop to her sides. "But I can't. And maybe it doesn't matter—at least he didn't get away with rape."

Her eyes were fierce. "I still love you, Matt."

"Erin, don't—"

"It's how I feel."

# ELEVEN

SYLVIA FOLLOWED THE procession of Rosie, Benji, and Velio Cruz as they passed under the metal bower of razor ribbon. They were in limbo between Housing Unit 3's exercise cages, the sally port, and the death house. It struck her as unlikely that the administration had approved a midnight full-moon healing ceremony in the close security yard. She half expected the tower guard, who was undoubtedly watching them, to start shooting. She was jumpy.

Moonlight sharply illuminated the hawklike features of Velio Cruz, the inmate shaman, who would try to reverse the effects of black witchcraft. Unlike a Spanish *curandero,* who was an all-around healer, Cruz was more like an *arbulario,* a practitioner who specialized in reversing bewitchment. Cruz borrowed his techniques from Native American, island, and Anglo cultures in addition to Spanish culture. If anyone could "cure" Benji, it was Velio, because, most important of all, he'd honed his prison survival skills: perception and observation, manipulation and power plays.

Velio Cruz had spent thirty-five of his fifty years behind bars. Currently he was an inmate at the penitentiary's North Facility, serving a life sentence for armed robbery and first-degree murder.

Cruz was tall and thin, as if intensity had stretched and

whetted his body to a spare minimum. Faded black tattoos snaked up his muscled arms and chest. His hands were large, his fingers long and tapered, but his knuckles were so swollen and deformed by arthritis that they resembled walnuts.

The healer's skin was pocked and discolored by acne. A handlebar mustache drooped over his thin stripe of a mouth. Sylvia had been instantly aware of his eyes. His irises were dark enough to be black, and he had *san paku*—a quarter moon of white was visible under each pupil. She felt their cold power.

Cruz stopped suddenly and pivoted toward Benji. "Here."

He had chosen his site. The maximum-security facility would be their scrim, while the death house and the sweat lodge, which had been built by Native American inmates for purification rituals, occupied the wings. Only the cedar sweat lodge seemed appropriate for the ceremony. Cruz had demanded the outdoor location. He insisted that the bad energy had to be released into open air. The most protected yard was here outside Housing Unit 3, which housed the most violent inmates at the penitentiary. Rosie maintained that she'd arranged for official permission; Sylvia didn't believe her friend.

Sylvia felt Rosie's hand on her arm. Rosie said, "He's starting." She turned toward Benji but froze when a distant scream cut the silence.

It came from Maximum. The inmates would not witness the ceremony; their cells were located on the far side of the cinder-block building and faced north or northeast. But by natural prison law they *knew* something was going on. They could sense action the way a pack of coyotes catches the first scent of its prey. The faint cacophony of their catcalls and howls hung on the night

air. Sylvia knew what the din must be like inside the unit.
She took a breath.

Again, she felt Velio's eyes on her skin. Earlier, in a
visitors' room, Cruz and Benji had completed their
*platica,* or discussion of the basic problems at issue—in
this case, a dark witch, or *brujo negro.* Even then, the
healer had watched Sylvia. Now, she heard his deep
voice and turned to stare. He had removed his shirt. The
tattoo that covered his chest depicted a crow, dark wings
open in flight.

Velio Cruz raised both arms, suddenly as fierce and
graceful as a panther. His voice was deep and sonorous,
and he murmured something that sounded like Latin. A
prayer.

Benji Muñoz y Concha moaned. He sat bolt upright
on the brown grass opposite Velio Cruz. His loose hair
fell past his shoulders. His body was lost inside a large
work shirt and blue jeans, both turned inside out. He
looked like a wide-eyed ten-year-old, not a prison
inmate.

Rosie, apparently engrossed in the ceremony, murmured softly, and Sylvia tried to shake off a sudden
feeling of dread. But when she looked away from Benji
and Cruz, her eyes settled on the death house bleached
white by moonlight.

JESSE MONTOYA—GRANDSON of Augustine Montoya,
a sixth-generation Montoya whose ancestors had followed Vásquez de Coronado's conquistadors through the
*Jornada del Muerto*—moaned as the motion of the truck
tossed him like a shell in the tide. He didn't fight the
momentum but let his body roll. Bruises would not
matter. Nothing would matter. The monster with the
painted face had made that clear enough. Jesse knew he
was going to die.

In his imagination, he made the sign of the cross. He made it slowly and carefully, just as he would if his hands weren't bound; his limbs had gone numb long ago. Perhaps by now they were poisoned by lack of blood. That wasn't something he could say; he wasn't a doctor. He could only guess at such things.

He thought about his grandfather, who had prayed for hours—days—that Jesse would stop hurting people. Jesse knew that his sins had caused great pain for his grandfather. But he had done so many bad things, the memories flowed together and filled his mind like one vast sea. He prayed now: *If you let me go free,* Madre de Dios, *I will never hurt another girl.* He started to cry.

And for a moment, Jesse believed he could honor his side of the bargain.

When he was finished crying, he tried to fight the fear. But he wasn't good at it—not without help from marijuana or Four Roses—and fear coursed through his body until he knew he would fail to die like a man.

So much had been wrong in his life. He didn't trust that the end could go better. He wished he had known his real mother. He missed his grandmother, his *abuelita.* He missed the voices of women as they chattered in the kitchen over great steaming pots of pinto beans and chile.

*Dios, ayudame*—help me. But it wasn't God who embraced him with great warm arms; it was his grandmother. She called his name softly: *Jesse, jito.* She told him she was waiting for him.

SYLVIA FOUND THAT she was falling into a light hypnotic trance, lulled by the deep voice of Cruz, the incense, the night air. Clouds had covered the moon in gray silk. The light was diffuse and rich with shadow. She lost track of

time and simultaneously became hyperalert. The opposing sensations reminded her of adolescent drug-induced
states. The first streak of acid coming on when she was
sixteen. The trip had been seductive and dangerous.

Her eyes caught movement as Velio Cruz rubbed
something white over Benji. An egg in its shell. Sylvia
heard faint chanting until Cruz finally threw the egg, and
it exploded against the cinder-block wall of the death
house.

The moon freed itself of obscuring clouds, and sudden
milky light poured down on the prison yard. Sylvia felt
sick to her stomach; a wave of heat rushed under her
skin. Her vision blurred until the moon was a watery orb
suspended in dark liquid. She reached out to Rosie,
touched her arm, and the sick feeling passed.

Cruz began to smudge rough lines with charcoal or
paste across Benji's high cheekbones, across his chin,
and his neck. When the healer was finished, he took
Benji's bare forearm in both hands and lowered his head.

He began to suck at the soft skin near Benji's elbow.

To Sylvia, it looked as if Velio were a wolf pulling and
tearing at the flesh of a deer.

As Cruz worked, Benji appeared to experience in-
creasing pain. He writhed on the hard earth. Abruptly, he
cried out, "Help me!"

Answering cries echoed from Housing Unit 3.

But Velio Cruz kept his mouth tight on Benji's arm.

THE PANEL TRUCK coasted to a stop on a rough forest road
just miles from Los Alamos. On either side of the road
cut, a wall of ponderosa pines denied trespass. The mature
trees—the veterans—stood twenty-five feet. The youngest
had grown together, entwined and crippled, in their quest
for the sun.

The driver's door opened, but nothing emerged from the truck except a thin strand of cigarette smoke. After several minutes, the forest's half silence was broken by the throb of a motorcycle engine. The noise grew louder until a Honda roared into view. Tree branches grazed the biker's arm and thigh. Motorcycle tires crushed infinite pine needles and stirred up fine, powdery earth. The bike drew even and came to a stop next to the truck. The biker climbed off the Honda and slowly removed his helmet. Kevin Chase ran a hand through his damp hair and gazed up at the trees.

The forest was alive, breathing, and seemed to take one step toward the road. Kevin closed his eyes as if waiting to be crushed by the dark, hunkering shapes. Maybe he heard them speak: *Tonight, you have the power.*

Finally, he walked around to the rear of the truck and opened the double doors. He saw Jesse Montoya curled up like a sick baby in the farthest corner. Kevin ignored the naked, bound man and stripped off his denim shirt. He had things to do.

When he opened the toolbox, the small containers of pigment were ready. He unscrewed one bottle and scooped out rust-colored paste with his thumb. Using the index fingers of both hands, he carefully smeared blood-lines along his cheek, forehead, and throat. A canteen of water had been strapped to a metal hook on the truck's left panel. He took the canteen and squatted outside the truck. With his palm, he wore down the earth between his feet. He dripped water into the hollow. Mixed, the dirt and water became mud, which he rubbed over his chest, arms, and face.

He hunched over the bike and stared at himself in the mirror. A bloody, aboriginal demon stared back. Good. Killer would approve.

When Kevin dragged Jesse Montoya from the bed of the truck, he got a surprise: Montoya was conscious. He heard the pleading whisper of Jesse's voice. The sound made him uneasy.

As he dragged Montoya away from the road, he followed spidery strands of moonlight on the forest floor. His feet were cushioned by the carpet of brown pine needles and rotted trees. Montoya's weight slowed him down. He was hot, sweaty, and irritable by the time he reached the clearing. He dropped Montoya, and the man groaned.

"Fuckin' rapist." Kevin spat on Montoya's exposed neck. Then he turned and retraced his steps. It was his job to carry the red gasoline can already filled with accelerant.

He reached the road just as Killer emerged from the truck in full paint: reddish brown and black covering face and chest. The owl mask was terrible. The grotesque predatory-bird features mesmerized Kevin.

Killer reached out one painted arm and flame emerged from between fingers. Like *magic*.

And then Kevin saw that Killer also held the video camera. The red light pulsed.

Hefting accelerant, Kevin led the way; Killer followed with the camera. By the time they reached Montoya, Killer was moving through the trees in slow motion, red light gleaming, body undulating in a private ritual of death. Wet with sweat, anticipating the coming death, Killer plunged deeper into some altered state.

Kevin watched the red light and his pulse began to race. He lifted the gasoline can and poured a mixture of paint thinner and kerosene over Jesse Montoya's bound, naked body. The fumes excited Kevin. He was overwhelmed by the reek of kerosene. He had memorized the explosion, the burst of flames.

But this time, he would risk the wrath of Killer. This time, the kill would be *his*. He had to prove he wasn't afraid; that he wouldn't be sick like the last time.

He stared down at the rapist. Jesse—coughing, sputtering—looked away and closed his eyes. The accelerant had soaked the tape bindings and glistened on naked flesh.

From the corner of his eye, Kevin saw Killer moving his way. The camera was on *him*. He didn't let himself think about his next move. Strutting hollowly for the camera, he pulled matches from his pants pocket. He was surprised at how numb he felt as he deliberately struck a match, let the book ignite, and tossed the tiny inferno in the air. It fell. Kevin saw it drifting in slow motion. Actually, it began in an instant. Jesse Montoya screaming as his body exploded like a fireball. Flames raced hungrily over skin and earth, gobbling up the trail of flammable fluids.

Kevin was thrown back by the blowout, his yell fueled by surprise and the rush of panic. But his cry ended abruptly when he felt the brunt of Killer's rage—one boot stroke across his temple.

BENJI MUÑOZ Y CONCHA experienced a moment of intense pain as the dark form of Velio Cruz melted in front of his eyes. The air was so hot it scalded his skin. He cried out, felt his body sucked off the ground until he was hovering above the death house. He looked down and saw Velio Cruz, Rosie Sanchez, and Sylvia Strange. They were huddled around a small dark form on the ground.

Benji knew he had become someone else. A stranger. A dying man.

For an instant, he thought death might be an eternity of pain, a burning hell like they told you in church. Then, the panic subsided, the smells, sounds, sensations eased off and he was flying. His body glided above the road, across the dark green reservoir, into the first soft rise of the Sangre de Cristo Mountains. To the west, the lights of the city shimmered like something alive. Each separate illumination was so intense, so beautiful, he had to turn his eyes away. He looked north and saw the Rocky Mountains stretching forward, the tortured spine of a great beast. He wanted to fly on forever except the sky was afire. Flames climbed one hundred feet above the ground where the air was thin, without taste. He could see sparks in the distance, blowing closer. The muscles in his arms and legs no longer responded to his commands. An owl matched flight with him, wings aflame, flapping in slow motion. When the bird looked his way, it had the eyes of Velio Cruz.

He heard the ponderous whoosh of air under the bird's wings. The owl's beak was sharp and black. It stretched out its body, beak tweezed open, and tore the flesh on his arm as it passed.

He cried out. Below him, he caught a quick glimpse of swirling gray wings—two witches fighting over a dead fox. No . . . the fox was a man. And he was burning.

Suddenly, he could no longer keep himself up, and he was plunging back to earth. As his body gained momentum, the ground flew up in his face.

KEVIN WRENCHED HIS pant leg away from the flames and rolled. Pain streaked across his cheek and skull. He swore as he slammed into a tree. Dazed, he hauled himself to his knees, then stumbled to his feet. He was overwhelmed by the sickening smell of kerosene smoke and burned flesh. Nausea stopped him. He vomited.

When he could, he checked for damage. His fingers

felt loose, wet skin on his face—*Hurts like hell*—and came away bloodied. Killer had cut him, knocked him, stunned him good.

He looked around, checked out his surroundings. Jesse Montoya's body was still burning—the stink was awful—and Kevin felt sick again. But the man was probably dead. Kevin turned his attention to the fire that had started in the nearby trees. The flames were moving quickly, all business. They darted up branches, danced in the pine needles and dry leaves.

He tried to get his bearings—which way was the road? He stumbled forty feet in the wrong direction, turned himself around, started off again. He lunged from tree trunk to trunk. It took forever to reach the road.

The truck was gone. So was his bike. *No, wait a minute, the bike is there.* In the stippled shadows he saw metal gleaming. His head had cleared enough so his progress down the road was almost steady. He straddled the Honda. Turned the key. Pressed the starter button and cranked the throttle. The bike roared to life.

That's when he saw the headlights in his rearview mirror. They blinded him. Coming from the main road. Killer had come back for him. Kevin balanced on one foot, spun the bike around, and accelerated toward the truck. Adrenaline raced through him. Then panic. It wasn't a panel truck. It was a pickup with metal tanks instead of a bed. Official vehicle. U.S. Forest Service.

He heard a man's voice call out. Saw the flash of shiny black metal. *A gun?*

But it wasn't a gun, it was a spotlight—and they caught him in the beam.

He revved the bike's engine and pushed off. The Honda 750 terraplaned over the washboard dirt road, shimmied across a Forest Service cattle guard, and grabbed the blacktop of Highway 4. Kevin kept the bike straight and smooth, his head clearing as the wind tore over his skin. The mountain landscape flew by in a blur of road, speed, adrenaline—and the ultimate thrill.

The truck was behind him, but slow. He was losing them.

*Jesus, I killed a man.* He accelerated to seventy, eighty, ninety.

The bike between his thighs was pure power. He saw the curve ahead. Saw the gleaming lights of Santa Fe a few miles in the distance. A hazy glow in a canyon of darkness.

Kevin slowed to fifty miles per hour as he approached the turn. He heard faraway sirens; they were after him, made him feel high. *I matter.* The cops were probably waiting at a roadblock. Waiting for him. Not Killer.

For all his size, Kevin became one with his motorcycle. He was a fluid and daring driver. He leaned into the turn. The wind stung his wounded face. He saw the lights of Los Alamos, and they looked almost within reach. There were other lights, closer. Red and pulsing, like the video camera, only big. Cops. Coming his way, up the road. He aimed straight for their headlights.

VELIO CRUZ RAISED his wet mouth from Benji's arm. Between white teeth, he gripped a long metal splinter. Rosie gasped. Sylvia caught her breath. Her first thought was that Cruz must have hidden the damn thing in his mouth. Her second thought was that Benji was healed. His clothes were soaked through, his hair lay damp against his skull, his eyes were bloodshot. But he was smiling wanly, and his skin glowed. He was a man reborn.

Sylvia swayed suddenly. The heat under her skin seemed unbearable.

Rosie placed her palms against Sylvia's throat and whispered, "You're on fire, *jita*." She wrapped her arms around Sylvia's shoulder. Velio Cruz walked toward them.

Sylvia brushed away her friend's arms angrily, and said, "I'm fine."

Cruz stopped in his tracks when he was three feet from Sylvia's face. He stared at her with his *san paku* eyes. The whites of his eyeballs were yellowed and bloodshot. He took the spike from between his teeth and held it like a needle.

He said, "This dark energy, this witch . . . it touched you, too."

They were face-to-face, neither one moving. Sylvia didn't know how long she stood there, but she was aware that her breathing now matched that of Cruz.

She whispered, "I'm not your patient, Velio."

His concentration didn't waver when a sudden shrill sound broke the air. Sylvia jumped, her heartbeat took off. It took her a moment to recognize the sound of her own pager. Relieved, she stepped away from Cruz and peered at the small digital numbers. She caught the last three digits: Matt.

She felt something pressed into her hand. Rosie's cell phone was cool against her fingers. Rosie shrugged. "I'm not allowed to go anywhere on the grounds without it."

Matt picked up on the second ring. He said, "I wanted to be the one to give you the news. They just found Jesse Montoya. He was set on fire, like Randall."

Sylvia pictured Augustine Montoya's weathered face, heard his whisper, *Vienen las llamas de juicio.* And he'd been right, the flames of judgment had come.

Matt said, "Deputies pursued a suspect on a motorcycle. He got away, but they ran the plates. Sylvia, it's *not* Dupont White. It's Kevin Chase."

# TWELVE

CAFÉ ESCALERA WAS filling quickly with the Friday lunch crowd, but there were two empty seats at the bar. Sylvia and Dr. Albert Kove sat on the tall stools, and the bartender set lunch menus in front of them.

The downtown restaurant was a study in spare elegance. Parallel runners of white canvas draped the ceiling in gently billowing fabric clouds. Tiny capped bulbs glowed like carnival lights. All this in a room that had been part of the old Sears department store a decade earlier.

Kove decided on a mixed green salad. Sylvia ordered a steak sandwich that came with a mound of Escalera's famous shoestring french fries.

While she and Kove waited for their food, Sylvia sipped tart lemonade and stared straight ahead into the long mirror that graced the wall behind the bar. The stark white tables, the tiny lights, and the view from the balcony windows on the opposite side of the room were all visible in the glass. Sylvia's gaze was drawn to the reflection of a slender woman with brunette hair and dark almond eyes that swallowed you up. It took her a moment to recognize herself.

Kove added a spoonful of sugar to his iced tea and gave Sylvia a slow sideways glance. "So, I had a call from the attorney general's office, and another from

Probation and Parole. They want to know if we had any 'warning signs' on Kevin Chase?" He kept his voice low.

"Albert, between you and me, I see warning signs all the time." Sylvia spoke in a furious whisper. "Most of the time, they come to nothing, but I *never* ignore them. Yesterday, Frankie Reyes agreed to begin Kevin's revocation process. But you and I both know that takes time." She had twisted her lemonade straw into a spiral; now she knotted the plastic ends.

Kove sank his chin in the palm of one hand. His words were careful. "Your client is a fugitive for two murders. Don't get snippy with me."

Sylvia shook her head impatiently. "Okay, Kevin's borderline. He's weird, he has bizarre relationships where he's the passive participant." The tortured straw flew out of her fingers and landed on the floor of the bar. "But if Kevin's involved in these murders, he didn't work alone. He doesn't have the aggressive drive to be a solo serial murderer."

Kove said, "Last night two Forest Service employees witnessed a man who fits Kevin Chase's description fleeing Montoya's murder scene. They were sharp enough to get his license plate number."

The bartender placed a new straw next to Sylvia's glass.

"I'm not saying he wasn't there. I'm saying he wasn't alone." Sylvia frowned. "Kevin needs to prove his manhood. That might make him vulnerable to someone like Dupont White." A part of her mind automatically continued the shuffling and evaluation of facts, and she guarded them like cards in a poker hand. Psychology wasn't a hard science: she did her best to understand a client's problems, stressors, cycles, and motivations; she did her best to predict future behavior. Then she made judgment calls that would affect the course of a human being's life. Sometimes, the whole thing was very messy.

Like now. The thought of a client under her supervision committing brutal murders made her sick.

She was startled out of her thoughts when Albert Kove patted her hand gently. He said, "Don't look now, but Marty Connor's coming this way."

Sylvia stared diligently at the mirror and spoke in a low voice. "Bend-over Marty? Marty-who-knows-everything-about-everyone? Marty the governor's bagman?"

"Be nice."

She turned and just had time to set a boundary with one hand. The Bagman actually made her skin crawl. She said, "Hello, Marty."

The Bagman placed his beer on the bar between the two psychologists. He grasped Sylvia's palm. She retained her composure—and extricated her hand. He was a scrawny man with a pink and shiny bald spot that was bordered by longish hair.

Marty signaled the bartender for another beer. He said, "Anchor Steam on tap. If you haven't tried it, you should." Sylvia noticed that the Bagman wore silver spurs on his cowboy boots—they jingled. His pants were cuffed, the center crease was paper sharp.

Albert sensed that Sylvia was about to insult the Bagman and he interceded. He tapped Marty on the shoulder, and the man turned, palm extended in a knee-jerk offer to shake. His tiny features worked themselves into a grave expression.

The Bagman's brows twitched and met above his nose. "So you poor children have a contract coming up for renewal." He noisily sucked the head off his beer. "A little late, I'd say. Me, I'd move at warp speed to put this Kevin What's-his-name thing to bed." He sighed as if to grieve the fact there was only one Marty "the Bagman" Connor in the world.

Sylvia took a slow sip of lemonade; her heart was down in her shoes. The Forensic Evaluation Unit's contract with the state came due every two years; the performance review for renewal had already begun. If Kove was going to retain the contract with the courts, it would happen by the end of summer. She knew what the contract meant to Albert. Everything. It meant just about that much to her.

The Bagman dripped beer on his paisley tie. "Since we're all friends here"—he lowered his voice and his lips stayed immobile—"you didn't hear it from me, but Burt Webster smells contractual blood, and he's making his move." He shrugged and his eyes narrowed to malevolent dashes.

Sylvia grimaced; Burt Webster was a show-off and a snob who wore navy suits with polka-dot ties. He was also a psychiatrist with a thriving forensic practice and demands for his services that took him far from his Albuquerque office. Burt Webster was very good at his job.

She said, "Burt Webster's a shark who drives a Range Rover."

The Bagman smiled and said, "He's a very chummy shark when it comes to the governor's wife. We all know she's carrying a torch for mental health in the Land of Enchantment. It's her raison d'être." It sounded like "raisin dooter" after it passed through Marty's lips.

Sylvia felt angry and mean. She couldn't resist mocking the Bagman, even though he was an octopus with tentacles reaching into every state agency. He was the governor's brother-in-law—and the man who made the midnight deals during the last election campaign. She smiled sweetly and said, "Her raisin dooter?"

"It's French," the Bagman barked.

Sylvia nodded seriously, then continued, "So I take it Burt Webster is lobbying for our contract?"

Sandwich and salad arrived, and Sylvia grabbed a french fry and doused it in ketchup. She was the newest member of the unit, and she was the youngest. And the most expendable. And right this minute, she was the most visible as far as the public was concerned; what she had was way too much negative exposure. She was the team's Achilles' heel, and Marty Connor knew it.

The Bagman pointed a small finger at Sylvia and gave her a look that said, *You fucked up, lady.* "Burt Webster claims he has seventy-five percent accuracy when he predicts future violence by offenders. He's got stats to prove it."

Kove waved his hand in disgust. "Webster's manipulating his numbers or else he's got a crystal ball. That's impossible."

The Bagman shrugged and extended a finger toward Sylvia's french fries. She wanted to slap his hand away but knew she couldn't afford the display of temper. In the queer and fickle arena of politics, the Bagman wielded enough power to ruin her ass; even worse, he could ruin Albert Kove as far as the state contract was concerned. If Burt Webster had the governor's wife in his pocket, the Bagman had the governor. She turned away from Marty Connor and whispered, "Lambe rosca."

If the Bagman heard the insult he just smiled, and tucked another french fry between his lips. "I'll do what I can for you, Albert, because you've always been there for me." His pupils were dark and glittery. When he leaned toward Sylvia, he smelled of stale beer and fries.

He whispered, "Today, this minute, I know several attorneys who won't use you until this mess is cleared up. Their clients are afraid of the 'killers' doctor.' "

He leaned even closer. "Malcolm Treisman was the

best. Maybe you bit off more than you can chew, trying to walk in his footsteps."

Sylvia didn't have a comeback for the Bagman's mixed metaphor. Treisman had been her colleague, mentor—and lover—who had died of cancer nine months earlier.

The Bagman leaned back and smiled. "Go out and get yourself some good press, lady." He winked. "And how about an attitude adjustment, while you're at it?"

As Marty Connor walked into the dining area, Albert Kove took Sylvia by both shoulders and stared at her intently. "What the hell is a *lambe rosca?*"

Sylvia shrugged. "Ass-licker, ass-wipe, brownnose, whatever."

Kove stayed perfectly still, but a few seconds later he stifled a laugh.

In the mirror, Sylvia could see the Bagman in conversation at his table across the room. She said, "That pompous little sonofabitch. I hope he chokes on his polenta." Her fingers worried a bar napkin until it was a damp wad.

She said, "It would take the heat off the team if I was out."

Kove was silent, but one eyebrow arched in speculation.

"I'm not quitting." She shook her head and carefully finished off an especially long fry. She motioned to the bartender. "Could I have another lemonade? And spice it up with a short shot of Absolut." She caught her partner's woeful expression.

"Don't worry, Albert." She glanced at her watch. "It's after noon."

He waved his hand, dismissing her words. "You feel you're jeopardizing this team?"

She cut him off. "Hey, I said I'm *not* quitting." Sylvia accepted the drink from the bartender. She took a long sip and then said, "But you should be aware of something. I've decided to fly to California for a few days. It's likely that Kevin Chase will be arrested and charged with two murders. I know he didn't work alone. If Dupont White is alive, if he dragged Kevin into this mess, I've got to learn more about him. An old friend of mine, Leo Carreras, works at Atascadero State Hospital, and he's already agreed to let me see Violet Miller."

"Dupont White's psychotic girlfriend?" Kove ran a hand across his wiry sandy hair, rolled his round eyes, and remained silent. Not for the first time, he reminded Sylvia of her terrier, Rocko. They were both resolute, unflappable, determined.

"You really think she can tell you anything?" He frowned.

Sylvia swung around on the stool. "Maybe she can *show* me something about Dupont's dynamic with his followers. I won't know unless I take the trip. This whole thing—Chaney, Dupont, the murders, Kevin Chase, it's messing with my mind, and it's ruining my credibility."

"But Sylvia—"

"I mean, I feel like some sort of contagion is affecting me. Until I know what's going on, it won't get better." She pulled away from her associate.

During the last half hour, the crowd in the restaurant had thinned; no one was seated next to them at the bar. Kove's voice never shifted from neutral. He said, "Sylvia, you're a very good forensic psychologist. If I didn't believe that, I would never have asked you to become a part of the unit." His eyes held the slightest glint of light. "You had a tough year, but you survived it. You did more than survive it. You thrived." He smiled now. "You're young, but you've got potential."

She rolled her eyes. "Thanks."

"If you need to go to California—go. But I want you on this team."

Sylvia kissed Kove's cheek. "Thanks." She pushed away the last of her vodka and lemonade. While Kove was busy with his wallet, she snitched a stray pack of cigarettes that had been left on the bar. Surreptitiously, she examined the occupants of the restaurant who were reflected in the mirror. Apparently, no one had seen her take the pack.

She rested her chin in the palm of one hand and let her eyes bore into Marty "the Bagman" Connor. Across the restaurant, he was gesturing, laughing, in general making a big production out of lunch with his cronies.

A lean, bushy-haired man in an expensive suit stepped next to Sylvia. He said, "Did you see a pack of cigarettes? I left them—"

Sylvia shook her head and her expression held friendly concern. "That's a bad habit. You should work on kicking it. I can recommend a counselor."

AFTER LUNCH, ALBERT KOVE had to attend a meeting with the director of the state's Mental Health Services at the Pera Building. Sylvia left him outside the restaurant and walked along Palace Avenue under the portal where Pueblo artisans displayed their jewelry and craft wares. She was glad to find this pocket of time to think. Her heels on concrete clicked out irritation. The Bagman's cheap power games were disgusting. *"Burt Webster claims he has seventy-five percent accuracy when he predicts future violence."* A voice nagged at the back of her mind: *Why didn't I see it coming with Kevin?*

As she walked, Sylvia brushed her hair off her neck; the great branches of a century-old elm offered brief but welcome shade. The heat settled low on the city and applied the brakes. Activity slowed, people became increasingly punchy. It was a kind of smoke and heat craziness.

When Sylvia rounded the corner and turned onto Grant Avenue, she saw a familiar figure. Ten more paces, and she recognized Erin Tulley.

Tulley said, "I just stopped by your office, but you weren't there." She looked keyed-up and her voice was running too fast.

Sylvia did a rapid calculation and figured that she had half an hour free before her next client. She said, "I'm just back from lunch. Let's go up and I'll make you a cup of really disgusting coffee. Actually, it's high-octane sludge."

Erin smiled. It was a weak effort, but the corners of her mouth did turn up, even if only a fraction. She said, "Could we just walk for a minute?"

Erin took the lead and moved quickly, with her head down. When they were a short distance along Grant Avenue, Erin tugged on Sylvia's arm and ducked through the double wooden doors that marked the threshold of First Presbyterian Church. Intrigued and puzzled, Sylvia followed.

The church interior was filled with pastel light and shadow. Sylvia removed her sunglasses and waited for her eyes to adjust. It was years since she'd been inside the church. The first thing she noticed were the modest stained-glass windows gracing three walls. Lambs wandered beside shepherds. Women clustered together, hands clasped. Praying women. Worried women. Everything was held in those plain, devout faces: isolation, suffering, sorrow.

Sylvia saw that Erin had settled in a pew, but she didn't move. Her eyes were on the altar. It was made of wood and marble. The lines were simple and the effect was surprisingly powerful. It was designed to draw the eyes up and out, to make one feel the cross before the eyes actually registered the intersecting lines. A sleight of hand, a trick of the eye or the mind, as if God must be felt before seen. It worked, but it made Sylvia uncomfortable.

She sat down on the cool, dark bench. She heard Erin breathing beside her. She said, "Do you attend services here?"

"No."

"Matt told me you aren't at D.P.S. any more. That must be a difficult change." Sylvia leaned away from Erin so she could see her face. She found it odd that they would be sitting together in an empty church. She felt empathy for this woman, but she also felt wary.

Erin gave a small laugh. "Difficult? My dreams went up in smoke." She swallowed hard.

Sylvia didn't like the desperate look on Erin's face. She said, "Are you seeing anybody to talk this out?"

Erin clenched her jaw. "Talking doesn't help." After a prolonged silence she continued, "I was afraid I'd lose my nerve."

"Erin, are you talking about the Randall case or the Title Seven action?"

"No." Erin's pupils were fat in their surrounding green orbs. Her lipstick was worn away at the corners of her mouth.

"Then what?" Sylvia glanced at her watch.

"I want you to hear it from me, that it's over."

"What's over?" Sylvia shook her head; she was puzzled and frustrated by Erin's cryptic behavior.

A tear squeezed out from the corner of Erin's eye. It stuck to her eyelashes. "It's over between Matt and me."

Erin obviously expected a verbal response from Sylvia; when it didn't come, she continued. "I thought you should know he called it off. I won't lie to you—I still love him."

Sylvia stared at Erin in disbelief—the woman was insinuating that she'd had an affair with Matt. Then

Sylvia's disbelief wavered—had Matt actually slept with Erin? She felt sick.

Erin was watching her intently. She said, "I thought you knew."

Sylvia met the other woman's gaze and held it. She said, "No, I don't think so. I don't think you're here to enlighten me." She stood and backed away from Erin Tulley. "I don't know what's going on with you, but I suggest you get some professional help before you go so far over the edge that you can't come back."

Sylvia left the church and stepped out into blinding light. She swore and pushed her sunglasses over her eyes. A homeless man scuttled toward her, but she shook her head sharply.

Dazed, Sylvia crossed the street and climbed the stairs to the offices of the Forensic Evaluation Unit.

Marjorie, the regular receptionist, had returned from her vacation the day before. She smiled at Sylvia and held out an envelope. "Mr. Chaney said you were expecting this." Her eyes narrowed in concern. "Are you okay, darlin'?"

Sylvia gazed down at the envelope and shook her head. She tore open the white seal. Inside she found a six-by-six-inch cutout of a map of California. Route 14, south of Palmdale, had been circled to indicate the approximate location of the ranch where Dupont White had spent his childhood summers. On a three-by-five file card Dan Chaney had written Roxanne White's number and address in Montecito, an area adjacent to Santa Barbara. Roxanne White was Dupont White's mother.

"Marjorie, hold my calls." Sylvia reached her office door. "And book me a flight to California tomorrow morning."

Marjorie's eyebrows disappeared under shaggy bangs. "Any particular city?"

"Santa Barbara."

"Okeydokey. Before I forget, Rosie Sanchez called you. It sounded important."

Inside her office, Sylvia sank into her chair and closed her eyes. After the conversation she'd just had with Erin Tulley, she didn't know where to start. She called Matt at his office, but a woman said he was out and could she take a message?

*Yes. Tell him his girlfriend wants to know if he fucked Erin Tulley, or is the woman crazy. Or both?*

"Thanks, I'll try him at home."

She rang Matt's trailer. No answer.

Marjorie found her a seat on Delta, departing at 9:05 A.M. Saturday.

After her last client of the day, Sylvia called Dr. Leo Carreras at his office in Santa Barbara and confirmed that she would see him within eighteen hours.

This time when she dialed Matt's number, he answered.

"Hey, I wondered if you were still at work. Want to catch a movie?"

Behind his voice, Sylvia heard the sound of running water and the chink of dishes or glass. All of a sudden, her entire body ached. She said, "Sorry, I can't. I've got an early flight tomorrow morning."

"Going where?"

"Santa Barbara."

He was silent; no sound of water, no chink of dishes. He would be standing at the sink, stock still, receiver jammed between chin and shoulder, eyes distant. Tom mewed in the background.

After a few moments, Sylvia said, "I've decided to follow up on Dupont White. I'll talk to his girlfriend in Atascadero Hospital. His mother. I want to go out to the ranch. You know . . ."

He said, "No, I really don't. I don't know if Kevin

Chase worked alone or not. I trust your instincts. But that's law enforcement business; you're a shrink." His voice was level and steady, but she heard the frustration as well as the pain.

"I'll be back the day after tomorrow." She took a breath.

Finally, in a voice she hated, she said, "By the way, I ran into Erin Tulley today." *By the way?*

"What did she have to say?"

Sylvia swallowed. "She's having a hard time."

There was a pause filled only by the sound of his breathing, then he said, "Sylvia, I think we should get away and really talk—"

"Let's talk when I get back. I'm tired. It's been a hellish day." She felt the miles between them, a gulf that had nothing to do with geographical distance.

While she was putting together the papers she wanted to take to California, she made up her mind she wouldn't think about Dupont White, Kevin Chase—or Matt—for the next few hours. Instead, she would go home, cool down, pack. Maybe she'd put on a video: *Double Indemnity* or *From Out of the Past*. And then she'd go to bed early. She needed a good night's rest.

AT MIDNIGHT SHE made herself a cup of herbal tea, barely touched it, and then poured the rest in the sink. Half a bottle of Absolut was in the freezer. Soda and lemon were in the refrigerator. She added two lumps of ice to the high-ball and carried the drink to the patio.

She didn't turn on the lights. From her chaise longue on the deck she could see the flare of the distant forest fires seep around the edges of a dusky, swollen sky. The clean, simple silhouette of her adobe home was more than a hundred years old. Although her father had fixed it up years ago, the lines had remained unchanged.

Sylvia took a long drink as a jagged slice of lightning cut across the ridge behind her house. The air smelled sweet and promised rain, but the thunderstorm was high in the stratosphere, and whatever rain fell never reached the ground. She watched the sky, considered the danger of fire, and that thought led her to physical craving. She left the patio and walked through the house to her bedroom where she retrieved the pack of cigarettes from Café Escalera. She'd stashed them in the top drawer behind her lingerie. She took one cigarette—moved the pack to a kitchen drawer—and walked back out to the porch.

It was six years since she'd been a serious smoker. When Malcolm was diagnosed, she'd started in again. He'd told her it was a stupid response to a lover's cancer. Since his death, it had been the intermittent cigarette. When she was stressed.

No one knew. Not Rosie. Not even Matt. She was careful to wash her fingers and brush her teeth after her hidden smokes.

The truth was, she liked her secret. She had always liked secrets. She liked the hiding, the watching. She understood how secrets took root and grew, twisting and turning, reaching the light sooner or later. Still, she enjoyed the tension they created internally.

On her way back to the patio, she found matches in a blue ceramic bowl. Outside, she breathed in ash-tinged air and plunked down in her chair. The skin on her bare legs broke into goose bumps. She snapped a match against the flint band of the box and locked the flame in her gaze for several seconds. Its violence impressed her. A minute chemical reaction that could expand almost instantly into a combustible beast.

With her lips she drew the flame to the tip of her cigarette, inhaled, and shook the match out. Smoke made her lungs ache. She imagined twin black clouds contained within her body without any avenue of escape. When the pressure became unpleasant, she exhaled.

THE CALL BROUGHT Sylvia out of the choppy waters of sleep. Her hand found the phone before her conscious mind registered, *Four thirty-eight* A.M., *my house, bed.* God. It had to be her mother calling from San Diego.

"Dr. Strange? This is your service, it's Alberta. I'm sorry to bother you so late, but he sounds like he might do something bad to himself."

"Who might do something bad?" Sylvia snapped on the hurricane lamp beside the bed and managed to find pencil and notepad on the table. Her first thought was of Kevin Chase.

Alberta continued, "He didn't give his name—I think he could be on drugs or something because he's so jumpy. He says he was a patient of Dr. Treisman . . . I hope I did the right thing?"

Sylvia pulled back internally. In his will, Malcolm Treisman had entrusted her with all his patient files. "You did the right thing. I'll talk to him, Alberta."

A sharp hiss signaled the line transfer. There was a long silence during which Sylvia feared the caller had been cut off. But a voice finally asked, "Dr. Strange?"

He had the breathless tone of a boy. He was clearly agitated.

"Yes, this is Sylvia Strange. Who are you?"

"I should apologize—to bother you so late, I didn't know what else to do—Dr. Treisman always told me—at the end, I—" Abruptly, he stopped speaking. For several seconds, the only sound was his ragged breathing.

Gently, Sylvia said, "Can you answer a few questions for me?"

"I'm so tired—" The words almost got away from him. "But I'll try to talk about it. . . ."

"Good. I want you to do that." Sylvia kept her voice low and soothing and listened for any change in his tone. She said, "Where are you calling from?"

"A motel."

"Which motel?" Pause. "Is someone there with you?"

"I'm alone. I thought it would be all right to call. . . ."

Sylvia reassured, mirrored. "It was all right to call."

". . . when I got crazy again."

She heard a young man who was hypertense, angry, scared, but coherent. The histrionic fiber of the voice worried her the most. Drugs, alcohol, the manic phase of a bipolar disorder, roller-coaster mood swings—any of these could give him that audible edge. All of them qualified as red flags when it came to the possibility of self-destructive behavior. Sylvia guessed at least one of them applied to the person on the other end of the line.

"I need to know, have you taken something?"

"No . . . but I've got to cut myself."

When a client threatened self-destructive behavior it was the therapist's job to take the threat seriously—and then assess the risk. On the phone with a stranger, Sylvia had no personal history, no personality assessments, no one-on-one experience to draw on. She had to function under the same directive as a cop facing a suspect in a dark alley: assume there's a weapon. She said, "Did you do something to hurt yourself?"

"I need to let it out. I need air—light to burn them out."

"Who? You need to burn who out?" The sustained silence was nerve-racking.

He asked, "Don't you know who this is? We've met."

She stopped breathing.

"What do we teach you, Dr. Strange? Crazy people— what do you see in us?"

Awareness seeped through her body like cold water—she was talking to Dupont White. Her heart scudded against her chest. She tried to keep her voice calm. "Dupont? I don't think you should be alone right now. I'd like to get you some help."

He laughed softly. "So you do recognize me. I'm glad. But I don't want anybody's help. Not even yours, Dr. Strange."

Click. The dial tone jarred.

# THIRTEEN

EIGHT MILES SOUTH of downtown Santa Fe, Benji Muñoz y Concha paced the yard outside Dormitory A at the penitentiary's Minimum Restrict Facility, the murf. The Saturday morning air was tepid because the sun had only been up for two hours. But already, the promise of intense temperatures was palpable.

Behind the bleachers Benji paced a small area of parched ground. In a center court two inmates were playing a game of one-on-one, and they smacked the basketball aggressively. They shouted challenges or encouragement to each other; sweat oiled their brown bodies. On the bleachers men sat in groups or alone, smoking cigarettes and talking.

Unlawful taking of a vehicle. That was why Benji had to do his time. He had taken the car—he admitted that much. But he wasn't really part of any car ring like the cops had claimed. And minimum-security time was still time, even for a first offense. He had one year, eight months, and four days to go . . . not counting good time.

Dust billowed out from Benji's feet as he paced. He couldn't find Rosie Sanchez anywhere. He needed to talk to the penitentiary investigator.

A horn honked; the perimeter patrol vehicle was bouncing over ruts and weeds next to the perimeter fence. From this distance, the correctional officer's head was the size of a pea.

On the other side of that fence, Benji could see *freedom*.

He couldn't stand still; if he did, he knew he'd catch fire on the inside and burn down to nothing. He had to get out—he had this bad feeling about the future. Not *his* future, but the future of Rosie's friend, Sylvia Strange.

To calm himself he closed his eyes and let his mind slip through the eyes of the chain-link fence, ascend over the security T-line, glide across no-man's-land, float once again through fencing, this time parallel panels topped by razor ribbon.

To find guidance. To find an answer.

Now he was a blue-white orb of energy hurtling through air. Past the National Guard armory, where the weekend trainees jogged the frontage road; across four lanes of I-25; over the racetrack where the first race of the day had just begun—*and they're off!* He didn't stop to place a bet on a white-legged filly named Run in Her Stockings, even though he knew she'd pay off fifteen to one.

He eased north, caught an air current and soared over the Caja Del Rio Plateau, past Bandelier National Monument, to choppier air currents above the Jemez Mountains. To his right the Valle Grande gaped. To his left he saw what the Dark Canyon fire had left in its wake. He knew this land, this earth—he'd been cradled here as a child.

He hovered over the ridge where he had seen the burning body. If the killer was human, he had driven in on the forest road; only a ten-minute drive from State Highway 4, it had been a good choice for a drop spot. It was the place Benji would have chosen. Somebody had known his way around . . . and there was nothing left now but scorched and smoking earth.

Benji glided directly across the mouth of the caldera over the peak of Cerro Grande, at 10,199 feet, and Pajarito Mountain, where the skiers would be busy next winter. San Ildefonso Pueblo was below him now. And then Pojoaque, Nambe, and the Rio en Medio.

As he approached Little Tesuque, he began to feel the first twinge of heat.

Fire.

But there was no smoke, there were no flames visible. There was no fire here, only the ashy remains of some past inferno. The ashes stretched as far as Benji could see. All the way to the tops of the mountains.

Some evil force reached out to probe Benji's soul as he soared over the Santa Fe Reservoir. His heart caught in his throat, but still he soared. And then he saw the ash begin to move. Here and there it stirred, shifted, pressed itself into a new shape. A human form. A corpse.

When Benji was directly overhead, the corpse sat up suddenly. It turned to stare at him, and he knew that it was a woman. It was Sylvia Strange.

THE BELLY OF the 737 skidded over invisible cross-currents while the ocean fifteen thousand feet below the aircraft stayed as smooth and still as blue glass. The pilot completed the wide, banking turn, and corrected the plane right, then left. Sylvia's stomach churned, her knuckles were white.

This trip to California had begun at five-thirty A.M. that morning. The phone call from Dupont White had scared her; it had also mobilized her into action. On the drive to Albuquerque she tried to reach Matt from her cell phone. She'd called him again from the airport terminal. When she couldn't track him down, she found herself wondering if he was with Erin Tulley.

With a sigh Sylvia snapped the airplane handset from the seat in front of her. She was careful to tuck in her elbows; the plane was full, and she was wedged between a "window" who overflowed his chair and an "aisle" who had managed to carry on and was now devouring a New Mexican meal, including tamales, enchiladas, green chile, and sopaipillas with honey.

Air-bus time.

So far Sylvia had managed to avoid a lapful of chile, but she didn't want to tempt the gods. Carefully she ran her phone card through the slot and dialed Matt's office. She could barely hear it ring under the deep throb of the airplane's engines.

She was startled when he answered.

"Sylvia? Where are you?"

"Coming out of the clouds over Santa Barbara." Sylvia pressed the handset tightly to her ear. Mr. Window was staring at her. She shifted forward in the seat. On the other end of the line she heard a faint, unfamiliar voice say, "Time to go, Matt."

She asked, "What's going on?"

"A photo lineup . . . Forest Service got a look at the fire setter at Tsankawi."

"I'll keep this short because we're about to land. Last night, Dupont White called me at home." She felt Matt's astonishment.

"He identified himself?"

"Yes." The engine noise increased. Sylvia squeezed her eyes shut, trying to hear.

"—get him on tape?"

"No. Listen, I'll be back on Monday—"

"Hold on."

"I can't—" But Matt was gone. Sylvia imagined she

heard voices, doors slamming, a phone ringing twelve hundred miles east, in Santa Fe. But in truth, she could barely hear herself think. She shifted her body toward the aisle and narrowly escaped a spoonful of cheese and chile.

Claustrophobia washed over her, and a sweat broke out on her forehead. When she lowered her head, she caught the compulsive jerky action of Mr. Window's thigh.

Suddenly Matt was talking again. "—going over to your house—want you to be careful—damn, hold on." After long seconds he came back on the line.

She said, "Let's do this later."

"Sylvia, come home."

"Soon. I miss you." She pressed OFF and snapped the phone back into its cradle.

The kelly green seat-belt sign blinked.

"Ladies and gentlemen, we will be landing in Goleta–Santa Barbara shortly. . . ."

For a moment Sylvia's thoughts settled on Benji Muñoz y Concha; she was still intrigued by his history, his spirit, his visions. She remembered a discussion with Malcolm Treisman about a client who made an excellent living as a psychic. Malcolm had described the man as a "well-informed intuitive." Did that describe Benji as well? She shrugged—she hoped the session with Velio Cruz had helped him. Then the 737 banked again, and she swallowed and turned her head to glance out the windows on the opposite side of the airplane. The sky was veiled by cirrus clouds. As the wing dipped lower, a picture came into focus: a sandy beach crowned by palm trees. Paradise on a postcard. Judging from the statuelike stillness of the trees, there was hardly any ocean breeze in this new world.

She exhaled as the plane's wheels slapped the runway.

She was the sixth passenger to exit. As soon as she stepped into the quaint Spanish-style terminal, she saw Leo Carreras.

He stood in the center of the walkway. His smooth, dusky skin set off rich brown, keen eyes and chalk-white teeth. He was lean and tall and easy to look at, hands shoved deep in the pockets of his linen suit. Sylvia noticed that several women cast lingering glances at her old friend. When she'd last seen Leo, five years before, he'd carried a few extra pounds and been minus the startling streak of silver just above his left temple. The wire-rimmed glasses were a new addition, too. No doubt they served him well when he was testifying in court. Professorial specs earned "smart" points with juries.

His smile widened as he walked over to her and kissed her cheek. "I'm still wondering how I got you here after five years of groveling."

It was her turn to smile. She pinched the sleeve of his jacket and shook her head. "Come on, I need fresh air."

Leo pushed open the glass door, and her first impression was of soft, salty air scented with camphor—her second impression was how deeply the humid warmth seemed to penetrate her pores. In New Mexico, high-desert light heightened visual perceptions; here, at sea level, the primary sensory experiences were touch and smell.

The golden flecks in her brown irises darkened a tad, and she said, "I'm here, Leo."

HIS SEA-GREEN LEXUS was parked at the curb in a no-parking zone. Sylvia raised her eyebrows, but Leo just laughed. He used a remote to deactivate the alarm and unlock the car. The Lexus bleated a plaintive greeting, then Leo opened the passenger door and offered Sylvia his hand.

She sat and eased her long legs gingerly into the car. The Lexus smelled heady, of warm leather and sandalwood. It was spotless, and Sylvia smiled when she thought of her own dusty, battered Volvo. She ran her fingers over the gray leather interior, and they came away free of even the faintest smudge. She noticed a thumb-size carved wooden crucifix resting in the compartment between bucket seats. She knew Leo's mother was a devout Catholic; Leo used to be a dedicated atheist.

He stowed her garment bag in the trunk and slid behind the steering wheel. A security vehicle pulled up next to the Lexus, and the uniformed driver motioned to Leo to clear the curb. The Lexus engine purred, and Leo eased the car into airport traffic.

Sylvia waited until they were safely away, then she held up the cross, which dangled from a beaded strand. Each small bead was smooth, nut brown, delicate. Together, they gave off the faintest trace of sandalwood.

"Did you change your mind, Leo?" She was surprised when he answered her seriously.

He said, "I find faith comforting after particularly grueling days at the hospital."

Sylvia studied her friend. Dr. Leo Carreras had published extensively and his most recent book was considered a landmark text, an integration of data—psychobiological and social—on human predatory agression. In a nutshell, Leo theorized that modern American society incubates its psychopaths. The lack of a resilient maternal bond combined with the shape of our image-obsessed, media-crazed, nonlinear society results in high anxiety and low levels of empathy.

In short, we are growing our very own monsters.

Leo said, "I made some calls. Atascadero State Hospital, and Dupont White's criminally insane girlfriend,

Violet Miller, are on this afternoon's agenda." He glanced at his watch.

Sylvia exhaled her impatience.

Leo laughed. "Still the same impatient Strange. I hate to disappoint you, but we're in the sight-seeing portion of today's schedule."

Sylvia looked contrite.

"That's better." Leo pulled back into the right lane. "Where to?"

"My toes are craving ocean."

"We can satisfy your toes."

Sheltered by palm trees, they ate mozzarella, tomato, and basil sandwiches while waves nuzzled the long creamy beach. Sylvia had left her suede pumps in the Lexus; she dug her naked toes deep into the sand beyond the edge of the blanket Leo had provided. A Route 66 baseball cap shaded her face. She loved the coconut scent of suntan lotion that radiated from nearby sunbathers. When she had finished her sandwich and two fat dill pickles, she lay back on the blanket and stretched her arms overhead. She must have dozed off for a few minutes; she was surprised to feel a tickling sensation. Eyes open, she saw Leo was trailing a thread of sand across the inside of her upper arm.

He smiled and brushed off the tiny particles. "We have an appointment at the hospital at one forty-five."

Sylvia glanced at her watch: eleven-fifteen.

He said, "I thought you might want to talk."

Business. She sat up, surprised to register how sleepy and relaxed she felt. When he handed her a bottle of mineral water, she drank gratefully.

Her sunglasses slid down to the tip of her nose; she pushed them back so they were square against her face. "I've got files in the car. I thought you might want to look them over. I could use your read on this whole thing. It's making me a little bit crazy. I told you about Dan Chaney, the special agent. . . ." Her voice trailed off when she saw that Leo had one eye closed. He was shaking his head.

He leaned back on both elbows. "Why don't you tell an old friend what's bothering you?"

A gull on a reconnaissance mission swooped overhead. Sylvia wrapped her arms around both knees. "I misread a client and now he's wanted for two murders."

"Is that all?"

"And I don't know if Matt is having an affair."

She told Leo about the events of the past week and a half, filled in details, including the Randall case, Kevin Chase, and her weird encounter with Erin Tulley. He let her stop and start and work her way around difficult thoughts. He didn't respond immediately when she was finished speaking. In the stillness, she watched his smooth tapered fingers sift sand.

Leo said, "You want some simple advice? This stuff with Matt is throwing you off balance. Talk to him, Sylvia. When you get back to Santa Fe, find out the truth."

ATASCADERO STATE HOSPITAL, which housed the acutely mentally ill and the criminally insane, was located several miles off Highway 101. The squat three-story main building was surrounded by ten-foot-high walls; barbed wire rimmed each face. Beyond the walls, the beige façade of the hospital had blackened at the edges. Small windows, gray and opaque, dotted the building like eyes. The wire grids embedded in the panes were invisible under layers of grime.

A uniformed officer stepped out of the security booth and waved Leo's Lexus through the main gate. They parked in a lot and walked across dirt and asphalt to the acute-care facility, where all intake was done. Another officer nodded to them as they entered.

"Good afternoon, Dr. Carreras."

Leo had already clipped on his photo-I.D. badge. He spoke to a woman at the reception desk and she produced a bright red temporary pass for Sylvia. Sunshine streaked through a high window and spotlighted the dust motes that swirled above the receptionist's auburn hair. Fascinated by their surreal motion, Sylvia stared at the tiny dancing particles as she fastened the pass to her collar.

"We're running late," Leo said.

They took a grim, tight elevator to the third floor. The building contained a maze of hallways extending off a central corridor, and Leo led the way through metal security doors, and past a series of treatment rooms and day areas.

Here, patients wearing institutional green wandered the halls or occupied day rooms. A young man spouting a schizophrenic word salad—verbs and nouns incomprehensibly diced, shredded, and tossed—stared at Sylvia through glassy eyes. A hyperthin woman with jaundiced skin directed traffic.

Finally, Leo ushered Sylvia into a soundproofed room that wasn't much bigger than a closet. She sat in one of three chairs and faced the tinted glass panel. Leo spoke into an intercom, "Hi, Mark. Mind if we watch?"

A young, pink-cheeked doctor in the next room waved cheerfully at the glass. His voice crawled through the speaker: "I always knew you were kinky, Leo."

"That's Mark Chism. He's been working on a project with violent female offenders for six months. He kindly agreed to let us observe this session. You'll get a chance to talk with him afterward."

Sylvia had just produced a pad and pencil for notes when the door to the treatment room opened. An orderly

escorted a female patient inside and left her alone with
Mark Chism.

Leo said, "Dr. Strange, meet Violet Miller."

Sylvia thought Violet must be about twenty years
old. She was delicate, and so pale that her blue eyes over-
powered her face. She might have been a fashion model
except for her unkempt, oily hair, and the pain and stress
that eroded her features.

Violet's wrists were secured at her belly by padded
restraints. For the moment, she seemed to have surrendered herself to external controls.

"She's not medicated, not on neuroleptics," Leo said.
"She's been here about six weeks. We're still eliminating
organic disorders. She's had several violent episodes
since intake."

Both clinicians kept their voices modulated even
though they could not be heard or seen by anyone on the
other side of the glass.

"Acute schizophrenia?" Sylvia asked.

Leo shook his head. "I think she's a borderline personality with severe periods of psychotic dissociation.
Apparently, over a two-year period she was participating
in ritual murders with her lover. At least she claims she
was. We don't believe she actively assaulted victims, but
again she says she took videotapes like the one you told
me about."

Sylvia asked, "What does the F.B.I. have to say about
all this?"

"Nothing. They refuse to talk about it." Leo frowned.
"We believe that only a few months ago, Violet was
a high-functioning borderline; the deterioration was
acute."

Sylvia nodded slowly. "Leo, I'll give you my guess—
the most critical stressor in her criminal career was
Dupont's alleged death. This is a woman who could not

handle the loss of her dominant partner, especially when he was a killer."

Leo raised his eyebrows. "I think you're right. She flipped when the F.B.I. began questioning her—right after that Las Cruces debacle."

"How does she act out?"

"Violet's with us because, when she was at the county jail, she tried to stomp out a guard's heart. *Literally.*"

Sylvia was mesmerized by Violet Miller's angelic countenance. The young woman's beauty was a startling contrast to her circumstances. Sylvia didn't look away from the glass when she asked, "Did she do much damage?"

"Other guards intervened."

Sylvia experienced a moment of relief until she heard Leo's addendum.

"And failed. The jailer died."

Thinned by the intercom, Violet's voice communicated pain and confusion. She was mumbling to Dr. Chism; three or four words seemed to hold a thought before her speech changed direction in a course only she could fathom.

Sylvia looked at Leo. "Why the restraints?"

"If we take them off, she tries to claw out her eyes."

*What do we teach you, Dr. Strange? What do you see in us?*

Leo said, "Mark Chism tried to interview her last Friday, but she deteriorated too quickly; the session had to be aborted."

On the other side of the glass, Chism was speaking softly. He said, "Violet, I know you're having a hard time—that a part of you is gone." Both patient and clinician were seated, facing each other across a rectangular table.

Sylvia was about to ask about Violet Miller's pre-morbid functioning, but her words died in her throat.

Violet began to nod her head arhythmically as she spoke. "He was my killer, he was my killer, my killer, my killer, my killer." The woman closed her eyes and shivered.

Sylvia felt the tingling rush of fear—the first taste of the natural and potent chemical adrenaline. She wiped sweat from her forehead.

Chism continued softly, "One of the things I'm curious about is what you're doing now, and its relationship to the killer. One possibility is that he gets to be the bad part of you, and you get to be the good part of him."

Violet's initial reaction to Chism's words was to stomp both feet in a bizarre, seated clog dance. The force of her action reverberated up her body to her face.

Violet Miller threw back her head, opened her mouth like a wound, and emitted a terrible nonstop screech. Sylvia watched the young woman's throat muscles contract under the strain; they pulled tight like ropes. Violet's blue eyes bulged, her cry reached glass-shattering intensity.

Violet rose from her chair the same instant Leo Carreras moved toward the door of the observation cubicle. Spooked, Sylvia watched as Violet sprang forward and up and landed on the seat of her chair with both feet; even without the use of her hands, she maintained her balance. Violet launched herself toward the table, and again, she landed squarely; she was fueled by rage.

Leo said, "Stay here," and then he was out the door striding down the hall.

Sylvia waited to see what would happen when he entered the treatment room. If the orderly wasn't nearby, he would need her help, but she didn't want to let Mark Chism and Violet Miller out of her eyesight.

Violet threw herself at Chism and he stumbled backward. Like a whirling dervish, the crazed woman whipped her head around and smacked her skull into his chest before he fell to the floor. She was in motion to attack the doctor again when Leo burst through the door.

Before he could get his hands on the patient, Violet impelled both legs straight out, and the heels of her shoes struck his groin. Leo doubled over in pain but managed to activate the panic button anchored to his belt.

Sylvia had no intention of waiting for staff to arrive. She rushed from the observation cubicle to the hall and the closed door of the treatment room.

Adrenaline was speeding through her system when she pushed the door open and stepped inside the room. The door slammed shut behind her. The room was stuffy, uncomfortably warm, and it smelled of urine and disinfectant. She turned to find herself face-to-face with Violet Miller.

The woman was flushed, drenched with sweat, and her eyes were hyperbright. While Sylvia watched, Violet struggled to focus—eyes bulging, eyes squeezed shut until they finally settled on Sylvia.

Sylvia's blood cooled instantly. She was facing all the pent-up fury of a deranged, enraged woman. She felt as if she had been cornered by a rabid dog. In her fear, fragments of the scene got special attention: the blood on Violet's head, the odor of almonds on the air, the soft moans coming from behind the overturned table.

Sylvia held out both hands in a calming, placating gesture. She was amazed that her voice sounded composed, gentle, even. Her heart rate had to be pushing one eighty-five. She said, "Violet, I'm here to help you. Everything's going to be just fine."

Without turning her head, Sylvia knew that Leo was

now standing somewhere behind her. Violet knew he was there, too. The woman gave a warning growl.

"Why don't you step back, Leo," Sylvia said soothingly. "We're going to be all right here. How's Mark doing?" She heard Carreras move away.

Without any real knowledge of the patient and her history, Sylvia had to tread carefully to avoid emotional flash points. She kept her energy centered on Violet Miller, but didn't approach or trespass on Violet's small territory, a space roughly four feet square. The woman had corrected her threatening stance just slightly when Leo withdrew. Now, her energy visibly dissipated. The change was dramatic: the blue eyes dulled, the breathing slowed, the muscles seemed to lengthen.

There was agony and terror in her tortured monologue: "I have, I need, I need, don't you see what they're doing to me? I feel, don't you, don't you need, they cut off my arms, cut off my arms, cut out my feelings, tear me apart, tear me down—" The litany went on for minutes without pause until, abruptly, Violet was silent. Her expression transformed, and lucidity realigned her features. She smiled at Sylvia and said, "I'm really okay. I remember you. . . ."

And then the Violet who was not psychotic disappeared again, like a woman who had stepped behind a door.

It was unnerving to observe the shift from close range.

Sylvia consciously regulated her own breathing so that it was somewhere between Violet's ragged inhalations and normal respiration. Her eyes never connected directly with the woman's pupils. She continued to recite soothing words, a verbal pabulum.

Violet's body telegraphed the arrival of hospital staff; her musculature stiffened when the door opened.

Without turning, Sylvia said, "We would appreciate a little space here."

A quiet male voice said, "We're not going to intrude."

"That's fine," Sylvia said.

"That's fine," Violet mimicked. She stared at Sylvia and laughed. "Dupont was my killer, he was my killer, he was my killer—" The phrase went on and on. Sylvia had a theory about what Violet meant: Dupont had been a carrier for Violet's darkness; he had acted out her murderous rage; in a sense he had contained it. But now that Violet believed Dupont was dead, her rage was her own, and it was wild, and it was consuming her from the inside out.

Sylvia murmured reassuringly, "He was your killer."

Abruptly, Violet stopped speaking, swallowed, and cocked her head toward Sylvia. "I know *you*—you're the killer's doctor."

It was an extraordinary moment—an instant out of time—when the world realigned itself. Sylvia said, "That's right, Violet. That's who I am."

"Did he send you?"

"Do you mean Dupont?"

Violet looked almost wistful. "He hates them—the government—hates doctors because you call him 'crazy killer.' He taught me to hate." She shook her head in bewilderment, opened her mouth, and whispered, "Help me." Her eyelids lowered, and she looked half asleep; she didn't speak again.

Leo managed to help Mark Chism from the treatment room. Five minutes later Violet allowed herself to be sedated. The nurse and one orderly escorted her back to her room. The other orderly attended to a shaken but stable Mark Chism. With Sylvia at his side, Leo limped out of the hospital.

\* \* \*

ON THE DRIVE back to Santa Barbara, Leo put Eric Clapton in the CD player and kept the car straining at the bit. San Luis Obispo, Santa Maria, Goleta: familiar places disappeared in their eucalyptus and oleander wake. The setting sun dipped herself like a woman into silvery Pacific waters.

Sylvia felt conflicted after the encounter with Violet. She was relieved and still experiencing the total rush; she'd chalked up a victory. At the same time, she felt totally enervated.

*I know you. You're the killer's doctor.* Both Dupont and Violet had the same unique way of saying, "You work with bad guys." And today, Violet had asked for help.

Maybe—with his cryptic messages, his Polaroids, his manipulative phone call—just maybe, Dupont White was finally asking for help from the killer's doctor.

Leo turned down the music and said, "When we get to town, I'm buying you dinner. Where are you staying?"

"The Biltmore."

"Nice choice."

"Let me buy *you* dinner. I really appreciate that you set up the visit to Atascadero for me."

"I owe you one." He shifted uncomfortably in the soft leather seat.

She said, "Hell hath no fury like a woman—scorned or not."

Leo gingerly tested his groin with his fingers. "No shit."

THE SANTA BARBARA Biltmore rose up like a Spanish castle in the center of an oasis. Tinted flood lamps illuminated acacia, gum, avocado, hibiscus, and giant prickly pears. Magenta and white bougainvillea seemed to explode out of the earth. A hundred feet from the main hotel, Sylvia's secluded bungalow was surrounded by palm trees.

Leo and Sylvia relaxed over cocktails on the patio and dined in the restaurant. The dining room's subdued elegance was an extension of the rest of the Biltmore, which dated to the late 1920s. Conservative shades of rose, cream, and walnut accented the rich mahogany fixtures. The restaurant's only primary colors were provided by immense floral arrangements.

It was well after ten when they left the restaurant and strolled down the carefully tended stone path to the hotel's private beach.

Breakers hit the shore with a fierce finality intensified by darkness. Already mellow from food and drink, Sylvia lost herself in the thunder of the ocean. She slipped out of her sandals and let the edge of each wave grab her by the ankles and tug her deeper into wet sand.

Voices drifted up the beach. Somebody approaching. Time to move on. She began to walk north along the shore. Leo was following several paces behind. He caught up with her.

He said, "When you came into the room with Violet, what did you experience?" She didn't respond immediately, and he continued. "I remember the first time I faced a violently aggressive patient, and the few times since then. It's always a moment of clarity; some jagged piece of myself rises to the surface."

Sylvia's voice wasn't loud, but it was clearly audible over the sound of the waves. She said, "I felt like I was witnessing the power of absolute destructive energy. It scared the shit out of me."

Sylvia felt Leo's eyes on her face. She said, "How is Mark Chism going to proceed with her treatment?"

"What would you recommend?"

Sylvia brushed a strand of hair from her face. "Next time, I'd have a woman conduct the interview."

"Maybe you should be the one to work with her." Leo paused and leaned over to pick up a long, slender stick that had washed up on shore. "Do you have dinner plans tomorrow night? I'd like you to meet some people."

"If I didn't know you better, I'd think you were trying to seduce me, Leo." She set her hands on her hips. "I should be free by late afternoon."

"Good. We'll go somewhere in town. Mark Chism will be there. And some other folks I'd like you to talk to."

"Fine." But Sylvia's mind had already shifted to her own plans for the next day: a visit to Dupont White's childhood home and his adoptive father's ranch.

Leo's next words brought her back to the present. "I'm making you a professional offer, Sylvia; I want you to come to work with me. I don't want to know your answer now. I'll call you in two weeks, and you can give me a yes, or a no."

With the stick he sketched numbers in the firm, damp sand. Sylvia gazed at the figure and sighed. It was more than twice what she made in Santa Fe.

Leo gazed at her face for a long moment. Finally, he said, "I'm not going to make it easy for you."

He walked her back to the door of her bungalow and kissed her circumspectly on one cheek.

"Good night, Leo. And thanks for a lovely evening."

His expression was dark and serious, and his eyes felt as though they penetrated deep beneath Sylvia's skin. Finally, he allowed himself a half smile.

She watched his thin shadow disappear between the trees and then she went inside and closed her door.

She lingered in a very hot shower until her muscles felt

rubbery. She slathered on moisturizer and slipped naked between fresh sheets.

Fighting sleep, she picked up the phone and dialed her service in Santa Fe. Rosie Sanchez had called twice; there were no messages from Matt. She called his trailer. No answer. She dialed her home number. When her machine answered, she entered her remote message-playback code.

A digital voice announced that she had ninety-six new messages—only three short of capacity.

Dazed, she pressed a key to receive her messages: click and a dial tone. Then another hang-up call. And another.

With mounting horror, she listened to an endless chorus of clicks and dial tones. She lost count after only a few minutes. That's when she first heard the crying. Someone was weeping. A woman? A boy? *Click.*

Another call, and another, until the crying had reached hysterical pitch. *Click. Click. Click.*

When the messages finally played themselves out, Sylvia lay rigid on the bed. She was numb, and her fingers were clamped around the receiver.

# FOURTEEN

SYLVIA WOKE AT SIX A.M. with a blinding sea-level headache and the lingering uneasiness caused by last night's phone messages. If Dupont White—or someone very close to him—had made the calls, they were an unpleasant reminder that Killer's domain extended beyond Santa Fe. She couldn't shake the feeling that he knew exactly where she was.

She rose stiffly from the bed. Sleep had eluded her most of the night. Instead, her mind had trailed stubbornly over familiar territory: Dupont vented his bloodlust, his need to torture and murder, in the guise of an omnipotent vigilante. The core of his obsession was the victimization of sex offenders—he offered up his own swift punishment when, in his eyes, the state failed to provide adequate justice. That type of obsession went well beyond the need for retribution; it was all-consuming, like a poison, like a fever that burned away the infected person's soul.

Sylvia sighed, pressed a wet washcloth to her forehead. Victims are always a mirror in some way for their killer. Follow that line of thought to its conclusion: Dupont White had himself been victimized. And he was channeling his urge to victimize others into killing sexual aggressors.

She opened the green-striped curtains that covered

floor-to-ceiling windows and saw soft unsettled fog and the shadowy shapes of trees. This white mist—not sunshine—was the typical day stored among her memories of southern California. Fog always made her feel as if there was something lurking just beyond her view, something she couldn't quite see; it was so different from New Mexico's harsh sunshine—a sun that exposed everything under its burning glare.

She made the first of two phone calls, this one to Rosie at home where the sound of Ray Sanchez's voice on the outgoing message made her homesick. She left a brief message of her own: "Hey guys, I'm out of town, back tomorrow. Miss you."

And she did. She felt lonely and isolated, but a part of her was relieved to be free of her responsibilities, her relationships. And she still had work to do in California.

On the doorstep, under linen, Sylvia found a silverplate tray, a large pot of coffee, and assorted pastries. She poured herself a coffee, smeared jam on a warm raisin scone, and opened the file on Dupont White. On top of the reports was the envelope she had received from Dan Chaney. She unfolded the map of California and traced the one hundred twenty or so miles from Montecito to Devil's Den Ranch. When she was satisfied she knew the route, she picked up the phone and dialed Roxanne White's phone number in Montecito.

Sylvia knew the area from the time she'd spent in southern California with her mother, seventeen years earlier. Montecito was just southeast of Santa Barbara. Huge estates from a more luxurious era claimed acres of verdant, rolling hills. Ornate stone mansions with formal gardens elbowed up to horse paddocks and postmodern steel and glass habitats.

No answer after a dozen rings; she hung up the phone.

A globule of strawberry jam fell on the edge of the envelope, and Sylvia spooned it off and returned it to her last bite of scone. Roxanne White lived at 13 Camino Suerte. Lucky Lane.

THE GATEHOUSE WAS empty, the security phone looked new, and the pitched metal gates were open. Sylvia turned off Camino Suerte and followed a circular brick driveway that continued for a half mile before it reached the hand-carved double oak doors of Dupont White's former home. Sylvia parked her rented Taurus next to a black Lamborghini Diablo VT. The vanity plate read VIP-1. She didn't bother to lock the Taurus.

The house had three stories, a yellow-and-blue-tinted Spanish hacienda; judging from its frontage, it looked as though it might cover five thousand square feet. A loggia ran the length of the second story, and palm trees brushed their sharp leaves against wide sandstone balconies. High windows on the top floor made Sylvia think of a strong-hold. At the hacienda's eastern corner, a Spanish-style bell tower rose above eucalyptus and palm trees. Beyond the edge of the tower, green-and-white canvas awnings delineated private tennis courts. Although some of the fog had burned off, there was still enough mist to shroud the scene.

It was hard to place Dupont White in these surroundings. Montecito was the land of the privileged, those whose crimes tended to be calculated, sterile, bought and paid for—not the messy hands-on rage necessary to castrate someone and then burn him alive.

She climbed stone stairs to the red stuccoed front entrance and rapped on the massive doors. After a few seconds they opened a crack. Enough to give her a view of a narrow strip of the gleaming tile floor. Enough to see a female face.

The woman smiled expectantly, her face devoid of suspicion or challenge. In fact, she looked delighted to see Sylvia. "You've come after all." Her voice was low and musical. She let the doors swing wide.

At a loss, Sylvia murmured a response. "Yes, I'm here." She guessed the woman was between forty and fifty years old; her body was small under blue overalls and a red sweater, her hair was tucked into a green turban. She was clutching an earth-dampened trowel in her gloved left hand.

"I'm Jilly."

Sylvia heard the anxious edge in the woman's voice, took in her vacant, glassy brown eyes, her placid face, and guessed that Jilly was suffering from depression, maybe some form of dementia. Psychological or organic? The result of Alzheimer's or Parkinson's or pathology?

She smiled and said, "I'm very pleased to meet you. My name is Sylvia."

Jilly cocked her head. "I'm just not myself anymore."

Sylvia nodded. Jilly repeated this bit of information like a parrot, and she had to compete with other voices. They were faint, muffled, emanating from a distant room, but Sylvia thought she could distinguish the rumbling bass of a male from the slightly higher contralto of a female.

Sylvia entered a high-ceilinged anteroom. Potted ginger plants with giant orange blooms graced each end of a tapestry-covered settee. The tiled floor was turquoise blue and polished so it gleamed.

Jilly's eyes widened with curiosity. "Are you a friend of Roxanne's? She's my sister."

"No, but I've come to speak with her about her son, Dupont White."

"Dupont died, and Roxanne's with her friend." With

measured gestures, Jilly placed her trowel on the settee, clapped together gloved hands, and shook loose residual garden soil onto the tile. She said, "I'll be right back, okay?" She turned and passed out of Sylvia's sight beyond the largest of three Moorish arches, roughly thirty feet away. The smack of her rubber soles on tile echoed and then faded away.

To enter the vast living room, Sylvia had to pass through a portal created by a pair of giant elephant tusks. Each of the ivory horns had been planted in a heavy brass base that in turn was bolted to the floor. Between the tusks, a zebra skin had been laid down like a cape. Sylvia tiptoed across the striped animal hide.

Below vaulted ceilings, the trophy heads of wildebeest, a pair of African lions, and a Cape buffalo were suspended on white walls. Sylvia walked over to the sadly majestic lion heads and stared at the huge oil painting displayed between them. It was a full-length portrait of a regal, blue-eyed blond woman dressed in a simple formal gown. Her golden hair fell softly to her shoulders in a flattering wave. Her oval face was delicately featured. But it was her eyes that caught and held the viewer's attention; they were large and soft and full of promises.

Sylvia stepped close and saw a name etched on a small plaque: ROXANNE GLADSTONE WHITE.

If this portrait was accurate, Dupont's mother was a very beautiful woman.

Sylvia continued across the room past a large powder-blue Chinese vase that looked like a museum piece. Here, the rugs were Persian and the chairs were French Empire.

A door at the far end of the living room banged loudly.

Sylvia followed the sound and came to a long hall. She

stopped, ready to turn back, until she heard a voice rise shrilly: "You think I'm stupid?"

A deeper voice murmured in a placating tone.

There were footsteps and then a door shut—slammed this time—somewhere down the hall.

Sylvia stood in the silence. She stifled a cry when she felt a tug on her sleeve. When she turned, Jilly placed a small snapshot in her palm. In faded color, three children posed proudly for the camera. They were all dressed in costumes; they all wore masks.

On the back of the photograph someone had printed HALLOWEEN, 1978.

Sylvia pointed to a boy of eight or nine who stood at attention in a Batman cloak and mask. She asked, "Is that Dupont?"

Jilly's brown pupils sharpened for an instant, and then they went soft again. She clasped her hands in front of her waist. "That's right. He was proud of that costume."

Jilly aimed her little finger at the tallest boy: a cowboy in plastic chaps and a white hat. "And that's Cole. This was taken at the ranch."

"Cole Lynch?" The Counselor.

"That's right. Fuller's little boy."

Sylvia knew that Fuller Lynch had been caretaker of Devil's Den Ranch for the last three decades. Apparently he still supervised the property. She gazed again at the photograph, noticing the stark California high-desert terrain in the background behind the children.

"And who's this?" Sylvia indicated the smallest child—the Green Hornet—hemmed in by the larger boys.

Jilly took the picture back and slid it into her coverall pocket. Sylvia was startled by the woman's expressive transformation. Her eyes filled with tears, her mouth quivered.

"They were so close," Jilly whispered. "But my little girl's gone away." She wiped her hands on the pocket that contained the photograph; the gesture seemed to finish something. Jilly shook her head stubbornly and walked toward the windows.

*So the little girl was Dupont White's cousin.*

Sylvia joined Jilly at the windows that overlooked the driveway. The fog had burned off completely, and the acres spread out, hill after rolling hill, until they reached the sharper peaks of the Santa Ynez Mountains. Closer to the house, the tennis courts and the turquoise swimming pool beyond were clearly visible. Sylvia could see her rented Taurus parked next to the Lamborghini.

"There's Roxanne." Jilly pointed outside.

Sylvia saw two figures appear around the corner of the house. Roxanne White was following a man. Even from this height, Sylvia could see that Dupont's mother was plump, a coiffed blonde, very well dressed—and not at all like the portrait in the living room.

The man was tall, ruddy, and gray-blond. He wore a black leather jacket and Levi's. His stride was insolent.

"That's Roxanne's friend," Jilly said. "I don't like him." She unlocked the window and pushed it open.

Sylvia saw Roxanne White reach out to touch the man's arm, but he pivoted on his heel, grabbed her by both shoulders, and shook her fiercely.

Jilly cried out, and both her sister and the man looked up. Sylvia stepped away from the window, but not in time.

"Jilly!" Roxanne White's voice rang out. "Who's that with you?"

Jilly said, "Oh, oh."

Sylvia walked quickly from the room and retraced her steps to the front door—she had expected a confrontation with Roxanne White earlier. She thought it best to face Dupont's mother without delay.

She opened the front door and walked down the steps just as the tall man reached the house. They almost collided.

From the drive Roxanne White said, "Who are you?"

The man said, "I'll handle this."

Stalling for time, Sylvia offered him her hand. "Sylvia Strange."

The man did not try to cover his irritation. "What's your business here?" he asked belligerently. "You're trespassing."

Sylvia wasn't about to end up on the bottom of the food chain under this contentious asshole. She stood her ground. "I came to talk to Mrs. White." Now, Sylvia directed her words to Dupont's mother. "When I knocked, your sister offered to entertain me until you were free."

"There is a security gate—"

"The gates are open, Garret." Roxanne White stepped forward, effectively dismissing the man, until she was arm's length from Sylvia. She eyed her cautiously, and asked, "Are you a reporter?"

"I'm a psychologist." Sylvia had a close view of Roxanne White. The woman was drastically different from her portrait. Her hair was dry and dyed and heavily sprayed. Her skin was thick with makeup a shade too orange. Her eyes were blunted, haggard, painful to see. Time and circumstance had not been kind to Roxanne White.

"A psychologist? Is this about Jilly?"

Sylvia shook her head. "Dupont."

"You people said you'd bring me his remains." The woman's eyes widened in alarm. "What's going on? When are you going to release my son's body?"

Sylvia guessed that Roxanne White had assumed she was an F.B.I. psychologist. She considered whether to tell the truth.

"Roxanne, don't talk to her."

"Be quiet, Garret." An embittered Roxanne White stared at the man who had shaken her roughly just minutes before. "Leave us alone."

His face reddened and he spoke furiously. "I'm not going anywhere."

Roxanne White shrugged. "Suit yourself." She took Sylvia's arm. "I want to talk to this lady."

The man named Garret grabbed Sylvia's other arm, but she shook him off just as Roxanne stumbled. Sylvia supported the woman's weight.

"Let her go," the man barked at Sylvia. "I demand to see your credentials."

Roxanne White's pale blue eyes were fierce. Fine lines were visible under her white powdered skin. She sputtered, "Meet Garret Ellington, the big man himself." She clutched Sylvia and breathed in her face. "Why don't you talk to him if you want *real* answers?"

Sylvia placed him now. Colonel Garret Ellington. Right-wing. Ex-marine, Vietnam vet. More recently, Mr. Ellington had spent several million dollars in a brief but highly publicized bid to become president of the United States. Although the man hadn't come close, his extremist ideas had attracted an unnerving number of supporters.

Ellington gave Sylvia the creeps.

Roxanne White pulled away from Sylvia abruptly. Clumsily she removed one leather loafer and hurled it at Garret Ellington. Sylvia ducked as the shoe flew past her shoulder and struck the man on the ear.

"Fucker," Roxanne mumbled. She stared at Garret Ellington defiantly as she addressed Sylvia. "You F.B.I.

people should go talk to Fuller Lynch again and see what he has to say."

Sylvia saw Ellington's body stiffen.

"Roxanne?" Jilly had appeared on the front steps. "Is he hurting you?"

Sylvia heard Roxanne White groan. The woman aged another ten years as she gazed up at her bewildered sister.

Garret Ellington called an order to Jilly. "You go back inside. This is none of your business."

Jilly started to cry.

With that, Roxanne White lunged toward Ellington, kicking at him with her stocking foot. She shrieked, "You can't talk to my sister that way!"

Sylvia tried to ward off Roxanne, afraid the woman would hurt herself in her rage.

Garret Ellington bellowed suddenly. "Stop it!"

The energy drained from Roxanne White. Her arms fell limply to her sides. She sobbed once, then held a hand to her eyes.

Ellington's voice was low and tense. He said, "Why would you upset Jilly? You know what happens when you do." Then he turned, strode toward Sylvia, and announced, "I want you to leave this property this minute."

Sylvia said, "Roxanne—"

Roxanne White held out a shaking hand. Her voice was low. "No . . . I can't talk to you."

"Has he threatened you?" Sylvia asked. "Do you need help?"

Roxanne stumbled to the top of the steps. She shook her head. Tears had streaked her makeup. Her eyes were red.

Sylvia said, "I'm registered at the Biltmore. Sylvia Strange."

"Get in your car, *now!*" Garret Ellington's eyes were murderous.

As Sylvia walked toward the Taurus, she saw Roxanne's shoulders sag.

Dupont's mother said, "I've talked to so many of you people. But not one of you can begin to tell me what went wrong with my boy." Then she disappeared inside her Spanish mansion.

TWENTY MINUTES LATER, as Sylvia passed Punta Gorda on U.S. 101, she realized a state trooper was following her Taurus. He was with her when she reached Ventura. She stayed at the speed limit and maneuvered with care. When he followed her onto Route 126 and was still behind her twenty miles later at Fillmore, she knew he was going to pull her over. Sure enough, his red light began to flash a few minutes later.

A deep male voice boomed out of broadcast speakers: "Pull over, turn off your engine, and stay inside your vehicle."

Muttering to herself, Sylvia eased the Taurus to the gravel shoulder and switched off the ignition. In her sideview mirror she saw the trooper adjust mirrored sunglasses, but he did not get out of his vehicle. Traffic was heavy on the highway, and the wake of passing cars buffeted the Taurus. With the engine off the air-conditioning didn't function, and the car quickly reached an uncomfortable temperature. Sylvia rolled down the driver's side window. She glanced at her watch and gauged that at least four minutes had passed since the trooper's summons. He was still seated in his vehicle.

Sylvia leaned back in her seat and gazed at the rearview mirror. It was beginning to sink in: Garret

Ellington was a powerful and well-connected man. He could certainly have a few cops in his back pocket.

The trooper had his radio transmitter in front of his face. On the roof of his vehicle, red lights pulsed an unsettling rhythm.

She stared at her watch again; six minutes gone. Through her open window she heard the faint chatter of the trooper's radio. By now, state computers would have pulled her name off rental agency computer files. With a little diligence, this trooper could find out if she owed money on her Visa card. He'd certainly know she wasn't an F.B.I. agent. Sylvia fanned herself with the refolded state map and cursed the age of computer technology.

When more than twelve minutes had passed, Sylvia had to force herself to stay inside the Taurus. She knew that the balance would shift sharply if she tried to force the trooper's agenda. She jumped when she heard his amplified voice issue a new set of commands.

"Remove your driver's license from your wallet, keep both hands in plain view, stay inside your vehicle."

Sylvia was fumbling with her leather wallet when the trooper emerged from his sedan. He was burly—in her sideview mirror, he looked huge—and his expression was sour. He kept one hand on his sidearm, and he stayed clear of the Taurus's open window.

She held the license out and he slid it from between her fingers. Then he disappeared back inside his car.

"Fuck." Sylvia clamped her fingers on the steering wheel. This was psychological warfare.

An additional eleven minutes passed before he finally tossed her driver's license through the open window. Then he tipped his hat with robotic precision and said, "Obey state laws, ma'am."

She started the Taurus and put some pressure on the gas pedal. The engine gave a snarly roar, a terrific sound.

No . . . she wasn't paranoid. Garret Ellington had her under very obvious surveillance. Either that, or California cops just liked to hassle women in rented sedans who drove the speed limit.

She shifted into first gear.

The trooper was back inside his vehicle, watching her, when she pulled into traffic. Her hands shook for the next fifteen miles, and she did not fully relax even when she reached the gravel turnoff to Devil's Den Ranch—and left the cop behind—about thirty miles east of Palmdale.

The terrain had gradually changed from green hills to desert plains. The wind had kicked up, and dust devils raced across the road. The map of California was open on the seat beside her as she guided the Taurus under the welded metal arch. Seconds later the car rattled over a wide cattleguard, past a dingy FOR SALE sign. The vegetation was scrub, the road was rough, and the four miles it took to reach the ranch headquarters seemed to take forever. Finally, three wide oak trees rose out of the ground like fanning beacons. The squat buildings were dwarfed beneath the trees. When she looked in her rearview mirror, she saw the Taurus was kicking up a long tail of dust. California had been as dry as New Mexico—inland, the drought was easily apparent.

She pulled into a clearing shaded by the oak trees and parked directly in front of a small white farmhouse. A large and faded red barn was situated a few hundred feet farther back. On the opposite side of the clearing was a second, much larger, rambling ranch-style house. Additional outbuildings were scattered around the property. But Sylvia saw no trace of people or animals. She got out of her car, shielded her face from the sun with one hand, and searched for signs of life.

Almost instantly she saw one. A large bulldog raced around the corner of the barn. It was charging her, massive head down, spit flying.

Sylvia clambered back inside the Taurus and slammed the door just as the dog hurled its body at metal. There was a thud. And then awful scraping sounds as the bulldog scrambled onto the hood of the car. He growled through the windshield and thick globules of drool smeared the glass.

"Boomer, git the fuck off the car!"

Sylvia flinched as a rock slammed into the Taurus and ricocheted off her door. Boomer yelped and jumped from the rental car's hood. He slunk off toward the barn. Before Sylvia could breathe any relief, she saw the dog's master.

He was wiry, mid-fifties, minus most of his teeth, and quite handy with his pitchfork.

Sylvia forced a smile.

He said, "You can git yourself outa there."

She studied the plain, unpolished man and saw a rancher who'd fallen on hard times. When she caught sight of his hook nose, she thought instantly of Cole Lynch, the penitentiary's Counselor; from this vantage point, Cole's Ivy League legalese seemed preposterous and poignant. This had to be his father, Fuller Lynch—caretaker of Devil's Den Ranch.

She climbed slowly from the Taurus, introduced herself, and said, "Roxanne White said you could show me around the place."

Fuller Lynch's eyes disappeared in a squint. "Why should I do that?"

"It's for sale, isn't it?"

Fuller Lynch spat in the dirt and raised a tiny puff of dust. "Yeah, but today's not a good day." He started to walk away.

Sylvia tried again, letting her speech roughen. "Last week, I visited your son Cole at the penitentiary. He was working in the law library, and he looks real good. Talks smart as a lawyer."

There was a long silence while Fuller weighed that information. His calculations were visible on his changing countenance. Finally, he grumbled, "And Cole's a whole lot more honest than most." His eyes softened up one notch. "Why'd you visit my son?"

"I'm a doctor, and I'm doing some research on Dupont White."

The corner of Fuller's mouth turned up derisively. He shrugged. "Go ahead and look around. There's nothing to find no more. Main house is all locked up." He jerked his head toward the rambling structure, and Sylvia followed his gaze. The sky caught her eye. Wispy clouds soothed a hard blue heaven. The sun had baked away any moisture in the air. The ranch house stood against the horizon like a false front on a movie set.

Sylvia's eyes followed a gliding buzzard or hawk. It circled lazily, cresting strong currents. And then it dove toward the earth. This was the place where Dupont White and his cousin had spent their childhood summers.

Fuller had been watching her. He said, "F.B.I. been all through the house, then they went and put a padlock on the door. See for yourself." He narrowed his eyes, looked down his beakish nose at Sylvia, then turned to walk away. Over his shoulder he said, "Watch your step. It's dangerous footing."

Sylvia waited until Fuller Lynch disappeared inside the barn, but she wasn't alone. Two children had appeared. They were playing hide-and-seek. The high notes of their voices carried easily on the dry air. Sylvia watched them for a moment before she turned and covered the distance to the trees and the ranch house.

Concrete steps still led up to the front stoop; they were cracked and overgrown with weeds, and she walked carefully. The front door was intact, but someone—presumably federal agents—had locked it with a heavy hasp and padlock.

She walked around to the rear of the house. The back door was locked, but the entrance to the basement gaped open. Sylvia stared at the cellar steps—they were clear and looked navigable—and she followed them down to the darkened doorway.

The basement was large, and it rambled like the house. Pipes ran through the foundation. Spiders had spun their webs in corners. Dead, dry leaves were thick underfoot. She thought she saw a rodent scuttling past her legs.

She wandered along a central hallway past various small rooms. She entered one that was as close and dark as a tomb. She wished she had a flashlight; it took minutes for her eyes to adjust to the darkness. Finally she began to discern shapes: a bench, a stool, pots and pans—no, they were trays. She was standing in a home darkroom.

She could hear a child's voice very faintly coming from outside. It was soft and high and plaintive. The sounds and the dark space spooked Sylvia, and she stumbled back along the hallway and up the steps, eager to reach open air.

Outside, clouds had thrown their veil across the sun, and the light had depth and shadows. With care, she made her way back around the ranch house. When she reached a picture window, she peered inside through dust. It was a long, low room, a gallery of some kind. It was all pine veneer, red leather, very masculine. Animal trophies lined the walls. No, they were masks. Sylvia wet her finger with spit and cleaned dust from a small circle of the window. Now she saw they were carved, painted masks that resembled ones she had seen from Mexico or South America.

While she stood absorbing the scene, she heard a noise from across the clearing. She turned and saw Fuller Lynch standing in the barn door. He made no bones about staring.

Sylvia waited without moving for several minutes—stubbornly, as much to see if the man would look away. He didn't, even when she walked in his direction.

Fuller Lynch met her at her car. He worried a stalk of straw between his teeth.

Sylvia looked him in the eye. She said, "You were right . . . there's nothing to see."

He nodded soberly. Satisfied. Sylvia thought he looked like a fat canary—the one that swallowed that poor old barn cat. Not a good man with secrets, she decided; he would deny anything and everything without finesse. Just a farmer fallen on hard times.

She said, "What happened to the little girl that used to come out here with Dupont and his stepfather?"

Fuller Lynch said, "Don't know about no little girl."

"Really? I just saw a picture of her with your son and Dupont . . . on Halloween, about 1978. That picture was taken here."

"Well, I don't remember no little girl."

Sylvia nodded. But her eyes widened as she glanced away. She was right—Fuller Lynch was definitely a rotten liar. She said, "So who used the ranch?"

"Dupont hid out here sometimes."

"When he was running guns with your son Cole?"

"When they were practicing the second amendment." Fuller Lynch sounded proud of his son. He eyed her.

"But you oughta know all that if you're doing research like you say."

"What about before that, when Dupont was young?"

"Mr. Roland White, Dupont's stepfather, and his gentlemen friends came out here."

"Gentlemen? When Dupont and his cousin were here?"

"You ask too many questions." Fuller Lynch turned and walked away.

Sylvia reached the Taurus and slid behind the wheel as the caretaker disappeared back inside his barn.

The engine turned over, caught. Just then Sylvia saw a flash of color. She looked out the window at wide, blue eyes—a child chasing a clattering can.

The child asked, "Is that your car?" She was about seven or eight years old. She stood with tiny hips jutting forward, aggressively curious.

Another child appeared out from behind the Taurus, this one a boy who was older than the girl by a year or so. He said, "My daddy's a lawyer."

The girl crossed her arms over her concave chest. "He's in New Mexico."

These must be the Counselor's children.

"What were you doing inside the crazy house?" the boy demanded.

Sylvia smiled encouragingly. "Crazy house?"

"It's haunted," the girl announced. She kicked at the can. "And now you're haunted."

"Yeah, you're haunted," the boy repeated.

The boy spit at something on the dusty ground, then he wiped spittle from his chin. "You go inside there, you get cursed . . . we saw you go in."

Sylvia stared at the children. The fading daylight seemed to turn them into little demons—bad seeds. She knew it was her mood, not the day.

Three minutes after she turned out of the ranch, the state trooper picked up her trail again. This time he stayed right behind the Taurus. Sylvia set her cruise control for sixty-four miles per hour and forced herself not to glance in the rearview mirror. At Ventura he pulled off the road and let her continue, apparently unescorted, to Santa Barbara.

She couldn't have been happier to see the Biltmore. Her bungalow, and the luxury of the hotel, felt like a refuge. From the day, from the world—for a moment. She would have plenty of time to dress for dinner with Leo, Mark Chism, and their business associates. Tomorrow morning, by eight A.M., she would be on a plane to Albuquerque.

There was a message on her hotel voice mail from Roxanne White. Dupont's mother had the slurred speech of a woman on depressants and alcohol. Sylvia thought she had probably needed chemical support to make this call. The message was brief and bitter.

*"If you really want to have some fun, ask Nathan Howzer about the Gentlemen's Club."*

JUDGE NATHANIEL HOWZER couldn't remember how long he'd been sitting in the dark. For the third time he let the telephone ring and ring until the jarring sound finally died away. It took a great effort when he lifted the crystal decanter from his desk and drained the last of the alcohol into his glass. This was the pattern of his recent days—to drink himself into a stupor that almost passed for sleep.

He was in his study with the timid Adobe sprawled beside his chair. His fingers touched warm fur and the Doberman whined gently.

The phone began to ring again. This time he picked up the receiver and listened.

"Nathan? It's me."

The judge recognized the fretful voice. He said, "Hello, Garret."

For his lack of caution he was rewarded with silence. He welcomed the space. He fantasized that Garret Ellington had turned into dust and blown away, leaving him in peace.

Howzer sighed. Garret Ellington was the least of his troubles.

Ellington said, "Do you know a woman named Sylvia Strange? She was here asking questions . . . and she went out to the ranch."

Judge Howzer grunted and took another sip of his drink. "Yes, I know her."

Ellington felt the other man's loathing, and he blurted out his complaint. "I thought you were going to handle Fuller Lynch. Now he's called Roxanne, and I think she's folding. She's catching on. You said you'd handle it."

"I am."

"I don't like to be pushed! Especially not by lowlifes."

The judge was enjoying Garret's discomfiture.

Ellington said, "From the beginning, I wanted to handle this *my* way. But oh no, *you* knew better. Well, I expect closure."

The judge grimaced and took a breath to calm himself. Through the French doors he could see the lights of the city intruding into a blackened sky.

He closed his eyes, kept his voice low. "I don't think you understand what's at stake here, Garret."

"I know damn well what's—"

"Shut up," Howzer snapped. Adobe whined and the judge patted the Doberman's head soothingly. "I don't want you calling here again. I don't want you mucking up the waters. Just stay out of this, and let me do what I was paid to do for so many years—keep secrets."

"Just remember your ass is on the line, too."

The judge smiled in the dark. He was pleased to discover how little he cared about his own fate anymore. He forced himself to speak. "I'll remember."

# FIFTEEN

IN A SANTA FE motel—on Monday morning—Kevin Chase aimed his .44 Magnum at the bouncing heads on the television screen—Samantha, on *Bewitched*, wiggled her nose, and her husband Darrin made a pug face. Kevin's finger caressed the revolver's stainless steel trigger—he imagined Darrin's head exploding—but he didn't apply enough pressure to fire the round and whatnot. He wasn't stupid.

When the Nickelodeon station break began, Kevin lay back on the bed and aimed the revolver at the light fixture overhead. "Ptoow. Ptoow, ptoow!" The meth he'd just snorted was kicking in, kicking him in the butt.

He flashed on how Killer knew so much about everything. Killer was a genius, like other chosen people. Had a mission. Like some kind of *god*. Sure, Killer got bossy or crazy sometimes, but there was always a reason. Kevin knew there was a reason for everything.

He aimed his gun, a present from Killer, at the cornflake girl on screen. She just grinned at herself in the mirror and wiggled her butt like she was swimming.

"Ptoow. Ptoow."

Kevin swung his legs off the bed and began to pace the motel room. He'd covered every inch of that floor at least a hundred times during the last three days. By now he should've worn a path into the rug. He began to hum a tune—off-key—his own special song. As he walked, his right hand swung the .44 Magnum like a parade salute, and his left thumb slipped into his mouth.

Kevin couldn't get Killer out of his mind: how they saw eye to eye the very first time they hung out and shared a bottle of tequila. They could talk for hours about life and death, how the biggest crime was criminals getting away with rape, and the murder of little kids and whatnot. How guys in Jersey and Idaho and Texas were starting to get smart and make justice happen. How the government had turned bad and the cops and the courts were all bad. The only one to trust was yourself and your partner. You could be your own god.

Long before the first kill, their partnership was established.

*Call me Killer.*

*Trust my will.*

*Know my discipline.*

*Follow my path.*

With Randall, they had sealed their partnership in blood.

Kevin didn't pretend to understand everything Killer said. But he was learning quickly. Maybe he was even ready to do something big on his own. Only Killer wouldn't believe it until it was already a success.

A sigh escaped Kevin's lips. He wanted to prove his worth, he wanted to prove to the world that he could carry out a mission. Make Killer stand up and be proud. And he would. Damn right, he would! "Ptoow." He had a pretty good idea how to do it. "Ptoow!"

He thought about his plan for a minute. A shiver of anticipation—and what he would never admit was fear—ran up his spine. His thumb popped busily in and out of his mouth.

And he smiled. Yes . . . it would work out perfectly and whatnot.


MATT PULLED UP in a parking slot outside the Law Enforcement Academy. As he got out of the car he heard the sharp, repeated ping of metal from the flagpole. Overhead, state and national flags were flapping in the hot wind.

"Matt."

He recognized Erin's voice before he saw her standing in the shade of a cottonwood tree. Her hair was loose and tousled, her clothes were clean. She looked much more rested than the last time he'd seen her. He glanced around to see if anybody was watching—since her suspension it was a bad idea for her to be here. He strode across hot asphalt. As he got close, he could see her eyes were clear.

Matt kept his voice soft. "What are you doing here?"

"Waiting for you."

"You shouldn't—"

She frowned. "Just listen. I've got something on the Randall murder." She swallowed as if her throat hurt, and she licked bare lips. "One of my people told me there's going to be trouble tonight. Another kidnapping."

Matt frowned. Erin's "people" were her snitches. She had always maintained a solid snitch file—the bad guys trusted her. And so they should, because, as far as Matt knew, she'd never given away an informant.

He said, "What's the deal?"

"You remember Manny Dunn?"

"Pedophile, got out of the joint a few months ago."

"Right. My guy says Manny's been in the market for kiddie porn, and he's making a buy tonight."

"Who's the supplier?"

"Kevin Chase and somebody he's working with." Erin

shook her head. "Manny has no idea he's the next target. Number Three."

"Where's this deal supposed to go down?"

"La Bajada rest stop. Men's toilet."

An appropriate choice. Matt knew that several murders had taken place at the rest stop in the past few years. It was frequented by transients, gang-bangers, voyeurs, and eighteen-wheel truckers who'd pay any out-of-luck kid for sex.

He said, "Who's your source?"

Erin turned away in disgust. "Damn you, Matt. This is the last place I want to be today." She turned and began to walk to her car.

Matt stopped her gently with one hand. "Erin, I appreciate what you're doing. You know I've got to ask."

"And you know I've got to protect my sources. Just because I've been through some hard times, I don't plan on not being a cop." She shrugged. "Do whatever you want with this, I don't really care anymore."


BENJI MUÑOZ Y CONCHA squirmed on the hard bench outside Dr. Cray's penitentiary office. From where he sat he could see inmates' vacant faces. They were staring out at him from behind screened glass. They were locked inside tiny examination cells waiting for a visit from medical staff. There was a physician's assistant on duty today. Benji liked her because she was nice. But he wasn't here to see the nurse. In fact, he shouldn't be here at all. He had an emergency on his hands.

Ten paces down the hall, an inmate moaned and plastered one cheek to the small window. Benji could see whiskers on flattened skin and the dark circle beneath a walleye. He hardly noticed. He was thinking about Rosie Sanchez, and how he couldn't find her anywhere in the prison. If he didn't find Rosie—well, he didn't know any other way to get a message to Sylvia Strange. He had already tried to call her three times, but she wasn't home, and her answering machine didn't seem to work right.

A door opened across the hall. Dr. Cray peeked his head out. He stared down at a clipboard. "Benji Concha?"

"Muñoz y Concha," Benji murmured.

"I was told you're having another problem?" Dr. Cray's face was stern.

"No problem." Benji shook his head.

Dr. Cray frowned in consternation. "Don't stand out there in the hall, come inside."

"I don't need to come inside," Benji said.

"Inside, right now!"

Reluctantly, Benji passed over the threshold into the doctor's office. It was dingy, a blur of dull colors and fading tile, the office of bland men who came and went with the seasons.

Benji stood with his hands behind his back, and his fingers tripped over one another nervously. "I don't need to see you. I need to see Rosie Sanchez, but I can't find her."

"This morning you made a spectacle of yourself outside her office," Dr. Cray said. "You had to be restrained."

"I just needed to talk to her. Where is she?"

"Why don't you talk to me?"

Benji set his lips and shook his head.

"Is it one of your *visions*?" When he didn't get a response, Dr. Cray let out a great sigh of exasperation. Just three days ago Rosie Sanchez had lit into him like a bitch with a new litter, and apparently, Benji was her favorite pup.

Cray stiffened at the memory of the penitentiary investigator's stinging words—she'd called him ignorant and patronizing. She'd accused him of cultural insensitivity just because he suggested a light dose of Thorazine for Benji. Well, this inmate was pathological, not *visionary*, dammit.

Unconsciously Cray made a face. If anything, he was *too* culturally sensitive ... that came from having a Polish grandmother and a French mother. *For God's sake, I know suffering, too.*

He tried for the severe but compassionate expression of a schoolmaster. "Benji, I'm sorry, but it's none of your business where Ms. Sanchez has gone."

"She wasn't here yesterday, either."

"I'll give her a message. How's that, Benji?"

Benji shook his head slowly and deliberately. And then he said what came to his mind. "Ms. Sanchez doesn't work here anymore."

Dr. Cray's eyes widened; Benji was right ... but there was no way he could know this.

Benji backed toward the door. This doctor was part of some plan to keep him away from Rosie Sanchez. Well, it wouldn't work. He would find her, and then he would explain that her friend the psychologist—Sylvia Strange—was in trouble.


SYLVIA DROVE FROM the Albuquerque International Airport to her house outside Santa Fe. She was grateful to be on solid ground. The aerial step-down to Albuquerque had been turbulent; it usually was during the warm summer months. Although she flew regularly, she rarely enjoyed the experience. Especially when she had so much on her mind.

All in all, the forty-eight hours spent in Santa Barbara seemed unreal. Especially her encounter with Garret Ellington, and the message from Roxanne White about the Gentlemen's Club and Judge Nathaniel Howzer.

Instead of finding answers, Sylvia had stirred up more questions.

She wanted to talk it all out with Matt—but they had some personal business to clear up first.

She considered whether to stop by his office, but decided against that plan. She wanted a little more time to consider her own feelings before she opened the floor to discussion on Erin Tulley's allegation. Anyway, state police headquarters wasn't the place to bring up Tulley's name.

She reached the edge of her twenty acres by noon and experienced a familiar sense of comfort, of coming home. Across the lane from her mailbox, crows monopolized a honey locust. Their loud caws sounded like insults hurled down from above. Blackberry avian eyes pierced the skin, jet bird feathers gleamed even through the haze. She had seen that morning's *Albuquerque Journal* headline in the airport newsstand, reporting two new small fires burning in surrounding mountain ranges. The dry heat felt foreign and harsh after the softness of ocean air. When she opened the metal box to pull out three days' worth of mail, she disturbed a layer of lacy ash. She stacked the letters on top of newspapers, drove the last hundred yards to her driveway, and climbed out of the Volvo.

In front of the house the lilacs were droopy, and the fruit on the apricot trees was tinged gray. Sylvia set her luggage on the front porch under the portal and moved the hose and sprinkler between two trees; their roots were desperate for moisture. She turned on the faucet, and water sprayed her bare legs and her shoes. She smiled when she remembered hot summer days in early childhood; her father was master of the garden hose and a stream of water—he would swing the jet like a jump rope while his small daughter squealed and jumped, dripping wet, deliciously happy.

She unlocked the front door and entered. The interior smelled stale, and she left her bags in the bedroom and immediately opened windows. Next, she twisted the cap from an icy bottle of Pete's Wicked Ale and read a postcard from her mother. The card showed a massive iceberg surrounded by gray-blue ocean. Her mother had penned a brief and humorous update of her Alaska cruise.

She spread peanut butter on an Oreo cookie and stared at the blinking light on her answering machine. *Fuck it,* she thought, as she jammed the cookie into her mouth. She had urgent business on her agenda: chill out, come down to earth, and water the damn garden. But first she wanted to smoke a cigarette.

She was in the side yard, barefoot, in shorts and T-shirt, when she heard a car pull into the driveway. She dropped the garden hose and stepped quickly toward the house. Then she recognized the roof of the Caprice and stopped. With both hands she pushed damp hair from her face. A smear of dirt decorated her chin and her shirt was dripping wet from the hose; she wrung water from the thin white fabric.

She wished Matt had given her another few hours to relax and pull herself together. Or at least enough time to get pleasantly high because that would be fine, too. She found her beer where she'd left it on the deck, drained it, and met Matt at the gate.

He smiled at her, kept his hands in his pockets, and kissed her lightly on the cheek. That was his compromise between warring instincts: to hold her or to fight. He was angry, and the anger had been building for weeks until his chest felt as though it was encased in concrete. Sometimes it was difficult to breathe. Like now. He knew the feeling of suffocation came from pushing down his emotions, keeping them below the surface, but his knowledge didn't help him. Always, when he tried to let his anger out, it got the best of him.

He leaned against the sagging coyote fence. After an uncomfortable silence, he asked, "How was Santa Barbara?"

"Weird." Her resolve to ask Matt about Erin Tulley wavered. She picked up the hose, aimed the nozzle toward the sky, and took a drink. Then she adjusted the spray over the flower bed, and began to speak—too fast.

She said, "Santa Barbara was *very* weird. Dupont's mother, Roxanne, is involved somehow with Garret Ellington—*the* Garret Ellington. And I drove out to Devil's Den Ranch; I found out Dupont had a cousin, a little girl, and both kids were out there in the summers—so were Roland White's cronies, and Fuller Lynch called them Roland's 'gentlemen friends.' Roxanne White left me a message that Judge Howzer is connected to the gentlemen—"

"Whoa. You're babbling. Slow down a minute." Matt took the hose from her fingers and set it down in a bed of cosmos. The water made a soft urgent sound. "Nathaniel Howzer is involved with Dupont White's family?"

"That's what I just said." Abruptly, Sylvia tipped her head and sighed. Then she raised both hands, palms out, and stepped away from Matt. "Stop. Wait. This is making me crazy."

"What?"

"Did you fuck Erin Tulley?"

Matt opened his mouth, closed it, then opened it again. His voice was soft. "Yeah."

"Jesus." Sylvia shook her head. Then, carefully, she picked up the hose and turned the spray on Matt. He jumped from cold and shock when icy water hit his face and chest. After a few seconds, Sylvia let the hose drop to the ground.

Matt wasn't sure whether to laugh or get mad. "Sylvia, it happened before you and I even knew each other."

"She's young enough to be your daughter." Sylvia swallowed hard, then she turned and walked past the salt cedar.

He followed her, tasting the dusty scent of the bush as he moved. "We saw each other for a few months. She said she was in love with me . . . but I didn't feel that way."

She stopped, pivoted, and let her eyes burn holes in his skin. Her voice was incredulous. "That's it? That's all that happened?"

His answer was a fraction too slow. "Almost. That's almost all."

"Dammit! Will you just give me a straight answer?" She stomped over a flower bed, crushing pastel cosmos underfoot.

Matt stood his ground. "We got together again in March."

Sylvia skirted the side of the house and slumped down on the wooden steps of the deck. Matt walked over to her and leaned against the railing. He thought he saw tears on her cheeks.

Her voice sounded very young, almost tremulous. "Was it after I told you I needed time alone to think about our relationship?"

"Yeah."

After a silence, she said, "Please don't make me ask."

He looked embarrassed. "We had drinks a few times— dinner."

"Did you have sex?"

Matt blushed. "Goddammit."

"Okay." She looked miserable. The crows in the yard

were crabbing; loud, heated squawks emanated from tree branches, fence posts, and the power pole. Their cousins, a family of magpies, joined the debate.

Sylvia barely heard the cacophony. She asked, "Did you sleep with her again?"

"No."

"Did you want to?"

"I wanted you. I love you."

She took a breath. "Why didn't you tell me when it happened?"

"I was going to . . . but you and I were back together . . . and there was really nothing to tell." Matt's forehead creased with concern.

Sylvia sighed. She studied Matt, and thought about the fact that she could have lost him. And she thought about the fact he was in love with her. And how good that felt.

She stood slowly and walked over to the hose. It was still running, and water had puddled around the walkway. Sylvia turned the nozzle on herself. Icy needles of water stung her throat and chest. She closed her eyes, let her head fall back until the sun burned a golden fringe around her eyelids. She felt Matt's hands on her shoulders, and she almost shook him off. Instead, she twisted her body, and pressed her cheek against his chin. The shaved bristles of his beard roughed up her skin.

Above the sound of the spurting water, she barely heard him whisper, "I love you."

Behind the fabric of his collar, she bit soft skin. His body tensed, and he scooped her breasts in his hands. When she found his mouth with her tongue, she forced his lips apart. Still, the hose gushed cold water between their bodies.

She pulled back for air, and mumbled, "Water's freezing."

Matt slid his hands from her nipples, down her belly,

to her thighs. He eased one finger between her legs. She moaned, but she pushed him away and pressed the garden hose into his hand. Her voice was a growl. "Get rid of this damn thing."

Then she knelt down in front of him, unzipped his wet pants, loosened his shorts, and pulled them down around his ankles. He was hard, pressing toward her face, and she took him into her mouth. His body swayed, and then he caught himself, balanced with one hand on her shoulder. Water still poured from the hose in his other hand.

Matt caught his breath sharply, and he dropped the hose. She had him inside, all the way to her throat, and her teeth were sharp.

She willed him to relax, ran her fingers gently over his bare butt. Gradually, he let go, gave in to the rhythm of her mouth. And, finally, he let her have her way.

IN THE KITCHEN, after a long, warm shower, they shared a beer. His muscles had turned into jelly. He leaned up against the counter and watched his lover pour potato chips into a bright blue bowl.

He said, "If you've got a craving, why don't you just smoke a cigarette?"

Her eyebrows arched, and she popped a potato chip into her mouth. Then she shrugged, opened the utensil drawer and scavenged a slightly-worse-for-wear cigarette from behind the spoons. She lit it with a kitchen match, inhaled, and exhaled in his face. "If you knew I smoked, why didn't you say something before?"

"I wanted to see if you'd volunteer the information." He gave a short laugh. "I'm going to stop acting guilty about my bad habits."

"Be my guest." Sylvia smiled, shook her head.

Matt eyed her quizzically, wondered how well he knew her, and what other secrets she might have.

Her fingers drummed the countertop. "Anything on Kevin?" Her voice was edgy. "I keep expecting him to show up."

Matt considered how much to tell her. He said, "You remember a pedophile named Manny Dunn?"

Sylvia nodded, then paled. "Don't tell me he's dead?"

"He's not dead, yet. But we got a tip that Kevin and whoever he's working with have set Manny Dunn up for a kidnapping tonight."

Sylvia's eyes shot wide. "Where?" She stepped forward, her body tense. "I want to be there."

Matt shook his head. "We'll have the place staked out. We'll be waiting when they show. They won't get away."

"Does Dan Chaney know about this?"

"Yeah."

Sylvia hunched forward nervously, and asked, "Will you call me as soon as it happens?"

"You bet." Matt wrapped his arm around her shoulders. "I'd feel better if you were at Rosie's."

Sylvia opened her mouth to protest, closed it again. Then she nodded.

"I'll call you the minute we've got them."

She stabbed her cigarette out in the sink. "Be careful."

She walked him to the gate. At the edge of the deck she stopped and stared up at the sawback ridge that sliced jaggedly into the sky behind her home. When she turned back to Matt, her face was soft with emotion.

SHE PUT ON her running shoes and took off on a jog along her regular makeshift course. It was much too hot for exercise, but she had so much pent-up energy that the run took twenty minutes instead of forty. Her route followed the dirt road, cut up onto the lower flank of the ridge back, and doubled back to the house.

The phone began to ring as soon as she walked in the back door. She shook her head, bent over to catch her breath, and heard the answering machine click on. The volume was down. She could ignore the world and this message. At the sink, she filled a tumbler with water, and then her fingers moved reluctantly to the machine. She turned up the volume.

Ray's voice was anxious, as he said, ". . . so call me, as soon as—"

She jerked up the handset. "Ray, what's happened?"

"Sylvia, I've been trying to find you for days. Rosie was fired."

"What? Shit." Sylvia set her tumbler on the edge of the sink. It fell off the edge and shattered, spilling water and glass shards. She jerked back, then stared at the mess. "When did it happen?"

"She heard about it Friday from Colonel Gonzales. The warden picked one of his little gringos to replace her. I thought Rosita called you."

"She did. But I was in California, Ray." She bit her lip. "Damn, I'm so sorry. Can I talk to her?"

"She's not here. She took off yesterday for Christ in the Desert Monastery."

"Alone?"

"She wouldn't let me come." Ray sounded heartbroken. "I can't help how I feel about her job."

Sylvia knew that Ray had always wanted Rosie out of the penitentiary. Her termination would not be all negative from his point of view. But Sylvia also knew what being penitentiary investigator meant to Rosie. She had pioneered the position—she'd taken the initiative to learn the forensic and investigative protocol that went with the job. Now, some young, three-piece chauvinist was probably sitting at her desk.

Sylvia said, "I'm going up to the monastery. I can leave here in ten minutes."

Ray protested weakly, but there was relief in his voice. "I know how much she needs you."

# SIXTEEN

THE MONASTERY OF Christ in the Desert had been built at the end of a breathtaking canyon that was traversed by a rugged Forest Service road. The Benedictine brothers offered travelers room and board for a nominal fee. Next to the chapel, the monks kept an open, unmarked, and empty grave; it served as a steady reminder of death. When Sylvia had visited two years earlier, she found the experience of staring into that deep grave unnerving.

Now, as she drove past the Santa Fe Opera on 285 north, she realized she felt as if she were on an adventure; the sensation was triggered by memories of childhood camping trips with her parents. The sense of adventure was sharpened by urgency. She was eager to reach Rosie, and the two-and-a-half-hour drive to the monastery was best completed before nightfall.

As she passed Camel Rock, Tesuque Pueblo land gave way to Pojoaque Pueblo's great clay gullies and gorges, called Los Barrancos, which were abruptly interrupted by the valley of Cuyamungue, a green slash of oasis on the west side of the highway. Beyond, and farther west, thunderheads streaked the sky above the Jemez Mountains. She said a silent prayer for rain.

She was headed north of Abiquiu, toward Georgia O'Keeffe territory. The artist had visited the region in the 1930s and had stayed for the rest of her life. O'Keeffe's

brush and palette—swirls of orange, pink, and ocher—
accurately caught the shapes, the hues, the drama of the
sandstone cliffs.

KEVIN CHASE WHISTLED while his fingers strayed to
the spot on his nose where a pimple bloomed. It was
easy to keep the Volvo in view along the stretch of
highway that traversed Pojoaque; traffic was dense but
her blue sedan stood out from the pickups, spuvs, and
low-riders.

He clamped both hands on the steering wheel and
sank lower into the seat of the white Nissan until the
metal springs groaned. He was like a tree stuffed into a
flowerpot—much too big to take root. The top of his
head brushed the roof of the stolen car. His left shoulder
butted up against the driver-side door.

Kevin stopped whistling, his hands strayed from the
wheel, and the Nissan drifted into the next lane.

A shrill horn brought him back. He glanced at the car
passing him in the left lane to see if anyone was staring.
When nobody seemed to think he deserved notice, he
inserted his thumb between his lips and stared straight
ahead. He watched the blue Volvo crest the hill about a
half mile to the north.

He had never liked Sylvia Strange. She was smart—he
admitted that grudgingly—and she acted like she cared
and whatnot. But he hated her snotty ways, her therapy
mumbo jumbo. *Do you think you might be angry at your
parents because they abandoned you, Kevin?*

As if he could be angry at people who were dead and
whatnot.

Kevin sucked his thumb, and the digit jerked in and
out of his mouth while his eyes glazed over. He was
oblivious to his own habits; he avoided the burden of
introspection. Not surprisingly, he'd dreaded the court-

ordered treatment sessions. Killer had insisted it was important. Although Kevin would never say so out loud, he disagreed.

*What does it matter why?*

IT WAS ALMOST EIGHT when Sylvia pulled off in Abiquiu at Bodes General Store, a roadside market that sold gas, groceries, and agricultural goods. Under tall cotton-woods, the air had cooled; now it was a refreshing eighty degrees. She filled the Volvo with unleaded, and then bought Oreo cookies and a cold six-pack of Coke. Before she left Abiquiu, she took a long look at her surround-ings: the alfalfa fields, the Chama River basin, and, in the distance, Triassic red beds and Jurassic sandstone cliffs. The sight was good for her soul.

For the next twenty miles, traffic on U.S. 84 was sparse. At the turnoff to Ghost Ranch, she passed a tour bus spewing diesel fumes. Farther along the highway, a few local farmers and ranchers were trucking goats and tomatoes, and day-trippers towed their speedboats toward Abiquiu Reservoir.

Two summers had passed since her trip to the monas-tery. There was no visible marker for Forest Route 151, but there was a new green-and-white sign: CHAMA RIVER CANYON WILDERNESS. She turned sharply and then her tires rumbled over the metal bars of a cattleguard. She remembered the distinct thought from the other time she had traveled this road: *You're on your own from here.*

The road was deeply rutted and bone-dry, but a respectable downpour could create an impassable mud slick within minutes. The Volvo passed under a canopy of cottonwoods; the great trees imposed their shadows over the road for thirty feet or so. Although it wouldn't get fully dark until eight-thirty, the deep canyon shut out the sun with unnerving finality. She glanced at her watch: she had another ten minutes of daylight at most.

The Volvo wasn't built for rough terrain. Sylvia kept the speedometer hovering at twenty-five as she ripped open the Oreo package and pulled out a handful of cookies. When she'd finished eating, she popped open a Coke and guzzled cold soda.

Six miles in, she began to wonder if she'd taken a wrong turn on a road that had no turns at all. She'd been driving forever, for hours, for years. The canyon was its own world, contained, feeding into the limitless, surrounding wilderness. For those humans who tested themselves against the wild country, distances were distorted; a mesa that appeared to be five miles away was actually fifty. Those who underestimated the overwhelming power of nature did so at the risk of their lives. People got lost here; they walked away and were never found.

The radio picked up static. On the north edge of the road the canyon's massive sandstone wall nosed up steadily until it angled more than four hundred feet. Pine trees somehow fastened to existence on the sheer rocks. To the south, the Chama River steadfastly continued on its muddy course, deepening the Cañon de Chama as it had for hundreds of thousands of years. The river was now designated wilderness, and launch stations had recently been provided for kayakers and rafters.

Both river and road appeared deserted. Sylvia gazed through her windshield at the last arms of sunlight as they pulled back behind Dead Man Peak and Capulin Mesa. Beyond those western mountains lay Jicarilla Apache Indian Reservation land and flat, dry fossil beds. And absolute silence.

Headlights suddenly clouded the Volvo's rearview mirror. She had company.

The vehicle gradually gained ground, and she adjusted the mirror to cut the glare. As it followed her trail and the curve of the road, it was gone, then reappeared like a ship riding rough waves. Suddenly, the lights were directly behind the Volvo.

She exhaled with relief when the vehicle pulled out at a widening of the road and streaked past. A rock pelted her windshield, and a tiny pockmark and crack appeared at eye level.

THE STONE FIT Matt England's palm perfectly, and he sent it spinning toward the industrial light overhead. The stone struck metal, there was a sharp ping, and then it landed somewhere beyond the barbed-wire fence. He picked up another stone from the gravel at his feet. He tested the weight, aimed, and threw an underhand curveball. For an instant, Matt was starting pitcher for the McNamara High Hornets. There was a satisfying pop as glass splintered, and his face disappeared in shadow. *Nice work for a cop.*

He was another stone's throw from the D.P.S. surveillance van. From his vantage point on the rise just south of the main rest area, he could watch each vehicle—and its occupants—pull into the Santa Fe Welcome Center. Earlier, a plainclothes cop had swept the entire property to make sure their guy hadn't already shown. Just another stakeout . . .

It had taken Matt several hours to convince Captain Elizer Rocha that it was worth a shot at Kevin Chase. Matt had lied about his source. Rocha would not be impressed with a tip from one of Erin Tulley's snitches— not after all the negative fallout on the Randall case.

Matt pulled his body back into shadow when Manny Dunn's white Buick appeared in his sightlines. The Buick braked to a stop under another industrial light, almost directly in front of the rest stop facilities. Matt shook his head. Manny Dunn was no genius.

The I-25 rest stop was located just north of the crest of La Bajada. The *bajada,* or descent, a one-thousand-foot drop from mountain to desert, marked the unofficial division between northern New Mexico and the southerly regions of the state. Vehicles heading north from Albuquerque climbed for an hour before they hit the crest of La Bajada, at which point the city of Santa Fe and its surrounds became visible, scattered below like children's toys.

Manny Dunn hoisted his bulk from the Buick and slammed the car door. He walked with a slow, rolling stride, hands in pockets, chin low. But Matt knew Dunn was watching everything and everybody around him as he moved toward the men's toilet. Matt and his team would wait for Kevin Chase to show. If he wasn't scared off, they'd have themselves a nice, neat collar. They'd even pop Manny Dunn for buying dirty toys.

A skinny guy walked out of the toilet and passed Dunn on the cement walkway. Matt could see Dunn's shoulder blades tighten beneath his cotton shirt, but the other guy kept walking without a word.

Matt checked his watch—8:08 P.M. The deal could go down any time now. Or never.

The night air was soft and soothing—the payoff of hot, sticky days. From where he stood he could see the lights of Los Alamos glowing like phosphorescent creatures.

More than an hour ago he had turned away from the faraway lights and traveled south across the plateau on foot, leaving the rest area behind. He had ducked under barbed wire, dodged cans, bottles, and other human debris. He had passed a large outcrop of rock. By the time he looked back at the interstate, the traffic had been reduced to a distant glow and a faraway hum.

He'd walked long enough for his mind to clear. The terrain, the sense of place, seduced and soothed. It reminded him of Oklahoma. There were antelope a half mile away, and a coyote was surely watching his long stride across earth. Unexpectedly he found himself picturing his wife's face. If Mary's soul was anywhere, it could be here, lured by open space. He still missed her, still felt her absence after all these years.

By the time he'd reached the rim of La Bajada, he felt almost peaceful. Out there, the earth dropped away and fell back like a receding wave; it gave him a view of the entire world.

Matt instantly put those thoughts from his mind when movement caught his eye; a girl skipped out of the women's bathroom. Her mother called to her from the parking area.

Matt glanced back over his shoulder. The D.P.S. surveillance van was parked between highway maintenance vehicles roughly fifty feet behind the row of picnic tables. He could communicate with the van via radio.

He looked back to the toilets—Dunn was inside and alone at 8:37 P.M.

Matt let a thin arc of tobacco juice squirt from the corner of his mouth. With his tongue, he readjusted the plug of chaw between gum and tooth. Now that Sylvia had smoked a cigarette in front of him, he didn't feel so defensive about his tobacco habit.

Another car drove into the parking area. A Jeep. Two kids got out . . . and then a woman. The kids raced over the grass toward the picnic area. The woman followed, calling them back in an irritated tone of voice.

Thirty seconds later, a gray truck rolled in and parked next to the Jeep. The low throb of the engine died away, but no one got out. The truck windows were tinted black, and it was impossible to see who was inside. Maybe, just maybe, Matt caught the faint glow of a cigarette behind dark glass.

His stomach churned uneasily. He was on edge. The plan was to wait until Kevin Chase was inside the toilet with Manny Dunn.

But what if Kevin didn't cooperate tonight? Ninety-five percent of stakeouts were busts. Long hours, boredom, fatigue, sore feet, a bad back. He had a sudden craving for a drink. He could almost taste the smooth bite of tequila, the lime, the salt—when his body tensed.

A dark van with tinted windows pulled into the slot on the far side of Manny Dunn's Buick. Headlights off. New Mexico plates. Music drifted from the radio—Bruce Springsteen.

Matt heard the car door slam, footsteps, and he glanced over at the D.P.S. surveillance van. Everything was quiet. Nothing that might scare off their guy.

The man was on the other side of the vehicle, walking around the front fender, heading toward the toilets. Matt squinted through the warm night air. Moths buzzed around the fluorescent safety lights. The contrast between dark and harsh light made it hard to see.

Five feet ten, one hundred seventy pounds, hair that brushed the collar under a low cowboy hat—and walking right into the women's toilet.

*That was a woman?*

Two seconds later, the same guy came out of the women's and walked into the men's. *Looked embarrassed as hell, like he'd screwed up.*

Matt tasted heat in his mouth—the whole thing felt hinky. Then his eyes were drawn to the high windows of the men's toilet. When had the light gone out?

SYLVIA WINCED AS the Volvo shuddered over a particularly nasty rut. Her window was open and the scent of salt cedar, fish, and desert flowers permeated the car. In midsummer the river was usually low; still, she heard the sound of water rushing over small falls. The road snaked right, then left, following the natural undulations of the Chama.

Her thoughts drifted to Matt, and she wished she was curled up on the couch, in his arms, watching an old black-and-white movie starring Carole Lombard or Jean Harlow. All at once it hit her, the melancholic edge that sometimes accompanied the liminal movements of twilight. As the Volvo rounded a corner, Sylvia saw the headlamps of a car parked by a river turnout. For fifty feet the parallel beams of light cut horizontal slices out of trees, rock, and earth; instead of reassuring, they only intensified the canyon's loneliness. When she followed the road around another bend, the lights were gone and the world returned to half-light.

She began to hum "Mi Corazón," a Spanish love song. She realized she'd chosen a song her mother, Bonnie, had sung to her when she was five or six years old. It was Bonnie's whistling-in-the-dark tune. She fingered the tiny scar by her left eye, her fingers tracing the familiar ridge of tissue.

She sighed, downshifted, and slowed to avoid the debris of a minilandslide that had peppered the road with rocks. She knew that boulders as big as cars had been known to land in the road. When that happened, road crews and front-loaders were summoned from Española or Abiquiu, and any traffic came to a standstill while the crews completed their laborious task.

She jammed on her brakes to keep the Volvo from colliding with a stranded vehicle that blocked the roadway.

A tire jack, lit by the beams from her headlights, was leaning against the rear bumper. The driver wasn't visible . . . and there didn't seem to be enough space for the Volvo to pass.

Sylvia wondered if the car belonged to hikers, kayakers, or pilgrims on their way to the monastery. She shifted into reverse, began to back up, to see if there was another route around the vehicle. As her headlights grazed the car, she realized that none of the tires looked flat.

She was instantly alert and rolled up the Volvo's window—the car was warm and claustrophobic and the engine ticked as it idled. She inched back, then forward, and back again. But the rear tires of the Volvo suddenly rolled over a barrier and spun out. She was high-centered; the car wasn't going anywhere.

Abruptly, a shape materialized beside her door. A tree of a man. When he yanked on the door handle, her foot hit the accelerator. The engine wailed but the Volvo didn't budge.

There was a dull crunch as a tire iron smashed against the side window. Sylvia jerked her head away and grabbed her keys from the ignition, but they dropped through her fingers. She reached automatically for the glove compartment and her gun before she remembered it wasn't there. She pushed aside papers and maps searching for anything that might serve as a weapon. Her fist closed around a long metal can opener.

With the impact of a second blow, the window caved inward. The tire iron thrust through glass—it was driven by a fat hand. Sylvia slashed at the man's knuckles and he cried out. She scrambled across the seat away from the driver's door.

Her attacker was verbalizing, but his words were garbled, choppy. Even in panic, Sylvia thought the voice sounded familiar. Her mind sorted out the reasons for his indecipherable tirade: he was drunk, high, enraged, and/or psychotic. None of the possibilities was encouraging.

*Thwack!*

The tire iron penetrated the window again and tiny particles of glass rained into the car. Sylvia wrenched up on the passenger-door handle and jammed her shoulder against the door. She stumbled out of the Volvo, regained her balance, and took off running. She knew he was pursuing her; she was moving fast and was terrified she would trip and fall. She headed uphill without thinking. Almost instantly she realized that many areas of the cliff wall would be impassable above fifteen or twenty feet.

With each stride her feet hit the ground on faith and her eyes barely made out the rugged trail. As she lunged along the path, she prayed it led up into the cliffs instead of dwindling to nothing or, worse, trapping her at a dead end. When she looked over her shoulder, she could no longer see a figure hurtling along behind her. Had she gained ground that quickly? Or had he taken some other route?

She caught her breath and listened. The rush of the river seemed far away. So did the civilized world. Pain crackled up her left instep; prickly pear spines had penetrated the leather of her shoe. She tried to pull out the thickest spine, but it stabbed the soft flesh under her thumb.

Her instincts told her it was too quiet and she dashed another hundred feet before she was exhausted, gasping for breath. She stopped again and heard the faint sound of sliding rock. Had it come from behind or overhead? She squatted behind a clump of chamisa that had clawed its roots into the cliff side. The stiff branches of the shrub scratched her bare arms and neck. Its sharp scent tickled her throat. She slowed her breathing, afraid her ragged inhalations would betray her location.

Something dark flashed overhead. A bat? An owl? As if by magic, shapes around her slowly emerged: rocks, rabbit brush, cholla. Her eyes strained, searching for the attacker who would lunge out of the shadows. She focused on a dead tree, arms extended like a man . . . a hulking piñon . . . a squatting juniper . . . a ghostly cholla. And then she saw the dark human shape, twenty feet away, as still as a tree.

Sylvia stayed frozen—she knew he was searching for her. A terrible minute passed before she felt his eyes settle on her body.

She bolted, scrambling up the hillside. Her hands grasped at any available shrubbery for purchase. She lost track of time, and her mind fell into that static space of nightmares: she was racing uphill, gasping for breath, muscles pumping desperately. She had the terrible sensation of running in place and going nowhere.

"Wait!" He was yelling at her as he ran.

Kevin Chase. She recognized his voice now. She kept moving higher and higher up the steep canyon wall until the trail finally jammed itself up against a mass of boulders. Unless she was ready to hoist herself from rock to rock, she was boxed in. She felt the fear crawl up her legs, take her by the throat—she was trapped. And she'd dropped the can opener somewhere on the trail.

She could see everything at once—stars overhead, the river flowing deep in the canyon, her own body standing on the cliff, Kevin coming closer and closer. A jolt of adrenaline shot through her muscles, and suddenly she was very angry and ready to fight.

She reached down and felt the rocks at the edge of the trail. Her fingers worked over several that were the size of a fist; then, with both hands, she gripped a rock as large as a human head.

Even in full darkness she saw her quarry forty feet away, walking—instead of running—up the trail; she heard the sound of his breath under his nonstop verbal tirade. Eerily, even the obscenities were delivered in a conversational tone.

When Chase had gained another ten feet, Sylvia yelled down at him. "Kevin, you sonofabitch, what the hell are you doing?"

Maybe he was surprised that she recognized him, maybe he heard his shrink talking—or maybe he saw the primitive weapon. For whatever reason, he came to a standstill.

Sylvia was shaking; a deep tremor passed through her body and played itself out. There might be a chance she could talk him out of this attack—

*No! Fuck him! I want to bash his skull in!*

He took a step. And another. Now, he was twenty feet away. She gripped the rock and raised it above her head so that he was staring up at it.

Seconds ticked away; they both stood in tableau. Somewhere up the canyon a pack of coyotes yipped excitedly. The sound was heart-wrenching and forlorn. It changed abruptly and became a command to go in for the slaughter.

Kevin Chase swung the tire iron with great force and it tore branches off a piñon. He darted forward, yelling out, "The whole government stinks—they all get away with murder like Killer says—there's no justice, no nothing—it's time—I'll show you what real justice feels like—"

Something tore loose deep inside Sylvia—some emotion that was sharp and dangerous—as she saw Kevin covering the last few yards. When he was three feet in front of her, scrambling toward her legs with the tire iron, she brought the rock down with all her strength.

# SEVENTEEN

THE MEN'S TOILET had gone pitch-black with Manny Dunn still inside.

Moths battered their fragile bodies against the yellow lights outside the cinder-block building. Behind a glass box, faded orientation maps showed visitors where they had come from and where they were going. The rest stop was quiet.

Matt whispered into his radio, "I'm coming down." Then he moved silently forward, closing in on the welcome center and facilities. When he was parallel with the D.P.S. van, his fingers played over the butt of his Colt, warming up.

All his energy focused on the darkened men's toilet as Manny Dunn appeared in the doorway. Illuminated suddenly by harsh fluorescent light, Dunn's face was haggard, his heavy shoulders sagging. He squinted into the night; it took him a moment to reorient.

A shadowy shape lurked behind Dunn; the second man had a hat pulled low over his eyes. His face wasn't visible.

Matt glanced over at the D.P.S. van and raised a thumb in a high sign: *Let's do it!*

One officer emerged from the surveillance van as Matt sprinted forward. The other man on his team closed in from the bushes on the north side of the building. In less than thirty seconds, they had both men restrained on the ground. Dunn was silent, but the other man was protesting loudly about his violated civil rights. He wasn't Kevin Chase.

Now, Matt could hear someone yelling from behind the cinder-block toilet. He took cover at the edge of the building.

He yelled, "Police! Come out. Put your hands on your head!"

Suddenly, there was silence. Just the swish of cars on the highway and the hum of powerful overhead lights.

Finally, a young teenage boy stumbled around the side of the building. He was followed closely by a hulking shadow: Special Agent Dan Chaney.

Chaney said, "I don't suppose this is your guy?"

Matt shook his head. "What the hell are you doing here, Dan?" He turned abruptly and found himself face-to-face with a frightened girl on her way to the women's bathroom. She glared at him suspiciously. He motioned her by, too distracted to explain he was a cop.

Chaney snorted. "The same as you. Trying to pop Kevin Chase. We got zip."

THE ROCK CLIPPED Kevin's left hand and mashed his knee. He toppled—rolled—and his head bounced off a juniper stump. A shower of tiny lights exploded behind his eyelids. He tried to stand but the pain in his leg made him fall back, heaving.

When his vision cleared, he could barely make out Sylvia crouched like a predatory bird twenty feet uphill. He groaned and reached out for a handhold, but surrendered when the earth began to give way.

SYLVIA WATCHED, GRIMLY triumphant, as Kevin was swept down with the wash of shale and arid topsoil. After he had disappeared from sight, small sounds—grunts and cries—reached her from halfway down the cliff side. How badly was he injured? She waited, prepped, ready to defend herself again. The sounds of the rock slide gradually faded away. It was quiet. Even the coyotes were silent.

Reluctantly she took the first few steps from the natural cul-de-sac. Her legs almost collapsed under her, almost refused to carry her forward. On the path, she was exposed and vulnerable to surprise attack; she prayed that Kevin Chase had taken the worst the primitive bludgeon could inflict. She cut off the path and headed across the hillside, away from the cars below.

Very recently, and very close by, a skunk had discharged its glandular toxins. The potent odor stayed with Sylvia as she continued down the cliff.

When she was almost to the road, she could see both cars, but they were just dim shapes in the distance. Her keys were back there somewhere—she prayed Kevin Chase was, too. She started west over rough terrain, toward the monastery.

All around, the sounds she heard were night sounds: crickets, owls, a fox. And under everything else, the never-ending rush of the dark river. She flushed a rodent from its nocturnal lair, and her stomach twisted uncomfortably when it scrambled through the underbrush. There was no sign, no sound, of Kevin, but she felt his presence.

She calculated that she had three or four miles to walk. If she pushed herself, she could make it in under an hour. The moon was just cresting the canyon rim. That gave her light; it also made her visible to Kevin. She would stay off the road and travel parallel to the river.

The terrain was much more hostile than Sylvia had imagined. Little black bugs attacked her bare arms and face, leaving red welts that she forced herself not to scratch. Clumps of rabbit brush clawed at her legs. She stumbled over tufts of buffalo grass, and once she tripped in what she thought was a gopher hole. Finally, fear that she would twist her ankle or wrench her knee forced her closer to the road.

She was rounding a curve when she heard the low throb of a car engine, and she dashed for cover behind a tree. She waited, heart in mouth, but no vehicle appeared. After a few seconds, she moved on cautiously. She found she felt safest when she walked on the shoulder of the road. While her body covered ground, her mind worked like a separate animal.

The sound of breaking branches shocked Sylvia back into her body; she was instantly aware of every breath she took. On her left, toward the river, something was moving through a stand of salt cedars. She stopped, her body rigid. The air, suddenly cooler, made her shiver. She screamed when a giant beast thrust its head through the brush and stared at her.

*A cow . . . a fucking cow.* She was so grateful to see the animal she wanted to throw her arms around its neck.

She took to the center of the road and maintained a slow, steady jog. When she had covered what felt like two miles, she stopped, caught her breath, and then looked up. The entire sky seemed to have burst open, spilling glitter—the Milky Way, the Dippers, and Venus. She rounded a corner and saw faint lights, earthbound and lonely; she hoped they belonged to the monastery.

WHEN VESPERS ENDED, it was the duty of Brother Ashok to close up the chapel. Although the warmth of the sun was now gracing his birthplace—Bombay, India—he sensed the last wash of light in the charcoal sky visible through the glass wall. That sky was what he loved the most about the monastery—glass kept the heavens available.

The door to the chapel stood open and Brother Ashok heard a scale of staccato yips, the excited and complex symphony of a coyote pack. He stood in the middle of the chapel floor, eyes closed, broom unmoving, and calculated the animals' distance at less than fifty yards. Hours earlier he had put out table scraps—although Brother Xavier had warned him against encouraging wild creatures. But he had spent hours tracking them during the days when he had free time.

Brother Ashok sighed, opened his eyes, and found himself staring at an apparition. A person—a woman—was standing in the doorway. Even in the dim light he could see that her eyes were wild, her hair and clothes disheveled, and she was breathing quick and hard. But her voice was calm when she spoke.

She said, "I just tried to kill someone." She seemed to hear her own words, and her dark eyes widened in disbelief. She shook her head. "No—he tried to kill me."

Brother Ashok lifted his broom several inches from the floor. He spoke softly to the woman as if she were an untamed creature. "What is the usual procedure in a case like this?"

"Call the police?" She shifted her weight, and braced one hip and shoulder against the door frame.

"Which police?" Brother Ashok asked. He saw she was trembling and he moved toward her and held out a hand.

"Española? The state police. A friend of mine is staying here; Rosie Sanchez." She spoke softly. Her pupils were dilated and her olive skin was flushed. Suddenly words poured out: "God, I wanted to kill him, but he tried to kill me, I couldn't do anything, but I know him, he's my client—"

The priest squeezed her hand firmly and nodded. "Let's go find your friend, and we'll use the radio phone. Española police, you say?"

She said, "No . . . Matt England with the state police in Santa Fe."


THE SKY PALED with gradual and diffuse light—a dark velvet sponge absorbing a smoky wash. The stars were extinguished like distant candles. Below the monastery, the Chama River aligned itself for the easy race through the shallows. From her place on the bank Sylvia was lulled by the soft, clear chanting of male voices. Her gaze settled on the meadow beyond the river; her eyes lingered on the buffalo grass and yellow daisies just becoming visible with predawn light.

She sat without obvious motion, but everything inside her seemed to follow the rhythm and flow of the river. Her mind balanced between each inhalation, each exhalation. There was nothing but the serenity of emptiness and connection.

She knew only that some time had passed when her thoughts pulled themselves from the watery silence, shook themselves off, and demanded attention. She let the stillness go.

What came to mind was Violet . . . in a padded cell in California.

*I know you . . . you're the killer's doctor.*

Sylvia had made a career of her ability to contain the most extreme, the most violent emotions of other humans. It brought satisfaction and it brought complications. Sometimes she believed it nourished her own darkness.

She felt a presence behind her just as she heard Rosie's voice. "Sylvie?"

Sylvia smiled, but she turned her face away and gazed out at the meadow. "I scared myself out there last night."

"He tried to kill you." Rosie sat next to her friend. Her face was highly expressive and her features changed constantly, but subtly, like colors in a sunset sky. The brothers had managed to work the radio telephone—never an easy task—and a call had gone through to Matt a little more than six hours ago. State police had discovered Sylvia's Volvo on the road. But they found no sign of Kevin Chase or his car. He was still a fugitive.

On the surface, Sylvia seemed to be coping well enough—although she was unable to sleep, unable to come down from the adrenaline rush. Rosie knew a distressed soul when she saw one.

Sylvia looked up at her friend. "I came here to help you. I came because you always help me—you're always there when I need you."

"I know." Rosie took Sylvia's hands and squeezed them gently. "*Jita*, you have this way of getting into trouble."

THE WOMEN BEGAN to walk when the first full rays of sun streaked the sky from the east. They made their way down to the rocky bank to stand at the edge of the river. Although the air was cool, they took off their shoes and socks and set them carefully on the shore. The initial touch of icy water sent electricity along Sylvia's spine; the charge felt good. She found footing on stone after smooth river stone. Once, she slipped from the rocks and a jagged submerged branch cut into her flesh. But the wound was slight and the cold water numbed any real pain. When Rosie reached the opposite shore, she stood on the rough bank and held one hand out to her friend.

They found a soft place to sit. After a few moments, Rosie said, "When I heard I was actually going to get fired, I forgot about taking rational, legal action, and instead I thought about tearing the warden's balls off."

Sylvia murmured, "That would get his attention."

"Then I thought about going to his house, waiting outside, and doing . . . something bad. I don't even know what. It's like my rage connected me to him. I felt this intimacy with this man I despise." Rosie shook her head. "It was weird." She sighed. "A woman's rage is much more frightening than a man's, don't you think?"

After a long silence, Sylvia spoke. "It's like looking into a well shaft . . . it has no end . . . it goes down and down and never stops." Her eyes had lost their shine; they were dull, lifeless. Then she blinked, and the pupils changed again—they gleamed.

Rosie tucked her fingers around her knees. "Since I've been up here I've had time to think. Women don't know how to deal with their own power and everything that comes with it—all the destructive forces." She sighed. "Maybe we feel more comfortable in the role of victim because we've had so much practice."

Sylvia turned to stare at Rosie.

"You know what Jesus says in the Gnostic text?" Rosie asked.

"When did you read that?"

Rosie smiled wryly. "When you question your faith every day, you read a lot. Even heresy."

"What does Jesus say?"

"If you bring forth what is within you, what you bring forth will save you. If you do not bring forth what is within you, what you do not bring forth will destroy you."

THE WOMEN LEFT the monastery before eight; they would reach Santa Fe by ten-thirty, give or take a few minutes. Rosie led the way in her husband's four-wheel-drive pickup. Sylvia followed in the Volvo, which was still smudged with a mess of gray fingerprint powder. As they drew closer to the highway, they passed vans loaded with rafters arriving to embark on a journey down the Chama. Some of the rafts were already in the water, bouncing and jolting over white waves. The riders looked sunburned, spirited, and intent on their work. But it was the stark majesty of the canyon in full sunlight that really drew the eye.

# EIGHTEEN

IT WAS ALMOST eleven when Rosie Sanchez parked in her own driveway. She walked into her living room and she saw her husband, Ray, and her son, Tomás, perched on the couch. Neither man noticed Rosie's entrance. Their eyes were glued to the television.

She looked at the screen. A titan—orange hair spiked, face painted white and purple—was pounding on a smaller man who was the color of milk chocolate and who sported a loincloth and feathered headdress. Both men were professional hulks and their arena was the world of pro wrestling.

The titan hammered his opponent's face into the floor, and Ray took that opportunity to glance up. His face brightened, and he stood and enveloped Rosie in his arms. Then he led her to the sofa where she claimed a place between the two men in her life.

Tomás put one arm around his mother as Ray asked, "How are you? How's Sylvia?"

Rosie had called her husband from Bodes General Store in Abiquiu that morning to tell him she was on her way home. Now she reassured him that both she and Sylvia were reasonably functional.

Ray squeezed Rosie's thigh with his big hand. He'd taken the day off from work at the highway department.

245

His concern for his wife overrode his sense of duty to the state.

Rosie yawned. After Sylvia's ordeal, her own worries, and a night without sleep, she was exhausted. She snuggled back into the sofa and felt a lazy and comforting sense of well-being. She was secure in her life, if not in her job.

On the television screen, the wrestler in the loincloth took a flying leap at the titan. While he flew through the air, his headdress buoyed out like a horsetail. At the last moment the titan shifted, and the other man slapped into the ropes. Both Ray and Tomás groaned loudly.

Ray stood and pulled Rosie up by one arm. He said, "Let me make you some lunch."

"Breakfast." She smiled, nodded, and followed him into the kitchen. She watched him work expertly, coffeepot on the burner, frying pan warmed, eggs cracked and scrambled. Before he could pour the eggs into the pan, Rosie stopped him.

She said, "Let's go into the bedroom."

Ray's eyes widened. "Now?"

"Why not? It's not every weekday we get to . . . hang out."

"You mean fool around?" He allowed himself to be led into their bedroom. Even with the door closed, the faint noise of the television was still audible. Rosie drew the floral curtains closed until there was just a narrow shaft of sunlight entering the room. She joined her husband on the bed where he had sprawled out against a soft pile of pillows.

She said, "Raymond, you know how much I love my work."

"Sure." He ran his fingers along her cheek and sighed. "But sometimes you've got to roll with the punches." His voice softened to a whisper. "You don't work for the Department of Corrections anymore, *jita*. Maybe it's time to face that fact."

Rosie pulled herself up from the feathery tangle of sheets. She wasn't angry that he wanted her off the job. For years he'd put up with the hours, the worry, and the stress that came with a job at the penitentiary. She was grateful for his patience, and for his love. Ultimately, he would go along with her decision to reclaim her position as penitentiary investigator, even if he didn't like her choice of job. And Rosie knew that Sylvia would support her all the way through the legal system.

She said, "I'm going to take this to the courts if I have to; Sylvia's going to talk to Juanita Martinez."

Ray shook his head cautiously. Martinez was a lawyer with a reputation for busting balls—actually, pulverizing *cojones*. He said, "Lawsuits and lawyers and dirty politics—we're not kids anymore."

Rosie held her hand to her chin. Against her olive skin, her maraschino nails shone with a hard gleam. "You think it's a midlife crisis? You think I want my job back so I can prove I'm not getting old?"

"You *are* getting old. So am I, *jita bonita*. Let the young people do the dangerous work." Ray batted at the rumpled sheets impatiently.

Rosie covered Ray's lips with her hand. "Tomás is young. You want a boy like our son in my job?" She spoke her son's name with the accent on the second syllable; his name was a worry bead collected from her grandfather, who spoke only Spanish and refused to embrace the Anglo world. "I think my age, my experience, gives me value, an expertise that a kid in a three-piece suit doesn't have, no matter what fancy college he graduates from." For a moment, anger sharpened her eyes and flushed her cheeks.

Ray put his arm around Rosie. He pulled her gently

to his body and hugged her. His heart turned over with helpless longing. Here was someone he loved completely.

In her ear he whispered what he felt.

Rosie raised her mouth to his. A shaft of milky light washed over their bodies as they fell into the familiar refuge of each other.

MATT STOOD IN the hallway of the Department of Public Safety's basement and listened to the *tap-tap-tap* of computer keyboards. Through the closest doorway he saw three women seated in front of computer monitors. They were entering data into the N.C.I.C. system from recent crimes and arrests.

As if she sensed his presence, Jackie Madden turned to stare at Matt. She looked the way she always looked—very neat and well dressed. Her pale, freckled skin was flushed, and her sandy reddish hair framed her face with baby-soft waves. She didn't look like a woman who was guardian of a fugitive wanted for murder and—most recently—assault. Matt nodded to Jackie and approached her workstation. Calmly she returned her attention to her computer screen and her hands tripped over white keys.

He touched her shoulder lightly because, like the other word processors, she was wearing a headphone. He said, "Jackie?"

Now her hands slowed to a stop. She removed the headset without looking up. Her voice was almost inaudible over the continued tapping of keys. She said, "Is Sylvia all right?"

One of the other processors—a petite woman with a long black braid—glanced up curiously from her work.

Matt said, "She's doing fine. Can we go somewhere and talk for a few minutes?"

Jackie Madden stood and followed him out into the

empty hall. She waited with her arms held stiffly at her sides, and distress flashed across her face. Matt ushered her into an empty kitchenette where employees took their coffee breaks.

He spoke softly. "The longer he's out there, the worse it gets. Where is he, Jackie?"

"I don't know. I haven't talked to him since they found Jesse Montoya's body. . . ." Her voice faded away. Her eyes focused on anything but Matt.

"Who were his friends? Who was he involved with?"

"I already told Terry Osuna, I don't *know*." She shook her head in frustration. "He wasn't that social. I mean, he hung out with someone in Pojoaque sometimes. But I never knew who it was. A woman, I think."

Matt hadn't been present when Jackie Madden was interviewed by Criminal Agent Terry Osuna, but he'd talked to Osuna after the fact. Jackie Madden had been a dead end when it came to Kevin's friends. Now, she was suddenly coming up with a place, a person.

He asked, "What made you think it was a woman?"

"I guess, the way he kept her a secret from me."

"Do you believe Kevin was involved in a sexual relationship?" Matt thought about the information Sylvia had relayed to him right after Jesse Montoya's murder: Kevin Chase had tried to hide chafe marks on his wrists.

"Why do you people keep asking me the same questions over and over? Can't you leave me alone?" Tears spilled from Jackie Madden's eyes. She brushed them away when a coworker, the woman with the dark braid, passed by the kitchenette and disappeared down the hall.

Jackie set her shoulders. "I thought he'd come back to me . . . I thought he'd tell me there was some mistake . . . there must be some mistake. Kevin can't be a murderer." She was crying softly. When she met Matt's gaze, she said, "Please go away. Just go away."

As Matt walked down the hall, he wondered why Jackie Madden had ever taken on the responsibility of Kevin Chase. He would be a burden for anyone. Certainly for a young woman who seemed to be without connections. But perhaps that explained it—Kevin was Jackie's *family*.

He turned the corner, and an arm extended out the doorway of the women's bathroom, and a tiny hand tapped him gingerly. The processor with the braid.

Her voice was faint, and he had to lower his head to hear her words. She said, "I think maybe I know why Kevin Chase would want to kill one of them."

Matt nodded encouragement.

"To kill a rapist." The woman pursed her lips in distaste after uttering the last word. "This is secret, but . . . Jackie told us she was raped . . . a couple of years ago. She never reported it, but Kevin knew." She lifted her chin and gazed at Matt.

He said, "Jackie Madden told you she was raped?"

The tiny woman looked embarrassed. "Well, no . . . not exactly, but I heard her talking to Kevin once on the phone. Don't tell on me, okay?"

As Matt left the D.P.S. building, he considered the best way to follow up on this new information. But right now, he had something that took priority.

He cruised across Cerrillos, past Villa Linda Mall, to Rodeo Road. Although he hit every red light along the route, it only took him minutes to reach Erin Tulley's home.

"Did your conscience get the best of you?" Erin Tulley stood in her doorway, arms crossed, and she allowed Matt a half smile. But when she saw the anger on his face, her smile faded.

She spoke quickly. "What's wrong?"

"You tell me." Matt pushed his way past her into the

house. He crossed the living room and entered a hallway. He thrust the bathroom door open with one hand. The small room was spotless, the air was hot and close from a recent shower.

Erin had followed him down the hall, and she confronted him. "Who the hell are you looking for, Matt? I'm alone."

He continued a few more feet to the bedroom at the end of the hall. The room was a mess, bed unmade, clothes strewn everywhere.

Erin grabbed him by the arm and pulled him from the doorway. She slammed the door and stood in front of it. "Do you think I've got another lover hidden away?"

"That's not my business anymore."

She set her hands on her hips. "I don't fall in love easily, Matt."

He shook his head impatiently. "I don't want to play games with you. Did you set me up?"

Suddenly she understood what he was asking. Her expression softened. She said, "Something went wrong with the Manny Dunn stakeout."

Matt was standing in the center of the hallway, feet planted. "Erin, I need to know who your snitch is." In the silence that followed his words, Matt heard the low hum of the swamp cooler.

Erin made up her mind. "Kiki Moore, at the Cock 'n' Bull."

Matt didn't hide his surprise. Kiki. The bartender he'd questioned last week about Anthony Randall's kidnapping and murder. The bartender who lived in Pojoaque. Just thirty minutes ago, Jackie Madden had mentioned that Kevin might be involved with a woman in Pojoaque.

Matt nodded brusquely to Erin and turned to leave. But she stopped him. She said, "That's it? You're just going to walk out?"

He glanced at his watch: ten-forty. "I'm going to the Cock 'n' Bull."

"You think I lied to you?"

"I don't know." For the first time since Matt had arrived at the house, he really looked at Erin. Her light brown hair was pulled back from her face and fastened with a turquoise clip. Her skin was still pale, but she had brushed a light coating of blush on her cheeks. Her lips were tinted with lipstick. She smelled of honeysuckle. Her Levi's looked freshly washed, and her cotton shirt had been pressed. He thought then how little he knew her, even though they'd been lovers.

She read his mind. She said, "It's impossible for you to trust me, isn't it?"

He didn't answer. And her voice was so soft, he barely heard her speak again. She said, "You're wrong about this."

Suddenly he doubted himself. Why did he have to blame Erin? Maybe Kevin Chase had set them all up. Or maybe the snitch was bad.

Matt felt something slipping away. But he couldn't quite let go of his anger—or his blame.

Erin walked past him into the foyer and held open the front door. As he stepped out, she was silent.

Sunlight hit him square in the eye; for a moment he was blinded. He heard Erin's voice clearly. "Please don't come back again."

And with that, she closed the door gently.

SYLVIA WALKED THROUGH her office door at a few minutes before eleven, and she knew instantly that she'd made a mistake. She should have driven straight from the monastery to her home.

Marjorie was frantically waving her bangled arm in the air. The receptionist had the phone handset pressed to her ear—she clamped one palm over the mouthpiece and whispered, "I think it's one of your clients, but I didn't get his name. He sounds bad. Line one."

Inside her office, she picked up the phone. "This is Sylvia Strange."

"Dr. Strange, I'm really sorry. . . ."

"Who is this?" Before she finished speaking she was at the door, signaling Marjorie to join her in the office. Then she moved back to her desk, found pencil and pad, and sank down into the chair.

He said, "I took some pills."

"What kind of pills?" Sylvia tried to keep her voice slow and steady while she scribbled words on the notepad. Marjorie stared down at the message: "Call Matt, tell him I've got Dupont White on the phone!"

"Are you there, Doctor? You care about me, don't you? You're still the Killers' Doctor. . . ."

Sylvia said, "I'm here." She watched Marjorie dart from the room. "How many pills did you take?"

"You know who this is, don't you?"

"Dupont."

"Call me Killer." His voice died to a whisper. "I don't think we'll have to go through this again, Dr. Strange."

"Where are you?" She didn't know what Dupont was up to, but she was damn sure he hadn't overdosed on pills.

He said, "Cerrillos . . . motel . . . the bird."

Sylvia tried to remember the names of the motels on Cerrillos Road. She grabbed the phone book from under her desk and flipped to motels. "Are you at the Thunderbird?"

"No . . ."

Marjorie was back, waving the handset, motioning a thumbs-up. Sylvia nodded to the receptionist and spoke into her own phone. "The Roadrunner?"

"The Roadrunner . . ." Killer was fading out.

"What's your room number?"

"Seven."

Outside Sylvia's office, Marjorie was whispering the information to Matt at D.P.S.

Sylvia said, "I'll be there. I'm going to send a paramedic team—"

*Click.* Killer was gone.

MATT'S CAPRICE AND A state police unit were parked a hundred yards south of the Roadrunner Motel on Cerrillos Road. Sylvia saw the two empty vehicles, cut across traffic, and guided the Volvo into the adjacent used-car lot. She slammed the door and strode toward the motel. She wasn't sure what to expect—a SWAT team, another murdered sex offender, a police barricade—but no one stopped her progress.

She slowed only when she rounded the side of the motel and saw an emergency medical transport vehicle in the middle of the lot. An E.M.T. walked out of Number 7. He was a young man, early twenties, and he wore the uniform of emergency response team personnel.

The E.M.T. shook his head when he saw her. "No one there."

Sylvia brushed past the man and entered Room 7. She almost bumped into Matt.

He said, "The door was open when we got here. We've checked the other rooms, but they're empty. No suicides."

Sylvia tried to center herself. She was still pumped up on crisis adrenaline, she was angry, and she was sick of Dupont's mind games.

The E.M.T. poked his head in the doorway. "You want us to hang around?"

Sylvia stared blankly at the man. Matt said, "Give us another minute."

The man shrugged and left the room. Through dirty windows Sylvia could see a dry, weed-ridden field, and a for-sale sign: 36 ACRES ZONED INDUSTRIAL/PARK AND PARK REALTY—WE BUILD YOUR DREAMS.

The Roadrunner had the dubious distinction of being the last motel over the age of thirty still standing on the south end of Cerrillos Road. It was shaped in a horseshoe and the undeveloped acreage butted up against the motel's southern edge. Beyond the field someone had tried to start a used-car lot, and wreckers still dotted the landscape. She could see her own Volvo; it fit right in with the other wrecks.

Although her view to the north was obscured by the motel's office, Sylvia knew that Sue-Ann's Curls and Cuts, Andy's Suds, and a shoe repair shop occupied a dejected-looking strip mall.

Through the open door Sylvia saw the E.M.T. lighting up a cigarette. Behind him Criminal Agent Terry Osuna strode across the lot from the office.

She stopped in the doorway and greeted Sylvia with a nod. The bulge under her thin jacket was a Colt .45. She said, "No one in the office, Matthew. Sign says they're out to lunch."

Matt said, "I bet they're always out to lunch. This place is a shit hole."

Sylvia turned her attention from Matt and Terry Osuna and surveyed the room. It was small and dingy: one room and bath. The stench of cigarette smoke lingered in the air. A varnished desk rested against the wall below the window. A Bible had been left on the desk. Pushed into one corner, a white-painted dresser stood like a fat man. A television was perched on the dresser. The bathroom and closet were situated off the adjacent wall.

On the other side of the room a sagging double bed had been made up; the green, fringed coverlet was smooth. Framed above the headboard: a faded print of an exotic saguaro cactus and a roadrunner. The artist had rendered dark mountains in the picture's background; Sylvia guessed they were the Superstitions outside Tucson. There was a small table and lamp on one side of the bed, a chair on the other. Two rag rugs covered much of the painted flooring.

She walked to the bathroom and stood in the doorway. The small porcelain sink was stained; water beaded and dripped, beaded and dripped in the mineralized aureole.

The shower curtain was drawn, and Sylvia experienced the abrupt, panicky thought that someone was hidden behind the curtain, in the stall.

She grasped a corner of the plastic curtain and tugged it open. The stall was empty.

The medicine cabinet contained only a glass tumbler, a pocket packet of aspirin, and a tube of acne lotion. The toilet had a permanent westerly list.

Sylvia stumbled out of the bathroom, suddenly anxious to get away from this dreary, anonymous catchall for those who were about to reach bottom after a long skid.

The E.M.T. now stood behind Terry Osuna. He said, "We're gonna take off unless you want to try something else?"

"No, I think you might as well split." Criminal Agent Osuna's voice faded as she stepped outside with the E.M.T. Matt followed them.

Without moving, he and Terry Osuna watched the orange-and-white emergency medical vehicle pull slowly out of view. Above the motel roof, black thunderheads had elbowed out the sun. A jagged silver flash of lightning cut across the clouds; distant thunder sounded seconds later. Drought and heat made lightning a very dangerous threat to forested land. As the rumble died away, Matt felt a sense of excitement and foreboding.

Sylvia could feel it: *I'm in the right room.*

And she was here at Dupont's invitation.

*No monsters waiting to jump out at me.*

But she would bet the acne medicine belonged to Kevin Chase.

Sylvia glanced outside—past Terry Osuna and Matt—just as lightning bolted across the sky. Her mind was racing. Why had Dupont gone through such an elaborate scenario to lure her to this motel? He didn't want to kill her—he'd already had the chance. If the room was a life-size puzzle created by Dupont White, every detail was critical.

Her gaze flew around the room and came to rest on the Bible. The book was unusually large. She walked to the table and saw that it wasn't a Bible at all. She opened the black cover, stared down at the first page of a scrapbook, and she saw newspaper clippings, yellowed and brittle with age.

A scrapbook of Dupont White's career as a vigilante killer. The headlines caught her eye: BURNED BODY DISCOVERED; SEX OFFENDER MURDERED; JOHN DOE SMOLDERS; PAROLED PEDOPHILE ASSAULTED BY MASKED VIGILANTES.

Sylvia used her fingernail to flip the pages. There were more clippings—these on the murders of Anthony Randall and Jesse Montoya.

The display on the last six pages in the book cut through Sylvia's defenses. They were a series of glossy color photographs. The first two pages held pictures of a boy. He was naked, posed ritualistically. His image had been caught on film with obsessive precision: hands by his sides; front view, side view, back view, side view.

Someone had written on the bottom of the photographs with tiny, up-and-down script, neat as typed letters: D.W. SIX YEARS OLD.

The next four pages held pictures of a young, fair-haired girl. In one series she was posed like the boy; naked with her hands by her side. The printing on the photos read: J.G. FIVE YEARS OLD.

The next series showed the girl with her arms raised overhead. J.G. SEVEN YEARS OLD.

In the last series, the girl was blindfolded and bound with tape and cord. The binding was obsessively neat, symmetrical, excessive. J.G. TEN YEARS OLD.

Sylvia recognized the compulsion reflected in the images; these photographs had been taken by a hard-core pedophile. Sylvia knew the boy was Dupont White. And J.G. must be Dupont's missing cousin.

She was startled when someone touched her arm; Matt stood next to her, staring grimly down at the photographs.

SYLVIA LEFT MATT inside the room and stepped out into the parking lot. She thought she felt a mistlike drop of rain strike her cheek. The wind had come up with the thunderstorm; the trees whipped their branches. She started the walk back to her Volvo. Matt and Terry Osuna would wait at the Roadrunner for the crime techs to arrive.

She turned the corner and moved quickly along Cerrillos Road. Someone honked a horn, and she glanced up. Traffic on the roadway was heavy, moving sluggishly.

Sylvia sidestepped a plastic bag driven across asphalt by wind. She reached her Volvo and opened the door. That was when she recognized the other car.

It was thirty feet away, parked next to a deserted trailer, in the used-car lot. It looked like the same car that Kevin Chase had used to block the road to the monastery. And someone was inside. A man. She could see his head and shoulders.

She felt fear climb her back.

Was Kevin inside the car? Or was it Dupont?

Sylvia started to run toward the road, but she stopped abruptly. *Walk. Go get Matt.*

But she didn't move. She kept her eyes on the car, on the man—she could feel his eyes on her.

She hardly glanced at the faces of drivers as they rolled down Cerrillos Road at fifteen miles per hour. She began to move slowly toward the parked car. Twenty feet, fifteen, eight feet. The man inside never moved a muscle.

She could see him clearly now; she leaned toward a side window.

She stared down into Dupont White's eyes. He stared back without blinking.

His face was smeared with paint. He was smiling. He was dead.

# NINETEEN

THE OFFICE OF the Medical Investigator was located on the north campus of the University of New Mexico in Albuquerque. Matt parked the Caprice in front of the three-story concrete building in a space reserved for visitors. Sylvia was out of the car before he set the emergency brake. As he followed her across the artificially lit parking lot, he surveyed their surroundings. Albuquerque's skyline had a grayish glow. Even at eight-thirty P.M., the air was warm and sluggish.

But the heat didn't dampen the sense of relief Matt felt: Dupont White was dead; his body had been transported to Albuquerque four hours earlier. That left one more person to deal with—Kevin Chase. Matt was amazed that Kevin had managed to take out a seasoned killer like White. Chase had more balls than anyone figured. *Still, we'll get the little shit soon.*

In the campus lot, the only sign of life was a student walking a tiny dog on a long leash. The animal skittered from shrub to hydrant to bike rack; at each pee stop it raised its rear leg in military salute.

Sylvia pushed open glass doors and then faltered slightly. This was her first visit to the O.M.I. and she didn't know which direction to take.

Matt led the way through the lobby and down a short

hall to a series of offices on the ground floor. He held open double doors marked STAFF, and she entered.

The room was large and cold, and even the powerful ventilation system couldn't erase the smell of chemicals and decay. Sylvia sidestepped a man-size floor scale designed for weighing corpses as they were transported on gurneys.

She and Matt continued past a massive refrigerator system that held the most recent arrivals. A young man in a white lab coat opened the thick refrigerator door; Sylvia inhaled Freon and glimpsed a leg and a tagged toe.

They entered the main autopsy area. Incongruously, it resembled an industrial kitchen. A shiny autoclave and gleaming counters lined one wall. The sinks were large as bathtubs. Three stainless-steel autopsy tables were positioned in the center of the room. There was a body on one of the tables. Sylvia didn't look closely at the corpse; she felt as if she were violating the privacy of the dead.

Matt spoke briefly to an assistant pathologist and learned that Dupont White's body had been moved to a separate and adjoining chamber where O.M.I. staff processed floaters and stinkers—bodies that were badly decayed or otherwise damaged.

The glass-fronted chamber was empty of living occupants. An overhead duct monopolized the air space, the floor was covered with rubber matting, and the work area was designed for maximum drainage.

Sylvia gazed through the glass window at the darkened remains of Killer. Even in death, his painted features were those of the man she had viewed on videotape: high forehead, powerful Roman nose, wide, cruel mouth. His stringy brown hair was shoulder length. His skin had a yellowish blue cast, and it was covered with dark body hair. His muscles had been well developed, his physique forceful. But dwarfed by the long metal table, Dupont's body wasn't as large as she had expected. He was a far cry from the arrogant, godlike persona he had projected on tape.

The man had been a sadist. If anyone fired a mercy shot into Anthony Randall, it wasn't Dupont White.

Sylvia caught a glimpse of her face reflected in the glass. Her eyes were cold with fury. Her mouth had curled derisively. She was startled by her own image and the intensity of her expression, one of loathing for a man who had used revenge as justification for torture and murder.

The sound of running water brought her out of her thoughts. Directly behind her, she heard the clink of surgical tools and the low hum of a saw. She didn't turn around until she heard Matt's voice.

He was talking with Lee Begay, the chief medical investigator, a compact woman with strong hands and beetling brows that hovered over vigilant eyes. Although the M.I. had known Matt for more than a decade—and considered him a friend—at the moment she did not look pleased to see him. Her naturally placid features were pinched, and she kept her voice low, but her energy was tangible.

"There will not be a postmortem."

Matt shook his head in disbelief. "Why not?"

Lee Begay said, "At least there won't be a P.M. in my office. Federal agents are on their way."

Sylvia stepped away from the observation window. "The F.B.I. is taking possession of Dupont White's body?"

Lee Begay nodded crisply. "Right."

Matt absorbed this information, and Sylvia could see subtle changes register on his face. He took Lee's arm gently and guided her toward the window and the view of Dupont White. "Talk to me, Lee."

She squinted up at Matt. "You know it's too early to tell you much. We've only had him a few hours." She paused, then said, "It *is* your guy. I like you, Matthew, so we hauled ass and managed to get a fingerprint match from A.F.I.S. I know you realize we did the impossible."

Matt acknowledged Begay, "I owe you one. What about an estimated time of death?"

Begay shook her head, sighed, and set both hands on her hips. "I'll give you a range. Since he was involved in the Las Cruces warehouse explosion, the Blowout, he was alive two months ago."

Matt gestured impatiently. "Right, now tell me something I don't know."

With her little finger Lee Begay tugged on her ear, poker-faced. "He's been dead at least two weeks. Possibly a lot longer."

"Two weeks?" Matt and Sylvia stood in stunned silence.

Matt said, "But there's no decomposition—"

"No decay," Sylvia protested.

Lee Begay said, "Right. I've never frozen a body, but he weighed in at about one-eighty. Considering a time-to-weight ratio, I'd allow a week to freeze him to the bone. And probably close to that to defrost him. Your corpse was one huge ice cube. He's defrosting externally—his skin is pliable—but his organs are frozen."

Matt kept his eyes on Lee. "Then he didn't kill Anthony Randall or Jesse Montoya?"

"And he didn't attack me in the trailer." Sylvia pivoted, pressed her face against the glass, and studied Dupont White's corpse again. "Where would you freeze a body this size?"

Begay said, "In a meat freezer after you move out the

venison. He's got freezing artifact—marks, redness—
where he was crammed into a tight space."

Matt addressed the M.I.: "What was the cause of
death?"

Begay made a face. "I'm guessing. The bullet wound
in his left shoulder. But that didn't kill him right away."

"After he was shot, how long did it take him to die?"

Begay shrugged. "You can't see from here, but the skin
around the wound is sloughed off. It's puffy and black.
That's infection. Sepsis. Gas gangrene. A clostridial
organism."

Matt tipped his head impatiently. He was thinking
about Chaney's assertion that he had managed to hit
Dupont White with one round at the warehouse. He said,
"To die from gangrene, would it take days, weeks?"

Begay frowned in consideration. "Several days."

Sylvia pressed the M.I. "Could he have driven from
Las Cruces to Santa Fe with a wound like that?"

Begay's face was impassive, and her response was
slow as she considered the facts and the probabilities.
"It's not impossible. But I can't answer that question
without more information. And I won't *have* more information, thanks to the feds."

A door slammed across the room, and loud footsteps
sounded. Sylvia, Matt, and Lee Begay all looked up in
expectation of the federal agents' arrival.

It wasn't who they expected.

Dan Chaney didn't look as though he'd just driven
over from F.B.I. headquarters. Sylvia sucked in her
breath when she saw his face. Although he had made
some effort to pull himself together, the fluorescent lights
lent his skin a sickly greenish cast. Still, his hair was
combed and he was clean-shaven.

Chaney approached Matt and demanded, "Where's the
body?"

Matt took Chaney by one shoulder. "Dan, the Bureau's got agents on the way. They'll be here any minute—"

Chaney pulled away, drawn to the window of the special autopsy room. He looked in, saw Dupont White's body, and spun around toward the door.

Lee Begay stepped forward to stop Chaney from entering the chamber, but the federal agent moved too quickly. He jerked open the door, a gust of stinking air escaped, and then he was inside.

The others followed: Lee Begay and Matt, to make sure he didn't compromise the remains; Sylvia, to watch his reactions.

In the claustrophobic chamber, Dan Chaney came face-to-face with the man he had obsessively pursued for months. He stared down at his enemy. His voice was hollow when he said, "That's him." He glanced at the bullet wound in Dupont's shoulder. "I knew I hit him. Did I kill him?"

Matt said, "Yeah, Dan. You got him."

Chaney nodded, then he whirled around and exited the chamber as abruptly as he had entered.

Sylvia followed Chaney out, and collided with him when he stopped outside the main refrigerator.

A woman, an assistant pathologist, was wheeling a gurney through the wide refrigerator door. The corpse had purple toes; a white number tag fluttered from the largest digit. The woman looked surprised to see two strangers in her work area.

"Dan, please." Sylvia took the big man by the arm. She managed to move him a few inches toward the exit door. Any minute, federal agents would appear. Sylvia didn't know what would happen to Dan Chaney if he encountered his fellow agents. Maybe they would leave him alone, but she didn't think so. She thought there would be a confrontation. And she feared Chaney would lose the last shred of control he had. She had a panicky feeling that he might end up dead.

Sylvia said, "Listen to me. You've got to get out of here."

Chaney turned toward her, and his eyes were blurred with tears. He gulped air, then lowered his chin.

Footsteps sounded in the hallway just as Sylvia felt Matt beside her. Then everything happened simultaneously. Matt pushed Chaney into the open refrigerator, two men in dark suits strutted through the STAFF double doors, and Sylvia held out a hand.

She said, "The chief medical investigator is expecting you." With authority, she pointed toward the other side of the large room.

The two federal agents looked slightly surprised, and one asked, "And you are?"

"Dr. Strange."

The agents crossed the room toward Lee Begay.

Immediately, Sylvia gestured to Matt, and then the two of them ushered Dan Chaney—anchored between them like a prisoner—through the double doors and out of the autopsy area.

Outside the building, in the night air, Matt exploded. "Goddammit, Dan. You almost got hauled in! What the hell are you doing?"

Chaney pushed himself away from the others and swung around. He pressed an envelope into Sylvia's hand. He said, "Nathaniel Howzer was Roland White's attorney from 1970 to 1985. He drew up the papers when White adopted Dupont. And he knew Garret Ellington."

Chaney was inching backward as he spoke. "The membership of the Gentlemen's Club is still a well-guarded secret, but I found out this much—Devil's Den Ranch was their playground—liquor, drugs, prostitutes, you name it."

Matt jerked his head toward the building. "You better beat it, Dan. They'll be out any minute."

Sylvia stepped toward Chaney, folding the envelope in her hand. "What about Dupont's cousin?"

Chaney nodded, still moving. "Jayne Gladstone. I tracked her through 1989—she was eighteen—and she was sent to a private hospital in Phoenix. The hospital won't release her file without an official written request. But I did find out she'd tried to kill herself enough times, the family had her committed for almost a year. After she came out, I don't know. She died, she vanished, or she became a new person."

Chaney was moving quickly now. Over his shoulder he said, "I wanted to kill that fucker Dupont with my bare hands. But goddammit, I got him. At least I got him."

"KILLER IS A woman." Sylvia lifted her martini glass and swirled the last of the vodka gently.

Albert Kove signaled the waitress for another round. He and his domestic partner, Carlos Giron, had snagged a table in the back corner of El Farol. Thirty years ago the historic adobe had been a rough-and-tumble pool hall. Before that it was probably one of several ranchitos that dotted the countryside around the Santa Fe River.

Carlos leaned closer to Sylvia and frowned. "*Who's* a woman?"

Sylvia turned to her left. "What do you think, Matt? Dupont's dead, and our Killer is a woman." Her words were slightly slurred.

After leaving the O.M.I.'s office, Matt had driven them up to Santa Fe, to El Farol, for drinks with Kove and Carlos. Sylvia was hyper, but he was exhausted, and the sour smell of liquor, cocktail garnishes, and smoke assailed his nostrils. The long narrow room was dark and close. Murals had been painted on the interior wall years earlier. The thick adobe structure sagged and listed after a century of use. Usually he enjoyed El Farol's funky ambiance; tonight it left him depressed.

He rested his hand on Sylvia's arm and said, "Maybe you should lighten up on those—" He nodded toward the martini.

"Why? I've got a designated driver." She shifted her body free and smiled at Carlos and Kove. She said, "God, I'm glad to see you guys. The last twenty-four hours have been totally insane."

"We love you, too," Carlos said. He reached out his left arm and gently massaged her shoulder. "You are tense, girlfriend."

"And hungry." Sylvia looked up as the waitress arrived with a large tray of tapas: red peppers and goat cheese, grilled chicken and garlic, roasted baby potatoes with leeks.

A waiter set another icy vodka martini in front of Sylvia, who mouthed, "Bless you."

Matt looked away, but Kove caught his eye and cocked his head quizzically. He kept his voice low and said, "She's letting off steam—and it's about time. Maybe you need a little down time, too."

Matt shrugged and took the head off his Tecate.

They began to eat—Sylvia selected peppers and cheese from the tapas plates. While she stuffed herself with food, she remembered childhood dinners at the old El Farol, an incarnation more recent than the pool hall. It had been one of her father's favorites—even with the occasional drunken brawlers. Her mother had preferred more civilized restaurants like the Palace.

Carlos propped both elbows on the table. He knew about the "Polaroid murders" because Albert kept him informed of details that never made the newspapers. He was also an incurable thriller addict—an aficionado of all things lurid—and he couldn't keep the excitement from his voice. He said, "We know this guy Dupont didn't kill Randall or Montoya. So Kevin Chase did both murders, right?"

Matt leaned back in his chair and crossed his arms.

"I'm not going to discuss Kevin." Sylvia drained her martini and started in on the new cocktail. "But it wasn't Dupont because he was dead . . . it had to be someone close to him . . . someone who took on his energy, his mission."

"Do we get a clue?" Carlos asked.

Sylvia popped an olive between her lips. "Jayne Gladstone."

Matt shook his head. "Come on, Sylvia, that's enough."

Carlos looked stumped. "*Who* is Jayne Gladstone?"

Sylvia stared defiantly at Matt. "Jayne Gladstone is Dupont White's missing cousin."

Albert Kove took off his glasses and rubbed the small of his nose. "Your female killer?"

Sylvia said, "Dupont White was an exhibitionist with an avenger-destroyer complex. He documented each of his kills. It was his mission to rid the world of sex offenders. But he was also a federal informant—and each time he murdered, he rubbed the feds' nose in shit."

She tightened her fingers around the base of the martini glass. "After he was wounded in Las Cruces, Dupont drove four hundred miles—he returned to Santa Fe to finish some business."

"Business with whom?" Kove narrowed his eyes.

Sylvia said, "Nathaniel Howzer, for one."

"That's enough, Sylvia." Matt shook his head.

Carlos popped a chile into his mouth and mumbled, "I can't see the judge stuffing bodies in his freezer."

Kove said, "Hush, Carlos."

Sylvia looked like an unruly child. She said, "But Dupont really came to find his cousin, Jayne Gladstone, because—ultimately—she was the person he knew the best. They shared the same family pathology, the same traumatic history—they both suffered the same abuse."

Matt thought about the photographs of the two children that had been left at the Roadrunner Motel. Dupont White and Jayne Gladstone had not only suffered the same abuse, it had gone on for years. Those photographs hadn't been developed at any commercial lab, and Sylvia found the remains of a darkroom at Devil's Den—

Sylvia's voice interrupted his train of thought. She was saying, "Jayne Gladstone came out of a psychiatric institution in 1989 or 1990 . . . with a new identity. Imagine she had an obsessive-compulsive overlay that made her outwardly functional."

"Maybe highly functional," Kove interjected.

Sylvia tapped the table. "But she was imploding internally."

"And Dupont White appears on her doorstep." Kove nodded.

Carlos blew air through his lips and said, "Like on *The X-Files*, when the alien monster jumps from one body to another." He took a drink of beer, and a foam mustache appeared on his upper lip. "Not a pretty sight."

Kove winked at Carlos and said, "I love you because you have a special mind."

Sylvia played with the remains of a pasilla pepper on her plate. Her hair was uncombed, her face free of makeup, and she looked like a teenager when she asked, "So why not Jayne Gladstone?"

Kove took a small bite of mushroom. "A woman's got the best cover in the world."

Sylvia stretched out her arms. She could feel the vodka relaxing her muscles; it was doing more than that—she was smashed. She stared at Matt as she said, "Any cop will tell you, women can be just as aggressive as men."

Matt took a sip of his beer. "But they're not running around burning sex offenders—unless that's a new trend I haven't heard about."

Kove clasped his hands and pointed both index fingers across the table in Sylvia's direction. "What do you typically expect from a male abused in childhood?"

"Adult abuser: he becomes like his tormentor." Sylvia nodded her head impatiently. "And a female who was abused as a child typically is *re*abused as an adult. She sets up her own children for abuse. She becomes self-destructive. I know, Albert. I've worked with so many victims—and they all have the same eyes—like a deer caught in someone's headlights."

"My point exactly. Victims, not perpetrators."

Sylvia popped a green olive in her mouth. "What about Aileen Wuornos? She killed six men."

Carlos said, "Equality at last."

Sylvia suddenly felt deflated. She took a drink of her martini just as Kove asked, "What about Kevin's guardian—Jackie Madden?"

Matt lowered his voice. "She could definitely be protecting Kevin." He thought briefly about the information he had gathered from and about Jackie Madden earlier that day. Because of Sylvia's personal involvement in this case, they had shared information. But he was glad he hadn't talked to her about the possibility that Kevin's guardian had been raped. Sylvia was drunk—talking too much—and this was not the appropriate time or place to discuss Jackie Madden.

A waiter set a third round of drinks on the table and began to remove plates. Although Sylvia still had vodka in her glass, she switched to the fresh martini. As the waiter left, she bit into a green olive.

Carlos spoke up: "Maybe your killer is a woman, Sylvia, but a *man* called you to the motel."

Sylvia slipped her fingers around the stem of her cocktail glass, and vodka sloshed onto the table. "It *sounded* like a man. But a voice can be disguised."

There was an embarrassed silence at the table. Then Matt said, "Sylvia, this Jayne Gladstone theory, it doesn't add up. Like Carlos said, it's like some bullshit from *The X-Files*—this woman *becomes* Dupont White?"

"She doesn't become Dupont White. She becomes an avenging *god*. But it's not working—and that's why she left those photographs at the motel, that's why she left Dupont's body for the Killers' Doctor." Sylvia waved her arm angrily, and her martini glass flew from the table and shattered against the plaster wall.

Abruptly, she stood up. "I need oxygen." She stumbled away from the table, her chair fell backward, and she moved quickly to the exit.

Outside she gulped air. Her face felt hot, flushed by three martinis. A nicotine hunger shivered through her body. She began to walk up Canyon Road surrounded by the sounds and scents of night. In chorus, the elms whispered like tall, thin women. The musty scent of river plants hovered on the breeze. The faint sounds of laughter and applause spilled from a small restaurant where a wooden sign advertised MUCH ADO ABOUT NOTHING.

Warm wind brushed Sylvia's hair from her face, and she was surprised to feel tears streaming down her cheeks. The images flashed through her brain—faces she saw when she could no longer find sleep. Faces of the dead and faces of killers. Victims and abusers. Flora Escudero. Anthony Randall. Jesse Montoya. Dupont White. They haunted her.

She whispered, "I can't do this anymore."

A shadow became two shadows, lovers standing arm in arm next to the road. She felt their eyes as she passed.

She moved quickly, almost frantically. *Jayne was the good child, Dupont was the bad. Black and white. Light and shadow. Total polarity. A splitting off, until Dupont died. His death created a psychic black hole that sucked Jayne inside. There must have been other stressors in her life—pushing her toward the edge. Law and order had already failed her. And she took over Dupont's mission.*

Sylvia cried out when she felt fingers close around her arm. She jerked around and stared into Matt's face.

He said, "What are you doing out here?"

"I had to get away."

"You're drunk."

"Arrest me." She pulled away from him, exhausted, sick. She knew she sounded ridiculous. Her head was throbbing with pain. She held out both wrists. "I'll help you control this situation. Do your job—cuff me."

He started to laugh, but the sound caught in his throat.

She rambled on, "The problem is, I need to figure things out . . . I always need to understand, to evaluate every-fucking-thing and get inside it until I'm crazy."

He shook his head impatiently. "Fine—"

"I know who killed Anthony Randall and Jesse Montoya."

"Right. Jayne Gladstone. We've been through this."

"Erin Tulley."

Matt jerked back as if he'd been punched.

Sylvia reached out one arm. "Just listen to me. It fits. Jayne Gladstone is Erin Tulley. She's the right age. She's in law enforcement—she's been exposed to violence. State police gave her the structure she needed to contain her rage, until she turned against it—"

Sylvia knew she was talking too fast. She swayed on

her feet, hazy from alcohol. And Matt just stared at her like she was crazy.

She drew back, stung by his reaction. "Why don't you say something?"

"I'm thinking."

She squared her shoulders, ran a hand over her rumpled shirt. "What?"

Matt sighed. "I'm trying to decide how much to tell you."

Sylvia stiffened. Hurt. And Matt's eyes were sad. Even in moonlight, she could see them clearly.

He spoke slowly, in a very quiet voice. "You're wrong about Erin. She has real problems . . . but they're not what you think." He was silent for a moment while he waited for a man and his dog to pass out of earshot.

Finally, Matt continued. "I'll trust you to keep this confidential. Erin's been in treatment for almost a year. With a psychiatrist in Albuquerque."

Sylvia blurted it out: "Who does she see?"

"Burt Webster." Matt bit his lip. He was ashamed of Sylvia's desperation, of her need to indict Erin for murder.

"Shit . . ." Sylvia bent her head and groaned. She didn't like Burt Webster, but she knew he was damn good at his job. He deserved his reputation as one of the best in the business.

Quietly, Matt said, "Your killer may be a woman, but it's not Erin Tulley."

KEVIN FELT HER fingernails dig deep into his flesh as Killer rolled him over and straddled his belly. She had that smile on her face. He turned his head away.

She whispered. "If you don't help me, I'll have to get someone else."

Silence. He could keep his mouth shut and whatnot.

"Don't I take care of you, Kevin?" Her voice had darkened, and now it held menace, made him shiver. "Look at me!"

He looked. And whispered, "Yeah."

"You're a murderer. You killed two men."

"No, I didn't—"

"You'll get the death penalty." She slapped his cheek, and he cried out. She said, "That's because you didn't listen. From the beginning you haven't trusted me. You haven't really surrendered yourself."

Slowly—his eyes never leaving her face—he slid his thumb between his lips. After his fiasco on the monastery road, she had agreed to take him back on one condition— follow orders.

And he'd done that. He left the car and its silent passenger near the motel. But even that wasn't enough.

She moved her mouth close to his and whispered, "That's right, baby."

The muscles in her short arms rippled. She was a medium-boned woman, but her body was lean and muscular.

"Bad boy," she crooned, "you're my bad boy." She stroked his chest. "Why don't you do what Killer tells you to do, bad boy?" She raked her fingernails gently across his nipples. "Shouldn't Kevin be good?"

As he sucked on his thumb, Kevin's eyes began to close; the whites of his eyeballs were visible under half-closed lids.

His eyes shot open as she raised herself up on her haunches.

He cried out, "No, don't—"

"Don't what?"

"Don't hurt me."

"Don't hurt me what?"

"Don't hurt me, Killer."

"Don't hurt me, Killer, what?"

"Don't hurt me, Killer, please."

Her voice was sweet and slow, but poison. She crooned, "That's what you like, Kevin. You like it when I'm strict with you." With one hand, she grabbed the roll of duct tape that was on the table next to the sofa. She slapped the silver tape around his wrists, once, twice, three times.

"It's time to be a man."

# TWENTY

MATT ALMOST COLLIDED with Nathaniel Howzer as the judge stepped out of the offices of juvenile probation services at the Santa Fe Judicial Complex.

"Watch yourself—"

"Sorry, Judge."

"Agent England." The frown evaporated from Howzer's countenance. His big hand clasped Matt's firmly, then his face clouded. "I heard about Sylvia's run-in with Kevin Chase. Is she recovering?" He stepped back to let a tall woman enter the probation offices.

Matt nodded. Both men began walking down the long corridor toward Howzer's chambers and the main entrance to the courthouse. The building was just beginning to come to life, and bailiffs, lawyers, and clerks all had a sleepy look about them.

Howzer said, "Are you here to testify in Judge Tafoya's court?"

"Actually, I'm here to speak with you."

The judge studied Matt for a moment, then nodded. "I see. I'm not due in my courtroom until eight forty-five." He glanced at his watch. "I can give you fifteen minutes."

The two men entered the outer sanctum of Howzer's chambers. Ellie Gomez, the judge's secretary, greeted both men with a quizzical smile, then patted a stack of pink message slips.

She said, "I'll hold your calls, Your Honor."

"Thank you, Ellie." The judge continued past her desk to the door that led to his private chambers. Matt followed.

Though the room was not large, it had wall-to-wall shelves to accommodate the judge's law books, and a spacious walnut desk was free of clutter. Healthy bougainvillea and lobelia plants added life to the room. A globe, beautifully crafted and brightly colored, had been placed on a stand beside the desk.

For a moment Matt studied the judge. He had appeared in Nathaniel Howzer's courtroom countless times as a law enforcement witness in robbery, assault, and even capital murder cases.

He didn't like the yellow tinge to the judge's complexion . . . or the dark circles under his eyes. There was a desperate spark in his light irises.

The door opened and Ellie stepped into the office. She stood staring at Howzer. The judge sighed and nodded. "It's all right, Ellie. I'm going to deal with it."

Ellie withdrew and closed the door quietly.

Howzer said, "Ellie wants me to admit to you that I've received unpleasant communications."

Matt eyed the other man; he wasn't surprised by the news, he was surprised by the admission. He said, "Why did you deny these—"

"—notes."

"Why did you deny these notes when we talked at your home?"

"I thought I was doing the best thing."

"For who? You've obstructed an investigation." Matt held out one hand. "May I see them now?"

"I destroyed them."

"Jesus, Nathan . . . " Matt shook his head. He took a few long breaths, then he pulled four photographs from his jacket pocket and placed them on the judge's desk. They were from the glossies Sylvia had found at the Roadrunner Motel—portraits of Dupont White and Jayne Gladstone as vulnerable, exploited children.

When Nathaniel Howzer gazed down at the pictures, a sigh escaped his lips. Matt read the expression on the judge's face: relief.

"Where did you get these?" Howzer asked softly. He extended a finger toward a photograph of Jayne Gladstone.

Matt said, "From a motel on Cerrillos Road. I think Dupont White brought them to Santa Fe." He braced himself for a reaction, some protest from Howzer. There was none. He continued, "Dupont's body was discovered yesterday, near that same motel."

The judge sat heavily in his leather chair. He reached out one arm and pushed at the globe. The colorful orb spun lazily with a soft *shuing* sound.

For the first time, Matt noticed a large animal beside the desk: the judge's Doberman, Adobe. The old dog struggled to raise itself on its haunches. Howzer reached out a calming hand. The dog whimpered gently under his master's touch, then settled again on his pillow.

Matt sat in a wide wooden chair opposite the judge. He placed one booted ankle over his knee, and he put both hands on his thighs. "You were Roland White's attorney in California?"

The judge ran a thick-veined hand over Adobe's smooth coat. His expression was twisted with derision. "I was the keeper of the family secrets."

Matt said, "Tell me about the Gentlemen's Club."

Howzer nodded, but no new emotion showed on his face. He began to speak as if he were in the middle of a very long story. "Roland White never loved his wife— she was far below his station—but he married her for convenience. He wanted access to her young son, Dupont . . . and he wanted access to Jayne."

"For this purpose?" Matt gestured to the photographs.

"Yes."

Matt knew that it wasn't uncommon for male pedophiles to marry women in order to get close to their children. The most extreme pedophiles could be calculating and radically patient predators; they would wait as long as necessary for their victim of choice.

Howzer continued, "For many years, I had no idea what had gone on at the ranch." Beside the desk, the Doberman moaned softly in sleep. The judge looked down at his dog, then he closed his eyes. "I don't say that to exonerate myself. I have no claim to innocence. It's a simple statement of fact."

"Were the children raped?"

"They were used . . . " The judge swallowed with difficulty. "I believe they were molested, yes."

"By Roland White?"

"Yes."

Matt leaned forward imperceptibly. "And by the other men?"

The judge touched his fingertips together. "The Gentlemen's Club included wealthy men with connections and power. There were a dozen members, give or take. They all had their excesses. But I only know of one other who may have shared Roland White's sexual appetites."

"Garret Ellington?"

The judge's eyebrows shot high into his creased forehead. He nodded slowly.

Matt shifted in the wooden chair and cleared his throat. The judge was implying that a right-wing presidential hopeful was a pedophile. Under his excitement, Matt felt the subsequent empty space—the next missing piece of the puzzle. It bothered him the way a missing tooth bothers a tongue.

He said, "All those years ago, and no one ever found out about any of this? No one ever tried to put pressure on the club's members?"

It was a slip of Howzer's body language that gave Matt his answer. Howzer was right-handed, and his dominant fingers contracted twice, unconsciously beckoning: *Come on, come here.*

Both men sat in silence for a moment, then Matt followed through. "When did Fuller Lynch and his son, Cole, make the first blackmail demand?"

"Two months ago; as soon as the story of Dupont's death and the Las Cruces debacle hit the media. But I have not been their primary target."

"Garret Ellington?"

The judge nodded slowly.

Matt asked, "What did the Counselor use for leverage?"

"I believe he had copies of these photographs. Fuller knew about the darkroom at the ranch. . . . I think he guessed long ago what was happening. As for true leverage, the Counselor plays a very good bluff."

"Why did they wait so long?"

Nathaniel Howzer frowned. "For years, Cole and Fuller were afraid of Dupont and what he would do if they acted on their own." He took a breath with effort. Sweat had broken out on his forehead. His color was now an unhealthy pink. "Dupont had grown into a paranoid killer. He didn't want his family secrets bartered and sold, and he had his own agenda."

"Which was?"

"*True* justice."

Matt was unnerved by the desolation in Howzer's voice. He said, "Dupont White is dead, Nathan."

"Oh, *I* know." The judge nodded, and his voice held

irony. "Dupont's death gave Cole Lynch and his father the freedom to pursue another source of income." He stroked fingers over Adobe's soft ears. "But while he was alive, Dupont planned to give the feds something on Garret Ellington."

"Did he have evidence to tie Ellington to these photographs?"

"I gave him proof. He came to see me right before he went to Las Cruces. There was one photograph that incriminated Ellington. But when I heard Dupont had died in Las Cruces, I thought it was all over." Howzer shook his head in response to the criminal investigator's searching glance. "I never heard from Dupont again."

Matt's self-control snapped. "Why the hell didn't you tell me this when I came to your house? Why did you destroy those notes? Weren't you going to do anything at all?" He pulled back and tried to interpret the expression on Nathaniel Howzer's face. He saw exhaustion and despair. Even so, he pushed the man further. He said, "Tell me about Jayne Gladstone."

Now Nathaniel Howzer shut down completely, his eyes went flat, his mouth tightened into a frigid line. He said, "I can't do that because there is no Jayne Gladstone. She no longer exists."

"That's not good enough." Matt shook his head, refusing to let it go.

Howzer said, "I'm afraid I'm due in court."

"You've covered up their secrets for fifteen years. It's all crashing down around you."

The judge smiled. His voice was calm. "I tried to erase the damage done to innocent children. I tried to erase the perversion, the sickness . . . but I only encouraged new sickness. Events must follow a predetermined course. There is such a thing as fate."

* * *

SYLVIA PULLED THE sheet over her head and groaned. Not only was she hungover, but she'd overslept. Not a good idea. If anything, she was more exhausted than ever. Her head ached, her body ached. Her mouth had a bad taste. She felt almost feverish. She rolled over in Matt's bed and lay still with her eyes closed.

Although her mind was barely functional, she tried to review the events of the previous day—and night: with Matt, Albert, and Carlos at El Farol. She'd made a fool of herself.

Matt was probably talking to Judge Howzer right this minute. Sylvia rolled over again and stretched her arms above her head. Her fingers touched the headboard.

She wondered how Nathaniel Howzer had reacted to the photographs of the children. Not with shock . . . he knew about their existence, she was certain. She was also certain Howzer had not participated in any abuse. His sin was silence.

Sylvia sat up in bed and rubbed her eyes. Matt and Terry Osuna would probably question Jackie Madden again because she was their best lead to Kevin Chase. But hadn't Matt said something about business with Chaney? *God,* her mind was really foggy. Thoughts were slow to clarify, and her brain wasn't connecting details. Finally it came to her: Matt and Chaney were going to check out the source of the bad stakeout tip on Manny Dunn.

She forced herself out of bed and into the kitchen to make a pot of strong coffee. Tom the cat greeted her with throaty demands for breakfast. She popped open a can of Mighty Dog that Matt had purchased by mistake. Tom didn't seem to mind.

After two large cups of coffee and a dose of CNN, Sylvia's mind refused to *stop* working. Manically it sifted and sorted details. The lack of peace finally drove her into action.

It was a day free of clients, so Sylvia had time to follow up a loose end that had nagged at her all morning. She didn't bother to shower. She washed her face, brushed her teeth, and stole a pair of Matt's jockey briefs. They bunched between her thighs, but they were clean. She pulled on Levi's and one of her lover's large cotton shirts; her blouse had been ruined at the monastery.

Then she switched on the handset of her cell phone and punched in the number for directory assistance in Albuquerque. Within sixty seconds she was dialing Burt Webster's office.

She bit her lip and waited while the phone rang a half dozen times. Only six days ago, Marty "the Bagman" Connor had bandied Burt Webster's name around Café Escalera. Webster was lobbying for the state's forensic contract. Webster was a schmuck, but he could accurately predict violent behavior. He had also served as national president of the American Psychological Association, he had been extensively published, and he testified in courtrooms all over the country.

Sylvia needed something from him; one bit of information.

A woman with a South American accent finally answered the phone.

Sylvia gave her name and asked to speak with Burt Webster.

"I'm sorry, Dr. Webster is busy."

"Is he with a client?"

The woman sounded offended by the question. "I can't say."

Sylvia told a lie: "He's expecting this call."

There was a small silence, but the woman did not hang

up the phone. She was debating which way to go. Finally, she gave in, grudgingly. "Hold, please."

Sylvia lay back on Matt's couch. The minutes ticked by. Tom jumped up on her stomach and dug his claws into her skin. She thought, *You have a way with women, cat.* And just then, she heard an arrogant voice.

"Sylvia Strange. What's up?"

"Burt. I'll jump right in; I need to know if someone is *not* your client." She realized she was ignoring professional and social protocol. She was doing this all wrong. Patient confidentiality demanded that a therapist not reveal anything about his or her patients—including identity—unless the circumstances were life-threatening.

Burt Webster cleared his throat. "Sylvia, when I receive written permission from my client—whoever that might be—to share information with you, then I will be willing to do so."

"I know the protocol. This is an emergency."

Webster sighed. "This must be connected to Kevin Chase. My sympathy goes out to you, Sylvia. But all inexperienced psychologists get burned once or twice in forensic practice."

She said, "The individual is Erin Tulley. Has she ever been in treatment with you?"

"Sylvia, please, I can't give you that information."

Quickly, clearly, Sylvia recited the number of her cell phone. She said, "If the answer is negative, all you have to do is call me and say, 'No.' "

As she clicked off her phone, Tom the cat jumped off her lap and stalked from the room in a huff.

TINY TAPIA'S WORK detail identification tag had a laminated color photograph—just like the tag of each of the other seven inmates headed out to pick up trash along the

Old Las Vegas Highway. Correctional Officer Suzanne Dillon, a recent graduate of the Corrections Academy, had supervised a work detail only twice in her life. In contrast, C.O. Abel Dietz knew his way around the system and the inmates. He had forty extra dollars in his pocket—and the promise of more installments. He was always willing to do a low-risk favor for a hardworking inmate.

Normally, two veteran officers took out the crew—today was an exception. C.O. Dillon didn't notice anything odd about inmate Tapia. But had she thought much about it, she would have realized that inmate Tapia had become much more handsome, a decade younger, and a good six inches taller than normal.

Benji Muñoz y Concha kept his eyes down as he and the other members of the work detail boarded the inmate-transport van. Supplies on this detail were minimal: rakes, plastic trash bags, and orange hazard vests. Benji settled into a seat in the rear of the van. No one else made eye contact with him—they didn't want anything to do with "Tiny Tapia's" new look. Then again, they weren't going to snitch.

Both correctional officers rode up front, and they bitched about eighty-hour weeks and low pay during the entire twenty-minute ride. Benji sympathized, but he had his own problems.

When C.O. Dillon parked the van by the side of the road, the inmates stepped out and plodded down the highway, bags in hand. They had been given orders to split up and cover the ground in teams. Full trash bags were to be tied off and left for later pickup. Benji and his partner worked the northeast roadside.

In the ninety-degree heat, they walked, gathered, and loaded assorted items of trash. Single shoes, a baby's T-shirt, used diapers, aluminum beer and soda cans, wrappers, and even a toaster made their way into the bags. Benji was proud of the three loads he and his partner had collected.

C.O. Dillon sat in the truck while C.O. Dietz walked the line placing sandwich-board signs: MEN CLEANING ROADWAY. Cars whizzed by in a steady stream of traffic. C.O. Dietz passed Tiny Tapia without a second glance.

Benji kept working, but his eyes were everywhere. On the old gray hawk that perched on the power line; that bird owned every square mile as far as he could see. On the three stray dogs that trotted down the road. The largest dog, a blue tick hound, raised his muzzle to catch a scent on the breeze. Pack leader, four-legged guide, the hound kept his followers from harm's way. Sure enough, when the animal reached the intersection of Arroyo Hondo Road and the highway, he turned east, away from the road, and began trotting up the wide arroyo. Beyond the arroyo, mountains filled a blue-black sky where lightning flashed every couple of minutes. The watershed. Exactly where Benji needed to go.

As soon as Benji saw a clear shot, he followed the tick hound. This was the way people in New Mexico had traveled cross-country for centuries. Barefoot, on horseback, or on mules—the sandy arroyos were natural roadways.

Benji began to jog. An observer would have seen a man with a peculiar gait and posture—arms hugging his body, chin tucked, and—if they were visible beneath the bill of his cap—eyes that were almost shut. He traveled that way—like an odd sort of water diviner—across a wide arroyo and up a small rise; his feet found steady purchase on the ground.

That's how he moved. Until he turned his hat around on his head and felt the rush of adrenaline—giddy, light-headed.

When Benji passed his first house, he stayed low and kept to the sandy arroyo. Two blond women passed him on huge white horses, but they were busy gossiping, and they failed to glance his way. Children raced a dog across the sand; they only waved.

The sun was halfway across the western sky, and Benji figured they'd missed him on the crew. But no sirens sounded, no alarms ripped the quiet.

He was just a nonviolent inmate from minimum facility. There would be no shotgun roadblocks for Benji Muñoz y Concha. Nevertheless, the authorities would not be pleased with his freewheeling behavior.

When he gazed around, eyes wide, he saw that he was on a journey that led eventually to the base of the Sangre de Cristo Mountains and the Santa Fe Reservoir. He was a firefighter—the best—and he had a fire to fight, even if no one else knew that it was burning.

# TWENTY-ONE

MATT WAS PASSING Cities of Gold Casino on U.S. 285 north just outside Pojoaque when he caught sight of Dan Chaney's Lincoln in his rearview mirror.

He could see Chaney's shoulders and head, and he caught the small, sharp salute that his friend offered up. He waved a return greeting, then accelerated around an eighteen-wheeler. He caught the rich smell of livestock, saw a few brown and white butts pressed up against the truck's slatted sides.

Maneuvering smoothly, the brown Lincoln stayed on his tail. Chaney was in a hurry to reach the Cock 'n' Bull. He was also having fun—probably for the first time since the warehouse blowout. The two friends had talked this morning, over coffee and breakfast burritos at Tia Sophia's. Chaney had announced that he was going to leave for Las Cruces the next morning. He'd already called his wife, and he'd notified his S.A.C. of his whereabouts.

Matt increased his speed to eighty miles per hour as a string of truck stops and eateries faded away in his outside mirror. For the first time all summer, he spotted what he thought could be *true* thunderheads beyond Black Mesa and Puye Cliffs. He watched the fat, dark clouds take command of the desert sky. They looked so good, he laughed out loud.

Suddenly, Chaney's Lincoln swerved around him, accelerated, and then turned off the highway in a swirl of dust and gravel.

"Shit." Matt checked right-lane access, cut in front of the livestock truck, and followed his buddy. Thinking about rain, he'd almost missed the last turnoff to the frontage road.

He darted past a drugstore and honked at a battered tractor that was nosing into traffic like a blind bull. The tractor's driver, a weathered Hispanic farmer, tipped his head in a half greeting, then shrugged.

Typically New Mexican.

Seconds later Matt zigged right onto a dirt road and zagged left into the parking lot of the Cock 'n' Bull. Chaney had already parked the Lincoln perpendicular to the road under a stand of cottonwood and elm trees. Matt pulled the Caprice alongside the empty Town Car and scanned the lot for a sign of his friend. *Shit, Dan is already inside.*

The double doors of the bar swung open, and Chaney strode out. He sprinted across the gravel toward Matt. When he reached the Caprice, he rested his elbows on the edge of the window and said, "Your gal Kiki's not working today."

Chaney dodged his head toward a trailer that was mounted on cinder blocks in the middle of a field adjacent to the bar, about a hundred yards beyond the trees. "That's where she lives. Meet me over there."

Chaney took off on foot and was already halfway across the lot when Matt guided the Caprice slowly out onto the dirt road.

As he passed the stand of tall trees, Matt's eyes skipped back to the farthest elm. A huge magpie was dancing on a high branch. Matt counted a flock of five black-and-white birds apparently involved in a family dispute.

Lightning jagged across the sky above Black Mesa. The air buzzed with electricity. Matt's car bounced onto a rutted dirt trail that meandered toward the trailer. He could see Chaney moving easily across the field, almost even with a narrow, deep arroyo that cut through the property. The closer Matt drew to the trailer, the more his stomach clenched. The last time he'd seen Kiki, she was cooperative. But now, things were different.

SYLVIA SAID GOOD-BYE to Tom, walked out of Matt's trailer, and locked the door. Before she reached her Volvo she stopped in her tracks. She could smell rain.

The sky was clear overhead and to the south, but when she turned north, she saw the thunderheads. They were so massive, so powerful, a shiver passed through her body. The arid earth was dusty, the rivers had shriveled to creeks, bears and deer had been drawn down from the mountains for food.

And the forest fires made everything worse.

She heard—then saw—two children riding their bikes out on the street. They called to each other in excited voices. A car backfired in the distance. A fast-food plastic lid scuttled across asphalt driven by a gust of wind. Traffic on Cerrillos Road accelerated with a low, urgent hum. The hair on Sylvia's arms stood up—the air was heavy with ozone.

She hitched her briefcase to her side and continued walking toward her Volvo. She was still feeling frustrated by her conversation with Burt Webster. She felt like a fool. Of course, he hadn't called back. Now her plan was to stop by the office to check in with Albert Kove and deal with some of the work that had piled up. After that, she would head home to La Cienega. She hadn't forgotten that Monica Treisman and her son, Jaspar, were going to drop off Rocko today. Sylvia was eager to see Jaspar, and she had sorely missed her terrier.

As she approached her car, she thought again about shopping for a new vehicle. The Volvo was trashed from age and accidents. She'd owned it since her return to Santa Fe, years earlier. It really was time for a new car. A pickup truck might do very nicely.

She unlocked the driver's door, shoved her briefcase across the seat, and settled behind the wheel. She had a moment of panic when she tried to remember where she'd left a stack of confidential psych tests.

She shoved the key into the ignition then rifled through her briefcase. She pulled the cell phone out and emptied the entire contents of the briefcase on the seat.

*Well, shit, where are those reports?*

She turned the ignition key, and the Volvo's engine turned over and caught. Sylvia gave the car a spurt of gas. The engine rumbled, rough but steady. She picked up a binder and opened the flap. The tests were stowed inside. Relieved, she shifted the sedan into reverse and backed away from the trailer. Just as her phone rang.

She stepped on the brake and grabbed her phone. Dr. Burt Webster said one word, and then he hung up.

*Erin Tulley lied to Matt about getting psychiatric treatment.*

In first gear, Sylvia accelerated toward the gates of the Salazar Elementary School grounds. She saw it then, trapped under the windshield wiper—a color Polaroid pressed against the outside of the glass. It was a photograph of a man, a blurred and familiar likeness. She braked the Volvo, jammed the gearshift into neutral, and was out of the car.

She didn't worry about fingerprints or the destruction of evidence, she just grabbed the photograph and stared down at words scrawled in a trail of thin ink: "Three for the Killers' Doctor. How does it feel to be part of the picture?"

She instinctively knew what she would find as she flipped the Polaroid over. Matt England smiled for the camera, and there were red and green balloons tacked to the wall behind his head. The D.P.S. Christmas party.

There was another person in the photograph. Standing behind Matt: Erin Tulley.

Sylvia climbed back inside the Volvo, clutched her cell phone, and dialed the number she knew by heart: Matt's pager.

MATT PARKED THE Caprice beside Kiki's trailer. As he stepped out of the car, his beeper began to vibrate, signaling an incoming message. He glanced down—saw the tiny LED numbers scroll by—just as the trailer door swung open. Kiki stood on the metal stoop.

Matt said, "Tell me about Manny Dunn."

"Who?" Kiki shook her head and looked blank. "Listen, I knew you'd be back. I mean I'm glad to see you."

Matt heard a pop. Instantly, he recognized the sound—the report of a firearm. He reached out and pushed Kiki back inside the trailer. Then he sprinted behind the Caprice and squatted down, gun in hand. Another pop gave him the chance to gauge direction—a single shot, coming from the southwest, directly behind where Dan Chaney had been walking.

Matt couldn't see Chaney in the field. He knew Dan would have taken cover by now—if he could. But the area was flat and open.

Another shot, and Matt saw the bullet hit the dirt roughly fifteen feet west of his position. At almost the same time he saw the top of Dan Chaney's head at ground level. The agent must have dropped down into the arroyo for cover when the first shot rang out. Or else he'd been hit.

Pinned behind his car, Matt aimed down the sight lines of his Colt .45. He scanned the parking lot and the trees for signs of the shooter. If he could get to his vehicle, he could radio for backup.

He heard voices and a group of people walked out the door of the bar. He yelled, "Get back inside! Call 911!"

# TWENTY-TWO

SYLVIA PUNCHED IN the main number for D.P.S. and caught Criminal Agent Terry Osuna as she was about to leave her desk. Quickly, she told Terry about the Polaroid and her attempt to reach Matt. "He was going to drive out to Pojoaque, to the bar where Anthony Randall was kidnapped."

Osuna said, "The Cock 'n' Bull. We'll find him, don't worry."

"Find Erin Tulley," Sylvia said bluntly. "She'll know where to find Matt."

Osuna was speechless for a moment, then she said, "I'll send a car over to Tulley's house, and I'll drive out to Pojoaque. Where can I reach you?"

Sylvia weighed the odds that Judge Howzer would tell uniformed officers anything about Jayne Gladstone, a.k.a. Erin Tulley.

They were nil. But she wasn't in the mood to take unnecessary risks.

She said, "I need to talk to Judge Howzer—he might know something about Erin."

Osuna cut in: "You're not going alone. Dispatch can get one of our officers over to the courthouse in ten minutes."

"You've got my number—I'll take my cell phone with me."

*  *  *

BENJI GOT HIS second wind as he raced over the base of
Moon Mountain. He was panting, and he could hear the
tiny breath of his life—flowing in and out of his lungs—
even above the rush of air.

To the north lightning shivered, and thunderheads
rolled across the blue sea of sky like great black ships.

For half an instant, Benji glimpsed his ancestors who
had covered this same terrain barefoot or in leather moc-
casins. They carried the news from pueblo to village.
They ran in the sacred ceremonies. In an emergency,
nothing but death had stopped the ancient runners.

He pictured Sylvia Strange—his vision of her as
a body made of ash. Nothing would stop him from his
mission.

He felt as if great storm winds were surging him forward, but almost at once they washed him back again.
Like ocean breakers. He imagined that a swimmer
trapped in a riptide must feel exactly as he felt. Lost.
Without bearing, without direction. Tempted to surrender
to the current—or the wind. Benji was terrified that he
would lose his way completely.

He squeezed his eyes shut to stay in touch with his
inner compass. Instead of direction, he felt the presence
of a great black void. Overhead he heard the roar of a jet
plane. The roar increased, growing so loud, so painful, he
believed it would rip open his skull and suck out his
thoughts.

He clutched his head with both hands, and his body
began to fall. Wind rushed up around his ears. When he
was sure he should have hit the ground, he forced his
eyes open. And he saw that the jet plane was a bird.

An owl with wings afire, and eyes that were as old and
deep as the earth.

*  *  *

ANOTHER SHOT RIPPED over Matt's head and raised a puff of dirt behind him. The shooter had to be on high ground, and his—or her—aim was improving. Whatever the weapon, it was powerful. The rhythm of the shots indicated a revolver.

From the impact point of the bullets, Matt figured the shooter was firing from a spot between a pile of old tires and a big metal trash bin on the northeast corner of the parking lot. If so, he had a good shot at Chaney.

Matt aimed toward the trash bin, finger on the trigger. From the corner of his eye he could see that Dan Chaney was inching his way along the arroyo toward some scrap two-by-fours and a thicket of chamisa. The federal agent was down on his belly, probably gauging his chances to make a break for cover.

Kiki yelled out from the trailer, "What the hell's happening?"

Matt opened his mouth to warn her off when he saw Dan Chaney's body jerked back by sudden impact. At the same time he heard the crack of gunfire.

Chaney was hit.

Over the buzz of highway traffic, Matt heard the rumble of a motorcycle. He followed the noise and saw the shooter hotdogging his way from the parking lot onto dirt. The bike almost went down when it jammed into a pothole, but the rider stayed on.

Kevin Chase!

Matt took aim as Kevin pulled his gun from between his thighs. He was roughly fifteen yards away; there was a faint flash as the gun exploded. Matt yelled a warning to Chaney but his words were lost under the sharp report of gunfire. One round whizzed past Matt's ear. He fired just before he threw himself behind the Chevy. His heart was hammering inside his chest.

The motorcycle accelerated and skidded out of the lot

onto the frontage road. Matt vaulted to his feet and sprinted to Chaney. The F.B.I. agent was seated on the ground. He had the palm of one hand pressed against his bicep. Blood had seeped into his shirtsleeve. He was white-faced, breathing rapidly.

Chaney said, "Go get that asshole!"

Matt called to Kiki who had cautiously emerged from her trailer: "Get an ambulance."

Then he raced to the Caprice, spun the car around, and tore out to the frontage road. He switched on his siren. As he passed the Pojoaque Market and Liquor Store, he radioed a Code 30 emergency: *Shooting. Officer down.*

Matt was headed north, traveling parallel to the highway; he had a clear line to the motorcycle, a Honda, two hundred feet ahead. But just beyond the Honda, cars turning off to the Burger King threatened to slow the biker's escape.

The Honda speeded into the left lane, passing a Cadillac and a flatbed truck. Instead of cutting back into the right lane, Kevin Chase banked the Honda even farther to the left onto the shoulder. A southbound Range Rover blared its horn.

Three seconds later, the speedometer in the Caprice hovering at sixty-five, Matt saw the reason for Kevin's detour: traffic in the right lane had come to a standstill. Low-riders, high-riders, and family station wagons were treading asphalt bumper to bumper.

Paper signs announced the reason for the slowdown: GRAND OPENING, BINGO AND SLOTS!

Matt swore through his teeth as he slammed the wheel to the right.

Seconds later, he saw an opportunity to escape. He snaked the Caprice into the lot of Tio's Mexican Food Restaurant. He pressed down on the accelerator and raced through the adjacent lot—barely avoiding a collision with a propane tank—then bounced off the edge of asphalt, across an acequia, and onto dirt. The motorcycle had gained another eighth of a mile.

KEVIN CHASE KNEW the cop wasn't far behind him. He guided the Honda along the shoulder over broken glass, trash, and rocks. He shifted his weight, pulled up, and jumped a drainage culvert.

He was sweating like a pig; the salt water stung his eyes and ran down his face. But he loved the warm electric wind, the flash of oncoming traffic, and the shrill scream of the cop's siren.

He'd been working up to this and whatnot; he only wished he hadn't missed his shot at Sylvia's cop. Too much adrenaline, and he'd jerked the trigger on the first three rounds—the rounds meant for Matt England.

He swerved to avoid a bag of garbage that had fallen from some asshole's truck. A stranded car just ahead seemed to come out of nowhere.

He had to jam the Honda to the right, cut across both lanes, and wind his way between cars turning into the parking lot of the Bingo Palace. He cut in front of a high-rider and clipped its chrome bumper with his helmet. He heard a horn, even over the scream of the siren.

"Fuck it!" Now, he had the high-rider on his ass. There was only one thing to do; he waved his middle finger at the driver and began a slalom race between parked cars.

When he was almost to the end of the row, a Toyota 4Runner pulled out in front of him: *I don't think I can make this—whoa!—shit!*

MATT NAVIGATED THE Chevy through a sawhorse barricade; he'd taken a shortcut into the Bingo Palace lot. He narrowly avoided a convertible jammed with kids; the girls in the backseat waved as he flew by doing forty-five. He only had time to catch a flash of pink and green and smiling faces. His eyes were on the Honda.

A high-rider mounted on gargantuan wheels was weaving between two lanes of parked cars behind the careening motorcycle.

Suddenly Matt saw the bike go down. It skidded under the belly of the high-rider and out of Matt's sight lines. Just then the Caprice plowed into a NO PARKING sign. The screech of metal made Matt cringe.

He reversed, worked free of the steel post, and covered the short distance to the spot where Kevin had gone down.

He saw the motorcycle. It was on its side, jammed between a Toyota 4Runner and the high-rider. The wiry truck driver stood, weight leveraged, pinning the stunned fugitive against the truck bed.

Matt skidded to a stop and slammed out of the car.

"I'm a police officer!"

The truck driver stared at Matt, not moving. "This asshole scratched my chrome."

Weapon drawn, Matt said, "Back off." He stepped up to Kevin Chase and twisted his arm behind his back. Then he snapped cuffs over the biker's hands and patted him down. No gun—they would find it somewhere on the road.

Kevin Chase stared at Matt with bulging, frightened eyes. He said, "Killer made me do it!"

"Who is Killer?" Matt jerked the cuffs and twisted them hard.

The words finally stuttered from Kevin's lips. "Erin . . . Erin Tulley."

# TWENTY-THREE

SYLVIA PARKED THE Volvo next to Judge Howzer's Mercedes in front of his home. She had been here before, most recently for a fiesta party almost a year ago—the night Zozobra, Old Man Gloom, had been burned in a traditional pagan ritual. She remembered that evening in detail; it was the night her friend and associate Malcolm Treisman had been admitted into the intensive-care unit at St. Vincent Hospital. Nathaniel Howzer had been kind to Sylvia; he'd taken her under his wing. They had talked for a while on the veranda while flames lit the sky over Santa Fe, and the fifty-foot Zozobra went up in smoke.

Sylvia stepped out of her car, slammed the door, and froze. What was she doing? The judge might not have a clue where to find Erin Tulley. He could refuse to talk. Or maybe it was too late to matter. . . .

Refusing to acknowledge her last thought, she glanced worriedly at her watch; someone from state police should be meeting her any minute. She'd left a message with dispatch: *Change of plan.*

But no vehicles turned onto the long driveway leading up to the house. And there had been no phone calls from Terry Osuna.

Sylvia walked up the flagstone path and climbed the steps to the front door of the house. No one answered her knock. When she rang the bell, she heard dogs bark inside the house; she recognized Adobe's deep bass. It was punctuated by the high-pitched whine of a smaller dog.

When Sylvia had called the courthouse fifteen minutes earlier, Howzer's secretary, Ellie, had told her that the judge wasn't scheduled in court today: "He said he was going home. I'm worried because he hasn't been feeling well."

Ellie obviously cared about the judge. That was understandable; although Nathaniel Howzer was reserved, he was known as a fair man—on the bench and off.

Sylvia began to walk around to the side of the house and the veranda.

"Sylvia?"

She pivoted, and she saw the judge standing on his front stoop. He looked groggy and disoriented. She wondered if he was ill or drunk.

She said, "Are you all right, Nathan?"

It took him a moment to answer: "I was resting. Won't you come inside?"

She followed him into the house. The floors were dirt—the expensive kind: pounded to the consistency of rock, polished to a bloodred sheen, and finished with acrylic. Four doors opened off the foyer. Beyond an arched doorway, Sylvia stepped into the large living room with its massive vigas and smooth plaster walls. She heard Adobe's frantic bark from the rear of the house.

Sun streaked into the room through partially drawn curtains. The air smelled of cedar. She sat in a high-backed chair opposite the judge. He seemed to have forgotten she was in the room. His gaze was intent on some distant point.

Where to begin? Softly, she queried, "Nathan?"

His eyes pounced on her, blurred, refocused. He said, "I don't have much time, and you want to know about Erin."

"Yes." The words Sylvia had rehearsed on the drive up—about Matt, the Polaroid, and Erin—died on her lips.

He nodded, his eyelids lifting with effort. "She was such a good child. All children are lovely—but she was exceptional. A golden child. And she and Dupont were inseparable . . . like sister and brother."

Howzer frowned as his mind drifted back to the past. He sighed dreamily. "I thought bringing her here would help . . . erase the past."

As if it were possible to erase anyone's past. She said, "You brought Jayne Gladstone here?"

The judge barely nodded. "I had the connections. . . . After she left the hospital, I gave her a new life, a new start as Erin Tulley. For a while, it seemed to work."

Sylvia shook her head. "She's killed two men." She leaned forward in the chair and said, "I need your help." She handed Howzer the Polaroid of Matt. He barely glanced at it.

Sylvia said, "Matt's in danger, Nathan. I think you're the only person who knows where to find Erin."

The judge looked up, his ruddy cheeks wet with tears. He whispered, "I'm so sorry."

Directly behind the judge the tall hand-carved door swung open, and Erin Tulley walked into the room. Her dark hair was loose, and her eyes were empty, as if she had stepped outside herself. She gripped a .38 caliber revolver in her hand.

BENJI THOUGHT HE'D never seen anything more beautiful than the old adobe walls of Cristo Rey Church. But he didn't linger; he followed the path of the great owl. The bird stayed with the river, parallel to Upper Canyon Road.

Each house along this stretch of the Santa Fe River had a different character. A cloistered eighty-year-old adobe stood next to a light-drenched solar house; farther on, a barnlike studio fronted a rustic stone cottage.

Benji raced past someone's yard and ornamental pond. He glanced down into dark water, and he saw a cluster of orange, white, and red koi, their tails undulating in unison. The rhythm of the fish mesmerized him, but he did not allow his pace to slow. He kept traveling toward the mountains.

When he had almost reached the entrance to the reservoir, he realized that his guide, the owl, had disappeared. Deserted him. Now he felt the immobilizing voice of fear. All the way to his toes he felt it. And it was the one thing that could take him down, the one thing that could destroy his flight. Fear was the only emotion that could rob him of his power.

He was surrounded by mountains. Beyond the reservoir and the ski basin there would be only wilderness. Benji could smell the sharp tang of ashes. Ash, smoke, fire.

He felt a presence behind him, turned, and spied the owl. It was perched on the branch of a tall pine tree near the mouth of a dirt road. Its powerful talons gripped the rough wood, its gray feathers moved almost imperceptibly with each breath. Ever so slowly, the owl rotated its blunt and feathered head one hundred eighty degrees to clutch Benji with its avian eyes.

SYLVIA GAZED AT the woman she'd known as Erin Tulley. She hardly recognized the eyes or the mouth; rage had altered Erin's features, turned them hard and cold.

Tulley said, "I've been waiting. What took you so long?"

"Erin, where's Matt?" Sylvia struggled to keep her words stripped of emotion.

Adobe howled from another room, a grating plea for release. The Doberman's paws scratched wood. The judge seemed to hear his dog for the first time. He looked worriedly at Erin, but she ignored him. Instead, she focused her attention on Sylvia.

Erin smiled. "It's time for the Killer to follow the path of judgment and destruction."

Her voice chilled Sylvia; it was Dupont White.

Erin said, "You can't be trusted, none of you."

Sylvia watched Erin carefully, trying to gauge where the madness stopped, where logic began. The woman was sweating, almost hyperventilating, and her body was rigid. But there was a canny spark of intelligence in her eyes.

She said, "After Las Cruces, Dupont came to me. He'd been shot. For three days, I never left him, not for a second. And then he died like a warrior. After that, I still kept him with me."

For a few moments, Erin was distracted by the sound of an airplane flying over the house; she stood stiffly as the engine noise faded away.

When silence returned, she whispered, "Nasty dreams . . . that never go away."

She began to unbutton her shirt. Paint was streaked across her bare throat and chest. A carefully designed bird had disintegrated into muddy smears of black and red across her small breasts. Sweat, repelled by the greasepaint, ran down her skin in rivulets; the waist of her pants was soaked through under her belt.

With her left hand, Erin pulled a buck knife from a leather sheath on her hip. She sighed, "They hurt me." She placed the tip of the knife to her chest, and drew the blade diagonally across smooth flesh. Blood beaded and ran; it flowed over her ribs. She didn't react to the pain;

her eyes were cold and clear as water. And her fingers stayed steady on the revolver's trigger.

She slid the knife back into its sheath. Then she scraped her thumb along her rib cage. Her focus didn't waver from her two captives as she smeared greasepaint mixed with blood across one cheek, then the other.

Sylvia knew what she represented in Erin's eyes: she had the man Erin had loved, she had professional standing, and she made a career of understanding the men Erin murdered. The Killers' Doctor.

And Erin had become a killer.

The revolver wavered now, but Erin forced herself to cock the trigger as she stepped closer to the judge. She whispered, "Why couldn't you make them stop? That was your job, all along. You were no better than they were." She shuddered. "That's why I let Anthony Randall walk out of your courtroom."

The judge didn't move. He had a faraway look on his old face—one of resignation and compliance. He said, "If you want to kill me, go ahead."

Erin's control crumbled. In an instant she looked completely bewildered, like a lost child. Sylvia thought of the little girl who had spent her summers at Devil's Den. That child was here, in the room, crazed with pain.

Howzer spoke again, and his whisper held puzzlement. "Jayne? Did you come to hurt me, child? Is that what you want?" He shifted his bulk in the chair and reached out one trembling hand. He was seriously ill. Sweat beaded on his forehead. His complexion had a florid glow, the kind of glassy tone that precedes a heart attack. His gaze was vacant and unfocused.

Erin pulled a photograph from her back pocket and tossed it at Nathaniel Howzer. It fell to the floor by his feet. She hissed, "You gave this to Dupont, but it's too late for your bullshit justice."

Sylvia stared down at the photograph. It looked like the ones she'd seen at the motel: a very young Jayne Gladstone, naked and bound. A travesty of the golden child. She felt Erin's eyes on her. She lifted her gaze. For an instant, those eyes belonged to the girl in the photograph—then the child was lost behind the grotesque and primitive mask of the killer.

The gun jerked to life in Erin's hand—spit fire and metal when she pulled the trigger three times. The first bullet came within inches of Sylvia's throat. The second bullet hit the wall behind Nathaniel Howzer. The last one shattered glass.

It took Sylvia a moment to register that the judge had not been shot.

Howzer looked up at Erin blankly. His arms went slack. The house was silent except for the Doberman's worried cry.

# TWENTY-FOUR

ERIN TULLEY JABBED the barrel of the .38 between Sylvia's ribs. "Stand up. Move."

She stood an inch shorter than Sylvia, but she weighed about one hundred forty pounds and much of her bulk was muscle. She had the added power of a woman who had cut loose all bonds that had anchored her to reality.

Sylvia knew that Erin's primitive psychological structure would allow her to move fluidly in and out of dissociative or fugue states when her consciousness, memories, perceptions—even her identity—were disrupted. She might sound coherent one moment but not the next. Any attempt to predict her ebb and flow would be like trying to pin down smoke. She also guessed that Erin had at least one more bullet in her gun.

Erin's eyes seemed to glow. She gave off an acrid scent. Her dark hair was matted with her own blood.

Sylvia said, "The judge is dying, Erin. A heart attack. We've got to get help—"

"Go!"

Sylvia took a deep, ragged breath and walked out of the house, down the flagstone path toward her car. The driveway was deserted. Dense trees blocked the view of surrounding houses or the road farther below. There was no one to see the bizarre spectacle of the two women— one half naked and painted.

Sylvia turned, waiting for a command.

Erin said, "This way." She tipped the revolver in the direction of the mountains behind the property.

Sylvia led the way alongside the house. Both women passed the veranda, a small manicured lawn, and a fruit orchard—apple, pear, apricot, and peach trees. Beyond the orchard they entered a thicket of pine and aspens. Sylvia thought they were on a trail that led to an outbuilding—perhaps a garden shed. But the path continued, and beyond the dense cover of trees it became a narrow, rough road.

Her heart sank; when someone finally came looking for them, there would be nothing to find.

MATT SLAMMED THE Caprice in gear and raced up Alameda Street on his way to Upper Canyon Road and Nathaniel Howzer's home. The state police dispatcher had relayed Sylvia's message to Terry Osuna.

*Why the hell did she go to see the judge on her own? When I find her, I'll kill her!*

Matt inhaled a Life Saver as he nosed the Caprice between a parked car and a tour bus. Metal scraped paint from metal. The Chevy had taken lots of punishment today—thank God it was a state car and not his own.

*Too close. Not going to make it.*

He floored the gas pedal, the Chevy bolted suddenly from the jam, and two wheels bounced through someone's carefully tended cactus garden. Prickly pear and cholla were crushed by tires.

He couldn't believe how blind he'd been about Erin. Blind and stupid.

There were only a dozen homes at the high end of Upper Canyon Road before the old Randall Davey estate. Howzer's was the last house on the road. Beyond the judge's property, you'd find mountains—the start of the Sangre de Cristos. The reservoir. And wilderness.

He turned sharply into Howzer's steep driveway, pushed the pedal to the floor, and the Chevy lunged to the top of the grade. Matt braked next to Sylvia's Volvo.

In a flash he was out of the car and up the walk. The front door of the house was open. He listened for sounds of life, then he entered with care. Nathaniel Howzer was asleep in his armchair. Somewhere in the house two dogs barked—a deep bass and a yipper.

Matt said, "Nathan?" It took him a moment to realize the judge was dead—he saw no obvious wounds; he guessed heart attack or stroke. A photograph lay on the floor near Howzer's feet.

Matt knelt down to take a closer look. It was another pornographic image of Jayne Gladstone . . . Erin Tulley. But there was something different about this one. There were two girls. No. It was a mirror image. Jayne and her reflection. And there was a second reflection in the mirror. The photographer had caught himself in the picture. The man was naked. The camera obscured half his face. His features were familiar: Garret Ellington.

Matt left the judge and searched the house from top to bottom. No sign of Sylvia or Erin, but at least three rounds had been fired. And there was blood on the floor. It looked like there might be another victim.

*Please, not Sylvia.*

Outside the house he tried to figure out where the women might have gone. There were trails leading away from various points on the property.

Matt could hear sirens of approaching vehicles. He knew Terry Osuna was on the way. He stood at a loss, then he made up his mind to take the Caprice and canvas the area. They had probably taken Erin's vehicle and cut back to the main roads. Matt sprinted across the property.

He was almost to the Chevy when a flash of color caught his eye and he turned. He saw a man beckoning to him from the edge of the orchard. The man stood between apple and pear trees. He waved both his arms frantically. His body was poised to take off at a run. He wore blue work clothes. He was slight and dark. And Matt had seen him before.

He was the firefighter, the inmate: Benji Muñoz y Concha.

Confused, Matt called out. His mind struggled to come up with an explanation for the inmate's presence.

Benji disappeared between trees.

Matt followed.

# TWENTY-FIVE

THE STEEP LANDSCAPE had gradually shifted from ponderosa pine to tall fir and spruce trees. It was cooler up here, but the sun was hot on Sylvia's back, and she was so parched her throat ached. Disoriented, she felt as if she had been traveling for hours; by her watch the uphill journey had only taken nineteen minutes.

She slowed her pace. She was a hostage, and because of that, time was her ally. The more minutes that passed, the greater the opportunities to defuse the situation, and, ultimately, the better her own chances for survival. Erin's agenda was chaotic and unpredictable—but Sylvia believed the woman intended to kill her.

It wasn't the possibility of her own death that made her sick—if and when the confrontation escalated, Sylvia would still have some control over her own fate—it was the fear that she would find Matt's body at the end of this trail.

At times, when the path widened, Erin walked beside Sylvia. She stared then, and she seemed to be memorizing Sylvia's features with a hunger. When the path narrowed again to a single track, she forced Sylvia to lead the way.

Now the trail grew even steeper. Sylvia's breath came fast and rough. Tree branches scraped her bare arms.

Sweat made her skin itch. Erin appeared unfazed by exertion.

They came to a wall of trees, and Sylvia stopped.

Erin spoke in a soft voice. "Go on." She pointed to a small opening at ground level between branches. Sylvia squatted down and forced her way through the natural entrance. Needles and twigs left welts on her skin and scratched her face. She expected to enter a small, tight space. Instead, she moved into a clearing roughly a hundred feet square. It looked like a squatter's camp. As Erin followed, Sylvia stared out at the view of Santa Fe in the distance, and closer, the river valley and Judge Howzer's house.

Here the wind blew fiercely, and streaks of lightning punched the sky. The ground was nothing but matchsticks—the shavings and needles of pines. For a moment, Sylvia wondered about the branches, dead and downed wood, that had been piled on either side of the entrance to the clearing—and the metal gasoline can—but something else seized her attention. On the far edge of the area, a white panel truck was parked beside an outcrop of rocks. She felt new fear.

She faced Erin, and said, "Matt?"

"Go on, look." With her free hand, Erin clicked open a metal cigarette lighter and held the flame arrogantly in front of her face.

Sylvia turned and crossed the clearing, breaking from a walk to a run as she neared the truck. Before she reached the rear of the vehicle, the wind shifted. The air spun around from the north like a cornered beast. Sylvia tasted grit and gasoline, then the sharp smell evaporated. Her hands closed around the metal truck handles. She yanked the doors wide.

The truck was empty.

Rage washed over Sylvia, she cried out in frustration, then swung around. She yelled at Erin, "Where is he?" The wind tugged the words from her mouth.

Erin didn't answer, she just stood planted on the other side of the clearing. Behind her the cigarette lighter lay on a pile of dry brush and a new fire sputtered, crackled, then whooshed for a moment when it encountered a green piñon branch. It died back almost instantly, retreating like a timid snake along the forest floor.

Sylvia's rage propelled her, and she lunged toward the other woman. When she had covered several yards she shifted direction, sliding sideways to a stop. She found herself transferring her weight from foot to foot. A primitive need to destroy overwhelmed her—just as it had in the canyon with Kevin Chase. She wanted to kill Erin Tulley.

Erin raised her revolver, clasped left hand over right, and aimed directly at Sylvia's heart.

Sylvia stopped in her tracks. It wasn't only the weapon that held her back. She had reached a threshold, a line she would not cross.

Erin saw it, too. In that instant of recognition the fury went out of her body. She raised the .38 until it was pointed at the clouds. She stood that way, as if the life had drained out of her limbs.

But Sylvia knew it was the will to kill that had deserted Erin—and, along with that, the will to live with all that she had done.

Almost drunkenly, Erin drew the revolver to her mouth, bit down on the muzzle, and fired. But nothing happened.

Incredulous, Erin pulled the revolver from between her teeth. She jerked herself into action. Her feet cut a track in the duff, just inches from the place where she'd started the fire.

Erin heard the flames before she saw them. There was life in her fire yet. She turned, watched yellow blades eat their way across the ground. A weed sizzled and caught. Another burned. And another.

Beyond Erin, the forest stretched green, untouched by flames. The trees looked pristine and vulnerable. The winds could spread a fire in minutes.

Leery, Erin circled the tiny flames. And then her eyes settled on the metal can just a few feet away. She moved toward it, all the time aware of Sylvia.

Sylvia called out. "I can help you."

"The way you helped Anthony Randall? And Jesse Montoya?" Erin drew her fingers down her paint-smeared face. The gesture made her look as though she was wiping away contamination.

Sylvia inched forward. She was now roughly twenty feet from Erin. She said, "You asked for my help."

Erin shook her head vehemently, pacing like a bare-foot child on hot sand. With each pass, she came a little bit closer to the metal gas can. Her damp hair was plastered to her head, the greasepaint on her cheeks had smeared into mud, her eyes glittered dangerously.

Abruptly, she stood her ground and hefted metal. She raised the container over her head, and the liquid bubbled to the end of the spout. Then, sluggishly, gasoline dribbled onto her hair and down her chest.

"Put the can down." Sylvia worked to keep her voice steady.

Erin stared at Sylvia and nodded. Carefully, she lowered the can and set it on the ground.

Sylvia raised one hand and reached out to Erin. Only fifteen feet separated the two women.

Erin seemed to become aware of the .38, still clutched in her right hand. She gazed at it dreamily, as if she was unsure of its use, its purpose. This time, when she squeezed the trigger, a bullet razed the ground six feet in front of Sylvia.

And then, Erin kicked out abruptly with her boot. The gas can toppled, and fluid ran from its supple nozzle. The scent of gasoline hung thick on the air. A dark puddle nosed its way toward the low flames.

"Don't do this." Sylvia brushed hair from her eyes. She tasted grit and salt. She knew that Erin had touched some-place deep in her shattered psyche—a place that gave her refuge from her need to kill others—but it wasn't strong enough to protect her from self-destruction.

The flames of the spot-fire were still low, just the skirt of a blaze, but they were only a few yards away from the steady flow of gasoline from the can. Even before the fire encountered the liquid, it shivered and grew, tasting flammable fumes with its myriad yellow tongues.

Sylvia flinched, and she saw that Tulley had stopped to gaze out at the growing flames with new fear. The gun fell from Erin's fingers, and Sylvia lunged forward. But before she could cover the short distance, the metal can exploded, and she was thrown to the ground by the terrible concussion of fire, alloy, and gasoline. The air was sucked from her lungs. Dumbfounded, she gasped for breath. Sticks and rocks bit into her hands and knees. Gasoline stung her skin.

Sylvia heard her own name—and screams—as the fire found Erin. She stood, stumbled forward, fighting against the vertigo.

She saw Erin's muscles contract as flames ate their

way up the legs of her pants. Her boots were lost in a dense, black smoke.

Sylvia's feet felt the scalded earth. Fire seemed to enter her body through the soles of her shoes. Just as another burst of exploding fire engulfed Erin, Sylvia reached out.

She grabbed Erin's arm—fought the pull of the flames—and stumbled backward.

Sylvia felt herself sinking into a numb inertia, and she cried out. Someone called her name. Then a man hovered over her. At first she wondered who he was—then she knew: the firefighter, Benji Muñoz y Concha. He pulled her clear of the fire then stripped off his shirt to smother the flames on Erin's legs.

Sylvia tried to breathe, but there was no air, just gray swirling smoke and ash. She felt weak and faint.

Matt's voice brought her back to consciousness. He yelled, "We've got to get out of here!"

She found herself on the ground near the van. She looked up and saw Matt coming toward her; he was carrying Erin.

Sylvia asked, "Where's Benji?"

"Start the van, we've got to get away."

She mustered herself and jerked open the driver's door. Hot pain shot up her arm. The keys were in the ignition, and she whispered a prayer when the engine caught and held steady.

The back doors of the van opened, and Matt placed Erin on the metal floor.

Sylvia saw that the fire was turning, preparing to gather force and momentum. She slid over as Matt jumped into the driver's seat. She asked again, "Where's Benji?"

"I don't know. We can't wait."

Matt drove, escaping smoke and burn, following a rough road down the back of the mountain. They were almost to the Santa Fe Reservoir when they heard the sirens of the fire trucks.

# TWENTY-SIX

IT WAS LIKE standing on the spine of a great beast. The ridge back scratched the sky and fell away to the plateau below. Sylvia and Matt stood on a flat chunk of granite that jutted out of the earth. From the narrow trail, Rocko, Sylvia's spike-haired terrier, stared up at the man and woman.

The breeze felt like water—cool and clean. On the northeastern horizon, the Sangre de Cristo Mountains, true to their name, were tinged pink. There was no sign of fire where thirty acres had burned ten days earlier.

To the west of the ridge back, black thunderheads shifted shape, rapidly approaching the Santa Fe basin. The air smelled of rain. A raven caught a current and sailed over the ridge. Rocko barked at the bird.

Sylvia felt tiny drops of water hit her skin—it was starting to rain. She thought about Erin, lying now in the hospital's burn ward. The doctors thought she would survive. If they were right, she would be sent to a private hospital. Judge Nathaniel Howzer's estate would easily cover Erin's expenses for life.

Sylvia hadn't been surprised to learn of Howzer's bequest. The man had lived with his own demons. She believed that in the end, the secrets he kept had killed him.

As for Erin . . . eventually, she would be evaluated by

psychiatrists to decide whether she was competent to stand trial for murder. It was possible that the case would go to trial—but not probable. Either way, Sylvia would be a witness, but not an expert. This time, she would not be the Killers' Doctor.

Rocko yipped, tail at attention.

Matt watched the terrier's frantic action. The rain felt good after all these months of dryness. Rain washed away all the dust and allowed for a fresh start. He was thinking about the photograph he'd found at Nathaniel Howzer's house. Matt nodded, unconscious of the gesture. Garret Ellington was one presidential hopeful who'd seen his aspirations wither and die.

Sylvia brought Matt out of his reverie. She said, "Garret Ellington should rot in prison."

"You a mind reader?" Matt took Sylvia's arm. He said, "At least Dan Chaney's having a hell of a time; he's going to testify before Congress at the hearings on Las Cruces. Dan's like a bear shaking a hornet's nest. I have a feeling the whole damn thing will come tumbling down." Matt's fingers grazed Sylvia's bandaged hand; the burn would leave a scar.

She took a breath, tasted rain, and pressed her head into his shoulder. "Matthew, there's something we have to settle. About kids . . ."

Down the ridge, Rocko barked excitedly as a lizard skittered across rock. The terrier lunged and darted at the air. The lizard was long gone.

"Don't you think we should get married first?"

Matt stared at her in surprise. Finally he said, "Yeah, I really do."

The silence between them stretched to minutes. After a time, she pointed down the rocky hill to a cluster of trees where some moss rock had flourished. She said, "My father tended those trees. He hauled in that moss rock. He always said he wanted to plant a garden there."

Matt smiled. "It's a fine spot."


WHEN SYLVIA STEPPED into the small yard next to Dormitory A at the murf, Benji Muñoz y Concha had his back to the world. He and two other inmates were each perched on stepladders, dabbing silver and yellow paint on the foam tips of a great wave. The wave began as a flat blue-green plate in the distant ocean; it built speed and weight until it finally came crashing toward the viewer.

In a wide-legged stance, Sylvia stood in the center of the yard. She was dressed in Levi's and a crisp cotton blouse that buttoned at the collar. She had a secret smile on her face as she considered the mural.

She stood for several minutes and watched as the waves took on a very realistic foamy hue. While Benji painted, he kept his nose to the mural and never acknowledged her presence.

The other two inmates stared at her from time to time.

Finally, Benji set his brush on the ladder. Without turning he said, "Yo, Strange."

She said, "You're psychic."

He backed down the ladder, reached the bottom, and turned slowly. He was grinning, eyes hidden behind black plastic sunglasses. In one hand he clutched a small mirror.

Sylvia laughed, and then her smile died away.

Benji glanced down. He said, "How's your hand?"

"It still hurts sometimes."

Benji nodded slowly.

"Let's sit down." Sylvia led the way to the bench that ran along one wall. Except for the two painters, they had the small yard to themselves. They sat side by side.

"Smoke?"

Benji nodded, and Sylvia pulled a pack of Camel filters from her shirt pocket. She shook one out; Benji accepted the cigarette. Sylvia took one for herself. They used Benji's matches to light up.

They smoked in silence until the burning ash drew close to their fingers. The smoke gathered in translucent layers only to be dispersed by the breeze. The sun felt good.

Benji sighed and squeezed the cigarette butt between his paint-smeared fingers.

Sylvia stared at him; her eyebrows were arched and the cigarette dangled from the corner of her mouth. She took a last drag and stamped out the butt on the concrete. "How the hell did you happen to be on that mountain?"

Benji looked the psychologist directly in the eye. "I was on that work crew all day. I never left. Ask anybody."

Sylvia tipped her head. "So they all say. Matt told me you showed him the way."

"You better see what your man's been smokin'."

"Three times, he's been out to measure the distance from Old Las Vegas Highway to Judge Howzer's house. He can't believe you made it up that mountain in time."

A faint smile crept across Benji's mouth. "But who can say, eh?"

"Me, I just wonder how you knew where to go?"

"For weeks those weather guys been saying the watershed was gonna burn by lightning."

Sylvia stood and nodded. Her sunglasses had slipped down her nose, and she nudged them up. *A well-informed intuitive . . .* That was one explanation.

She turned to Benji and held out her hand. He took it, and they shook solemnly. Then he walked back to the wall and his work.

When Sylvia was almost to the gate, she heard Benji's quiet voice.

He said, "I had another dream last night. . . . I got a message for you." She was still perfectly visible in his handheld mirror. Her eyes were wide and deep. Her posture was strong.

She said, "What was it?"

"It's time to find your father."

SYLVIA WAS SITTING under the piñon in her side yard, reading, when she saw Rosie and Ray's Camaro pull into the drive. Rocko sprinted toward the car, barking ferociously.

Rosie waved as she stepped out. Ray slid out the passenger's side, but he stayed beside the car. He had a peculiar look on his face; he also held something in his hand.

A leather belt.

*No, a leash.*

And Rocko was going crazy—barking, growling, tail wagging.

Sylvia set down the book, stood, and moved a few feet to the right. The leash disappeared around the rear of the Camaro. Ray tugged on it and smiled.

Sylvia was already thinking of some way to protest; she knew what was coming. She raised up both hands, palms out. "No way!"

The leash strained, then gained some slack. Finally, a shepherd appeared from behind the Camaro. The dog was lean, and her fawn-colored coat was matted. She kept her head low and bared her teeth.

Sylvia recognized her from the kennels at the penitentiary. Nikki, the drug dog who couldn't keep her mind on her work.

Rosie said, "Nikki's probation was revoked when she couldn't sniff out a joint in a cell."

Sylvia said, "I don't need another dog."

Rosie set her hands on her hips. "But Nikki needs a home."

"This dog's a nervous wreck."

Rosie said, "She just needs someone who will love her. She just needs a family of her own."

The fur on Nikki's back stood up straight and she began to bark. The sound was sharp and frightening. Rocko growled, hackles up.

Sylvia groaned, but she could feel her resistance weaken.

Over the noise, Sylvia said, "I talked to the Bagman. I called him for a conference."

Rosie nodded uncertainly.

Sylvia said, "Don't worry, the lawsuit looks good, but it may not come to that." Her eyes narrowed as she remembered her meeting with the Bagman. He'd been seated at his massive desk. On the wall behind his head, a photograph of the governor. And the Bagman chattering away: "I have to admit I underestimated you, Sylvia. Malcolm would be proud of his spunky protégée."

Sylvia punched Rosie's arm playfully. "I couldn't believe he actually called me 'spunky.' But he's going to help us. I think the warden's *pendejo*-in-a-suit may be out on his ass very soon."

A wide smile transformed Rosie's face. "Thanks, *jita*."

Now the dogs were sniffing each other gingerly, nose to butt.

Ray shrugged and held out the leash. He said, "It's the beginning of a beautiful friendship."

**Outside Santa Fe, New Mexico**

The girl gripped the steering wheel with both hands. Her fingers were pale where knuckles stretched skin; her arms were thin as sticks. Bones—not flesh—defined her body. Toes on toes, her bare feet pressed the accelerator flush against the Honda's floorboard. Her head scarcely topped the dashboard, but she saw the narrow horizon of blacktop change suddenly to desert and barbed wire. Raising a wake of dust, the car hurtled headlong off the highway toward a fence. Bits of gravel and rock smacked the windshield.

The world careened past the moving car—low trees, jutting rocks, rolling terrain—as the fence loomed closer. The child's chest heaved, but all sound of her breathing was smothered by a song blaring from the radio. The music rose tinnily above the rattle of loose metal and the high-pitched whine of the hot engine.

The girl jerked the steering wheel to the left, straining her muscles, frantic when the vehicle didn't respond the way Paco had taught her it would. She was sure the car would crash and she would die in flames and twisted metal. For an instant, she imagined giving in to the black night. But she was a fighter and so she focused the last reserves of her energy on steering the car. Finally, she felt the shudder of tires forced back onto the hard surface of the road.

Dim yellow headlamps filled the rearview mirror of the Honda, and the child's heartbeat stuttered. It was *el demonio*, the demon—with his dark hungry face. The lights glowed like the eyes of a crazy animal. A sudden memory jolted through her mind: fingernails scratching her neck just as Paco's strong arms pulled her from the demon's reach.

But there were no grown-ups with her now—and no safe place. Just the yellow glowing eyes of her pursuer growing larger in the rearview mirror.

Blood smeared the girl's cheek and lip. Dried blood where she had slammed her cheek against metal, fresh blood where she bit her lip in fright. A deep blue-black bruise darkened the inside of her left thigh. Beneath the delicate chain and the silver medallion around her neck, the skin was red and scratched where the demon had torn at her with long, cold fingers.

Suddenly, there was a new danger—bright flashing lights in *front* of the Honda—coming at her! The new lights snaked across the road, blocking the Honda's path. The child was trapped. Her eyes opened wide, and panic stole her breath away.

What was it? A truck? A bridge? *A train!*

To avoid the train she swerved the Honda and hit the brakes again—but too hard. The car went into a skid, across the road toward barbed wire and tracks. She couldn't escape the metal snout of the train engine.

A cry of terror escaped the child's mouth, just as a fat hunter's moon broke over the foothills of the Sangre de Cristos. The moon's glow suffused the night sky. She whispered the first words of the prayer.

*Our Mother, Nuestra Madre—*

And then she squeezed her eyes shut as a solid wall of moving metal caught the front end of the Honda. The noise of rending metal and a shower of sparks raked the night as the train pushed the car fifty yards along the track.

The dark green Chevrolet Suburban slowed on U.S. 285 just south of Lamy, and Lorenzo Santos Portrillo gazed toward the ruined Honda, a moonlit mess of smoke and dust and twisted metal roughly a quarter mile ahead. Just beyond the wreck, he saw the flashing lights of the railroad crossing where a train blocked the road.

His eyes were invisible in the unlit interior of the vehicle. His even white teeth were clenched. The smell of citrus cologne clashed with the uncharacteristic tang of nervous sweat and blood. Despite his agitation, Lorenzo's physical movements remained tightly controlled; but his mind refused to harness information with its usual discipline. He'd seen a ghost tonight; at first he believed she'd returned from the grave to do him evil.

But her terror had persuaded him she was merely human.

He saw the lights of the train, but he almost failed to register a car, hazard lights blinking, pulling off to the side of the road opposite the scene of the accident.

The warning message squeezed through to his consciousness: *More people to deal with tonight.* They were crossing the road, shining flashlights over the terrain as they approached the accident.

Was the girl alive or dead?

Lorenzo drove slowly. In the time it took the Suburban to gain the quarter mile, a man—lantern in hand—swung himself down from the train's engine and darted toward the wrecked Honda. The car had been forced along the track, crushed by the massive engine.

Lorenzo's gloved fingers grazed the Suburban's steering wheel; the gloves were cheap leather throwaways. On his left wrist, the thick silver bracelet—etched with the face of "Serpent Skirt"—was smeared with Paco's blood. That was the problem with knives.

The blood had a dull sheen visible even in the darkness of

the car. He remembered to check his face in the rearview mirror. When he snapped on the overhead light, he saw the droplet of blood above his lip. He wiped the stain away.

# DESPERATE SILENCE
## by Sarah Lovett

**Published by Villard Books.
Available in hardcover February 1998.**